PRAISE FOR *THE BONES OF MAKAIDOS*

It is fitting for the last book in the Oracles of Fire series to be the best. *The Bones of Makaidos* captured me from the very beginning. Bryan Davis's ability to vividly depict scenes is at its best in the final installment of his bestselling fantasy series. You will not be able to put the book down!

GRANT MILLER

Beloved characters, both new and old, grace the pages of this tale and beckon you to enter their world one last time as they fight against the growing darkness around them. The tapestry masterfully woven is finally complete. But is it really the end?

ANNE K. RILEY

After reading the rest of the Oracles of Fire and Dragons in our Midst books, I find *The Bones of Makaidos* to be a smashing ending. It's so nice to find not one, but two book series that are so enthralling, adventure-packed, inspiring, and God honoring.

REBECCA VATH

I laughed; I cried; I shared with each character's joy and suffering. I could not put this book down, even to go to bed. *The Bones of Makaidos* pulled me in from cover to cover. Bryan Davis has saved the best for last! This book is definitely one you don't want to miss.

SARAH PRATT

This book is absolutely amazing. It's thrilling to join in with all of these characters' adventures once again! I can't keep my hands away from the book. It's sad to know that this will be the last one, but it's great anyway! A must-read for sure!

DANIELLE DIEZ

Bryan Davis has done it again! I knew Mr. Davis was an excellent author, but I was amazed to find myself double-taking and rereading pages as my jaw dropped. You will be up late into the night reading *The Bones of Makaidos* telling yourself, "just one more chapter" over and over again. Possibly Mr. Davis's best yet!

JACOB EGGERT

The Bones of Makaidos is, in my opinion, the best book that Mr. Davis has written yet! The events in this book left me bewildered, and they completely change your outlook on this entire series. It's a work of art!

ANNA BJELLA

In *The Bones of Makaidos*, action will spike your adrenaline; suspense will urge you to read on; sacrifice and salvation will bring you to tears, and the characters will encourage you to trust in God more than ever before.

REGAN HICKMAN

I've cried more in this book than the other seven put together—some were tears of sadness, but most have been tears of joy. Each time you read it, it'll be just as powerful as the first time, if not more. All loose ends will be tied, and when you read the last page, you'll be left with a sense of peace that's hard to describe.

CONNIE WOLTERS

If you don't think the Oracles of Fire series can get any better, then think again. This book outdoes the rest! Prophecies are fulfilled, and any questions from the last seven books are answered. *The Bones of Makaidos* is my favorite of Mr. Davis's books, and I know it will be yours too.

TAYLOR WARD

The Bones of Makaidos is a fitting end to the best series of books I have ever read! In the ultimate battle of good versus evil, I felt joy at surprise reunions and sadness over the loss of loved ones. In the end I was left with a happiness that can only come from experiencing God at work in this world of ours.

RACHEL TETTLETON

The Bones of Makaidos is a tale of love, courage, sacrifice, and redemption; a wonderful end to an awesome series. All I can say is: What a ride!

T. McCARVILLE

"I want you to win my heart. I want you to fight for me, sweat for me, bleed for me. . . ." *The Bones of Makaidos* captures the hearts of readers, brings them into the lives of all the characters, and shows that God is always there, and if you have faith, he will reward you.

KENDRA WILLIAMSON

In *The Lord of the Rings: The Two Towers*, King Theoden said, "If this is to be our end, then I would have them make such an end, as to be worthy of remembrance." Mr. Davis has accomplished this and then some.

HAYLEY COX

The Bones of Makaidos is an epic adventure that brings the wonderful elements of the series together into an ultimate climax. Well done, Mr. Davis!

KENNY DONOVAN

The Bones of Makaidos is my favorite book. There's adventure, excitement, and romance all mingled together. At times I feel like all the characters are real, like I'm going right along with them in their adventures. Most of all, these books have strengthened my faith. Thank you, Mr. Davis!

JENN MORGAN

Throughout the first seven books, Billy, Bonnie, Walter, Ashley, Sapphira, and Elam have grown closer to each other and stronger in their faith in Elohim. Now, together with the rest of the Oracles of Fire, they face their final battle, the fiercest challenge, preceding the ultimate reward.

BRYCE McLEMORE

In this rousing conclusion, Bryan Davis has penned a tale of betrayal and endurance, of faith, hope, and love. Of humor. Of other worlds and of a majestic people in whom the lights of chivalry and honor have not gone out. Indeed, *The Bones of Makaidos* is a masterpiece of Christian literature.

HOLLI HERDEG

FROM THE ASHES:
THE BONES OF MAKAIDOS,
PART 2

Dragons in Our Midst Story World Reading Order

Dragons in our Midst

Raising Dragons

The Candlestone

Circles of Seven

Tears of a Dragon

Oracles of Fire

Eye of the Oracle

Enoch's Ghost

Last of the Nephilim

Refining Fires: The Bones of Makaidos, Part 1

From the Ashes: The Bones of Makaidos, Part 2

Children of the Bard

Song of the Ovulum

From the Mouth of Elijah

The Seventh Door

Omega Dragon

Dragons of Camelot

The Sacred Scales

The Memory Stone

Other Books by Bryan Davis

The Reapers Trilogy

Reapers

Beyond the Gateway

Reaper Reborn

Time Echoes Trilogy

Time Echoes

Interfinity

Fatal Convergence

Dragons of Starlight

Starlighter

Warrior

Diviner

Liberator

Tales of Starlight

Masters & Slayers

Third Starlighter

Exodus Rising

Standalone Novel

Let the Ghosts Speak

The Oculus Gate

Heaven Came Down

Invading Hell

My Soul to Take

On Earth as It Is in Hell

Wanted: Superheroes

Wanted: A Superhero to Save the World

Hertz to Be a Hero

Antigravity Heroes

Astral Alliance

Across Astral Realms

The First Starborn

At the Speed of Mind

Not So Famous Dog Tales

All Dogs Go to 7-Eleven

Mission Impossible

If You Give a Dog a Dictionary

A Series of Unfortunate Dogs

The Wizard of Dogs

AUTHOR OF THE BESTSELLING SERIES DRAGONS IN OUR MIDST

BRYAN DAVIS

THE BONES OF MAKAIDOS

PART TWO

FROM THE ASHES

ORACLES OF FIRE

BOOK FIVE

wander™
An imprint of
Tyndale House
Publishers

Visit Tyndale online at tyndale.com.

Visit the author online at daviscrossing.com.

From the Ashes: The Bones of Makaidos, Part 2

Previously published in 2009 by Scrub Jay Journeys under ISBN 978-1-946253-78-1 as *The Bones of Makaidos*. First printing by Tyndale House Publishers in 2026.

Designed by Jennifer L. Phelps

Published in association with Cyle Young of C.Y.L.E. Agency, LLC.

Library of Congress Cataloging-in-Publication Data

A catalog record for this book is available from the Library of Congress.

ISBN 979-8-4005-1382-4

Printed in the United States of America

32 31 30 29 28 27 26
7 6 5 4 3 2 1

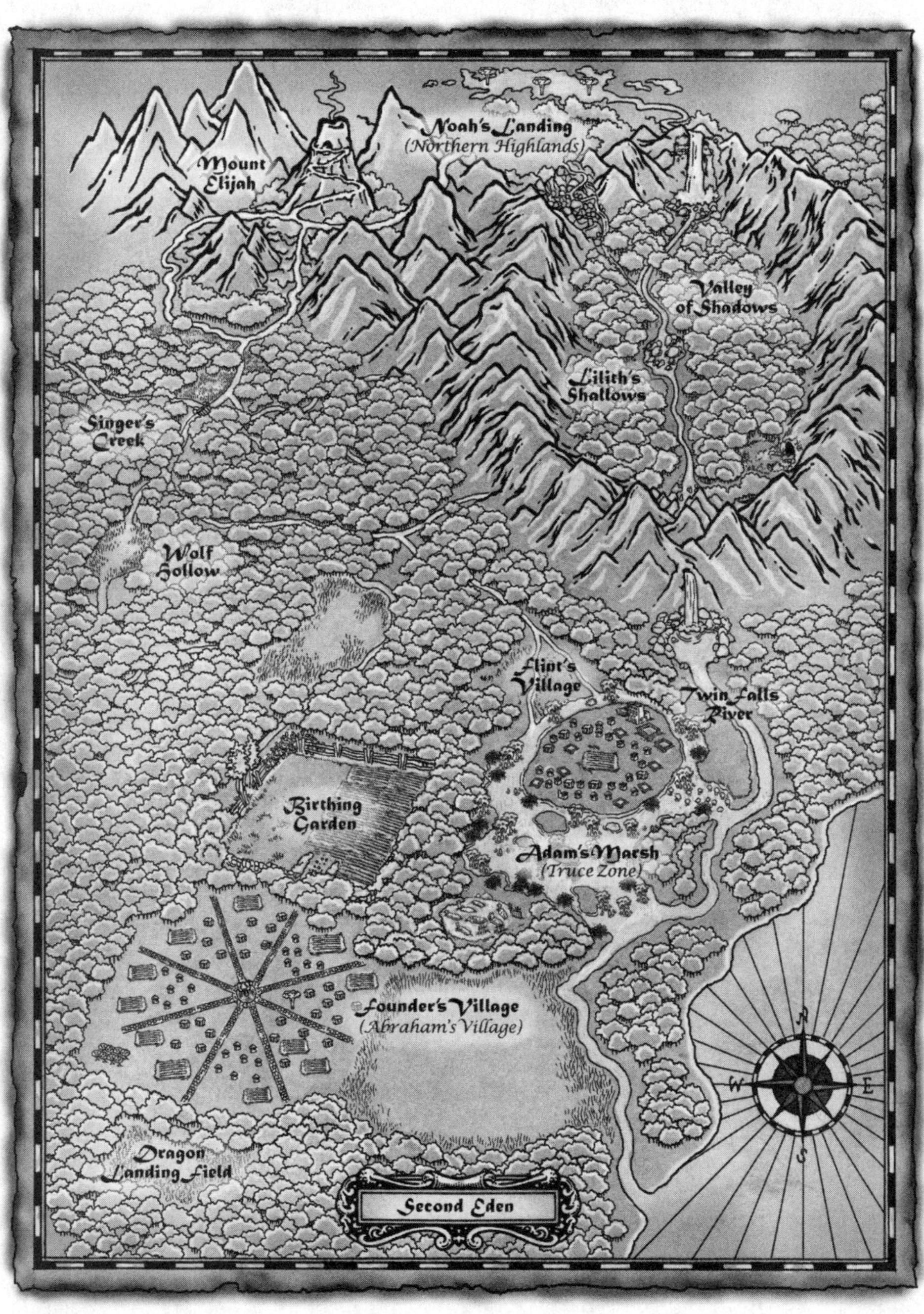

Mount Elijah
Noah's Landing
(Northern Highlands)
Valley of Shadows
Lilith's Shallows
Singer's Creek
Wolf Hollow
Flint's Village
Twin Falls River
Birthing Garden
Adam's Marsh
(Truce Zone)
Founder's Village
(Abraham's Village)
N
W
E
S
Dragon Landing Field
Second Eden

DRAGON LINEAGE

Human offspring are represented on leaves.

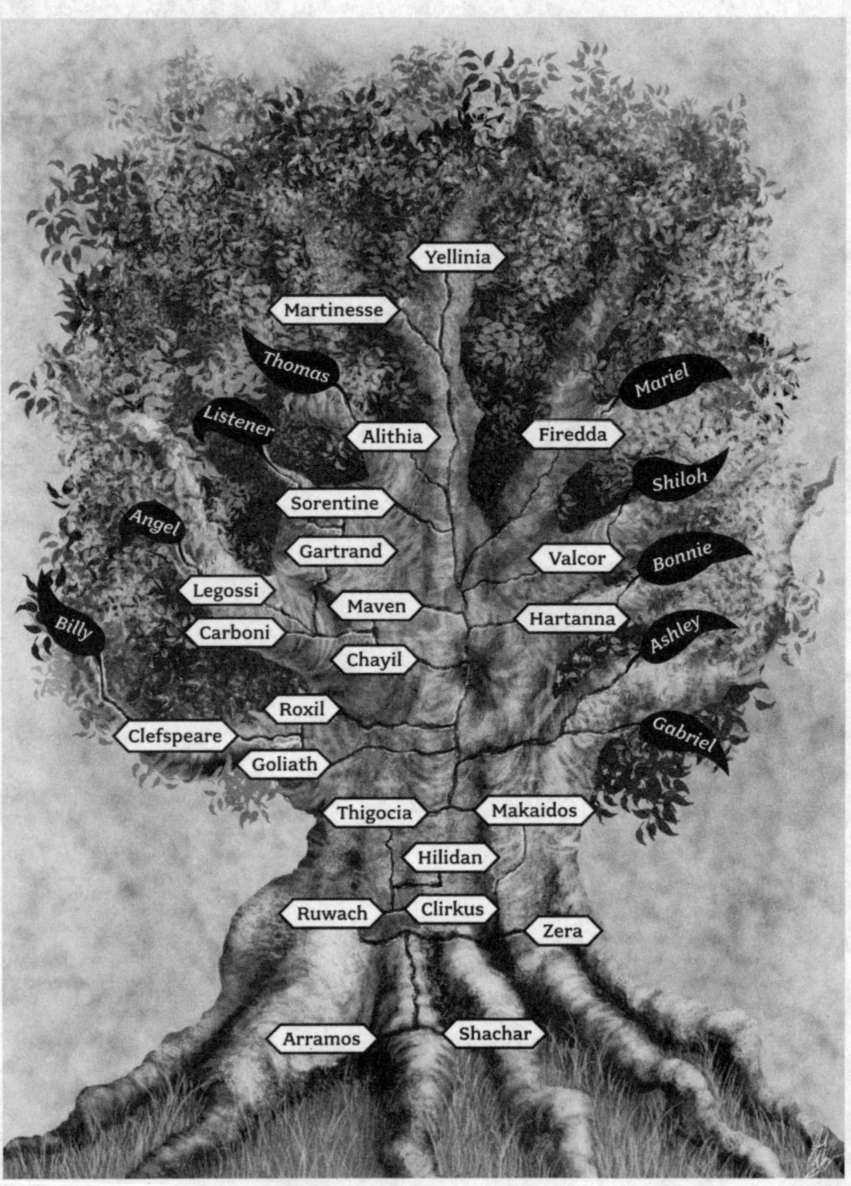

Cast of Characters

Abbadon—a powerful angel of the Abyss who takes the form of a dragon

Abigail—the human name of dragon Roxil; previously called Jasmine as a human

Abraham—the human name of dragon Arramos; reborn in Second Eden as the Prophet (not to be confused with the physical dragon form of Arramos later possessed by the devil)

Acacia—an Oracle of Fire; twin to Mara (Sapphira Adi)

Adam Lark—a teenage friend of the Bannisters

Albatross—a dragon of Second Eden

Alithia—a dragon; as a human goes by the name Kaylee

Angel—formerly the wife of Dragon; widowed mother of Candle and Listener

Arramos—a dragon; mate of Shachar; father of Makaidos; grandfather of Thigocia; died in the flood but his body is possessed by the devil while his soul was reborn as Abraham, a human in Second Eden

Ashley Stalworth—daughter of Timothy and Hannah (Makaidos and Thigocia)

Billy Bannister—son of Jared (Clefspeare) and Marilyn

Bonnie Silver—daughter of Irene (Hartanna); previously known as Bonnie Conner

Brogan—the human name of dragon Hilidan

Candle—son of Dragon and Angel

Carboni—a dragon; as a human goes by the name Elise

Carl Foley—a friend of the Bannisters; husband of Catherine; father of Walter and Shelly

Carly Masters—a friend of Bonnie's

Catherine Foley—a friend of the Bannisters; wife of Carl; father of Walter and Shelly

Charles Hamilton—a former teacher of Billy, Bonnie, and Walter

Chazaq—a giant; Mardon's commander

Clefspeare—a dragon; son of Goliath and Roxil; as a human goes by the name Jared

Cliffside—a guard of the birthing garden in Second Eden

Cornelius—leader of the unicorns

Dallas—the human name of dragon Firedda; mother of Mariel

Dikaios—a talking horse

Dorian—the human name of dragon Yellinia

Dragon—the husband of Angel; father of Candle and Listener; the human form of Goliath in Second Eden

Elam—son of Shem; grandson of Noah; went by the name of Markus for a time

Elise—the human name of dragon Carboni

Ember—a mare in Second Eden

Emerald—a widow in Second Eden

Enoch—a prophet

Firedda—a dragon; as a human goes by the name Dallas

Flint—Abraham's rebel apprentice

Gabriel—son of Timothy and Hannah (Makaidos and Thigocia)

Glewlwyd—the gatekeeper of the Bridgelands

Goliath—a dragon; son of Makaidos and Thigocia; mate of Roxil; goes by the name Dragon as a human in Second Eden

Grackle—a dragon of Second Eden

Hartanna—a dragon; daughter of Makaidos and Thigocia; as a human goes by the name Irene

Hunter—a false name for Mardon

Irene Connor/Irene Silver—the human name of dragon Hartanna; wife of Dr. Matthew Connor, mother of Bonnie

Jared Bannister—the human name of dragon Clefspeare; husband of Marilyn; father of Billy

Jordan—the human name of dragon Martinesse

Joseph of Arimathea—a guide for lost souls

Karen—adopted sister of Ashley; died in battle

Karrick—a dragon; son of Goliath and Roxil

Kaylee Saunders—the human name of dragon Alithia; mother of Thomas

King Arthur—king of Camelot

King Nimrod—an ancient king; father of Mardon

Larry—Ashley's supercomputer

Legossi—a dragon; as a human goes by the name Rebekah

Listener—daughter of Dragon and Angel in Second Eden; birth daughter of Tamara; adopted by Mantika after Dragon's and Angel's deaths

Makaidos—king of the dragons; son of Arramos and Shachar; mate of Thigocia; as a human goes by the name Timothy

Mantika—a lowlander; wife of Greevelow; mother of Windor and adoptive mother of Listener and Candle

Mardon—an ancient scientist; son of King Nimrod and Semiramis; master of the Nephilim; disguises himself using the name Hunter

Mariel—daughter of Dallas

Marilyn Bannister—wife of Jared; mother of Billy

Markus—a name used by Elam for a time

Martinesse—a dragon; as a human goes by the name Jordan

Matthew Connor—husband of Irene; father of Bonnie

Monique Bannister—adopted daughter of Jared and Marilyn

Morgan—a witch; sister of Naamah

Naamah—a witch; sister of Morgan

Noah—a patriarch who built an ark to save humans and animals from the great flood

Paili—an underborn; wife of Patrick; sometimes known as Ruth

Palin—Sir Devin's scribe and squire

Patrick—the human name of dragon Valcor; husband of Paili

Pearl—wife of Steadfast; a medical worker in Second Eden

Rebekah—the human name of dragon Legossi; mother of Angel

Roxil—a dragon; daughter of Makaidos and Thigocia; mate of Goliath; mother of Clefspeare; as a human goes by the name Abigail

Ruth—an underborn; wife of Patrick; sometimes known as Paili

Sapphira Adi—an Oracle of Fire; twin to Acacia; previously known as Mara

Semiramis—mother of Mardon (Hunter)

Shelly Foley—daughter of Carl and Catherine; sister of Walter

Shem—son of Noah; father of Elam

Shiloh—daughter of Patrick (Valcor) and Ruth (Paili)

Sir Devin—a knight; a slayer of dragons

Sir Winston Barlow—a knight of Camelot

Sorentine—a dragon; mate of Gartrand; as a human goes by the name Tamara

Stacey—adopted daughter of Jared and Marilyn

Steadfast—husband of Pearl; a medical worker in Second Eden

Stout—a villager in Second Eden

Tamara—the human name of dragon Sorentine; mother of Listener before she was sent to Second Eden

The Maid—a fiery teenage girl who lives in the Valley of Souls

Thigocia—a dragon; mate of Makaidos; granddaughter of Arramos and Shachar; as a human goes by the name Hannah

Thomas—son of Kaylee

Timothy—the human name of dragon Makaidos, husband of Hannah; father of Gabriel and Ashley; also called Captain Autarkeia

Valcor—a dragon; son of Makaidos and Thigocia; brother of Hartanna; as a human goes by the name Patrick

Valiant—a village leader in Second Eden

Walter Foley—a friend of Billy's; son of Carl and Catherine; in the line of King Arthur
Windor—son of Mantika
Yellinia—a dragon; as a human goes by the name Dorian
Yereq—a giant; one of the Nephilim
Zane—a shadow person who was banished

An Oracle's Call

A tender heart that burns with fire,
A contradicting blend;
With words of heat, I scald the soul,
And with my words I mend.

An Oracle of Fire born
To sacrifice and bleed,
For hungry souls, I spend my life
To meet their every need.

Yet, Oracles of Fire burn;
They pierce, they scald, they sear
Corrupted souls in dark abodes
Who cower there in fear.

The light has come! Begone, you shades,
Who hide in blackest mire!
I free the captives, loose their chains,
And give them holy fire.

While some will carry vibrant light,
The fearful drop the torch;
Courageous souls absorb the fire,
While others fear the scorch.

Yet, flames from God must pierce your breast
To purge the dross of sin
And make your silver wholly pure
And light the flame within.

A bridge awaits, a risky path,
The cross of Christ displayed
A broken body, blood, and tears;
A tomb for us inlaid.

I call you now to cross the bridge,
To take the scarlet key.
To gain the burning, tender heart,
And walk the path with me.

CHAPTER 1

TONGUES OF FIRE

Billy crouched behind a bushy tree, Walter on one side, Ashley on the other, and Elam guarding their backs with a drawn sword. As twilight faded into darkness, they huddled without a sound. It was finally time to make the boldest move yet. It had taken months of preparation, and tonight, with neither Pegasus nor Phoenix rising to reveal their presence, they would launch their plan.

After being dropped off by Clefspeare, Hartanna, and Thigocia, they had hiked a mile to get to this point. Although the enemy stayed behind a wall of fire, it was impossible to know if they could see anything beyond the flames. If they could perceive the shadow of a dragon, they would likely be on the alert for any activity near the wall, and that might ruin everything.

For now, the dragons had to stay back and meet them later at the southern rendezvous point, the river's exit from the flaming wall. Even there, they would need dragons for passenger transport only if their plans didn't work out. Candle was supposed to fly Merlin, the Bannisters' airplane, to the rendezvous and park it nearby for Billy's use when they arrived, and Ashley brought a transmitter for calling either the airplane or the base radio station in case they needed help.

So, with their powerful winged friends absent, it was time for Billy and company to be quiet and wait for the cover of darkness. That would be their greatest ally.

Billy peeked between the velvety green leaves. This "ghost lily tree," as the locals called it, reminded him of the rhododendrons he once hid behind in West Virginia while trying to stay out of the dragon slayer's sight. Ahead, just ten paces separated them from the towering wall of flames near the northern boundary of the Valley of Shadows. To their right, Twin Falls River, maybe fifty paces away, flowed under the fire and rushed toward the valley for about a quarter mile before plunging from a height of several hundred feet into the land of the shadow people.

Now that the sound of thundering water crashed into his ears, he couldn't help but shiver. Although he had grown accustomed to the never-ending frigid weather and frequent snowfalls, the thought of taking that plunge into the domain of shadowy fiends brought an icy chill.

He reached to his back scabbard and fingered Excalibur's hilt. It was still there. Why wouldn't it be? Checking it every few minutes served no reasonable purpose. Yet, somehow touching it settled the goose bumps.

Ashley whispered, "They know we're here."

"They?" Billy asked, also whispering. "The shadow people?"

"No. Abraham and Angel."

Billy looked at the wall of flames. Of course, it was more than flames. Ever since Abraham had marched around enemy territory four years ago, his and Angel's life energies had fueled this barrier, a living wall with two embedded souls. "Are they communicating with you?" he asked.

"In a way. I don't sense words, only impressions. They are weaker than when I first sensed them. Their energy will soon be spent."

Elam joined them in the low bushes. "Do they approve of our mission?"

"I'm not sure." The fire billowed upward in Ashley's wide eyes. "I don't sense *dis*approval. It's more like a contented sigh. They are at peace and happy to see us."

"Will they help us?"

"They will do what they can, but I'm not sure how. I get the feeling that they aren't able to make a hole in the wall without falling apart completely."

"At least we'll have fired-up cheerleaders," Walter said. "Can't hurt."

Elam straightened, picked up a shoulder bag, and motioned for the others to join him. Raising his hood over his bushy hair, he said, "I think it's dark enough. Let's go."

After raising their own hoods, Billy and Walter each hoisted a hefty pack while Ashley picked up two smaller ones, more like leather briefcases than the canvas haversacks the others toted. All four carried swords, either in a belt or in a back scabbard, though none had brought along shields. They already had as much as they could handle.

With Elam leading the way, they marched over packed snow that marked a deer trail they had scouted out earlier, perfect for a silent approach. Under the cover of trees, some just dry woody skeletons from the perpetual winter and others still green and vibrant, they followed the river's call.

Soon, they broke through the forest edge, and, hunched over and jogging, they hurried to a point near the intersection of the flaming wall and the river. A guard on the other side of the river stood next to a weak torch sticking up from the beach sand. He stared but said nothing. He knew the plan. No words. No gestures that might signal a guard on the valley side that something unusual was taking place.

Billy quietly set down his pack. Walter, Elam, and Ashley did the same with their loads. When Elam's bag clinked, everyone froze. The metal-on-metal sound had plagued their trial runs, but it couldn't be helped. Although the snowboards were merely part of a backup plan in case the raft failed, they had decided to bring them. No matter how confident they were in Plan A, it didn't make sense to forsake Plan B, even with the risk of the telltale sounds. They had hoped the river's noise would mask them. Now the theory would meet the test.

They stared through the flames. No shadows moved. Yet, since plumes of vapor shot up at the river's entry point, it seemed impossible to know if any guards on the other side had noticed their presence.

Elam waved his hand, the signal to continue. Billy untied his bag, withdrew a large raft, and unfolded it on the beach. Inflating it would be the first step. Ashley had installed a tiny motorized fan that would draw in surrounding air. Since they couldn't risk a loud sucking noise, she opted for a quieter, slower fan energized by a battery she had fashioned from local metals.

Billy flipped the switch and listened to the low whir as the raft inflated. It would take quite a while, but at least it was quiet.

Walter tied a rope to a hook on the left side of the raft's front, one of the guidelines for the parachute. There would be three other ropes, one on the opposite side of the front and two in the back. During their tests, mastering a directed fall had taken longer than any other step, but after so many successful trials, everyone seemed confident. Still, the swirling winds in the valley's sheltered bowl could be far less predictable than at their test range. This wouldn't be easy.

Elam laid four snowboards and eight ski poles in the raft, careful to keep the poles' sharp tips away from the sides. The metal points had been wrapped with a blanket just to be safe. One hole would end their mission before it began.

Ashley attached the transmitter to the back of the raft. As she adjusted the eight-inch antenna with one hand, she looked at a signal meter in her other hand, the flames from the wall giving her enough light to see. She flashed an okay sign. The transmitter was working.

When Walter tied the last guideline in place, the foursome unfolded an oblong parachute, laid it over the raft, and attached it to the lines. It had taken weeks to design the canopy's shape to allow for precise guidance, and their low-level trial jumps had cost the test pilots a few bumps and bruises, but with each new design, they were able to launch from higher elevations until all four had mastered the skill from the necessary height.

Elam raised three fingers—three minutes until the raft would be fully inflated. After thousands of years of life, his internal clock had become flawless. With Walter and Elam at the front and Billy and Ashley at the rear, they carried the raft to the river and set it in the water.

All four waded into the icy flow. While the men held the raft in place against the swift current, Ashley threw back a rear corner of the parachute and stowed their packs. The men's bags were nearly empty now, while Ashley's still carried the gadgets they would need later. She then crawled under the parachute and stationed herself at the raft's right rear corner.

Elam entered next, followed by Walter. With the raft now barely buoyant under the added weight, Billy shoved it toward the center of the river, pushed an anchor into the sandy bed, and jumped in. In the darkness, he had to squirm as he slid under the parachute as quietly as possible. For a moment, Excalibur caught the canopy, but Ashley pried it free and guided him the rest of the way in.

When he finally settled in his corner, he pulled the parachute over his head and waited in silence with the others. With the wall's firelight radiating through the protective covering, he could see each taut face. Elam had planned this pause, a time for everyone to slow down and collect themselves.

He held up a pair of fingers—two minutes. Again, this precision-minded warrior chief would run this mission like clockwork. Yet, the next sequence of events would require guesswork. Five seconds till they hit the fire, a minute and a half to the waterfall, and thirty seconds till they floated safely to the river again. They hoped.

Safety through the flames, however, was certain. The parachute's retardant chemicals worked. The first few tests using volunteers who braved the wall with chemically coated cloaks had been painful failures, but Ashley's newer formulas proved extremely effective. The tests had also drawn Flint's troops to their attempted penetration points on the south side of Adam's Marsh. With Valiant and Candle making another attempt an hour ago, they hoped even the shadow people might have migrated from the valley to help guard that region.

With the current pushing heavily and chunks of ice bumping the rear, the raft rocked back and forth. Elam paid no attention. His head bowed and his eyes closed, he seemed to be praying.

Billy nodded. Elam had never failed to begin every trial run with prayer. He wasn't about to take the real plunge without it.

Reaching over, Billy took Ashley's hand. She gripped it tightly and tapped Walter's. Soon, all four joined hands.

Taking in a deep breath, Billy prayed silently—for their dangerous mission; for his mother, whom he hadn't seen in four years; for Bonnie, wherever she was, that God would watch over her and bring them together someday; and even for Flint, that somehow he would realize how his actions had brought them to the brink of all-out war, that he would have a change of heart, and when the wall of fire faded, that he would come out with an olive branch instead of a spear.

Soon, Elam pulled his hands back and pointed at Billy. That was the signal. It was time to fly.

Billy untied the anchor. The raft shot forward. Elam splayed his hands and counted down the seconds.

Four fingers. The light inside the raft grew brighter.

Three. The raft jerked and kicked.

Two. The temperature shot up.

One. A sizzle erupted—water striking fire.

Elam closed his fist. Ashley squeezed Billy's hand. A whoosh sounded. Crackles, pops, and sizzles beat against their ears as steam warmed the floor of the raft and lifted them into the air. The wall was thick here, an impossible scenario to duplicate in tests. They would just have to ride it out.

Sweat dampened Billy's armpits and trickled down his back. Soon he would be soaked, and facing the frigid wind during their upcoming plunge would be torture. Yet, they had trained for that as well by spending several weeks sleeping outdoors with minimal clothing and covering.

Finally, they dropped back to the river with a splash. Their raft bounced twice before settling into a gentle rocking motion. Staring through the parachute's material, Billy listened. Had anyone out there heard the commotion? During their planning, no one had talked about the steam's elevating surge. But now it was too late to worry about it. They would just have to ride it out.

As they rushed away from the wall, the light faded. The sizzles died away. Coolness filtered in. For the next minute or so, they would wait in silence. It would do no good to peek out and watch for the upcoming drop. It was just too dark. And this section was uncharted. No one knew the exact distance between the boundary and the waterfall. Only a brief sense of flying and a sudden drop would signal their arrival.

During their tests in complete darkness, Billy had tried to use his danger sensing gift to guess when the fall would come. But it seemed that darkness and constant danger somehow blunted his ability to sense a coming peak. Knowing exactly when the moment would arrive seemed impossible.

Billy slipped out of Ashley's grasp and reached for the left rear guideline. She, Walter, and Elam held their lines, as well. They had practiced this in the dark before. They could do it again, four parasailing pilots flying an overloaded raft into a valley of death. No problem.

Every bump felt like "the" bump. Every sudden jerk made them flinch. Finally, it seemed that the river fell away. Then, they dropped.

Elam and Walter threw their lines out first. The parachute flew upward, billowed out, and grabbed the air. Billy and Ashley cast out theirs. The entire canopy beat above them, sounding like a dragon trying to hover in place.

As their descent slowed, falling water splashed in from behind. Gusts of wind blew the spray all around. Without a visible target, they had to use dead reckoning, listening to the roar of water and constantly adjusting to stay at the center of it while gliding away from the waterfall itself.

At this point, they had decided that necessary commands could be given. The background noise would have to drown them out.

"Left five degrees," Elam grunted. "There. Keep it there."

"Tilting right," Ashley called. "Billy. A few inches slack. . . . Perfect."

Soon, they slid back into the river with a barely perceptible splash. Billy gave Ashley a silent high five, almost missing her hand in the darkness.

As the chute began to droop behind them, Billy and Ashley reeled it in and folded it into a wad at the center of the raft. With the masking noise dying away, it was time for silence again.

Darkness enveloped them like a heavy blanket. Billy searched for Ashley's eyes. Nothing. Total darkness.

Her hand touched his. He slid his fingers under her palm and rubbed her knuckles with his thumb. The touch felt good. Reassurance. Comfort. In spite of the darkness, they were all in this together.

Billy kept his ears trained on the water's flow. It had died down to a consistent, low-level rush. Now he had to listen for another rise in volume, their only signal that the next waterfall, the exit from the Valley of Shadows, was fast approaching.

He pulled Excalibur from his back scabbard, taking care not to make it glow. Because of his four years of training and physical maturing, he had become one of the best, if not *the* best swordsman in their army. So, taking into account Billy's expertise with Excalibur, Elam appointed him the mission's strong-arm man. Everyone else would work while he stood guard.

After a few minutes, the water's percussion began to increase. Elam tapped Billy's knee. Billy tapped Ashley's. He tried to watch Ashley pass the signal to Walter and Walter back to Elam, completing the cycle, but it was too dark. Of course, there was no doubt. They passed it along, and now everyone knew the first water-ride phase was coming to an end.

Seconds later, the front side of the raft lifted. Elam had slid into the river, as planned. The raft turned to the left, lifted again, and, with a sliding noise at its floor, came to a stop.

Billy lifted his leg over the side and felt for solid ground—beach sand. Although the valley had likely received as much snow as any other place, the rise and fall of the river probably scoured any snow from its beach.

When he had steadied himself, he helped Ashley step out. As they had practiced many times in the darkness, Walter handed the packs to Elam and Ashley while Billy walked a few steps away from the river, listening.

No unusual noises. In order to prepare his ears, the younger villagers had tried to imitate the sounds the shadow people made. Candle had sent a chunk of ice sliding across a table, but he admitted that the shadow people were quieter. In reality, the dark creatures crawled along the ground with more of a hush. Windor poured oil on the table and tried again. That was closer, they decided, but still too loud.

Finally, Valiant offered a hint that all agreed was the best. "Hear them?" he had said. "Yes, you can hear them, but once you do, that will be too late. By the time the first breath reaches your ears, they will have you in their clutches. You *feel* them first. The hair on the back of your neck rises, and a tingle on your skin tells you that a dark hand is stretching out to drag you into their swarm of devouring black oil."

Billy shook off a shiver. It was time to concentrate. He reached out with his danger-sensing "radar" and tried to feel for the signals. After a few seconds, he shook his head. Nothing. And no sound, either. Even the expected noises of his fellow spies didn't rise over the river's din. Maybe the shadow people had no clue that intruders were present, and the months of training had paid off. But maybe their silence wouldn't be enough. Valiant had said that those creatures could smell a human a mile away.

Billy sniffed the air. Wood smoke. Something burned somewhere close by. Maybe that would mask their presence, too.

As he let his thumb rub across a gemstone embedded in Excalibur's hilt, a memory rose in his mind, the event that birthed the plans for this mission in the first place. Stout had found this rubellite on a tiny raft floating through the southern wall boundary. It had been tied down by wire, and a resin-coated note had been attached, obviously prepared by someone who wanted to keep it safe through the fire.

In an almost illegible scrawl, the note read, "Found in valley cave. Roxil."

A note on the other side, written in beautifully familiar penmanship, said, "Billy, if by some miracle you get this, here is an update. We have finally rebuilt Apollo. We found a portal near the mines that, according to Larry, emits signals that are not of our world. I attached his note to the missing stone from Excalibur's hilt. If it goes through the portal, we will begin working on strengthening Apollo to the point where we can make a hole big enough for Gabriel to go through. Then, if he is successful in finding Second Eden, we will send the other dragons. We are praying for you. Please tell your father that I love him."

Billy imagined Roxil tying the gem and note to the little raft. If only he could have replied! But now, months later, his mother had no idea that they had received it. He couldn't tell her that they had worked every waking minute since that time to get safely to the cave. And did anything happen in the meantime? Did she manage to open a bigger hole? Did Gabriel try to come through? If so, he would have been trapped. With no way out of enemy territory, he would have been taken prisoner . . . or worse.

Yet, most of the note's news had brightened their outlook. Mom was working hard to get the dragons into Second Eden, and putting the rubellite in its proper place had given Excalibur more power than ever before.

A hand touched his shoulder. Billy jumped but quickly settled down when Walter whispered, "We're ready."

Billy raised his arms and allowed Walter to tie a rope around his waist. The others would hang on to the lead rope and tag along with Elam at the back, guiding the raft along the shallows, as planned. He had to let it drag a bit on the sand to keep it from taking off in the current, but the noise wasn't discernible above the water's constant rush.

Billy drew a map in the darkness in front of him. Candle and Listener had created a nearly life-sized copy of the cave's surroundings, including a man-made stream with precise bends; rocks that protruded from each side of the river, signaling the exit waterfall; and the most important landmark, a head-high boulder embedded in the beach sand. Once they reached it, they would be even with the cave. They would then turn left, walk through the forest about fifty paces, and search for the opening in the mountain face.

Unfortunately, the boulder sat an unknown distance away from the river's edge, so they had to fan out, Billy on the left, then Walter and Ashley, and Elam on the right. Depending on the river's current level, it could be anywhere from one to ten paces from the edge.

Billy crept along, keeping his left hand out in front as he tried to feel for anything solid. At the same time, he kept his danger radar going. Using every sense but sight had been hard to learn, but the training was paying off again.

Finally, he touched a rock. With a quick tug on the rope, he brought everyone to a halt. He groped higher until his hand moved over the top. Yes, it was just about head high.

After giving Elam a moment to pull the raft fully on shore, he led the way toward the forest. With every step, he lowered his boot carefully. The terrain underneath would provide important clues that might reveal his location. The beach sand ended abruptly, giving way to soft turf of some kind. After tugging the rope again, he stooped and felt the ground. A thin layer of snow covered long, stiff leaves that crumbled as he pinched them.

Billy brought a sample to his nose and sniffed. Musky. Candle had said that the callow ferns couldn't have survived the weather. They always died back during the season of death, and with this season lasting four years, they would all be dead. He also warned that walking on them would raise a crackling racket as well as a musky odor that would alert the shadow people to their presence. Their only hope would be a deep enough layer of snow to mask both.

The river, however, had kept this section relatively free of a protective snow layer. Deeper snow, and safer ground, likely lay farther away, but how far?

Billy gave the rope two more tugs, letting everyone know that it was time for Ashley's magic. As soon as he returned Excalibur to his scabbard, he felt her hand touch his. She put Walter's MP3 player in one hand and a spray bottle in the other. Only days ago, she had captured the river's distinctive rush using the airplane's radio transmitter, which she had modified into a digital recorder. Now, they hoped, replaying the recording at this point would wash away the crackling noise.

After turning on the player and setting it on the snow, Billy began spraying the bottle's contents on the ground as he walked gingerly forward. The liquid emitted a strangely sweet fragrance that quickly vanished. Since the same species of ferns once grew near the village, Ashley had been able to formulate a counter odor that would, as Walter loved to put it, "mask the musk." Fortunately, no one had to reinvent an Earth spray bottle. They had found a bottle of window cleaner in the airplane.

When he reached deeper snow, Billy stopped spraying and passed the bottle back through the line. He withdrew Excalibur again and marched on. The snow under his feet made almost no sound at all, but he still had to be careful. With trees ahead, protruding roots could trip him up, and their mission would be over.

Keeping the sword in front, he waved the blade back and forth in a wide arc. Soon, it brushed against something. A low branch? Probably.

He signaled with another yank on the rope. They had arrived at the forest. Since Candle had reported that most of the trees were not evergreens, they likely had no leaves and had allowed the snow to fall through. The march could continue in silence.

A slight tingle crawled along Billy's skin. It wasn't much, but it was very real, definitely danger. The shadow people were in the forest, but where? Since they couldn't live in sunlight, wouldn't they take refuge in the evergreens where the boughs would give them shelter?

Billy drew in a long breath through his nose. The smell of pine was pretty strong. If it got any stronger, they would have to find a new path. After another minute or so of dodging roots, evergreen scents, and danger signals, the blade touched something solid that felt like stone.

Pulling the rope, he gathered the other three into a huddle. "We veered right," he whispered. Then, setting his hand on the cliff, he turned left and followed the mountain's stony face, his fingers feeling the crags for any hint of a recess.

The scent of pine grew stronger. The danger alarm heightened, but now was no time to find another route. He had to go on. Should he allow just a bit of glow? He could slice a few attacking shadow people with Excalibur's newly restored beam, but could he handle the storm of darkness that thousands of those creatures would bring? It wasn't worth the risk, at least not yet.

After a few seconds, the cliff fell away from his guide hand. He leaned and reached farther. Still nothing. This had to be the cave. Now it was time to plunge into the depths of another mysterious darkness.

CHAPTER 2

THE PORTAL HOME

With three tugs, Billy signaled the others. It was time for the next step. While he stood with Excalibur at the cave's entrance, Elam would start the new march inside. He had been in this cave before, and since the shadow people feared it, or at least everyone hoped they still feared it, they would not be likely to venture into its depths.

As Ashley passed by, she touched his hand again, prompting him to smile. What a comfort she had been during the four-plus years he had been separated from Bonnie. Now that he was twenty and his tough training had molded him into a man, he longed to fulfill the prophecy and marry Bonnie. Surely she would be ready, too. She was always far more mature than anyone else her age.

He turned and followed the pull of the rope. He could sense Ashley in front of him, and she likely sensed him as well. She always did before. Over the years his emotions had let her know that he needed a woman's support. Of course others had wanted to help. Several fathers of village girls had inquired about his availability, which explained the friendliness of some of the twentysomething females and the giggles rising from teenaged girls as he walked by. But there was no way he could offer them hope. He and Bonnie would eventually get together. Even if it took a hundred years, he would wait for her.

For the time being, Ashley had been able to tell when he needed a boost. A kind gaze, a caring smile, a soft touch—she gave each one at the right time, never hinting that her gestures suggested anything beyond a sister's love. She was salve for a Bonnie-sized wound.

After nearly a minute, the rope's steady pull slackened. Elam had stopped. Billy turned and set his feet, taking his stance as rear guard while Walter unfastened everyone from the line and let it drop to the ground.

With the rush of water now a distant whisper, every footstep and every popping joint sounded like thunderclaps. Ashley ventured a whisper of her own. "I'm going to let you know what I'm doing step by step. Right now I'm examining the cave's back wall with a photometer. It's definitely showing readings that are consistent with what I have seen at other portal locations. The key is in finding the strongest signal." A few quiet seconds passed before her whisper continued. "Ah! I think I have it."

After a rustling sound crackled in the motionless air, her volume rose a notch. "I'm setting my flash unit on the ground at the focal point, and I'm about to turn it on. There's no way to stop the noise." A click sounded, and a low hum reverberated in the cave. "Billy, I'll let you know when it's ready. The last time I tested it, the light-bending ions took twenty-three seconds to charge. We'll assume the same now. Elam will give us a five-second warning, and we'll all stand back."

As Billy faced the cave entrance, the tingle returned. Its level of intensity grew quickly, and his danger alarm spiked. Something was coming, something deadly.

He turned on Excalibur's glow to maximum and searched the nearby floor. Nothing.

"Billy," Ashley said, "it's not time yet."

"I know, but we have company." He turned on the beam. It shot into the cave's ceiling and bored into the rock. The brilliant light cast a wave of energy out onto the cave floor. A skittering mass of black halted about ten paces away, then began a slow retreat.

"Looks like a bunch," Walter said. "I counted six sets of beady eyes in the front line."

"Five seconds," Elam called as he and Walter and Ashley backed toward the side walls. "You'll have to risk turning the beam this way," Elam said. "It's do or die now."

"Great choice of words." Billy flexed his biceps and swiveled toward Elam. "Ready!"

Elam chopped down with his hand. "Now!"

Billy copied his motion, slicing downward with the beam. As it cut a vertical line from top to bottom on the back wall, sparks exploded as if he had cleaved a high-voltage cable. He angled his head away from the arcing fireballs and finished his sweep. The beam struck Ashley's ion box, a baseball-sized black cube with mirrors on the top and sides. As sparks continued to fly, he kept the beam in place. Yellow bolts shot from the top of the box and cut jagged lines all across the back wall.

"Is this supposed to be happening?" he called.

Ashley stared wide-eyed at the fireworks display. "No! The ion box was supposed to open a portal, but I think that wall was already a gateway of some kind, like a portal that just needed a burst of energy."

"Keep it up!" Elam shouted. "At this point it's better to go forward than back."

Billy firmed his grip. The tingling sensation mounted. His danger alarm blared. "Something's behind me!"

"Uh-oh." Walter leaped and hacked with his sword. "Just keep energizing that gateway. I've got your back."

Sparks flew everywhere. Light poured from Ashley's box, creating a rectangular aura on the rear wall that looked like a glowing door.

Ashley raised a hand. "That's enough!"

Billy swung the beam up and turned. Walter was hopping and

hacking his sword against the floor so fast, it looked like he was dancing a violent jitterbug.

"Get back!" Billy called. "I'll fry the vermin."

Walter jumped out of the way. Billy chopped down with the beam and waved it back and forth across the stony ground.

Sizzles and squeals echoed, and purple smoke filled the cave with a burnt carrion stench. The shadows melted away, leaving a scattered collection of flat white bones.

Billy spun around. Ashley and Elam stared at the aura, which now looked like a golden painting on the back wall, a door as wide as the cave itself, stretching from floor to ceiling and as bright as Excalibur's beam.

"Our portal?" Billy asked, shielding his eyes.

"I think so." Ashley pushed her fingers against the wall. Her hand disappeared up to her wrist.

Walter joined her. "Feel anything?"

"Just air." Ashley retrieved her hand and flexed her fingers. "I think it's safe to go through."

"Will the shadow people follow?" Walter asked.

"Not likely." Billy put Excalibur away. "They risked a lot by coming this far, but going through a door of pure light?" He shook his head. "I don't think so."

Elam gave them a firm nod. "No time like the present." Leading with a hand, he walked into the glow and disappeared. Ashley followed, then Walter. After a final look at the steaming pile of bones on the floor, Billy joined them.

He broke through into a bath of cool air, though not nearly as cold as what they had left behind in Second Eden. A quick scan revealed a high wall encircling him, its perfectly vertical face interrupted only by a pile of rocks at one point of the base. A tent big enough for two campers had been set up in front of the pile, and a campfire smoldered a few feet from the tent's entrance flap. Nearby, a huge man slept on the ground, obviously Yereq.

Ashley grabbed Billy's shirt. "This is the old mobility room where

Walter and I found Sapphira." Her voice pitched into a squeal. "We're in Montana! We're home!"

Walter slapped Billy on the back. "You did it!"

Billy let his mouth drop open. The portal opening hovered in place, a brilliant rectangle sitting an inch above the ground right over a large *X* that someone had painted in black. On one side, the portal was bright and shining, an obvious doorway, but from the other side it seemed that nothing was there at all. The window to the other world was completely flat, invisible from any angle beyond ninety degrees in either direction.

Everything made sense. His mother had found the portal at this spot and had marked it to make sure she could find it again. She was probably the one camping out, maybe waiting for some kind of response after sending the rubellite, and Yereq, her guardian, slept close by.

Smiling, Billy rubbed his hands together. A reply to her note had arrived. Pressing a finger against his lips, he crept toward the tent. Judging from the sun's angle, it was getting close to midday. Why would she be sleeping so late? Maybe they had been up most of the night.

As he approached, the tent flap pushed to the side. His mother came out, stooping to fit through the opening. With her head down, she didn't notice Billy. Carrying a cooking pot, she shuffled to the campfire, picked up a small log from a nearby stack, and threw it onto the embers.

Billy walked to within reach and looked at her from the back. Her hair was shorter, grayer, and her posture just a bit more stooped. Was it from the heavy burden of losing her husband and son and trying to retrieve them from an invisible world for more than four years, or had those years physically aged her body that much?

She crouched and stirred the ashes with a stick, deathly quiet. Billy's memories drifted back to another morning when his mother prepared breakfast, the morning he kissed her cheek and left a burn, giving her proof that he was different, that he was genetically a dragon child. She was humming that morning, her sign of peace and contentment, but now, not a sound.

Billy spoke softly, yet clearly. "Mom. I'm back."

She stopped stirring but neither spoke nor turned. Yereq woke and sat up with a start, his eyes wide as he stared at Billy.

Trembling, his mother straightened. The stick shook in her hand. Then slowly, ever so slowly, she turned. For a moment, she just stared. Her eyes darted, first side to side, then up and down, as if drinking in every detail. A teardrop fell from one eye. She laughed, then sucked the breath back in, her lips quaking.

Finally, she raised a hand and caressed Billy's cheek. A smile breaking through, she spoke with a hoarse, tremulous voice. "Who is this handsome young man who looks so much like my son? You are taller, your face is thinner, your body more muscular, and . . ." Her voice cracking, she shouted, "Oh, Billy!" She threw her arms around his neck and wept. "You're here! Oh, thank God you're here!"

Pulling her into a tight embrace, Billy patted her on the back. "Yes, Mom, and you're the reason."

She pushed herself away and looked into his eyes. "I am?"

He gripped her shoulder. "We found the rubellite."

She gasped, and her eyes grew wide. "You did?"

"Yep. I don't know where you got it, but it was made for Excalibur's hilt." He flicked his head toward his back scabbard. "Now it lights up like nobody's business."

She stared at him for a moment, blinking. Her head tilted, and her voice dropped to a whisper. "That was six months ago."

"Well, it's complicated. You see—"

She looked past him and locked her gaze on the others. "Then you didn't come with Gabriel?"

"Gabriel? No. Why would we?"

Her voice spiked. "Because we sent him through the portal to find out what was over there!"

Ashley, Walter, and Elam joined their huddle. "How long ago?" Walter asked.

Her eyes darted back and forth between Walter and Billy. "Late last night, maybe eight hours ago." She nodded at her tent. "That's why we camped out here. We finally got Apollo to open a large enough portal, so we did it as soon as we could, even though it was at night. I hoped to follow when he reported that it was safe."

"It's far from safe," Walter said. "There are these shadow people that—"

Ashley nudged his ribs. "We'll find him. Since he can fly, he's probably fine. He just won't be able to get past Abraham's wall."

"He won't be fine if Goliath sees him. Gabriel's probably not as fast as—"

"Walter!" Ashley nudged him again and looked back at Billy's mother. "Don't worry, Mrs. Bannister. We'll find him."

Billy's mother touched his cheek, tears again falling. "How is your father?"

"He's doing great. He has a shelter and a regeneracy dome, and ever since the dragons started taking turns resting by Abraham's wall of fire, they've all stayed strong. But I guess you didn't hear about the transformation, did you?"

"I heard he's a dragon again and that you have your fire-breathing back. When Acacia came through the portal, she told everyone in the mines, and Gabriel told us."

He slid his hand into hers. "Then you also know we need reinforcements. We think an army of giants and shadowy beasts are going to attack some peaceful villagers soon, so we need more dragons."

"Yes, the former dragons are lodging close by. Yereq can have them here in less than an hour."

Billy looked at Elam. "How much time do we have?"

"First light of dawn is about two hours," Elam said. "We still have to parasail down to the marshlands and then float out the southern wall, but I think we can make it." He glanced at the glowing portal. It was still bright and showed no signs of weakening. "We can wait an hour."

Billy laid a hand on Elam's back. "I almost forgot. Mom, this is Elam, son of Shem, grandson of Noah."

She nodded and offered a weak smile. "I'm glad to finally meet you."

"Likewise," he said, bowing. "I appreciate the politeness, but we should hurry. The longer we wait, the more danger for Gabriel."

"Yereq!" Marilyn called.

Yereq walked up and replied in a deep, echoing voice. "Yes, Marilyn."

"It's time to summon Kaylee, Tamara, and the others. We're going to Second Eden."

Elam raised a finger. "We can take only one at a time. Our raft is too small for more."

She gave him a quizzical stare. "Raft?"

"We have to navigate a river," Billy said, "but we'll explain the whole thing while we wait. We talked it over and decided it would be best to start with Dorian. Then we'll come back for the others, one each night until Pegasus rises too early in the evening."

"Pegasus is our moon," Walter added. "We need at least four hours of total darkness to do this safely."

"I think Dorian will be happy to be first. Kaylee is burning up the Internet and the phone lines searching for her son and Dallas's daughter. Elise is helping, so they'll want to keep working on that."

Yereq pulled a cell phone from his trousers pocket. "I will climb into cellular range and summon Dorian." Tromping with heavy footsteps, he headed for the wall where a rope ladder dangled from above.

Billy's mother let her head droop. "When will I be able to come with you?"

"Well," Billy said, glancing at Elam, "we talked about that. You see, we have to get five dragons into Second Eden. By the time we get the fifth one in, Pegasus will—"

"We'll get you over there," Elam said. "By that time, maybe we'll be faster and can do it in a shorter window."

Billy looked into his mother's eyes. She desperately wanted to come to Second Eden and see her husband. "Elam's right, Mom. We'll make it happen."

With her gaze still on the ground, his mother sighed. "Only five more days. I can live with that."

After a few seconds of silence, Billy took in a deep breath. It was time to ask the question he had been avoiding ever since he arrived. "Uh . . . Mom? Have you heard from Bonnie?"

She compressed his hand, a new tear sparkling in her eye. "Not a word in more than four years. Some of the Caitiff chased her and Sapphira in the mines, but every tunnel is flooded now, so there was no way we could keep searching. Even when the waters were rising, we sent in cave divers, but we didn't find any sign of either of them."

Billy tensed his jaw. He couldn't say a word.

A gentle hand rubbed his back—Ashley. She, too, stayed silent, but her touch said it all. "Don't give up hope," she was saying. "We're here for you."

As usual, Ashley's healing hand did wonders. His muscles loosening, Billy touched the string of beads around his neck. "Acacia and I found this on the ledge while the floodwaters were rising. Since it wasn't broken, I was thinking she left it there on purpose, like a sign that she's okay."

"There is another clue," his mother said. "When I arrived at the overlook in the mines, I thought I saw Bonnie flying Sapphira off the ledge, but it was dark, and it happened so quickly, I wasn't sure. But Yereq found one of the Caitiff, and it confirmed what I thought I saw. Bonnie and Sapphira were definitely there, and they did jump."

Elam pointed at himself. "I've been through a portal in that river. The magma was cool back then, and it got too hot later. But now that it's water—"

"They could go through it," Billy finished. "And that means we can go, too."

"I'm game," Walter said. "Compared to what we just did, diving through an unknown portal at the bottom of a flooded chasm should be a piece of cake."

"You can't." Billy's mother flattened her hands and set one on top of the other. "According to our diver, the magma hardened in layers. You have lava rock, then water, then lava rock, and so on. We don't know how many layers there are or how thick each one is."

Billy ground his teeth together. All the clues led to the same lousy conclusion. Even if Bonnie escaped through a portal, she was stuck somewhere without a way to call for help. Obviously, in four years, she would have contacted her friends if she had been able.

"And we haven't heard from Shiloh," his mother added. "Not a word since she was kidnapped."

"And Acacia's missing, too," Billy said.

After several seconds of awkward silence, he motioned for everyone to sit around the fire. While they waited for Yereq to return with Dorian, he related the story of how he, his father, and Acacia found Shiloh in the protected ghost town and failed to rescue her, and worse yet, how Acacia fell into the prison herself and disappeared with Shiloh.

As the minutes ticked away, all five exchanged stories, including how Billy's mother, Adam, and Carly had reconstructed Apollo. It had taken over three years to get a working model, and it would have taken longer if not for the help of a dead physicist who made them promise to keep his identity secret because of his shame. Obviously, being a resident of Hades meant that all his brainpower had been for naught. He had lost his soul. Still, he was willing to help. Why? He never said, and no one thought it proper to ask.

Shelly was now married and living in Morgantown. Since she was pregnant with her first child, she had to excuse herself from the adventures and make her home ready for the new arrival. Walter's parents were in Castlewood watching Monique and Rebecca. His father retired from his law practice and was running Ashley's computer company, Stalworth Enterprises, with help from a local computer wizard named Fred. For a while, people asked where Ashley and Walter had gone, so Walter's father kept brushing them off with a story about them traveling somewhere with Billy and Jared on a secret mission. Eventually people stopped asking.

Stacey was attending the local community college now, so she was relatively independent. Carly moved into the Bannister home on a fostering basis and later began attending the same college part-time while still working on the Apollo project. Adam and his father started an electronics supply business, which helped in finding parts for Apollo.

"Speaking of Apollo . . ." Ashley excused herself and returned a moment later with the hourglasslike portal device. As the storytelling continued, she looked it over, practically taking it apart and reassembling it with her practiced fingers.

Billy's mother touched Walter's hand. "Your father walks with a cane now. He took a bullet in his spine and was in physical therapy for months. He's doing great, considering the circumstances."

A tremor ran across Walter's face. He looked at Ashley. She took his hand and interlocked their thumbs.

Walter fished a small, rolled-up parchment from an inner pocket. "Mrs. B, can you give him and Mom something for me?"

"Yes, of course. I can mail it to them." She took the scroll and looked at it. "It's sealed with wax."

"It's personal." A distinct jitter rattled his voice. "I want them to be the first people on Earth to read it. Then they can tell you what it's all about."

"Okay." She laid the scroll on her lap. "But that makes my brain go wild with speculation."

Billy suppressed a grin. Since Walter was being so secretive, it wouldn't be right to give anything away. The message explained to his father that he had asked Ashley to marry him, and he hoped that somehow his family could come to Second Eden for their wedding. Of course, they were waiting for the expected war to be over first, so maybe it would be safe when the time came.

After a few more minutes of storytelling, Yereq climbed down the rope ladder, followed by Dorian. Billy and company greeted her and explained the transformation procedure. They had figured out long ago that each former dragon had to wear a rubellite ring while in the garden. Yet, Patrick was still unable to transform into Valcor, even after borrowing one of the rings Elam still had in his possession.

"I do not have one," Dorian said, showing them both hands.

"I have two." Elam pulled a ring from his pocket. "This one used to be Ashley's. She's wearing her mother's now."

Dorian slid it over her finger. It was a little loose, but manageable.

After they had gathered at the portal, Billy kissed his mother on the cheek, careful to hold back his scorching breath. "I read your note, and I told Dad that you love him. Is there anything else you want me to tell him?"

She nodded, her eyes sparkling. "Tell him scales or skin mean nothing; my love will never fail." She returned his kiss and, raising a fist to cover her mouth, said no more.

Ashley read her photometer. "The doorway deteriorated a little bit. At this rate, it will be gone in about three and a half hours. Yereq should guard it to make sure nothing comes out from the other side. You won't like what resides over there."

"Flat shadow critters." Walter twisted his shoe on the ground. "Yereq can probably stomp them like cockroaches."

Drawing his sword, Billy led the way through the portal. When he stepped back into the cave, it was darker and colder than before, but no shadow people slithered about, likely frightened by the portal's glow and the sight of their fellows' bones.

When the others joined him, Walter again fastened everyone together with the rope, Billy in front, then Ashley, Walter, Dorian, and Elam. Billy strode ahead, quickly at first, but when the portal's light faded, he slowed, listening for movement and tuning his danger radar. Since the shadow people had been alerted to their presence, they might have amassed at the cave's entrance. An ambush seemed likely.

Soon, the exit arch came into sight, barely visible now that the portal was well behind them. The tingling sensation crawled along Billy's body, and his alarm sounded. They were close, very close.

He halted. Ashley bumped into him, but only lightly. She tugged on his shirt and breathed a ghost of a whisper in his ear. "I sense a presence."

Billy pointed at himself, trying to signal, "So do I."

From her belt clip, she pulled a flashlight, modified for use with her homemade batteries. "It's real close." She shone the light at the base of the wall. A dark form turned its ribbonlike body away from the light and shivered as it emitted a series of high-pitched clicks.

"That's strange," Billy whispered. "It stayed here alone."

Ashley stooped. "It's scared, but it wants to communicate." She flicked off the light. "What do you want to say?"

The portal at the back of the cave painted a dim glow on Ashley's profile. As more clicks sounded, she nodded several times. "This one seems quite intelligent," she explained. "I sense mostly feelings. That noise it's making doesn't mean anything to me, but I'm getting a few words from its mind."

Billy glanced back and forth between the shadow person and the cave exit. His danger alarm heightened. Could this one be a decoy, told to get their attention while the others massed for an attack?

Ashley looked up at Elam. "I think he knows you. He said something about being sorry for not building the fire."

"The fire," Elam repeated in a whisper. "Where could that have been?"

She half closed one eye. "Does 'skotos' mean anything to you?"

"It's a forest in the Bridgelands." Elam crouched beside Ashley. "Does he have a name?"

Ashley turned back to the shadow. "What is your name?"

A short burst of clicks rose from its dark face.

Ashley shook her head. "He's saying it with his language, but I can't pull it from his mind."

"Zane?" Elam asked. "Is your name Zane?"

CHAPTER 3

THE FACELESS PROTECTORS

The clicking noise pulsed rapidly, sounding like an excited cricket.

"Slow your thoughts," Ashley said. "Your mind knows English. Just concentrate on each word and say it inside as forcefully as you can."

After a few seconds, she began nodding again. "Okay. I see. That's good to know." She rose to her feet with a sigh. "Apparently he was banished here when he lost his courage during the battle against the giants, and now he wants to make up for his faithlessness by giving us a warning. There are a few dozen of his people immediately outside the cave entrance, but the rest of them, thousands maybe, have gathered on the main path between here and the river. So if we want to survive, we'll have to go another way."

Elam slid his hand under Zane's paper-thin head. "Thank you for the help. Is there anything I can do for you?"

The tiny eyes turned toward Ashley. Once again nodding, she spoke while shifting her gaze between Zane and Elam. "He says he had his chance in life, and he chose the ways of the hypocrite, so it's too late for him. When the others learn of his treachery, they will tear him apart and end this phase of his suffering, which will be all for the better. Just go in peace and remember that he finally did something right."

Elam kept his hand in place, apparently struggling in his mind.

"We can't take him," Ashley said. "Among us, he would suffer all the more."

Drawing his hand away, Elam rose to his feet and whispered, "So be it."

"If they're gathering at the path we took to get here," Billy said, "we can use all the light we want to go around them. We won't run into them."

"Until we get to the river," Ashley said. "They'll see us there."

Billy untied the rope. "Just stay close." He took in a quick breath, lit up Excalibur's beam, and ran. Swiping the laser back and forth across the floor, he flew through the opening. Sizzles again erupted, and the now familiar stench of roasted shadow people permeated the air.

He stopped just outside the arch and mowed the ground with a blast of flames from his mouth. The firelight revealed at least thirty shadowy forms, some writhing in pain, others fleeing along the ground.

Billy waved his arm. "This way!" With his sword lighting the path, he headed straight into the forest, dodging low-hanging branches and leaping over roots. When he broke into the clear and found the beach, he sprinted along the boundary between sand and snow, running parallel to the river. On his left, a sea of black shadows boiled with activity. The escape raft floated on top of hundreds of black fingers.

When his four companions joined him, Ashley now leading with her flashlight, Billy waded into the blackness. "Stay here and get ready to grab the rope." He blasted a wave of fire on the ground and slashed the beam back and forth. Dark body parts flew in all directions.

"You're not going without Elam and me!" Walter called.

When Billy reached the raft, he grabbed the rope and tossed it past Walter and Elam as they cut and hacked at the ground. Ashley caught it, and she and Dorian dragged the raft toward the river. "We got it!" Ashley called.

A hand reached out and grabbed Elam's ankle. He sliced its arm with his sword, but five more hands latched onto his legs. As if running in glue, he lifted his feet in slow motion, constantly swinging his sword behind him.

Billy sprinted up to him from behind and yelled, "Jump!" He swept the beam along the ground. Elam leaped over it just in time. The dark arms snapped like rubber bands, and the sea of bodies underneath melted into a steaming oil slick.

"Run!" Billy and Walter jumped over the black mass, and Elam joined them in stride. Following Ashley's waving flashlight beam, they ran in leaps. When they arrived at the raft, it had been pushed out to the river's edge, and Ashley and Dorian were already inside. Dorian sat in the center with the empty bags in her lap.

"Get in!" Ashley shouted. "The parachute's almost ready."

While Walter climbed in, Billy doused and sheathed the sword. Now in total darkness, he slid into his corner and checked his guideline. It was good and tight. "Did you get your noisemaker?"

"Check," Ashley said. "And my musk masker."

"Launching!" Elam called as he shoved the raft fully into the river. He leaped aboard and settled in place. The current sent them hurtling forward.

"What may I do to help?" Dorian asked.

"We're the flight attendants," Walter said. "Just relax and enjoy the flight."

Elam snapped his fingers. "Silence!"

A hush fell across the raft. Elam seemed tense, in turmoil. Seeing Zane and leaving him behind had shaken him badly, and now it would be only seconds before they would launch over another waterfall where a new danger lay, Adam's Marsh, the home of Flint, Goliath, and the Nephilim.

Billy slid two metal tubes from one of the bags and fastened them end to end. He then put on a pair of fireproof gloves. There would be no time later.

Suddenly, the river fell away again. As before, Elam and Walter caught the air with the front of the parachute, and Billy and Ashley let out their guidelines to allow the canopy to fill. This fall would have been shorter, but their plan was to stay airborne and use the persistent breezes to fly as far away from the pool as possible in case enemy soldiers guarded the valley exit.

A queasy feeling churned in Billy's stomach. Was it fear? Not likely. He had made it this far without getting sick from fear. It was a deeper sickness, a nausea that seemed familiar somehow, but this was no time to figure it out. It was time to put their plan into action.

After filling his lungs, he lifted the connected tubing, hoisted one end near the apex of the billowing parachute, and pressed the other against his lips. Mixing in the gasses from his belly, he blew with all his might. The flames shot out the opposite end of the tube and struck the middle of the parachute, giving it an upward boost. The tube shielded the fire stream from any onlookers. Of course, a few orange tongues were visible at the exit point, but someone would have to be looking directly at it to notice.

Heaving in breaths and shooting more fire, Billy helped the raft stay aloft. Ashley had slid in behind him to control both rear guidelines. Since they had practiced this procedure many times, she had no problem steering the back of the raft.

When he began to feel dizzy, he pulled the tube down, broke it apart, and put it away. It was time to come in for a landing. Where? With nothing but darkness all around, they could only guess. Since this part of the river meandered, the best they could do would be to follow a straight line and listen for the rush of water as they descended.

He grabbed his guideline again. Looking below didn't help. The darkness was complete, and the wall of fire was too far away to provide any light at all.

After sailing at least a thousand feet, they settled on a patch of sand. The river splashed along on their left about ten paces away.

Billy jumped out and lifted his corner. The raft was light. Good.

Walter had already guided Dorian to his corner and helped her disembark, just as planned. They carried the raft to the river, and all five slid silently back into place.

After securing the wadded parachute next to Dorian, Billy picked up the two tubes, still warm to the touch, and reached one forward. Someone took it, probably Walter. He was supposed to use it to push off from the right front corner and Billy from the left rear in case the current rammed them into a beach.

Billy kept the far end of his pole in the water. Of course, he wouldn't be able to see any bends coming, so he had to navigate by feeling the river's depth.

As they rode the current in silence, Billy kept his stare fixed on the right-hand side. Adam's Marsh lay there, and if anyone would challenge them, the attack would come from that direction.

A pair of torches came into view, maybe a stone's throw away. Billy ducked low. As the raft passed the lights, he peeked up. One of the Nephilim stood next to a bitternut tree, his torches planted in the sand. As he ate one of the fruit, a torch fizzled out. He plucked it up and extended the top toward a dark mass. "Light it," he growled.

A blast of fire shot out and coated the torch, illuminating it with a vibrant flame. A dragon sat on the beach, a small dragon, too small to be Goliath or Roxil, and it couldn't be a Second Eden dragon. They breathed ice.

The dragon's eyebeams fell on Billy's cloak. He desperately wanted to brush them away, but that would just make him more obvious. Whoever this dragon was, it had spotted them, but it made no motion or sound, and the Naphil didn't seem to notice.

When they reached a bend to the left, Walter pushed off the beach, and they passed out of the dragon's sight. Billy let out a long sigh. Ashley took his hand and gave it a gentle squeeze. She knew. Something strange was going on. That dragon could easily have sounded an alarm, but for some reason, it chose silence.

After pushing off the edge a few more times, Billy rested. The river had straightened, and the southern part of Abraham's wall came into view. It was time to get ready for another plunge through fire.

Of course, the dragons had tried several times to blast through, but it repelled their blows, as if their bodies and the wall were similar magnetic poles. Was it their scales? Their photoreceptors? No one knew. But the effect was likely for the better. If Clefspeare and Hartanna couldn't get in, then Goliath couldn't get out.

Billy stared at the flames, searching for a shadow, any hint of Flint's guards. So far, nothing. If all went according to plan, Valiant and Candle were now raising a ruckus a hundred paces to the west, close enough to lure any guards away.

Elam tapped Billy's knee. Billy sent the signal along. They spread out the parachute again, and everyone ducked underneath. As before, the light grew brighter. Their raft was now exposed. The most dangerous part of the journey had arrived. If any guards were on duty and paying attention, this voyage was doomed.

Someone shouted. Another answered. Something whizzed above. Was it an arrow? A dull *thunk* struck the parachute, then another.

"Time to fire back," Ashley said. She pulled a thin cylinder from her bag, yanked out a strand of twine from one end, and tossed the cylinder out from under the parachute. Within two seconds, it exploded. While more arrows rained down, whizzing by or piercing their covering, she threw out three more. With each explosion, the number of attacking arrows lessened.

The temperature spiked again. With a loud whoosh, blinding light flew over the raft from front to back. The arrows ceased. Tongues of fire shot through the chute's holes and licked at their bodies. Finally, steam lifted the raft. The front tipped down, and the rear slung the passengers headlong into the river.

Billy tumbled through icy water. After a breath-stealing surge, he thrust his head above the surface and searched the turbulent river for the others. Ah! Ashley was treading water within reach, her wide eyes reflecting the nearby flaming wall. He grabbed her around the waist with one arm and began to swim for shore with the other, but something pulled his collar and jerked him up. Swinging toward Ashley, he locked his arms and legs around her. She relaxed and allowed herself to be dragged along.

Within seconds, he felt his body sliding on the beach. As strong arms helped him stand, he hoisted Ashley to her feet.

"Are you well?" came a deep, strong voice.

Billy looked at his helper. "Valiant! Thank you!"

"Yes," Ashley said as she wrung out the fringes of her cloak. "We didn't expect you to be here."

Valiant draped a blanket over Ashley's head and back. "I will explain soon. I must help Candle tend to the others." He ran downstream, firelight dancing on the back of his cloak.

"He's dry," Billy said, shivering.

Ashley drew the blanket together. "I noticed. Then who dragged us from the river?"

A hot breeze swept across their bodies. Billy spread out his arms and let his wet clothes flap in the luxuriant draft. "I think we have our answer."

Hartanna blew the stream of hot dry air while Clefspeare sat at her side. "Yellinia is hurt," Clefspeare said. "Thigocia and Candle are tending to her."

Billy translated his father's words. Yellinia was Dorian. One of the arrows must have hit her, but she hadn't made a sound. "How bad is it?" Billy asked.

"It does not appear to be a deep wound." Clefspeare inhaled and took a turn blowing a warm wind.

Ashley pushed her fingers into her hair and shook out the water. "I'll check on her in a minute."

"I think your smoke bombs did the trick," Billy said. "They couldn't shoot what they couldn't see."

"I was afraid one of those arrows would puncture the raft." Ashley let a smile break through. "When you think about it, every part of the plan worked pretty well."

Walter and Elam joined them in the warmth, both shivering and wet. "Valiant thinks Flint got wind of our mission," Elam said. "He and Candle tried their diversion, but no matter how much noise they made, only one Naphil stood guard at that part of the wall. When Valiant heard the ruckus over here, he and Candle ran to try to help, but there wasn't anything anyone could do."

Billy stripped off his cloak and let the heat radiate through his inner tunic. "But if they had a spy, wouldn't they have stopped us a lot earlier?"

"I would have thought so," Elam said.

"Did you see that dragon at the side of the river?" Walter asked. "Could he have flown ahead and warned them?"

Turning to give his back a chance to dry, Billy nodded. "I saw him, and I'm sure he saw us. If he betrayed us, why did he wait?"

"And who could he be?" Elam asked. "He was too small to be Goliath or Roxil but he was almost as big as Grackle."

"A youngling?" Hartanna asked. "Has Roxil given birth?"

Clefspeare let the breeze die away. "There has been ample time to have two younglings by now, though only one could be old enough to fit the description."

"I'd better check on Dorian now." Ashley pushed her hair back and fastened a rubber band around it. "She might not be able to make the hike, so we'd better bring Merlin closer."

"On my way." Billy ran downstream with Ashley and stopped for a moment to check on Dorian before continuing into the prairie. As he hustled through the snow-covered grass, light from the wall dimmed. At least the dangerous part was over. Lions no longer hunted these fields, having migrated farther south. All he had to do was taxi Merlin across the snow, pick up a few human passengers, and fly back to the village.

Although cold air dried his throat, he pressed on. At one time, running a mile would have winded him, but now, even tromping with heavy boots through snow, it seemed like nothing. A warm rush flooded his body. His mother had noticed the change—taller, more muscular, she had said. He had become a warrior, and her affirmation felt good.

After jumping into Merlin and starting the engine, he eased it into a low-speed taxi and settled back in the pilot's seat. What would they do now? Of course they could patch the parachute, but with Flint's troops knowing how they had breached the border, would it be possible to try again the very next night? If not, how could he get word to his mother that they would be delayed? She would be expecting them. And what about Gabriel? Without the ability to penetrate the wall, how could they search for him?

The silhouettes of his comrades moved about across the backdrop of the towering wall of flames. Somehow the view seemed appropriate, faceless shadows hustling about under the watch of an immeasurable light. Without desire for recognition or acclaim, these small, nondescript forms served the light's will. Would they live through the trials? Die in the effort? Those questions seemed unimportant. The only end that mattered was whether or not the purposes of the light would be fulfilled—to protect the innocent ones and hold back the fiends who would drag them away to slaughter.

Billy locked the scene in his mind. He would draw this portrait someday, maybe in charcoal with a splash of color for the background. Yellow and orange pigments from sempian bark would do nicely. He would call it, "The Faceless Protectors."

As he drew closer, one of the dragons spread its wings. With no other features visible, the shadow brought Bonnie to mind . . . again.

Four years and no word. Where could she be? Had Arramos's goons captured her? Maybe she was with Shiloh and Acacia in yet another world. And what about Sapphira? Could all four be together?

Billy stopped the plane and flopped back against the headrest. His mind raced with jumbled thoughts. Bonnie's face, so young and lovely. What did she look like now? The marriage prophecy, odd words that many agreed pointed to their eventual union. But did they really? The words seemed less certain than ever.

Gabriel came to mind. Someone had to rescue him. Sure, he was one of the faceless shadows, and he knew the dangers of his mission, but that didn't matter. No warrior should be left behind.

Pulling his hood up, Billy hustled to the back of the plane, hopped down the airstair, and marched toward Walter. "Are you ready?"

Walter raised his own hood. "Time to find Gabriel?"

Billy glanced at Valiant and Ashley helping Dorian into the airplane. Dorian was on her feet. That was good news. "Right. I think everything's under control here."

"Yes!" Walter said. "Another wild water slide!"

Billy shook his head. "By the time we get there, they'll have posted plenty of guards."

"Then what do you have in mind?"

Billy thrust out his fist. "Punch straight through the wall at an unguarded point."

"With just our cloaks to protect us?" Walter tapped himself on the head. "Did that tumble in the river rattle your brain?"

"Look, we already tested the cloaks partway into the wall, and the raft proved that we could go the rest of the way. We just need to get enough momentum."

"A dragon could throw us, maybe with its tail," Walter said. "Then we could—"

"Cool your jets, boys." Ashley walked up, inspecting a broken arrow. "Your plan won't work."

"Why not?" Walter asked.

Ashley pushed the arrow between her fingers. "A dragon might be able to propel you through the wall, but how are you going to get back?"

"I was just about to say that Roxil could shoot us back through," Walter said. "We're hoping she's still on our side, right?"

"If you can find her. If you can dodge Goliath and the Nephilim. You can't rely on help from allies who don't even know you're coming."

"But we have two allies who know we're coming," Billy said.

Walter and Ashley both stared at him. "Who?" they said at the same time.

"Abraham and Angel. I think we won't need a dragon at all. Just running with a full head of steam ought to do it. I'm counting on our allies to thin out the wall for us."

"Well . . . maybe." Ashley crossed her arms, her brow bent low. "You're missing one ally in your plans."

"I'm starting to sound like an owl now," Walter said. "Who?"

She elbowed his ribs. "Me, silly! How else are you going to find Gabriel in the dark? I should be able to detect his presence."

"Fair enough," Billy said. "But we'd better get back to the village first. We should reapply the flame retardant to our cloaks and get a fourth one for Gabriel."

"A big one," Walter said. "We have to cover his wings."

"Good point. We can't cut holes in the back, or the fire would get through."

Walter rubbed his stomach. "And I'm starved. Blasting through walls of fire really burns the calories."

"Food sounds good. And a quick nap. We'll go back in the middle of the day. Flint won't be expecting us to come back so soon and in broad daylight, and we won't be bothered so much by the shadow people."

"From the north," Walter said. "Climbing up from the south would be impossible. Besides, we didn't get to use the snowboards."

Ashley rolled her eyes. "The boards were Plan B, in case the raft didn't make it through."

"Plan A, Plan B, what do I care? I practiced too hard. Let's boogie on those boards!"

CHAPTER 4

SEEING THE INVISIBLE

Billy lay awake on his straw bed. With thoughts of trying to rescue Gabriel dominating his mind, getting to sleep would probably take a while. Their next mission could be the most dangerous yet, but they had no choice, and Gabriel might be out there dodging shadow people and Flint's troops, so they had to go as soon as possible. He had to make this nap a short and efficient one.

Although dawn was breaking outside, only a bare candle near his pillow illuminated his surroundings. The hut's window had been sealed tightly for the cold weather, so total darkness had become a way of life. But it was better that way. It would help him employ his usual plan for falling asleep.

He blew out the candle and settled in. Darkness gave him a canopy for painting pictures in the air, a way to begin his dreams. He would mentally draw Bonnie's face, and, since closing his eyes made no difference in the darkness, she would stay in his mind's eye as he drifted off to sleep.

Soon, his portrait expanded. Bonnie, now fully drawn from head to toe, knelt at her bedside. This was definitely one of his favorite scenes. Years ago, back when her father had come to West Virginia to take her home to Montana, Billy had found her praying in this position, her hands folded on her bedspread. Back then, her wings were hidden in her backpack, but now, in his imagination, they spread out behind her in all their glory. With her blonde-streaked hair draped over her back, and her sparkling eyes lifted up toward Heaven, she looked like an angel.

Billy walked into the bedroom scene and listened to her lovely voice as she prayed out loud, her cadence lacking rhythm as the words missed their obvious metric beat.

Call to me, and I will answer you;
Say my name, and my light will shine.
Draw me out, and I will rise again;
Take my hand, and I will be thine.

Billy let the words echo in his mind. These were different, not her usual prayer, and her lack of rhythm felt odd, like a drum striking at the wrong time. Normally she asked for help to escape whatever prison she was in, and she often prayed for him, for his safety, courage, and enduring faith. This was the first time his mind ever invented the scene with her praying a poem. And the opening line was familiar, the words on her poster, the phrase that helped him understand that he had to call for a doctor instead of Makaidos.

Makaidos. Billy let that name bounce around in his thoughts. Twice they had changed the poem and called for someone else, and now that the season of death had arrived and stayed, and with Acacia's energizing light no longer available, a third opportunity never arose. The eclipses had ceased, and with clouds and snow often obscuring the sky, they rarely saw Pegasus or Phoenix anyway. The moons would sometimes peek through breaks in the clouds, and their light would bathe the covering blanket in a silvery glow. Even with those glimpses, the villagers agreed that until the season of death finally ended, the cycles would never return to normal. And no cycles, no Makaidos.

Bonnie sang her prayer again, this time with more emotion. Every word seemed drenched with sorrow, yet buoyed by hope as they rose toward the sky as an offering to God. And Bonnie glowed. Oh, yes, she glowed, far brighter than Pegasus, and with a shimmering radiance that outshone a regeneracy dome, even with all the glittering gems the dragons had gathered over the years.

He reached for her, but, as usual, a barrier stood between them, invisible, yet impenetrable. He would have to wait still longer. Someday it would be broken. Eventually it would dissolve . . . Wouldn't it?

Bonnie turned and stared at him. Billy gasped. She saw him! This was new. They had never made eye contact before.

She opened her mouth, and a harsh call burst forth.

"Billy!"

Something shook his shoulder.

"Billy. It's me, Walter. It's time to blast through the fire."

Yawning, Billy blinked his eyes open. "Already?"

Walter stood over him with a lantern in hand. "You said three hours, and you got an extra five minutes."

Billy looked at the bed on the other side of the hut. Elam had still not slept. "Where's our warrior chief?"

"Interviewing Yellinia. He never gives up on our missing-in-action troops, so he's trying to get every clue he can about Sapphira and Bonnie." Walter threw a cloak over Billy's legs. "It's got a fresh coat of fire-be-gone. You're all set. I told Ashley we'd meet her at her hut."

Billy climbed to his feet, put on the cloak, and strapped on his scabbard. "When does Elam want to try the transformation?"

"It's done. That's why I called her Yellinia instead of Dorian. They decided it was better to go ahead and transform her so Thigocia could heal the arrow wound."

"Great! Now we have six dragons."

Walter nodded toward Billy's scabbard. "I put Excalibur back, but you might want to move it to your belt for this mission."

"Right." As Billy made the adjustment, Walter pushed open the door and allowed Billy to go through first. Still working on the belt, he blinked at the morning light. Snow was falling again, but not heavily. "If the beam worked on the garden soil, I guess the bones of Makaidos are still functioning."

"They sizzled up a storm. Excalibur worked great."

Billy and Walter jogged toward Ashley's hut. "Any effect on the two plants?" Billy asked.

"Zero. They're both still bulging. The ugly one looks about ready to pop."

When they reached the hut, Ashley was standing outside the door, her arms crossed tightly as she bounced on her toes. "Which dragons are we flying?"

"Grackle and Albatross," Walter said. "They're good and rested."

Ashley shivered hard. "Perfect. Heated scales."

Walter picked up a duffle bag near Ashley's feet. "Does this one have the snowboards?" he asked.

She nodded, tight-lipped and still shivering. "And more flame retardant and a few smoke bombs, just in case."

"Are you okay? It's not any colder than usual."

"Just tired, I think." She bundled her cloak tighter against her body. "That makes me colder."

"What did you get? One hour of sleep?"

"Maybe two." She nodded toward the door. "My other bag's inside, the one with a cloak for Gabriel, and my ion box."

"I'll get them." Walter disappeared inside.

Ashley smiled at Billy but said nothing. A ring glittered on her finger, a new one Walter had given her when he proposed marriage.

Billy grinned. Even after three months, it was still hard getting used to thinking of his old buddy as an engaged man. For most of the four years they had lived in Second Eden, Ashley had said many times that he wasn't old enough, that their ages were too far apart, but when he single-handedly mowed down four Vacants who had trapped her in one of the greenhouses, she changed her mind.

Sure, he was still only twenty, but living in the rigors of this world had definitely made a man out of him. He had helped Ashley design the farming greenhouses and suggested a great way to funnel geothermal energy to a heating coil system throughout the greenhouse network. Although digging through the frozen ground was bitter, backbreaking work, he never complained or took a day off. And his ability to organize and teach the villagers the intricacies of the technology was amazing. He had translated the scientific jargon into the common language so that everyone understood well enough to work without constant supervision.

And the results spoke for themselves. Without Walter's labors, by now everyone might have starved, but their food supply had proven to be more than adequate. So one day while he was showing Ashley his new idea for keeping snow from overloading a roof, he took her to the top of one of the greenhouses where he had built a snowman kneeling in front of a snowwoman.

As Billy and Ashley continued waiting for Walter, Billy imagined the roof scene, having heard every detail from Walter a dozen times.

* * *

"What's going on here?" Ashley said as she pushed off the top ladder rung and stepped onto the roof.

"The snow dude is asking the snow dudette a question." Walter touched the kneeling snowman's head. "But he's younger and a whole lot dumber, so it took him a long time to get enough courage. That's why he took her up on the roof, to do it privately. Down on the ground there's always someone asking a question or needing help."

"I see." Ashley crossed her arms and looked back and forth between Walter and the snow sculptures. "What question did he ask?"

Walter got down on his knee, mimicking the snowman. "I'm not a hundred percent sure. That's the reason I brought you up here. I was wondering if you could read his mind and figure it out for me."

"Is that so?" Ashley stood in front of him and copied the snowwoman's stance. "Judging from their facial expressions, my guess is that he's asking her to have a cup of hot cocoa with him."

"I doubt it. They'd both melt."

"Good point." Ashley stroked her chin with a gloved hand. "I guess I'll have to do a little mind reading."

As new snow began to fall, Walter pushed his finger into the snow dude's ear. "You'd better hurry. I'll bore a hole into his head so his thoughts will leak out."

After several seconds, Ashley shook her head and gave a mock sigh. "I just can't imagine what he's thinking. His brain must be so cold, it totally choked."

Walter took off his glove and then Ashley's. Taking her bare hand, he looked into her eyes. "For years I felt like a snowman in your sight—stiff, stoic, and stupid."

"Alliteration?" Ashley said. "Very clever."

"Shhh. I worked on this a long time."

"Oh, sorry." Taking on a doe-eyed expression, she gazed at him lovingly. "Please go on."

"Anyway, I felt like a snowman. I knew I was too young for you and too immature, but as I worked year after year, I grew up a lot faster than I would have at home, and I melted away my shallow shell until I became limber, lithe, and loquacious."

"Loquacious?"

"Right. Elam gave me that word, but he wouldn't tell me what it means. Anyway, . . ." He pressed a button under his coat. A sizzling sound rose from the snowman, and the snow covering his outstretched hand melted, revealing a metallic coil holding a ring. Walter took the ring and extended it to Ashley. "I have no doubt that I am now ready to be a husband to an angelic anthrozil." Swallowing, he paused for a moment to steady his voice. "Since your father isn't available, I asked your mother for her blessing, and she gave it without hesitation, so now I ask you. If you believe me to be worthy of taking your hand in marriage, I vow that I will never let it go. We will be side by side in everything we do, together in every adventure, just like we said when we clasped hands after you sang 'Amazing Grace' for your grandfather. I now ask for your grace." He cleared his throat and spoke the final words with power and clarity. "Ashley Stalworth, will you marry me?"

* * *

As Billy let the image melt away, Ashley smiled at him. "I hope you don't mind," Ashley said, "but your thoughts were so vivid, I listened in."

"Was that the way it happened?"

"Word for word, except you didn't finish. My answer was, 'O worthy warrior, you need no grace from me, for your request fills my heart with joy. I am the one receiving the blessing, for a noble knight has asked for my hand, the same knight who willingly laid down his life for me time and again. He melted my heart of ice so that I could hear the heralds of Heaven proclaim the amazing grace of God. I gladly accept, and it is most appropriate that you brought me here, for I want to shout from the rooftops that Walter Foley has asked for my hand in marriage."

"I know. You shouted so loud I thought the war had started."

As they laughed together, Walter exited Ashley's hut, her bag in hand. "Sorry," he said. "Emerald's father stopped me. He wanted to give me some pointers on being a good Adam."

Billy patted him on the back. "No problem for a noble knight."

The three hurried to the dragon launching field. Listener had already strapped on the seats and waited next to Albatross.

"I explained your mission to them," Listener said. "They know what to do. They promised not to get scared if Vacants show up."

Even from where he stood, Billy could feel heat from the passenger dragons. They would definitely provide a comfortable ride, but since they had disappeared after the battle with the Vacants, Elam wasn't comfortable with using them for important missions. When they finally came back after several weeks, they seemed contrite, so they were allowed to return to service in non-battle situations.

Albatross lowered his head, allowing Billy to climb his neck. Walter and Ashley mounted Grackle, Walter taking the front seat while Ashley tied her bags to the back.

Listener let out a shrill whistle and slapped Albatross on his flank. As the two dragons beat their wings, she yelled, "I'll be waiting at the radio station. We'll be praying for you!"

"Thank you!" Billy shouted. As they rose, he gazed down at the little girl. Well, not so little anymore. Although not much taller than when he first met her, she had definitely blossomed into a young lady, filled with love and laughter and no hint of the terrible wound she had suffered at the hands of the spear-wielding Vacant.

As expected, the dragons' heated scales helped immensely, making the flight through the snowy skies bearable. It would be a long journey. Flying north, they planned to stay well west of Adam's Marsh and the Valley of Shadows before circling east to the northern border of the valley, again wishing to avoid being sighted from within Abraham's wall. That would put the enemy on alert, and Goliath would see to it that every guard around the perimeter kept close watch, especially at the river entry.

With Twin Falls River in sight, they landed in a woodlands clearing about a mile from the valley's northwest border. Several years ago a landslide had flattened a section of the protective mountain range, so a thick blanket of snow would make that slope into the valley passable for someone on a snowboard.

After dismounting, Billy watched the dragons fly away in the same direction they had come. Since they had no idea when this mission would be accomplished, they planned to use Ashley's transmitter to call Listener at the village's radio station, and she would send the dragons back for them.

Walter joined Billy at his side. "Checking out the weather?" Walter asked.

"Just watching the dragons and thinking about the return plan."

"You do that. I'm still trying to figure out the meteorology here." Walter nodded toward the protective barrier, easily visible as its flames rocketed skyward. At the point the cloudbank collided with the wall, the fire seemed to absorb the vapor. "How do the clouds get inside? Shouldn't the heat evaporate them?"

Billy shrugged. "Beats me. It was dark when we went in there, so I couldn't see the sky, but the snow wasn't as deep in there as it is out here. Maybe the clouds redevelop inside."

When they had strapped into their snowboards, Billy and Walter each carrying a bag on his back, Ashley raised her hood and tied it closed. "Do you remember wearing those cloaks that protected us during portal jumps in the Circles of Seven?"

"Yep," Walter said. "The ones with the microchips."

"Same principle. When we get to the fire, keep your head low, and try to cover up as much as you can."

Billy raised his own hood and checked his gloves. Every article of clothing smelled of the freshly applied flame retardant. The odor wasn't strong enough to detect beyond a few inches, so the shadow people probably wouldn't notice, at least that's what he hoped.

With a little jump, they started down an easy slope that would lead them to the wall. As they dodged trees, some toppled from decay and heavy snow, Billy traced the course in his mind. The slope's angle would increase, allowing them to pick up speed for their plunge through the wall. Then, if they survived and stayed on their feet, they would use their momentum to slide as far up the valley's protective ridge as they could. From that point, they would hike to the lowest summit, the point where many of the rocky peaks had broken off and contributed to the landslide.

Whizzing past stumps and boulders, Billy led the way. Of course, Walter would want to stay at the rear where he could keep an eye on his fiancée. That worked out fine. Billy would cut through the powder and make an easier trail for both of them, and Ashley could save her energy for probing the forest in search of Gabriel's thoughts. And since Walter had been busy with Dorian's transformation, he couldn't have gotten much sleep. There was no use taxing his body further.

As they closed in on the flames, the snow thinned. According to Valiant's scouts, there was a slight rise within several feet of the wall that spanned a thirty-foot-wide section. The slope protected the side facing away from the fire, so it should be snow-covered, but the strip of land between it and the wall would be bare. They would have to slide up the rise at full speed, curl their bodies, and fly through the wall.

Billy scanned the forest. The rise had to be close by. If he didn't find it in the next few seconds, they wouldn't have a decent launch pad, and they would have to turn back and try again.

Ah! There it was, a short, sharp incline. Perfect. But would Abraham and Angel see him? Would they thin out the wall for his entry? Would he land in snow on the other side or crash onto bare ground?

He crouched low. They would all find out soon enough.

Giving his body an upward jerk, he launched over the rise and flew through the air. As the flames zoomed toward him, searing heat chafed his face. He ducked low. Unable to watch the collision, he tightened his muscles and prayed for balance.

The sound came first, the now familiar whoosh of flames, then heat, scorching heat that sent a shock wave straight to his bones. He bit his lip. *No screaming. Just . . . get . . . through it!*

The whoosh faded. Coolness freshened his skin. He opened his eyes just as his board pounded down on snow-coated grass. Bending his knees, he absorbed the impact and continued hurtling down the slope.

With clear sailing ahead, Billy looked back. Ashley burst through the flames, then Walter a split second behind her. With twin *swishes*, they landed and followed his trail.

Ashley's hair had blown loose, and one section was on fire. Since the burning ends flew behind her, she likely didn't even know it. Needing to stay quiet, he couldn't yell, and Walter couldn't catch up, even if he was able to see the problem.

Leaning over, Billy scooped up a handful of snow and threw it at her. He missed the flaming hair but caught her attention. She bent her brow and mouthed, "What's wrong?"

He jerked down his hood, pointed at his own hair, and formed the word, "Fire!" with an exaggerated alarm in his eyes.

An annoyed huff blew from her lips. She batted the flames away with her gloved hands, as if her hair catching fire was an everyday occurrence.

The terrain, a grass field speckled with tall pines and dead deciduous trees, flattened out and then rose in elevation. Soon, they came to a stop and unfastened their boards. The rocky ridge lay ahead, a short hike, and not too strenuous. The slope was fairly steep, but with only a little snow covering the ground, the rocky projections would make for an easy climb.

As they pushed silently against the incline, Billy looked up. The air rushing through the fiery wall at cloud level quickly transformed into white vapor and formed billowing clouds that joined into a thick dark blanket drifting away from the fire.

When they reached the top of the ridge, Billy peered into the bowl-shaped valley. Several hundred feet below, the river carved the floor into two halves and spilled out through a narrow divide at the southern end. On either side, trees filled the landscape. The evergreens seemed healthier here, perhaps a result of less snow and proximity to the surrounding wall's warmth. Even the deciduous trees seemed alive. Although none carried any leaves, only a very few had fallen prey to rot and the domino tumbling that had plagued the higher elevations outside the wall.

Walter and Ashley joined him, one on each side. Ashley let her hair flow in the stiff breeze, only a few ends showing signs of the earlier scorching. "I don't sense anything," she whispered. "At least nothing as intelligent as Gabriel. Just a mass of senseless beasts, hungry, craving, violent. Zane was different. These feel more like a pack of wild dogs than anything."

With the wind blowing the treetops, the shadows on the valley's snow-covered floor shifted back and forth, creating a hypnotizing dance of black on white. It wasn't hard to imagine those flat beasts lurking within the splotches of black.

Billy sat on the top of the ridge, set his feet on the valley side, and strapped into his snowboard again. Of course, these boards weren't as fancy as those on Earth. With leather straps, unvarnished boot braces, and no steel on the edge, they looked rough and primitive, but a special wax for the base made them tough and fast. When they first discovered it, Walter joked about bottling the wax and selling it to the snowboarders on Earth, but as the months and years passed, his jokes about what he would do at home diminished. He had settled into life here as if he would never return home.

As soon as all three were ready, Billy touched Ashley's back and whispered, "Your turn to lead."

She nodded and pushed off. Walter followed, and Billy trailed. On the valley slope, the new alignment made the most sense. Ashley would probe for Gabriel's presence and steer toward him, while Billy would watch for shadow people. Even if Ashley slid right over them, they likely wouldn't be able to react in time to hurt her, so Billy and Walter would be the ones to quell any uprising.

All three zoomed down the steep wall. Pointed rocks jutted out here and there, but they were easy enough to see in the treeless span. Ashley rode her board expertly, digging in for sharp turns and dipping and rising while riding over bumps and ridges. With her cloak flapping around a sword at her belt and her hair flowing back, she looked like a snowboarding elf straight out of a Tolkien story.

As the slope began to level out, she straightened and looked left toward the river, her stare fixed on something, though nothing seemed apparent in that direction other than the water tumbling from the top of the valley wall.

Digging in again, she turned that way. Now that they were near the floor, trees dotted the area, and shadows waved back and forth on the snow. Ashley glided past a tree and across the first shadow without harm and stopped in front of a tall pine. With her eyes wide and her mouth open, she slowly swiveled her head, like an antennae searching for a signal.

In a spray of snow, Walter and Billy slid to a stop next to her, listening. The waterfall roared in the distance, more of a background hum than a dominating thunder. Wind buzzed through the trees. A hawk let out a shrill call and flew from the highest branch of a pine to a perch at the top of a nearby deadwood tree.

Finally, without breathing a word, she took off again, this time slowly as she wound past trees and rocks on her way to the river. Billy kept glancing at the ground. Still no sign of life. Maybe the shadow people congregated in the denser woods during the day.

When they arrived at the beach, Ashley unfastened her straps, kicked out of her board, and marched across the sand. Billy and Walter did the same. Unable to figure out what Ashley was doing, they gave each other a shrug and hurried to catch up.

As soon as they reached the edge of the swiftly flowing water, Ashley allowed her voice to rise above a whisper. "I sensed something in the direction of the waterfall, but there were too many trees that way, so I thought we'd come down here and walk back upstream."

"Good thinking," Billy said, glad to uncork his throat.

Walter hustled back, retrieved the snowboards, and quietly set them next to the river. Ashley began a slow march, her head turning from side to side. Every ten paces or so, she stopped and listened, then continued, but since each step brought them closer to the waterfall, all other sounds surrendered to the tumult ahead.

When they drew close enough to feel the spray, she halted and turned in a full circle twice, her brow bent in confusion.

"What's up?" Walter asked.

She pointed at the ground. "I sense a powerful presence, right here, right now."

Billy searched the area. No shadows. Just sand and small patches of snow. He looked at Ashley and Walter in turn and gave each a nod. They were definitely on the same wavelength. Gabriel was here in his light energy form. Leaving Hades had caused him to lose his physical body.

Ashley withdrew her ion box from her cloak's inner pocket and opened a lid on top. "Gabriel, if you're here, would you please enter this box? I'm not sure how small you can squeeze yourself, but this indicates the presence of light energy, and it will allow us to carry you out of here."

Holding the box in her palm at chest level, she waited. After a few seconds, a glow emanated from the mirrors on each side.

Walter pumped a fist. "We got him!"

Smiling broadly, Ashley spoke into the opening. "Hello, dear brother. The circumstances could be better, but I'm glad to be with you again. I'm going to close you in. It's the only way to keep you safe when we jump through the wall of fire."

She began pushing the lid down but stopped. Her brow furrowed deeply. "What? I don't understand."

Billy looked at Walter. Obviously she was talking to Gabriel. Her ability to pick up words had been increasing all the time.

Ashley glanced back and forth between Walter and Billy. "If you stay in Second Eden, you'll just be light energy." Between every response, she paused, listening while the box's glow pulsed, as if energized by Gabriel's words. "Theory? What theory? . . . So how would you find the way? There was no trace of Shiloh . . . I see. Did you hear that Acacia went with her? . . . But how would Flint know? He's stuck behind the wall . . . Oh. So we're not the only ones using the river that way . . . Who?"

Her eyes grew wide as she riveted her gaze on Billy. "Gabriel's been listening in on Flint's conversations with Goliath. Apparently someone is getting messages through the wall, but they haven't said who's doing it. Flint and Goliath talked about what happened to Shiloh and Acacia, so Gabriel wants us to get him out from behind the wall so he can find them."

"But how?" Billy felt a twinge in his belly. Was it danger? He gave the sky and ground a quick scan but saw nothing. "There's no portal out there for him to go through."

"Not that we know of, but in his energy form he can sense a portal, and maybe he'll be able to go through it."

Billy nodded. That would be worth a try. He might even be able to locate a way to find Bonnie and Sapphira. "Sounds good. So let's pay my mom a visit and let her know what's going on, and then we'll—"

"Incoming!" Walter grabbed his sword and pointed it toward the sky. "Two dragons!"

CHAPTER 5

RETURN TO EARTH

Billy pulled Excalibur from its scabbard and looked up. The dragons, both bearing red scales, flew over the mountain boundary. The larger of the two was clearly Goliath, and the smaller one had to be the dragon they saw at the side of the river. "Think they've seen us?" Billy asked.

Ashley snapped the box's lid closed. "I sense anger in their minds, but nothing violent."

"Stay still or run for cover?" Walter asked.

She nodded toward a tree that stood about thirty paces away. "Slowly. Very slowly."

As they crept along the river's beach, Billy kept his stare trained on the dragons. The smaller one had its eyebeams turned on and was sweeping them across the valley floor.

The moment Billy set foot on the snow-covered turf, the beams brushed over his body. A loud screech rode the wind. Goliath's roar followed, and the two dragons dove toward them.

"Get under the tree!" Billy lit up Excalibur's beam and sliced the air, barely missing the smaller dragon. The dragons broke from their dive and separated. Goliath sped to the right, and the smaller one wheeled around one of the tallest trees to Billy's left.

Walter ran with Ashley to the tree before returning in a sprint to Billy's side. "Back to back!" Walter said. "Just like Sir Barlow taught us."

They pressed their backs together. Billy swiped the beam at the smaller dragon but missed again. "He's quick!"

"Turn it off and wait till he gets closer. He'll shoot fire, and then you can nail him. But if you miss, watch out for his tail."

Billy let the beam die away but kept the blade glowing bright. The dragon zoomed down, its mouth wide and its teeth bared. "He's coming! Cloaks up!"

Walter ducked low. "Goliath's coming, too!"

Both men let their cloaks cover their exposed skin. Torrents of fire lit up Billy's darkened vision, and heat blistered his face. The moment it passed, he leaped up and shot the beam from Excalibur's blade. The smaller dragon zoomed toward him, only two seconds away. He reared back and swung, but something smacked his head and knocked him to the ground, dousing Excalibur.

As he sprawled, still clutching the hilt, he covered himself again. Was it a tail? Goliath's tail?

A sudden pull jerked him to his feet and set him upright. A beige dragon sat next to him, spewing fire into the air. When the flames died away, she growled, "I will protect you from my mate, but I cannot allow you to use that weapon to kill my son."

"Roxil?" Billy rubbed his head. "I'm just trying to save my own skin."

Walter jumped to his feet and stood next to Billy. "You okay?"

"Yeah. Better check on Ashley."

Walter ran to the tree where Ashley stood, her sword drawn. She seemed fine.

Goliath landed on the other side of the river, and the smaller dragon joined him. "Roxil!" Goliath called. "You are not allowed to fight with the humans. Your vow is to stay at my side."

Roxil shot her eyebeams toward Goliath. "At *your* side? I stopped him from slaying our son. Even now he has the power in his sword to slay you, but he stays his hand because of my presence at *his* side. Do you really want me to leave him and allow him to disintegrate you?"

Goliath growled but added no words.

"Then be off," she continued, "and I will lead them out of this place."

"Only to return with that sword," the smaller dragon said.

Goliath's ears rotated toward him. "An excellent point, Karrick. If your mother were really on my side, she would kill that cockroach now and be done with it."

Billy pushed Excalibur's tip against Roxil's underbelly and shouted, "If she tried to kill me, she would be dead before you could blink. Just do as she says, and I'll let all of you live." He whispered out of the side of his mouth. "No offense, Roxil."

A growl masked her response. "None taken, but he will not be persuaded."

"Feel free to kill her," Goliath said. "I have my son, so I have no need of her any longer."

Billy caught a glimpse of Walter and Ashley skulking his way. He whispered again to Roxil. "What now?"

This time she didn't try to cover her words. "I am under a vow that I cannot break. I cannot fight with you. The only reason I was able to fend them off was because of my duty to protect my son. I knew you would slay Karrick if I did not interrupt the battle."

"So are we at an impasse?"

"Not for long. If you delay, he will attack the other humans. If you defend them, I will stop you from hurting my son, and your friends will be doomed. He knows this, but he is likely waiting to see if you will kill me. Since he is faithless, he does not trust me, so he wants me out of the way."

"But if you stop me from defending Walter and Ashley, I would have to kill you."

"Precisely." Roxil's eyes followed Walter and Ashley as they approached, but she seemed not to be concerned. "And after killing me, you would turn your sword on Goliath and Karrick, but they might have killed your friends already, and you would have to fight two dragons alone."

Billy made eye contact with Walter. Walter took Ashley's hand, whispered something to her, then nodded at Billy.

With a burst of strength, Billy jumped to Walter and Ashley, and the trio stood back-to-back-to-back in a triangle, all with swords at the ready. Billy turned on Excalibur's beam and slashed at Goliath, but he jumped out of the way and took to the air. Flicking his wrist, Billy swiped the beam over Karrick's head before he could follow. When the younger dragon ducked low, Billy stopped the buzzing laser within inches of its neck.

He shouted at the top of his lungs. "Don't move, or I'll disintegrate him!"

Roxil roared. "If you do, you will die! Goliath will kill you, but only if I do not kill you first!"

Eyeing Goliath as he circled overhead, Billy shot back with a growl. "We're willing to do battle to see if either one of you can kill us. Don't underestimate our abilities."

Karrick trembled. He looked up at his father with terrified eyes. Goliath landed on Karrick's side of the river but far enough away to keep Billy from shifting the beam to him. With a spiteful snort, he said, "Even with that weapon, you cannot defeat Roxil and me when we fight together. If you kill our son, her rage will be beyond anything you can imagine."

Walter mimicked Goliath's snort. "Then we'll provide a lesson in anger management at the point of a sword!"

"Walter!" Ashley hissed. "Cut the trash talk."

"I'm trying to get them mad. They won't think straight."

Roxil aimed her beams directly into Billy's eyes. "Are we at another impasse?"

"Not necessarily." Billy averted his gaze. Her eyebeams weren't blinding, but they had a dizzying effect. "Just let us go, and we'll all stay alive."

Roxil spat a ball of flames on the sand. "Fool! Even if we agreed to allow you to leave in peace, Goliath would break the vow and attack you when you are most vulnerable. He is a liar."

Goliath snorted again, louder this time. "You are a witness, Karrick. Your mother, the faithful dragoness, is displaying her undying loyalty!"

"Karrick already knows of your lying ways all too well." Roxil pawed deeply into the sand. "You cannot deny it."

"But *I'm* not a liar," Billy said. "Will you trust me to keep a deal?"

Roxil dipped her head. "You are the offspring of Clefspeare, and therefore the son of my son. I will gladly assume that he has passed on to you his undisputed integrity."

"I will hear your offer first," Goliath said. "With death hanging over my innocent son's head, it is difficult for me to believe that your integrity is as high as Roxil assumes."

Billy glanced at Roxil. "Is Karrick able to carry a passenger?"

"He is able," she replied with a suspicious stare, "but he has had only a little practice with one of Flint's men."

"Good enough." Keeping the beam in place, Billy pulled away from his companions' backs. "Roxil, fly Walter over there."

Walter sheathed his sword. "I'm not sure what you're up to yet, but I'm game."

"Karrick's a youngling," Billy said. "He should still have a vulnerable spot where his neck meets his back. Have him fly you to the cave and keep the point of your sword on that spot."

Walter cocked his head. "I didn't know you've been studying dragon anatomy."

"I guess you skipped that class." Billy suppressed a grin. Listening to his father's dragon stories for the last four years had paid off. "Just keep your hostage at the cave entrance. I'm sure you can persuade him to help you fight off any shadow people. Ashley and I will meet you there."

"And what do you offer in exchange for my trust?" Roxil asked.

"Simple. We won't kill your son. This way, we don't have to worry about Goliath breaking any promises."

"Then how will you leave this place? You cannot safely navigate the river in daylight, and Karrick is unable to carry more than one human."

"Once we get to the tunnel, we'll take our chances from there."

Roxil lowered her head to the sand. "Very well. In the name of my son, Clefspeare, I will trust you."

Walter scrambled up the neck stairway and settled on her back. "I'm ready."

"You are playing the fool!" Goliath shouted. "Your loyalty is with me, yet you are making deals with the vermin."

"I have conflicting vows," Roxil said as she raised her head again, "and I will honor my obligation to Karrick first."

While Billy held the beam steady over Karrick's head, Roxil flew with Walter over the river. Ashley drew close to Billy's side, trembling, but she stayed silent.

"He'll be all right," Billy said. "He's a true warrior."

"I know." Her voice shook. "Billy, I love him so much."

He nodded but stayed quiet. He couldn't add anything to such a profound statement.

As soon as Walter dismounted Roxil and climbed aboard Karrick, he set the point of his sword against the dragon's neck. "Ready!" he called.

"Okay. Get going!" Billy turned off the beam but kept the sword raised. "Roxil, if you will carry Ashley and me to the cave, we can finish this quickly. Otherwise, we have to cross the river at Lilith's Shallows and walk all the way."

"I will carry you." Roxil turned to Karrick. "Just do as he says, and all will be well."

"Fool of a dragoness!" Goliath shouted, still keeping his distance. "Your loyalty to these sewer rats will be the death of you!"

Roxil paid no attention. She and Karrick launched into the air at the same time. While Karrick headed south, she flew over the river and landed at Billy's side. "Let us fly immediately," she said as she made a neck stairway. "Goliath is no fool. He will devise a counter plan."

"I agree." Billy put his sword away and hustled with Ashley onto Roxil's back. As soon as he got a good grip on the spine in front of him and Ashley wrapped her arms around his torso, he yelled, "Let's go!"

Roxil took off and made a beeline toward the cave. In the distance, Karrick was already descending toward the river near the exit waterfall. Walter would get there less than a minute ahead of them.

"We have but a moment," Roxil said. "I must tell you something very important."

Shivering in the gusting wind, Billy gritted his teeth again. "Go for it!"

She turned her head back toward them as she spoke in rapid-fire fashion. "Someone smuggled in soil from the resurrection garden along with one of the bones of Makaidos, and Flint now has a resurrection garden. Since Goliath was once in a place called the Valley of Souls, and calling him out of there allowed him to rise in the garden, he deduced that we could resurrect others who reside in that realm simply by energizing the bone and calling for the resident to come forth. Goliath learned that I was carrying an unborn youngling when I died, though I did not know it myself, and it seems that he discovered this youngling's existence in the Valley of Souls. He likely also learned what kind of fire was necessary to energize the bone, and he reproduced it with his own breath."

As Roxil began her descent toward the river, Billy looked past Ashley's flying hair. Yes, Goliath was following, but quite a ways back.

"So," Roxil continued, "Goliath, being his father, assigned him a name and called him to this world, but he needed me to care for him, because he was ill equipped to handle an infant dragon."

Billy nodded. "I was wondering where he came from. I thought maybe you and Goliath—"

"No!" Roxil turned her head to the front. "My vow was to stay at his side. Nothing more."

When they landed on the river's beach, Billy and Ashley slid down

Roxil's side and sprinted toward the cave, both drawing their swords as they ran.

"I will stay here and fend off Goliath," Roxil said. "Restore my son to me, and all will be well."

Now tromping over a thin layer of snow, Billy looked back. "You have my word."

The ferns crunched underneath their weight, raising a musky odor. "See any shadow people?" Ashley asked as she ran two steps behind him.

"I sense danger, but it's not real close. My guess is that they're holed up in the cave in the daytime. It's the darkest place around."

"Perfect. Dragons ready to scorch us outside the cave, and a horde of shadow people ready to strangle us inside."

When they reached the cave entrance, Walter stood just outside the dark arch, his sword planted against Karrick's underbelly. "We had a good talk," Walter said. "You might say that he gets the point."

Karrick snorted the same way his father had. "I fear to die only because it would break my poor mother's heart. If not for that, I would do battle with you cowardly worms."

"And he has his father's charm," Ashley said.

Billy lit up Excalibur's beam and stepped inside the cave. "You do well to honor your mother. Go to her now, and I advise you to heed her counsel and not your father's."

Karrick spat a stream of sparks. "And I advise *you* to drink your own poison." With that, he shuffled away a few steps, then used his wings to help him scoot to the edge of the forest.

Waving Walter and Ashley inside, Billy marched ahead. "Let's see if we can get to Earth."

"Reinforcements?" Walter asked.

Billy looked back. "Are you a mind reader now?"

"Nope. Just guessing that you had a reason for walking into a cave full of spooks with no way out but into a dragon's mouth."

"Speaking of spooks." Ashley pointed into the darkness. "I sense something ahead."

Billy swept the sword's beam across the floor. Sizzles echoed through the cave, along with mournful cries. "They're here, all right."

"They're in pain," Ashley said. "Aren't we invading their territory?"

Billy took several steps into the cave and motioned for the others to follow. "Elam told me they're like vermin. Abraham said so himself. This is more like exterminating rats than anything."

Ashley sighed. "If you say so. I know it didn't bother me last time, but things seem different in the light of day, especially after talking to Zane."

Billy looked at her sad eyes. Again, her thoughts were clear. Goliath had called the three of them vermin, and he was ready to kill them, and now they were doing the same to these creatures, whatever they were. They had Abraham's word, but was that enough?

As the cries of the dying shadow people faded, Billy touched Ashley's cloak. "Better let Gabriel out."

She pulled the box from her pocket. "Why now?"

"We're going to make a run for it."

"Run for it?" Walter asked. "Through that mass of snakes?"

Billy nodded. "No use killing more than we have to."

"Gabriel," Ashley said as she opened the ion box's lid. "Have you been listening?"

The glow inside the box pulsed.

"Good. Hop out. After we open the portal, we'll see you on the other side."

A surge of danger flooded Billy's senses. As he turned to the entrance a dark form shaded the opening.

Walter swallowed. "Running for it works for me."

A blast of fire shot into the cave. Walter ducked his head and fanned out his cloak just in time to cover Billy and Ashley.

"Run!" Walter shouted.

As another flood of fire rushed in, the three sprinted farther into the cave, Billy leading the way with Excalibur's glow. Sticky hands grabbed at their feet and ankles. It felt like running through tar, but their momentum allowed them to snap away from the dark predators.

Soon, the end of the tunnel came into sight. Billy turned on the beam and slashed it vertically across the back wall. As before, sparks flew, and a rectangular aura took shape.

"It's open!" Ashley called.

Billy waved a hand. "Everyone go!"

While Billy kept the shadow people at bay, Ashley leaped into the glowing doorway, followed by Walter. As he turned off the beam and jumped, a dark hand grabbed his ankle, but his thrust carried him through the portal. He broke into daylight and landed on his side, the black limb still attached and stretching into the cave. With a quick jerk, he pulled away, and the arm sprang back and disappeared.

Squinting, Billy looked around. Ashley propped herself on hands and knees. Walter, a new abrasion on his forehead, helped her rise to her feet, then reached for Billy.

As he rode Walter's pull, Billy looked at the portal. A radiant human shape passed through and instantly solidified into Gabriel. He stretched his wings and lifted his legs up and down. "That box was a tight fit even for me."

Ashley ran into his arms. "It's so good to see you!"

Pressing his palms on her cheeks, he kissed her on the forehead. "Thought you got rid of your brother for good?"

Grinning, she swatted him on the backside. "Behave yourself!"

Billy called toward the tent, still staked out in front of the mine entrance. "Mom! Are you there?"

"Are we going to bring home another dragon?" Walter asked.

Shaking his head, Billy called again as he circled around the portal and headed for the tent. "Mom, it's Billy!"

A woman crawled out of the tent and looked at them, blinking. "I am Tamara," she said meekly.

"Oh, sorry. One of the dragons, right?"

"Yes." She tilted her head. "Do you seek Mrs. Bannister?"

"Yeah. She's my mother."

Tamara pointed at the pile of rubble that blocked the entrance to the mines. "In there with Yereq. The flood is . . ." She rolled her eyes upward, searching for a word. Finally, she looked at Billy again. "Receding."

"Thanks." Billy ran to an opening in the rubble. Just as he took a breath to yell, his mother walked out, her shoulders slumped, her face dirty, and her hair wet.

"Mom!" Billy hugged her close. His mother's arms slid around him, weak at first, but they tightened to a firm embrace.

She pulled back and looked at him. "I thought you'd come later. Is it night in Second Eden already?"

He shook his head. "Change of plans. Listen. We're going to need all the firepower we can get, and we can't wait to take one dragon at a time. Are there any other dragons available?"

She glanced at Tamara. The former dragon picked up a stick from the fire, then jerked her hand away and licked her finger, apparently nursing a burn.

Billy's mother whispered. "Tamara is available, but Kaylee told me she's not exactly the brightest bulb in the chandelier. When Devin killed her, she was carrying a message from Patrick that allowed Devin to find the courier and track down other dragons. She was supposed to destroy the message immediately after reading it. The former dragons would never have learned about the mistake if not for Devin's bragging about it to Patrick. But since Morgan wouldn't let Devin kill Patrick, the dragons were able to change the way they communicated."

Billy drew a picture in his mind of the slayer grinning as he read the message, but he quickly shook the image away. "If Tamara can breathe fire and wants to fight for our side, then I don't care about her IQ."

"Oh, she's loyal to a fault, and she's as loving as the day is long."

"Then sign her up." He looked back at the campfire. Walter, Ashley, and Gabriel had gathered around to warm themselves and were chatting with Tamara. "Anyone else?"

"No. You said you could take only one at a time, so I told the others they could follow up a lead Kaylee found about the missing younglings."

"Fair enough." Billy looked into the tunnel. "Is Yereq around? We could use him."

"He'll be out soon. He loves Sapphira so much, he'll never give up looking for her."

Billy dragged his boot across the stony ground. "I know exactly how he feels."

"You mean Bonnie?"

"Yeah . . . Bonnie."

She embraced him again and laid her head on his chest. "I know how you feel, too."

As he patted her on the back, he looked at the portal. "I can get you to Second Eden, but I don't know if I can restore Jared Bannister for you."

For a moment, she said nothing. Her body trembled slightly, but after a few seconds, the tremors died away. "When do we go?"

"We'll have to wait for Second Eden's nightfall. A couple of dragons out there are waiting to fry us."

She took his hand and pulled him toward the campfire. "Then let's sit and make our plans."

CHAPTER 6

THE EMPTY VALLEY

Bonnie thrust her sword. Sapphira blocked. When the two blades crashed together, they pushed against each other, grunting. Metal slid on metal until the two hilts met. With their hands blazing a pulse of flames, the two girls locked stares. Now that Bonnie had been an Oracle of Fire for more than four years, she could see through the fire easily, as if the flame coating were no more than an aura of light.

Flashing a grin, Sapphira looked up at Bonnie, her blue eyes sparkling in the midst of her fiery aura. "Giving up?"

"Never!"

Bonnie dug in and pushed with her legs, but Sapphira didn't budge an inch. Bonnie glanced at the smaller girl's bulging shoulder muscles. So much strength in such a small package!

After several seconds of stalemate, Sapphira glanced away and gasped. "Oh! Will you look at that?"

Bonnie tilted her head upward. "Look at what?"

"The sky!" Sapphira planted a foot in Bonnie's stomach and shoved her backwards.

Bonnie fell on her bottom with a thud and nearly completed a somersault before flattening herself on her back. "Such a fiend!" she shouted, a laugh shaking her voice. "Thou hast deceived me, rogue!"

Sapphira marched forward, set her foot on Bonnie's stomach again, and spoke in mock lament. "Oh, woe is me! I am smitten with anguish over my dastardly plot to fell this fair maiden! I deserve nothing but scorn for my vileness."

Bonnie grabbed her ankle and pushed her away. As Sapphira stumbled, Bonnie jumped up and shoved her again, knocking her flat. Then, with a mighty heave, Bonnie plunged the sword between Sapphira's fiery chest and arm and into the turf behind her.

Splaying her limbs, Sapphira cried out, "Thou hast delivered thy revenge in full measure, O virtuous maiden. If perchance I see you in the hereafter, I will be your eternal servant!" Her head lolled to the side, her tongue protruding. For a moment, she didn't move. Then a giggle erupted and grew into a full belly laugh.

Bonnie yanked out her sword. A dozen corny replies came to mind, but when she tried to speak, she just sputtered and laughed. This show was definitely over.

A third laugh joined theirs, then a clapping of hands. The Maid, her aura as bright as the sun, sang out with delight. "A wonderful performance, my friends! Your swordplay was excellent and your footwork exquisite. You are now the finest of sword maidens."

Sapphira climbed to her feet and saluted with her sword. "And the best of actors, don't you think?"

The Maid smiled. "Of all the sword-bearing actors I have seen in this realm, you two are the best."

Bonnie gave her an exaggerated bow. "You do us an ambiguous honor, fair Maid."

After another round of laughter, Bonnie slid her sword into a scabbard at her hip. "Can you tell us now?" She stared into The Maid's eyes. Her fiery orbs turned solemn, pensive. She had told them earlier that she had received a message from Abaddon, but she wasn't free to release it until the final swordplay examination was complete. They had studied every stance, every move, even every verbal joust from "En garde" to their dramatic Old English wordplays. They were ready for the next step.

The Maid nodded. "The time has come, my dear friends."

Sapphira hooked her arm around Bonnie's and leaned against her. "To go to Second Eden?"

"Perhaps. Abaddon has learned that your friends now have enough information, and their wisdom will likely guide them to attempt a call. At the very least, you should prepare for the journey."

Bonnie looked down at Sapphira's ovulum, still in its pouch. "So we'll shrink down into eggs, too?"

"Not you," The Maid said, "for the two of you entered here alive."

Bonnie shook her head. "I guess I don't understand all the rules. Will we arrive fully grown? I assumed my father did, because they needed a doctor, but I heard that most of them show up there as babies."

"The rules, as you put it, are fairly simple. One who has died goes to Second Eden in the form in which he or she arrived here. Most were killed as unborn babies, so they go to Second Eden in uterine plants that complete the gestations. Your father was too big for a plant, so he simply appeared in his adult form, like a flower sprouting from the soil. There are, however, a few exceptions. Roxil came here as Abigail, a human who died in a terrible plunge from the Bridgelands to Second Eden."

She raised a pair of fingers and continued. "Since that was her second demise, she passed into a state in which her body had to be regenerated by other means than the usual straightforward resurrection. Abaddon decided to use a birthing plant. He thought it would take a full nine months in the plant, but her rebirth was nearly instantaneous."

"Do you know why?" Bonnie asked.

"I have a theory." The Maid touched her sternum. "A crystalline egg dangled from her necklace. I know not what it was, but it had the aura of life within, so I assume that it provided the energy to regenerate her body."

Sapphira looked up at Bonnie. "That's the egg I told you about, the one that formed from the diamonds I collected when Timothy's tears fell from the sky."

"What about Timothy?" Bonnie asked. "He died three times. Does he need an egg's energy, too?"

"Abaddon and I have discussed this, and he thinks Timothy, or Makaidos, as we came to know him, will need that and more. His sacrifice was singular in that he gave up his right to have his soul resurrected. Even now as his body grows in a birthing plant, it will not come to fruition without three steps." The Maid raised a finger. "The first step is the call. The plant will wither and die without his name being verbally called by those who need his aid." She lifted another finger. "The second step is the crystal, for the body inside will not quicken without the necessary energy from his previous life. And the third step," she said, raising another finger, "is a sacrifice, the willing death of an innocent lamb, and the blood of the lamb must be applied to the plant to restore the soul of the one being reborn."

Sapphira gave her a quizzical look. "A sacrifice? Who?"

"Ah! But that is not for you to know. Since the lamb will make the decision without coercion either to sacrifice or withdraw, no one will be told ahead of time; neither you, nor I, nor Abaddon, nor even the lamb." Like a glowing tong touching a flaming coal, The Maid caressed Sapphira's cheek. "Who knows? Perhaps even you will be the one to offer your body to the wolves of Second Eden."

Bonnie watched as Sapphira stared at The Maid, their faces glowing and fresh, yet so serious. Was Sapphira thinking about becoming the sacrifice? Had her thousands of years of life and suffering been a preparation for an ultimate sacrificial act? She had to be in turmoil. She wanted to be united with Elam, but if that was really what God wanted, why weren't they together already? Why was it taking so long?

Filled with a blend of joy and heartache, The Maid's eyes communicated empathy. Somehow she understood the impact of her words, what it meant to be offered to the wolves. At the center of each pupil, a flame erupted. Shaped like a teardrop, the fire consumed something in its midst, a girl . . . a weeping girl.

Blinking away the image, Bonnie cleared her throat. "But there's something strange about all this. The Second Edeners couldn't have known about the three things necessary for Makaidos to be reborn. If they had called him too soon, he would have—"

"Come back as a corpse," The Maid said. "And that would have been tragic, truly tragic."

Sapphira shook her head as if throwing off a trance. "So . . . I guess it's really fortunate that it worked out the way it did."

"Fortunate?" The Maid laughed again, her eyes merry. "You may call it that, but nothing in this matter has been left to chance. You heard Abaddon tell the story. Were you surprised that Elam allowed Angel to tell the lie? And did it seem odd to you that he commanded Paili to alter the poem?"

"I was surprised," Sapphira said. "It didn't sound like something Elam would do at all."

"Elam prayed for wisdom. He received it. When God gave those words to Paili through Enoch, the delivery of the crystal and the sacrifice were planned, but certain events transpired that necessitated a change."

"Planned?" Sapphira repeated. "I know Ashley had a crystal, but who was supposed to be sacrificed?"

"Once again you ask the identity of a potential lamb, but consider for yourself the damage that could be done if you were to learn who the sacrifice was supposed to be, and then he or she chose not to walk the path of blood and fire."

Sapphira lowered her head. "I see what you mean."

"So Elam ordered the change," Bonnie said, "because not everything was ready for Makaidos to rise."

"Yes." The Maid's flames heightened. "Is it not an exciting thought to ponder? Even Elam was unaware of the reason, yet God moved his heart to do what appeared to be a mistake in many eyes."

"Especially since it gave rise to Goliath," Bonnie added. "That still looks like a mistake."

"Indeed it would to eyes that see through a glass darkly. Perhaps if you are called to that world, you will witness how the results of that decision unfold. Even the return of Goliath has a reason behind it." The Maid laid a hand over her heart. "Every call to life is an echo of a longing in the heart of the caller. It is like a thunder within, a drum that beats without a rhythm, yet it searches for the power to set the thrumming into a new heartbeat for the resurrected loved one. It combines words of love with the music of sacrifice and the rhythm of a disciplined purpose. All of these create passion, a heart set on fire, and without that fire, no one can be reborn."

Bonnie let the lovely words soak in. They seemed true, yet mysterious. Maybe they would become clear later when she needed them. "But will we remember what we learned here?" She lifted her sword. "It would be a shame to forget all the fighting techniques and the stories you and Abaddon have told us."

"Since you are alive, there is no need for you to revert to the form with which you entered this land. You will go to Second Eden four years older and four years wiser, remembering all that happened here. In fact, you will not even need the ovulum. Its usefulness has now passed away."

Bonnie looked down at her body. Although ripples of fire coated her clothes and skin, there was no doubt about the changes—subtle, yes, but she had definitely matured from a girl to a woman.

"Shall we go to the resurrection table?" The Maid asked as she extended a hand to each of them.

Sapphira removed the ovulum from its pouch and set it on the ground. "I'm ready," she said, taking her hand.

Bonnie slid her hand into The Maid's. When they touched, it seemed that a holy warmth radiated from her fingers and pulsed throughout her body. "How long will we be there?" Bonnie asked.

"Until they call you." The Maid walked with them along the edge of the river. "There is nothing more to tell."

As they walked, the image of the hourglass entered Bonnie's mind. The dragon's scaly hand would grip it and turn it over, beginning the process of waiting for the Second Eden dwellers to make the call. When the last grain of sand fell to the lower glass, their transport would take place, but how many times would Abaddon have to turn the hourglass over?

Bonnie checked the staurolite dagger in a sheath at her belt. It didn't really make any difference. No matter how long they had to wait, she and Sapphira would be ready.

* * *

Billy stood with his back against the cave's dead end wall. It had taken hours to gather everything they needed, and transporting them to Second Eden had been a nightmare. Since the portal opening contracted every hour or so, he had to reopen it four times. Twice he stepped back into the cave to reopen it with Excalibur, and twice he opened it from the Earth side using the new Apollo.

He looked around at his companions. Each one held a light of some kind to help ward off the shadow people. Yereq, who had to hunch way over to avoid the cave's ceiling, carried two sets of scuba diving gear, two tanks under his arm and the other pieces in a backpack he lifted by a strap on his shoulder. Billy's mother and Gabriel had used the equipment several times in the flooded mine tunnels, but not lately. Only Yereq had not given up the search. Since he was able to hold his breath for almost ten minutes, he dove without gear.

Billy's mother, decked out in a scuba dry suit, had packed her clothes and her pistol in a duffle. She carried a two-person inflatable raft, though they hoped to squeeze three inside for the dangerous journey. Since Elam had told of his own survival after plunging down the exit waterfall even during flood stage, it seemed reasonable that three in a raft could make it, especially with three others swimming in the river to help them right the boat if it capsized.

Ashley held up the ion box and spoke into it. "Gabriel, are you ready?"

The box pulsed with light.

"Everyone else?" Ashley asked.

Lifting his legs up and down, Billy looked at his mother. "I could use another lesson, and this diving suit doesn't quite fit, but I'm ready."

She set her hand over her nose. "Just don't forget to hold your mask and regulator in place. When we splash down after the falls, the impact might jerk them off."

He gave her a thumbs-up. "Gotcha."

Walter stepped out in front, Excalibur in his grip. The beam shot out into the darkness. "My guess is that with all of us here, the shadow people might not bother us, but let's go double time anyway."

Kicking into a fast jog, he led the way. Yereq followed, still hunched over as he pounded his huge boots, apparently trying to ward away any shadowy lurkers.

Billy ran a few steps behind the giant. The combination of Yereq's thudding feet and his own squeaking suit sounded strange, like bats succumbing to hammer blows. He waved a scuba flashlight back and forth along the cave floor. No sign of shadow people. Where could they have gone? Since it was now dark outside, maybe they were congregating between the cave and the river again. Not knowing where they were seemed worse than facing them. The advantage of surprise was on their side.

When they reached the cave entrance, Walter paused and searched the area, using the beam to illuminate the ground and nearby trees. Again, no shadow people.

He resumed jogging, slower now. Yereq straightened his body and followed, obviously taking care to silence his thunderous gait.

Billy suppressed a laugh. Such a huge man running on tiptoes seemed comical, but this was dead serious. He had to keep a straight face.

When all six arrived at the river, Billy dug the scuba gear out of

Yereq's pack, while his mother turned on the raft's inflation motor. Although the rush of the river was loud enough to drown out the motor and any whisper, no one spoke a word.

Once Billy and his mother had strapped on their gear, including an air tank and buoyancy compensator, they waded into the river with Yereq. Billy clenched his teeth together, forcing them not to chatter. Even with a scuba dry suit, the chill seemed to plunge knives into his bones. He clipped the waterproof flashlight onto his belt and let his body shiver. At least that was a quiet way to suffer.

While Ashley, Walter, and Tamara climbed into the raft, Billy searched the sky and the surrounding sand. Still nothing. No shadow people or dragons. Something was up. Something big.

Yereq swam into the flow and dove under. With a final kick, he disappeared. He would be the first to brave the plunge to the next level and wait in the pool to support the raft when it fell.

Walter pulled Tamara's hood up for her. Since she was wearing Billy's cloak, the hood and sleeves seemed to swallow her body. It would cover her well when it was time to blast through the wall of flames.

Billy looked over the surrounding mountains, but Abraham's wall was not in sight. The clouds must have been very thick tonight to mask its usual glow.

Walter doused Excalibur, leaving the area in total darkness. Billy pulled his mask down and inserted the regulator. It was time to go for it.

Placing their hands on a rope attached to the back of the raft, he and his mother guided it to the center of the river and let the current take over. As they picked up speed, he listened to the waterfall's heightening rumble. Within seconds the icy river would send them hurtling through the air and then straight down.

Suddenly, the water fell away. Holding his mask and regulator in place with one hand and the rope in the other, Billy twisted and dropped feetfirst. When he plunged in, he pulled on the rope to haul himself back to the surface. A light flashed on from the bouncing raft, and Ashley's face appeared at the back. She shone the beam in his eyes.

"Are you all right?" she whisper shouted.

Billy pulled out his regulator. Spray from the pounding water flew all around and tossed droplets on the flashlight's lens. "I think so."

Ashley shifted the beam to Billy's right, illuminating his mother. "You okay, Mrs. B?"

"Fine. And Yereq?"

"He's good. He's getting ready to guide the front end."

The light flicked off. As the current pushed the raft forward and out of the deep pool, Billy reinserted the regulator and dove underwater. He grabbed his flashlight, turned it on, and pointed the beam up at the raft's bottom, allowing him to follow its course. Immediately to his right, his mother set her beam on the riverbed. Although it was made up of sand and pebbles, they had to watch for sharp projections that might rise up ahead.

The flashlights' glow provided a view of Yereq's feet as he kicked. Since the river was only about four feet deep here, his powerful legs churned up sand at the bottom, clouding their view.

Soon, the channel deepened, and the bottom cleared again. Instead of sand, slabs of rock appeared, black with sparkling crystals embedded within that made the bed look like a star-filled nightscape. A hole appeared ahead, so deep, the bottom of the river seemed to fall away into nothingness. The hole's surrounding walls were covered with the same crystalline stars.

Billy studied one of the crystals. It didn't merely reflect the flashlight; it seemed to radiate a light of its own.

As they drifted over the hole, the bitter cold jabbed deeper into his body. Queasiness turned his stomach. He shivered hard, so hard his beam shook on the bottom of the raft.

His mother aimed her light at herself and raised her eyebrows as if to ask how he was doing. Billy laid a hand on his stomach and shook his head. Whatever the problem was, it seemed to be getting worse, a lot worse.

She dove and shone the light on one of the crystals. Billy followed her progress with his own light. After a second or two, she hurried back and caught up. Reaching out of the water, she jerked on the rope and surfaced, pulling Billy with her.

Keeping her light under water as they floated with the raft, she whispered, "I think they're candlestones!"

Billy pressed a fist into his gut. "No wonder I'm so sick. There must be a hundred of them down there."

Ashley whispered from the raft. "What's up?"

"Candlestones," Billy said. "Lots of them."

"Did you feel sick when we came through before?"

"We flew over this part, but I remember getting sick while we were in the air. It's worse now, a lot worse."

"Let's hope they're only in one spot," his mother said.

Billy pulled his fist away from his stomach. "Could be. It's easing up already. But since Goliath's been here four years, he probably felt them, too, so you can bet Flint knows about them."

"Something else has me worried," Ashley said. "I haven't seen the wall's glow since we came back."

"I was thinking it was cloud cover." Billy looked up at the sky. "It's pretty clear now."

"It's all adding up. No shadow people in the valley and no one guarding the river. They're probably massing their troops somewhere. Abraham's wall must be dwindling."

Billy let out a long breath. The pain was almost gone. "I guess we'll find out soon."

"Right." Ashley set her transmitter on the raft. "Hold this for me. I'm calling Listener. They need to know right now."

Kicking with his fins to stay upright, Billy held the small box and antenna in place, while his mother kept her light trained on his hands.

Ashley tapped her jaw and began speaking in a hushed tone. "Listener, can you hear me?"

As he held it, the antenna turned slowly. Their tests had worked several times before. Ashley's tooth transmitter sent her voice to the box, which boosted the signal, but since the antenna needed to point in the right direction, she had to find the correct angle as she spoke.

"Listener," she said again, this time a bit louder. "Are you there?"

A static-filled voice sounded from the box. "I'm here, Ashley. I can barely hear you."

"I know. The river noise is terrible. Is Candle with you?"

"He's right outside the door."

"Have him call Valiant and Elam immediately. This is an emergency."

"I'll be right back."

Ashley looked at Billy, a worried frown on her face. Behind her, barely visible in the flashlight's glow, Walter and Tamara looked on. Both stayed silent.

Listener's voice returned, clearer now. "Ashley, Candle is on his way."

"Good. Now here's what I want you to do. Run to Clefspeare and tell him that the wall of fire is either weak or gone. Flint's army is getting ready to attack, and they might have candlestones."

"That's awful. Billy told me about those."

Ashley kept her voice steady and calm. "We also need a ride back to the village, enough dragons for six passengers."

"But if Flint attacks," Listener said, "won't Elam want to keep the dragons here to help?"

"Good point, but it'll take us too long to walk."

"I can send Candle in the airplane."

Ashley looked at Billy. "What do you think? Can he fly in the dark?"

"He can do it. If we light up a landing strip, he'll be fine."

Ashley set her finger on her jaw again and looked toward the village. "Listener, that should work. Have him come to where the river meets the wall on the south side. It might not be there anymore, so he'll have to look for our signal. When we hear the engine, we'll shoot Excalibur's beam into the air."

"I'll tell him."

"If the tank's almost empty, there's a new barrel of fuel in greenhouse number four."

"Got it. I'm on my way."

Ashley breathed a sigh. "Four years of preparation are coming to an end. I hope we're ready."

"We didn't count on candlestones," Billy said.

Tamara tapped Ashley on the shoulder. "Walter says he sees the wall. It is weak and not as high."

"Okay," Ashley said to Billy. "We'll cover up. Maybe now it won't be so bad for the three divers when they go through the barrier."

Billy glanced ahead. The fiery wall did seem weaker, and there was no sign of a guard anywhere. But even with the prospect of an easier-than-expected exit, the thought of imminent war brought a new wave of shivers. Soon, good men would likely die. Soon, the once innocent and naïve villagers would learn if their hardened muscles and honed skills were ready for a real battle, a battle for blood.

When they drew within a few seconds of the wall, Billy and his mother submerged. The water grew warm, then hot. After spiking to a scalding peak, it suddenly cooled again.

Billy surged above the water, and he and his mother, working in concert with Yereq in the front, pulled the raft to shore. He took his mother's hand and led her to the dwindling flames, a wall that now rose to about thirty feet in height. Basking in the heat, they stripped off their dry suits and straightened out their wrinkled clothes. Yereq joined them, and the three dried out their hair and shook out the river's chill.

Ashley drew near, walking at Walter's side. "I can hear Abraham and Angel again."

"What are they saying?" Billy asked.

She edged closer to the wall, so close it seemed that the flames might reach out and scorch her skin. As she stared straight at the fire, she took on a strange tone, like a song, except all in one note, and breathed, not spoken, a breeze with blended voices. "It is time for us to go. We have protected you these many months, and our energy is spent. We will now fly to the Father of Lights, but we leave you three gifts. One is a final burst of energy that will release Second Eden from the shackles of the season of death, and your dragons will find new strength in the warmth of this world's first true summer. The other two gifts you will find as wisdom guides you."

She stepped back and again took Walter's hand. Then, smiling, she let out a long sigh. "They're so happy, happy to be together and happy that they're going to Paradise."

Suddenly, the wall of fire brightened. Like a rising curtain, it shot into the air, an irregular ring of flames that once drew a boundary around enemy territory. When it reached the remaining clouds, the fire absorbed every trace of vapor. The sky cleared. Stars twinkled. And far away, Pegasus peeked over the horizon, offering a scant glow over the dark area.

A loud shout sounded from somewhere in Adam's Marsh. A dragon's roar followed, then silence. Only the river's splashes reached their ears.

Billy pulled Walter and Ashley close. "Flint's troops. They're getting ready to march."

"How much time do you think we have?" Walter asked. "The shadow people are pretty slow, but we need time to set the trap."

Billy watched the clouds over the village dwindle and disappear. "How long will that take?"

"Setting the nodes will take maybe fifteen minutes. But we still have to spread the net with the airplane before we place the nodes. The fuel lines are already in place."

"If I'm flying Merlin," Billy said, "and you're spreading the net on the ground, who'll use Excalibur to energize the bones and get Tamara transformed into a dragon?"

Billy's mother joined their huddle. "Just tell me what to do. I can fly Merlin for whatever that prep run is."

"Mom, that's perfect. Candle can show you what to do. The maneuvers are too precise for him to do the flying, but the two of you together can pull it off."

"I'll help Walter," Ashley said. "That'll speed up his part. Cliffside can run the magneto."

Billy pointed at himself. "Then I'll get Tamara to the birthing garden, but everything depends on Candle getting here soon."

"There's one thing I missed," Walter said. "When you told us what Abraham and Angel were saying, you mentioned three gifts. What were the other two?"

Ashley flicked on her flashlight and aimed it at the ground. "I got the impression that it would be—" She dropped to her knees. "Here they are."

Billy looked over Ashley's shoulder. In her palm she held a ring and a small white object that looked like a bone.

Rising to her feet, she slid them into her pocket. "Maybe Valiant can give us an idea of what these—"

A new voice erupted from the radio. "Ashley? This is Elam."

Ashley touched her jaw. "Elam, did you get the word?"

"Yes. We're all hustling to get prepared. Is there anything else we need to know?"

"The wall's completely gone now. We heard a lot of commotion, so they're probably getting ready to march."

"Seen any shadow people?"

Ashley stared into Adam's Marsh. "The valley's empty. We can assume they'll be coming in full force, but it'll probably be a slow march. They might send a dragon as a scout, so you'll have to stay alert."

"We'll be ready. We're keeping the village lights at normal levels for now. Better to make them think we don't know they're coming."

"Unless Merlin gives us away," Billy said. "But we've done nighttime reconnaissance before. If they hear a motor, they might not think anything unusual is happening."

Ashley lifted a finger. "One more thing. You probably noticed the clear skies. Before the wall vanished, Abraham and Angel spoke to me. They said the first true summer will be coming to Second Eden."

"We noticed," Elam said. "It's a lot warmer. We'll discuss how to use that to our advantage."

"I have some ideas cooking. I'll let you know when we get there."

Elam's voice faded as if he had stepped away from the microphone. "It shouldn't be long. Candle has already taken off."

"Okay. See you soon." Ashley withdrew the ion box from her cloak. "I'd better let Gabriel out."

Walter stretched, popping his back. "Yeah, I get a backache just thinking about being stuffed in there."

She opened the lid and spoke into the opening. "Gabriel, do you remember the directions?"

The glow within the box dimmed. Ashley's gaze shifted upward as if watching something rise, apparently following the source of Gabriel's voice.

"Good." Ashley pointed upstream. "That's due north, so try to keep your bearings. When you find the lake, you shouldn't have a problem locating the boulder with the *X*. If the portal's still there and you can't get through it, come back and let me know. We can send some dragons to try to open it again."

As Ashley put the box away, she looked at the river. After a few seconds, she turned toward Billy. Breathing out her words in a sigh, she said, "He's gone."

Billy searched for any sign of Gabriel's light, but, of course, nothing appeared. "I guess there's no other way he can help us in that condition, but my father and Hartanna tried to open that portal at least three times. What makes Gabriel think he'll be able to get through?"

Ashley smiled. "Do you need a lesson in the power of love?"

"What do you mean?"

"Love believes all things. This is a love journey, you know."

"You sensed that?"

A trembling smile bent Ashley's lips. "Very deeply."

"Acacia or Shiloh?"

"Oh, it's Shiloh. Definitely Shiloh. When he said her name, I could feel his love."

Billy nodded. It made sense. Gabriel had watched over Shiloh for a long time, so developing an attachment was normal. And since they were both much older than they looked, their differences in age didn't really matter much.

He waved for Yereq and Tamara to join them. "Yereq, I have a dangerous assignment for you."

Even in a whisper, the great giant's voice seemed to shake the air. "Speak it. I will do whatever I must."

"Flint has no idea you're here. Since you look so much like the other Nephilim, and since it's still dark, you can try to infiltrate their troops. See what you can do to sabotage their plans, but don't give yourself away. The longer you can work behind the lines, the better for us."

"It will be an honor." Yereq rubbed his chin thoughtfully. "I will attempt to subdue one of my kinsmen and take his clothing."

Ashley pulled a white hair band from around her head and gave it to Yereq. "Use this as an arm band so we'll know which one you are. In the heat of battle, I doubt Flint's troops will notice."

"Very well." He took the band and pushed it into his pocket. "Yet, if you see me in the heat of battle, I am likely to be noticeable as the Naphil who is killing Goliath with his bare hands."

Billy handed Yereq his diving flashlight and grasped the giant's wrist. "We'll see you at the victory feast."

Yereq gave Billy a sad sort of nod and walked into Adam's Marsh, following the direction of the earlier shout.

Heaving a sigh, Billy laid a hand on Tamara's shoulder. "When we arrive at the village, I will rush you to the birthing garden to get you transformed into a dragon. Are you ready and willing?"

Her eyes sparkled in the moon's strengthening beams. "I am both, and I am also excited."

"Great. The other dragons will teach you everything you need to know."

Ashley took off her rubellite ring and slid it onto Tamara's finger. "You'll need this."

"Thank you." Tamara lifted her hand and looked at the gem. "Some of the other dragons had one. I did not."

After a few minutes, Merlin's familiar drone reached them, steadily increasing. Billy ran out to a flat area, lit up Excalibur, and pointed the beam at the ground. It drew a long line through the snow, creating Candle's runway.

As soon as the plane rumbled to a stop, Billy hustled everyone on board. His mother jumped into the pilot's seat, while he settled into the copilot's. "Think you can take off in the dark?" he asked.

"Just watch me, flyboy." With a wink, she throttled up and rolled Merlin down the bumpy runway. A few seconds later, they were airborne.

Billy nodded at the windshield. "See those pinpoints of light way out there?"

"Yes. What are they?"

"The village's lanterns. The birthing garden is on the north side; that's to the right. There's room to land, but you'll have to make a quick drop and stop. Then you and Candle will take off again."

She pushed the airplane toward top speed. "Let's get it done."

CHAPTER 7

THE HYBRID'S SEED

Billy climbed the stairs to the village's rampart, an eight-foot- high mound Valiant and Sir Barlow had constructed a year earlier to provide a good view to the northeast where Adam's Marsh lay. He crossed the rough beams that made up the rampart's eight-by-eight-foot deck and stood next to Windor behind a waist-high parapet. The teenaged boy had stayed at his lookout post for hours, his keen eyes surveying the field in the light of the moon.

After four years of bitter cold, the temperate air felt stifling, though it was likely no more than sixty degrees Fahrenheit. Billy aimed Listener's spyglass toward Adam's Marsh. Since Enoch's gift had not provided prophetic glimpses in years, Listener had stopped using it so frequently, but it still provided a great view of the surrounding area.

With Pegasus casting its radiance over the fields and forests, Walter and Ashley were easy to find. Riding Firedda northwest and southeast along the village's northeastern border, they were spreading out a thin-filament net across a field.

In preparation for the construction of the rampart, the villagers had cleared the dead and dying trees just outside the village. They hoped to be able to see the enemy coming, and now they had room for the huge net. Coated with iron filings, it would serve as a heating coil for the unsuspecting shadow people who were likely to make up the first wave of invaders. Then, when the second wave arrived, the villagers could spring trap number two, the fuel lines that lay underneath the net.

Firedda landed gracefully. Walter and Ashley jumped off and dashed around for a few seconds, pulling the net and staking it down. After camouflaging it under the melting snow the best they could, they climbed back on Firedda to fly to the next spot.

Billy looked at Pegasus, still low in the sky. At this rate, Walter and Ashley would be done pretty soon. Ashley's idea was brilliant, as usual, but would it work? No one knew exactly what the shadow people were made of, so all this preparation might be worthless. At the very least, it should light up the enemy, allowing the villagers to better attack their shadowy bodies.

He shifted the spyglass to the south and spotted Merlin. His mother and Candle had made the initial drop of the net and were now flying toward the dragon launching field. Soon he would be able to reunite his mother and father, but not right away. Clefspeare would be gathering the dragon air force and their pilots together for battle, and his mother volunteered to work with the women of the village. They and the children were preparing for their part in the battle, setting up the hospital, which once flew high above but now sat just outside the village's western border.

Nodding at the progress in the field, he lowered the spyglass and looked at Windor. "Report to Elam and Valiant and tell them the net's in place. I see no signs of enemy troops yet."

"I will tell them." Windor hustled down the rampart's five wooden steps and nearly ran into Elam.

Elam grabbed the teenager's shoulders and kept him from falling. "I heard the message. You will find Valiant with the dragons at the launching field."

When Windor disappeared in the darkness, Elam joined Billy at the parapet, carrying a lantern and wearing the village's battle uniform. The lantern's flame seemed to be mimicked by the sunburst design on Elam's tunic, a symbol of the fire God had given both man and beast, a demonstration of power and light from above.

Billy pointed with the spyglass. "The shadow people are probably on the front lines."

"Hoping to strangle us in our sleep, I assume."

"That's what I would guess."

"The dragons sense them," Elam said, "but they say that danger is closing in from the north at a faster rate, and it's a different kind of danger."

"The Vacants?"

Elam nodded. "We already caught a scout. The conspiracy between them and Flint's army has now reached its climax."

"Who's watching the birthing garden?"

"Sorentine."

"Sorentine?" Billy shook his head. "That won't work. My mother said she's . . ." He paused, searching for a kind word. "Well, she's not exactly a genius."

"Don't worry," Elam said, laughing. "Patrick's with her. With his brains and her brawn, they're a perfect combination."

Billy breathed a sigh. "You scared me for a minute."

"Give her a chance. Courage and love are more important than brains." Elam set his hands on the parapet. "So now we wait."

"Yeah. I guess so." Billy eyed Elam. Those words stung. Again it seemed that the ages-old warrior chief oozed more wisdom than Billy could learn in a lifetime. And he was right. He needed to give Sorentine a break. She was doing the best she could.

"Are we missing any steps?" Elam asked. "Can you think of anything else you heard or saw behind enemy lines that might help?"

Billy began counting on his fingers. "You already know what Yereq's doing. You know about the candlestones and Karrick."

"Right. Since we don't know who has candlestones, we decided to split up the dragons. Most of them will assist on the northern side against the Vacants, while Clefspeare and Legossi patrol the northeastern front. They should be enough to fight Goliath and Karrick. When we figure out if Flint has candlestones and how he'll use them, we'll decide how to shift our dragon army. In the meantime, it's best to hold Thigocia back until we have a handle on the situation. We don't want our dragon healer injured."

Billy touched a third finger. "There's one more thing. I didn't tell you how Karrick was born. Somehow Flint got some soil from the resurrection garden and one of the bones, and Goliath used them to call Karrick from a place called the Valley of Souls. When Devin and Palin killed Roxil, her unborn youngling went to that valley, and all they had to do was call him out to resurrect him."

"But when could they have done that? We haven't had another eclipse cycle."

"They must have done it at the same time we resurrected Dr. Conner," Billy said. "I guess they already had their garden by then. I described Karrick to my father, and he says four years old is about right."

"But who provided the soil and bone?"

Billy tightened his grip on the spyglass. "I already know what you think."

"Look," Elam said, grasping Billy's arm, "I'm not blaming you for putting any trust in Semiramis. If she stole soil and a bone, she must have done it before that night. You're in the clear."

Billy nodded. It was true. Semiramis had convinced him to find Shiloh after they called for Dr. Conner, so Flint must have already had his garden set up. Then why would Arramos need to plant something in the village's garden if they already had one of their own? Was Semiramis able to transport the bone and soil under the wall at the river but unable to transport the plant's seed? Or did she have some other reason for making sure their plant grew in the original birthing garden? "All that aside," Billy said, "there's another issue. With the season of death over, we're bound to have another eclipse cycle, so we can call Makaidos and probably anyone else in the Valley of Souls."

"Anyone else?" Elam raised his eyebrows. "Do you know who's down there?"

Billy looked away for a moment. Explaining this part wouldn't be easy. "It's like this. I've been having dreams where I see Bonnie praying. Sometimes she's alone, and sometimes she's with Sapphira, but she keeps praying the same thing over and over." He paused for a moment. A lump was forming in his throat, and he had to get rid of it. Just before a life-or-death battle was no time to get so emotional. "She always says, 'Call to me, and I will answer you.'"

"You've mentioned that before. That's on Bonnie's poster."

"But there's more. In the dream she mentions rising again if I'll say her name."

Elam nodded and stretched out his reply. "Oh, I see."

"I know, I know. You think I'm probably conjuring up some kind of hopeful daydream, but this one's not like that. You'd have to experience it to understand."

"Trust me. I've had dreams about Sapphira like that, especially one where we're dancing near a fountain, sort of like the fountain in our village, only it's in a ballroomlike setting." He tilted his head upward and inhaled deeply. "It's so real I can almost feel the spray."

"So you get what I mean. Maybe our dreams are prophetic."

"Hard to say for sure," Elam said, shrugging. "But if Bonnie and Sapphira went to the Valley of Souls, it would explain why no one's seen them."

"Then is it worth a try?"

"Maybe, but we don't know when the next eclipse is supposed to be."

"True." Billy looked at Pegasus. It seemed bright, similar to the brightness it had shone after the first eclipse, but since they hadn't seen its fullness in years, it was hard to remember for certain. "Valiant would've kept up with the calendar, but if tonight's the night, we can't wait to ask him."

The moon's glow reflected in Elam's eyes. "If it is, the moon's already getting close to the crucial angle."

"Do you think I have time?" Billy touched Excalibur's hilt. "I have all I need to energize the soil."

Elam looked toward Adam's Marsh. "Probably plenty of time before Flint's troops arrive, but it's such a long shot. According to the prophecy, it's possible only two nights out of the month."

"Wouldn't it make sense for Abraham and Angel to time their departure for the very day we needed to use the garden? We can't miss this opportunity."

"But if Abraham planned it that way, he would want us to resurrect his son. We can't miss another chance to call back Makaidos, especially when your idea is based on a dream."

Billy tensed his jaw. Elam's logic was right on target. How could a message in a dream overcome basic common sense? Dreams were just wishful thinking more often than anything, but sometimes they meant something more, and his vision of Bonnie was so deeply rooted, this dream had to be one of those times.

Years ago, he had read Bonnie's prayer in her journal, and a vision of her appeared in his mind, her wings spread in full flight. She begged him to take Excalibur from her hands. Not long before that vision, Professor Hamilton had said of Excalibur, "It was bestowed to you as a gift from above. It was meant for you to wield in battle." But he had refused the professor's wisdom, and rejecting divine revelation when it defied his ill-informed logic had led to a huge mess.

Elam shook Billy's shoulder. "Hey, we can't wait forever. If you want to give the garden a try, you'd better go now."

Tightening his muscles, Billy set his feet. "Elam, your reasons for calling Makaidos are right on the mark, but I think something's going on, something we don't understand. I'll go to the garden, and I'll do what you told me, but I'm asking for a little slack."

Elam set his stare on Billy and held it for several seconds. Finally, he exhaled and nodded. "I expect you to call Makaidos, but if wisdom guides you otherwise, you may do as you see fit."

"Thank you." Billy hustled down the stairs. "Don't start the war without me."

"If we get attacked," Elam called. "I'll send up a flare. But don't forget. The Vacants could show up from the north at any minute."

"Got it!" As Billy jogged along the path to the village, he imagined the resurrection procedure. Would he have to get Ruth to recite the poem? Apparently Flint performed a rebirth without her, but could Goliath have provided the words? He was at his own resurrection, but not really physically present until after the poem's recitation. Maybe they forced Roxil to sing it, but exactly when she showed up during the ceremony wasn't clear at all, and how could she have memorized it in one hearing?

When he arrived at the central circle, he stopped and pulled off his cloak. The air was getting warmer by the minute.

A sweet voice reached his ear. "Billy?"

"Listener?" Turning, he found her standing by a street lantern. She was dressed in the village's uniform, much like Elam's but without the marching dragon, signifying that she would not be in the battle. A troubled frown wrinkled her face. "What's wrong?" Billy asked.

"I was napping, and I had a strange dream. An elderly man asked me to do something. He was kind and gentle, so I hope it comes true someday, but I didn't understand his request. It was so puzzling."

Billy ached to take the time to hear more, but he couldn't delay much longer. "Dreams are like that sometimes. Maybe it'll become clear later."

"Where is your uniform?" she asked.

Billy clutched his tunic. "I haven't had time to put it on, and now I have to go to the garden."

"I can bring it to the garden for you."

"That would be great. Would you also ask Ruth to come? I need her to recite the resurrection poem."

"Really?" In the light of a dozen street lanterns, Listener's eyes sparkled. "Are you going to call Makaidos?"

"Yeah." Billy cleared his throat. No sense in letting her in on the other option. "Anyway, that's the plan."

Listener ran toward Billy's hut. "I'll meet you there!"

He watched her young legs, so light, so strong. No conflicts did battle in her mind, while his own conflicts made his legs feel like slabs of concrete.

Pushing his feet forward, he trudged toward the birthing garden. No use hurrying. He couldn't do anything until Ruth got there.

As he walked into the bordering forest, his view darkened. He had forgotten to carry a light, but it didn't matter; he knew the path well. With blackness ahead of him, his dream of Bonnie took over his senses, and the first line of her song repeated, *Call to me, and I will answer you.* Her delivery was quiet, as if she called from another world, yet it was forceful, a plea that reached from heart to heart.

Billy clenched a fist. It had to be real. It just had to be. But how could a dreamer convince anyone of a feeling? Elam had made his wishes clear, so Billy had to make those his priority, but how could he ignore the inner turmoil? He had said, "Don't start the war without me," but it felt like the war had already begun, at least in his mind, and this decision might be the first salvo for either side, and maybe a decisive one.

When he reached the field and the path to the garden, he forced his legs into a jog and focused on a single lantern light in the distance. His shoes squished. The surrounding snow was obviously melting, and the ground felt like a blend of dead grass and mud.

"Patrick!" he called as he drew close. "It's Billy." He slowed to a stop, sliding a bit in the mud. Patrick stood at the garden's edge while Sorentine sat on her haunches behind him.

Patrick's bushy white eyebrows arched up. "I'm glad to see you, William. What brings you out here?"

"We need to try a resurrection."

Patrick looked up at the moon. "I was just thinking about that. The shadow angles are precisely what they were when we began Dr. Conner's ceremony. I suspect that, if not for the season of death, we would have had a normal eclipse last night or perhaps the night before."

Billy cocked his head. "Really? You remember details like that?"

"Oh, yes. Charles Hamilton and I were both avid astronomy buffs, so I take careful note of celestial events."

As Billy looked up at the stars, a memory flowed into his mind, the early morning when he and the professor were in England waiting for Bonnie to arrive with Clefspeare and Hartanna. Prof pointed out Ursa Major and Polaris, as well as another star Billy had never heard of. The wise old professor definitely knew the celestial sky.

"Listener is bringing Ruth." Billy touched Excalibur's hilt. "I suppose I can go ahead and energize the bones."

"Ruth might not be able to come. She has taken ill, and I believe Dr. Conner is examining her as we speak."

Billy looked toward the village. Listener strode quickly down the path, alone, sloshing through the mud. When she arrived, she slipped and nearly fell, but Billy caught her in time.

Breathless, she handed Billy his uniform. "Ruth is too sick to come. Dr. Conner says it was probably something she ate, and it will pass soon, but she is so nauseated, she can hardly move."

Billy stripped off his tunic, leaving him bare-chested. He had learned long ago that the people of Second Eden had few modesty standards, so Listener wouldn't give his appearance a second thought. "So what can we do?" he asked as he pushed his arms through a long-sleeved red shirt. "If this is the second night, we won't have another chance until next month."

"True," Patrick said, "but must my wife be the one to sing the words?"

"Well, no." Billy put on the second layer, a short-sleeved silver shirt made of a woven cloth as tough as chain mail. "At least I don't think so."

"Then we have a solution." Patrick patted his torso, speaking slowly as if distracted by his search for something buried in his clothing. "Ruth has practiced it many times since her previous recital. I helped her by writing it down and following along while she practiced, and when the season of death ended, she asked me to find the transcription, so I located it . . ." He pulled a wrinkled piece of parchment from inside his coat. "Ah! Here it is."

Billy looked at the palm-sized scrap. Patrick's handwriting was sloppy but readable.

"The only problem that remains is the tune," Patrick said. "Do you know it?"

"No. Didn't Ruth practice it?"

"Only the words. Adding the tune slowed us down."

"Maybe the tune doesn't matter," Billy offered. "The words have the power, right?"

"I wouldn't be so certain, William. Music has great power. One tune can make a man rise up with his muscles flexed, while another can sap his energy."

"May I see the song?" Listener asked, reaching for the parchment.

"Certainly." Patrick handed it to her. "Have you heard it?"

Listener shook her head, her eyes trained on the words. "I wasn't at the garden either time, but I heard Ruth humming a tune many times, and I told her it sounded like one I have had running through my head for as long as I can remember. I wanted to see if the words fit."

"And?" Billy prompted.

Looking up from the parchment, she nodded. "I think so, but I should practice first to make sure."

Rapid-fire thoughts raced through Billy's mind. They couldn't drag Ruth out there on a wild hunch that it might be the appropriate resurrection night, and if Listener, the little girl who was known for her listening and memory prowess, was sure, then maybe her tune was the right one. Besides, they had to hurry. The battle might start at any minute. "Okay. Listener will sing the words, and I'll light up the bones."

"Is there any way I might be of service?" Sorentine asked.

Billy looked into her hopeful eyes. How could he find a way for a not-so-bright dragon to do something useful? "Uh . . . how about if you help Listener practice? Every singer needs someone as a sounding board."

Sorentine's brow drooped, and her long neck swung her head away. "Very well."

Billy's heart sank. He had hurt her feelings. She might not be brilliant, but she knew a veiled dismissal when she heard one. Yet, what could he do about it now?

He took Patrick's arm and guided him a few feet into the garden. "I have a dilemma," he said in a low tone. "I've been having these dreams that Bonnie wants me to call her. I think this is where I'm supposed to do it, but Elam thinks it would be wrong to bypass resurrecting Makaidos for the third time just because I've been dreaming about Bonnie."

Patrick stroked his chin for a moment before answering. "Do you have any corroborating evidence?"

"You mean, something more than just the dream?" He shook his head. "Not really. Just that the phrase Bonnie sings in the dream is the same one that led me to suggest calling Dr. Conner from the garden."

"Ah, yes, and that worked out quite well. We needed a doctor far more urgently than we needed Makaidos that night."

"True, but we sure could use Makaidos now."

"Indeed." Patrick looked down at one of the garden's pregnant plants and used his shoe to push soil over an exposed root. "It seems that, absent corroborating evidence, you should heed Elam—"

"Billy," Sorentine called. "I must tell you something."

He looked back at the village. No flare yet. "Sure. What is it?"

"Listener's song. I know the tune."

"You know it?" Billy walked back to the edge of the garden where Listener was staring up at the dragon with wide eyes. "How could that be?"

"It is a lullaby we dragons sing to our smallest younglings. Before the transformation, I sang it to my unborn little one. She moved so much inside me, I thought she must have heard my voice."

"She?" Billy asked. "How did you know?"

"When the time gets close, we dragons sense the gender. Yet, I know not what happened to my little one when I was transformed. Her movement slowed greatly, so I sang nearly all day, hoping to wake her up, perhaps to regenerate her as I was regenerated. But I never learned why she was so quiet. The slayer killed me before she was born."

As Billy looked at her serious face, a tingle ran across his skin. Something strange was happening. The mysterious dragon and the even more mysterious girl couldn't possibly know the same tune. "How . . ." Billy swallowed. "How does your song go?"

"It is not exactly the same as other dragons sing. I . . ." She looked up as if searching for a word. "I invented the last part, because my youngling was yet unborn, so it is not as good as the rest."

"It'll be fine," Billy said. "Please sing it."

"Very well." Sorentine moved her head directly in front of Listener, and, looking into her eyes, sang in a low, yet feminine voice.

When younglings play so hard all day,
They need to rest in mother's care.
Regain the light your play has spent;
My bed of gems I now will share.

So leave your eyes as open doors
To gather truth, to gather light,
For truth and light will call as one,
"Rebuke the false and scatter night."

And now I call to you in song;
Regenerate within my womb.
Above all gems you are to me,
I call you from your hidden room.

Tears flowed down Listener's cheeks. Sniffing, she petted Sorentine's neck. "That's the exact tune, and some of the meanings are the same, too."

"Yes," Patrick said. "The theme of calling to rebirth is similar in both."

Billy let the lyrics sink in. *I call to you . . . Above all gems . . . Your hidden room* . . . There was so much there! Each word seemed to reach into his heart and play its note from within. Furrowing his brow tightly, he turned to Patrick. "Which gem is the most valuable?"

Sir Patrick tilted his head. "A surprising query, William, but the answer would depend on a number of factors, such as color and clarity and how it is cut."

"Forget about cut." Billy stared hard at the ground. "What if it had perfect color and perfect clarity?"

"I suppose it would be a ruby. A flawless ruby usually fetches a higher price than a diamond of equal size and quality."

"A ruby?" Billy looked up at him. "Not a sapphire?"

"William, a sapphire is the same gem. They are both corundum. A red deposit is a ruby, and any other color is a sapphire. They have the same basic chemical composition, a type of aluminum oxide."

While Billy pondered the words, Patrick added, "It seems to me that we have discovered the reason for Listener's knowledge of the song."

"We have?" Billy looked up at him again.

"Indeed. My guess is that a certain unborn dragon was not completely transformed when her mother underwent her transformation. After the youngling died as the result of her mother's death, she resurrected here, much later, to be sure, but we haven't learned much about the timing of these events, so that should be no surprise. Since Listener was born with two companions, one of which gave her dragonlike scales, there seems to be only one explanation. Listener and the youngling are one and the same. The song is the binding tie that proves the connection. After hearing it in her mother's womb, Listener, who never forgets what she hears, remembers it to this day."

Listener covered her mouth with her hand. As more tears flowed, she reached up and touched Sorentine's cheek. "Mother?" she said meekly.

A large teardrop fell from the dragon's eye. "My little one?"

Listener rose to her tiptoes and wrapped her arms around the dragon's neck. "Mother!"

Sorentine wept. "Oh, my darling! At last we meet!"

As they nuzzled cheek to cheek, Listener spoke through her sobs. "Acacia said she thought my mother probably killed me before I was born. She wasn't really sure, and I always hoped she was wrong, and now I know you never stopped loving me. Never!"

Billy bit his lip. If he kept watching these two, he would start crying with them. Poor Listener had lost two mothers, first Sorentine and then Angel. Yes, Mantika was a fine surrogate mother, but this was different, a bond that lasted for centuries, tied together by a song that a tiny youngling never forgot.

Billy pulled Patrick away again. "You mentioned that we needed corroborating evidence." He nodded at Listener and the dragon. "Does it get any clearer?"

"If I am following your thinking, William, you are connecting the lyrics to our situation. Since Sapphira is linked to a sapphire, you are suggesting that we call her instead of Makaidos."

"Exactly. I was hoping I could call Bonnie, but I guess we'll have to wait for another time."

"I see." Patrick began stroking his chin again. "This is most extraordinary. I have to agree with your assessment."

Billy spread out his hands. "Elam is the warrior chief. He told me to follow wisdom, but is this enough proof to go against his wishes?"

"If he heard the evidence, he would likely acquiesce, but we have already lost so much time. Searching for him now with an army pressing in on us would cause too much of a delay, especially with Pegasus nearly at the crucial point in the sky."

"Then what do we do?"

Patrick raised a hand. "I will vouch for you. Since he long ago submitted to my authority as my servant, Markus, and has not rescinded that duty, he will trust my judgment. I hereby call upon you to change the name in the song from Makaidos to Sapphira."

A flare arced across the sky, brightening the field. "The signal!" Billy withdrew Excalibur, lit up the beam, and took Listener's hand. "We have to hurry."

They ran into the garden, passed by the plump weed they had been protecting for Shiloh's sake, dodged the dozen or so other plants, and stopped in front of the one Elam had grown from a seed.

Billy touched the soil with the beam, careful to avoid the plants. The light crawled across the garden like flame on a dry prairie. The bones began to glow, as if burning within and emanating a chemical fire that oozed radiance. Soon, the garden came alive with sparkling white embers, the bones of Makaidos again providing energy to the soils of rebirth.

After putting Excalibur away, Billy laid a hand on Listener's head. "Sing it now, daughter of Sorentine. Sing it with all your heart."

Blinking away tears, Listener began the song, not bothering to look at the parchment.

When phantoms knock on doors of light
To open paths to worlds beyond,
A friend replies, "Insert the key
To leave the dark and greet the dawn.

"The key is light, the words of truth;
No lie can break the chains of death.
A whispered word of love avails
To bring new life, the spirit's breath."

So now I sing a key for you,
The phantom waiting at the door;
We call for you, Sapphira who
Will join us now in holy war.

As she rolled up the parchment and held it in her fist, the garden's glow ran up her legs and painted an aura around her body. She was the new Paili, another prophetic songstress in a petite shell.

Billy steeled his shaking legs. What would happen now? She had called for Sapphira, but leaving Bonnie out felt like a stab in the heart.

Could they call for two at once? No one had said they couldn't. Bonnie's name didn't really fit the poem's meter, but did that matter? Resurrection couldn't hinge on singing perfectly placed syllables, could it?

Shaking his head, Billy glared at the shimmering soil. So many questions! And too few answers.

The ground shook. Just a few paces ahead, a bump formed between two rows. For a moment, it grew, like an expanding molehill. When it reached a foot tall, the soil began spilling away, revealing a head of hair, dirty, yet obviously white. Then, a face appeared, and two blue eyes blinked away the dirt.

CHAPTER 8

THE REUNION

"Sapphira!" Billy rushed forward, and taking her hand, helped her step out of the erupting garden.

Brushing dirt from her clothes, Sapphira looked around. "Where's Bonnie?"

"Bonnie? I thought she might have been with you."

Sapphira's eyes widened. "Didn't you call her?"

"Not yet. I wasn't sure how—"

She wrapped her arms around him and laid her head on his chest. "Billy," she cried out, "I feel your thundering heart. It is a drum that beats a call, a call for Bonnie. Can't you hear it? Can't you feel it?"

Billy lifted his arms and looked down at her soiled white hair. What a strange reaction! His heart racing, he stumbled through his words. "I . . . I do feel something. I just don't know what to do about it. We thought you were the one we were supposed to call."

"I was the one." Sapphira released him and picked up one of the glowing bones. "Rebirth has its genesis in love. Makaidos demonstrated that love by dying for the sake of his daughters, and he left behind the power to bring others to life. Yes, the prophetic song is one way to call specific people back from the Valley of Souls." She swept her arm across the garden. "But look around you. It is love that calls these little ones to spring forth from the valley of dead souls. Just sing your own song of love and call Bonnie from the valley."

A shout sounded from the village. "Billy! The Vacants are attacking!"

Billy spotted Walter swinging a lantern at the edge of the village's bordering forest. "I'll be there in a minute."

"A minute!" Walter's voice spiked. "We need Excalibur now! Goliath was seen flying this way!"

Billy gritted his teeth. War would have to wait. He spun toward Sorentine. "Are you willing to go with Walter?"

"Willing?" Sparks flew from her snout. "I will fight with the best of the dragons!" She dipped her head to the ground next to Listener. "Mount, my precious one. I will take you to safety, and then I must go to battle."

Listener scrambled up her neck and settled on her back. New tears gleaming in her eyes, she nodded at Billy but said nothing. The potent mixture of emotional filling and catharsis had drained her of sound.

Sapphira took Billy's hand. "You must call her now before it's too late. I will pray for the words to leap from your heart."

"Okay." His heart still racing, he closed his eyes. Again, the song from his dream entered his mind, yet this time spoken in his own voice.

Call to me, and I will answer you;
Say my name, and my light will shine.
Draw me out, and I will rise again;
Take my hand, and I will be thine.

As he added the tune, he let his new thoughts fill in the words, and he sang them out.

Hear my call, and I will raise you up;
Heed my words, and look at my eyes.

He stretched out his arm, his hand open.

See my love, and know my words are true;
Bonnie Silver, I bid you rise.

The moment the last note died away, the ground shook again. Billy searched the soil for another rising bump, but the shadows cast by Pegasus overwhelmed Patrick's lantern. He reached for Excalibur, but just as his fingers touched the hilt, something slammed into his body and knocked him flat.

Billy looked up from the ground, his head throbbing. "What was that?"

Spreading out her arms, Sapphira shielded him with a ring of fire. "Stay back, foul dragon!"

A deep growl sounded, but it was too dark to see the source. "I am not here to trifle with boys and girls. Stand aside so that I may collect my prize."

Strong arms lifted Billy to his feet. "Get up, brave knight." The voice was soft and gentle, but not Sapphira's. "Don't let this lizard defeat you with mere words."

Billy tried to focus on his helper. "Bonnie?"

As a pair of wings spread out behind her, her beautiful smile shone in the moonlight. "I heard your call, and now I'm looking into your eyes. I see a man, not a boy, a man who can stand up to this scaly bag of hot air."

Her words pulsed through his body, hardening his muscles. He embraced her and whispered into her ear. "I'm glad to see you, but I have to take care of business right now."

She kissed him on the cheek. "Go get him, tiger!"

Flexing his biceps, he turned toward the intruder. Now able to see the dragon in the shadows, he called out, "Goliath! Leave it to a coward like you to wait for the dragon guard to fly away."

"I will wait no longer for my prize." Flames shot from Goliath's mouth and slammed into Sapphira. Her body bent backwards, and her hair and clothes streamed as if flapping in a strong gust of wind. The fire arced around her, missing Billy and Bonnie, but it splashed into three plants behind them.

"No!" Billy lunged for one and batted the flames away with his hand. "You coward!" While Patrick ran to tend to the other burning plants, Billy rose to his feet, withdrew Excalibur, and took three heavy steps toward Goliath. Sapphira stood at his side, the balls of fire in her hands swelling.

"What is this prize you want?" Billy growled as he summoned the beam.

"Merely a weed. I am sure you have seen it." Goliath reached down and wrapped his clawed hand around the supporting stem of one of the plants. "It is very different from this one, which I will incinerate if you do not put away that sword. I wager that I can kill its fruit before you can strike."

Billy scowled at him. He didn't have much choice. Goliath had already proven that he would kill these unborn babies without a thought.

He doused the beam. "Okay. What next?"

"That's a good boy." Goliath released the plant and stretched his neck to see around Billy. "There is my prize. Stand aside, and I will take it and be on my way."

Billy glanced at the weed without moving his head. Of course, he didn't care a whit about the plant itself, but if Goliath took it, what would happen to Shiloh? If Arramos created the life connection between them, did Goliath's appearance mean that its fruit was ripe and could be harvested safely?

"I can't let you uproot the plant," Billy said. "I don't want you touching it."

"I understand what you fear. Open its leaves, and bring the fruit to me, but if you do harm to it, I will destroy every plant in this garden."

Bonnie touched Billy's shoulder. "I'll do it. You and Sapphira can keep an eye on him."

Billy nodded toward the plant. "It's the ugly weed with a big pouch on top."

Glancing back at Goliath, Bonnie hurried toward the edge of the garden and knelt. "This one?"

Patrick set his lantern down next to her. "Yes. We have been watching it for four years."

While Billy and Sapphira eased closer to get a better look, Bonnie peeled back one of the leaves. A sac with a gauzelike, semi-transparent shell tipped into her hands. As she rose to her feet, she held it out for everyone to see.

Billy eyed the strange object, an egg the size of a large cantaloupe. The ovular sac began to glow. Inside, a man pressed his palms against the lining.

"It's too fuzzy to see his face," Bonnie said. "But it looks like he's trying to get out."

Goliath let out a low growl. "Bring it to me."

She looked at Billy. "Should I?"

He tightened his hands into fists. "I guess we don't have much choice."

Beating her wings, she floated over the other plants. With every second, the egg grew larger and brighter. By the time she set it down next to Goliath, it had already doubled in size.

The dragon scooped it up, and as he rose into the air, he grabbed the back of Bonnie's shirt with his clawed foot.

Bonnie screamed. As her outer shirt rode up to her armpits, she beat her wings and kicked wildly.

"Insurance," Goliath said with a low rumble.

Billy thrust Excalibur back into its sheath and sprinted along a row, chasing them. Goliath rose higher. Bonnie's feet dangled only six feet above the ground, but Billy couldn't catch up enough to reach her. And with the dragon's tail swinging back and forth, he had to duck to keep from getting swatted to the mud.

Finally, with a leap and a desperate stretch, he grabbed her shoe with one hand. As his fingers began slipping, he swung up with his other arm and latched onto her ankle.

A rip sounded. He looked up. Was that her shirt tearing? Another rip reached his ears. Suddenly, they dropped. Billy landed into a snowdrift, breaking his fall. Less than a second later, Bonnie landed softly next to him, her wings fanning the air.

Scattering the slush around him, Billy scrambled to his feet. "Sorry, but I have to leave you. There's a war to fight."

She glared up at the escaping dragon. "Get me a sword. I'm going with you."

"A sword?" He laid an arm on her shoulder. When his fingers touched bare skin, he pulled back. "I'm not sure you understand. This is life or death fighting and—"

"Just trust me, Billy." Bonnie pulled her torn shirt higher on her shoulder. "Sapphira and I have been training with an expert for four years."

He took a deep breath. "Okay. I trust you. Ask Patrick to take you to the outfitters and meet me at the rampart."

"The rampart?"

He nodded at Sapphira and Patrick, who were now hustling toward them from the garden. "Patrick will show you."

As Billy turned to run, Bonnie took his hand and pulled him back. "Thank you for calling me."

Drawing closer, he took her hand into both of his. "I'm sorry. I called Sapphira first. There was this song—"

"Don't explain. We watched everything from the Valley of Souls. You did exactly what you had to do, and you *did* call me. I heard every word."

Her loving tone sent tremors through his body. "I hope Elam understands. I went against his wishes."

She looked at their clasped hands and smiled. "You did?"

"I was supposed to call Makaidos."

Her eyes snapped back to him. "And if you had called him, he would have died."

"Died?" He squinted at her. "How? Why?"

"Just trust me." She pulled his hands close and pressed them against her cheek. "Now get going. I'm looking forward to fighting alongside you."

Billy ran toward the village with her face and shining eyes still in his mind. In spite of the warming temperature, a chill ran from his toes to his head. *Bonnie's alive! And she's here in Second Eden!*

With renewed strength, he sprinted down a village street, now crowded with people as they made ready for their defense. Women and children rushed toward the western side carrying towels and basins. Ashley and Dr. Conner marched together, Ashley holding a basket of medical supplies with both arms and Dr. Conner lugging a cot under each arm.

When Billy reached the path to the northeast, he ran past the border of the village and bolted up the rampart's steps, nearly colliding with Walter and Elam. "Sorry I'm late," Billy said, breathless.

Elam looked through the spyglass toward the northeast but said nothing. Blood on his uniform and a deep scratch across his chin proved that he had just come from the battle.

Walter whispered, "Did you resurrect Makaidos?"

"No. It's a long story, but—"

"Save it. We're here because the Vacants on the northern front seem to be trying to draw us away, so Elam wanted to check out the path to Adam's Marsh."

"A diversion?"

"That's what we're guessing. Maybe you should take Excalibur to the northern front and show those Vacants a little diversion of your own. Valiant's troops and the dragons are handling it, but if you could sweep through the Vacants with that roasting beam, the battle would be over in a heartbeat."

Still looking through the spyglass, Elam raised his hand. "No. Wait."

Walter leaned on the parapet and peered into the dim landscape. "What do you see?"

Elam kept the spyglass trained, moving it slowly for several seconds before answering. "A dragon is flying away from us, and he seems to be heading for a dark mass in the distance." He handed the tube to Walter and pointed at a draconic silhouette sinking toward the ground beyond their trap area. "Do you recognize it?"

Walter guided the spyglass. "It's hard to tell, but I think it's red, so it's got to be—"

"Goliath," Billy said. "I just had a scrap with him out in the garden."

Elam narrowed his eyes. "Goliath was in the garden? What happened?"

"He wanted the fruit of the weed."

Elam pounded his fist on the parapet. "I knew it! They were growing something they wanted to use in the war."

"Whew!" Walter patted Billy on the back. "Good thing you were there. I guess you sent him off with his tail on fire, right?"

"Well, not exactly. You see—"

"Elam!"

The new voice was loud and joyful. All three turned. Rapid footsteps clopped up the stairs, and Candle burst into the moonlight's glow. "The Vacants retreated," he said, breathing heavily. "The battle on the northern front is over."

Walter interlocked wrists with Candle. "Great work! We have them on the run."

"I don't think so," Billy said.

Elam looked at him. "Why not?"

"It's the timing." Billy walked to the parapet and looked out at the field. "Ask yourself. If it was a diversion, why didn't Flint's troops attack from the northeast? They didn't even send the shadow people. With the dragons distracted, the conditions were ideal. My guess is that they lured the dragons to the north, so Goliath thought it would be safe to get the plant's fruit. They didn't know we have Sorentine now."

"So what happened out there?" Walter asked. "You're dancing around the bottom line."

"Well, it's a long story." Billy tapped his knuckles on the parapet's stone top. "You see, we never called for Makaidos."

"You decided it wasn't the proper night?" Elam asked.

Billy shook his head. "No. It's the night after eclipse. You see, there's this song Sorentine used to sing—"

"Hello, Elam. Hello, Walter."

Every head turned toward the voice. Bonnie climbed the stairs, slowly and with deliberate footfalls. Dressed in the village's orange and red uniform, a sword at her hip, and her hair tied back, she halted at the top and took a soldier's stance. "What are my orders?"

Billy tried to smile, but she looked so radiant he could barely keep his jaw from dropping open. "Elam," he said, working hard not to squeak, "I'd like for you to meet Bonnie Silver."

"It's a pleasure, my lady." Elam offered a formal bow. "I'm glad to finally meet you."

Bonnie bowed in return. "The pleasure is mine, son of Shem, grandson of Noah. It is truly an honor to serve under your command." She then leaned close to Billy and whispered, "Have you told him about you-know-who yet?"

Billy shook his head. Bonnie's impish grin indicated that she wanted to have some fun with Elam. He wasn't about to spoil it.

"You've learned a lot about me." Elam brushed his hand across the dragon on his tunic. "You're dressed as a warrior. Do you intend to fight?"

With a lightning-fast move, she withdrew her sword and set the tip near Elam's chin. Flashing a wide grin, she said, "Only in your service, my liege."

Elam touched the end with his finger. "I get your point."

She slid the sword back to its scabbard. "Since my point is well taken, may I ask the warrior chief if the current crisis is under control?"

"It seems to be. For the moment, at least."

"Then come with me." She reached for Elam's hand. "An old woman has begged me to request an audience with you on her behalf."

Elam allowed her to lead him down the stairs. "An old woman? A lot of the women here are well over a hundred, but no one looks that old."

Nudging Walter, Billy whispered. "Come on. This is going to be very cool."

As they followed, Candle trailing the group, Walter laid his arm around Billy's shoulders. "You're as cool as a snowball. You haven't seen Bonnie in four years, but you're acting like she's one of the guys."

"Hey, Mr. Engaged Man, I have no idea what to do. Should I just go ahead and ask her to marry me?"

Walter pointed at him. "Perfect. But don't build a snowman. It's not cold enough, and, besides, you should be original."

"Thanks for the advice. But just thinking about asking her to marry me makes my knees knock together."

"Good. It ought to." Walter gave him a light punch on the arm but said nothing more.

Still holding Elam's hand, Bonnie led him southwest down the street leading toward the village's central circle. To the left, a fountain gushed sparkling water several feet into the air. Normally they kept the pressure low at night by blocking the feeding stream, and in the daytime the children would romp in its spray. But ever since the stream froze, they had to chop the ice to get any flow at all. Apparently the rising temperatures had thawed the blockage, and no one had bothered to dam it up.

Bonnie pulled Elam onto the dead grass and closer to the fountain. "This is the place," she said.

When she released his hand, he fidgeted and pressed his fingers together, more like a little boy than a centuries-old warrior. "So . . ." He cleared his throat to arrest his high pitch. "Where is this old woman?"

Smiling, Bonnie just stepped away and pointed at the fountain.

Veiled by the spray, Sapphira stood with her hands folded over the hilt of a sword, the tip resting on the ground. Dressed in the village's orange and red, her hair as white as hailstones, and her face aglow in a fiery corona, she looked like a radiant angel.

She stepped through the mist and stopped three paces from Elam, her hair and cheeks sprinkled with tiny droplets that glittered in the moonlight. A tear dripping from one eye, she lifted a hand and wiggled her fingers.

Elam's jaw dropped. His arms trembled. He took one step toward her, but his other foot seemed anchored to the ground. He, too, wiggled his fingers, his voice barely more than a whisper. "Sapphira."

She walked another step and stopped again. Her eyes followed a moth as it flitted across the space between them. "It's good to see you again," she said with an air of nonchalance. "It's been a very long time."

"A long time," he repeated. He seemed distant, as if lost in a dream.

Billy winked at Bonnie. She covered a wide grin with her hand.

"So, I was wondering . . ." A coy smile spread across Sapphira's face as she stepped within reach. "I asked for this audience, because I was wondering if there's a place in your army for a five-thousand-year-old woman."

Elam mouthed the words, "five thousand," but no sound came out. His chest heaved through rapid breaths. Finally, he leaped toward her, gathered her into his arms, and twirled. Her sword clattered to the grass, and her petite legs, covered by the uniform's green trousers, swung out as she and Elam laughed and cried.

Stopping the wild ride, he laid a hand behind her silvery hair and pressed her cheek close to his chest. "Oh, my dearest Sapphira, how I have longed for this day!" As he caressed her hair with his cheek, sobs shook his entire body.

Sapphira wept with him. As her own body trembled, she stroked his arm. "Elam, before we go out to battle, I have something to tell you."

He pushed her gently away and lowered himself to one knee. "Please tell me, and then I have a question to ask you."

"Elam," she said softly as she caressed his cheek. "Elam, I lo—"

"Warrior chief!" Valiant ran toward them from the direction of the rampart. "The enemy is advancing from the northeast. We must activate the trap immediately."

Elam raised his hand. "No! I have waited for this moment for thousands of years, and I will not delay it again. I'm not moving until my Sapphira has said what she must say."

Walter gave the spyglass to Billy. "Take your time, Elam. Candle and I will make sure the trap's ready to go."

Valiant bowed his head, a grave expression on his face. "I will see you on the battlefield." Then with a twinkle in his eye, he added, "Or perhaps floating above the battlefield."

When Walter, Candle, and Valiant departed, their footsteps faded in the distance. Only the gentle sound of spraying water filled the nighttime air.

Elam, still resting on one knee, looked into Sapphira's eyes. "Now, what did you want to tell me?"

Still trembling, she twirled a lock of his hair around her finger. "Thousands of years ago I threw morsels of food on the floor for a little mouse I named Qatan. The food disappeared, so I knew he had to be around somewhere. Little did I know that a lost and lonely boy was pushing his hand through that mouse hole and gathering the tidbits just to keep from starving. When I learned about that boy, I fed him stew from my own hand, and he licked my fingers clean."

She lifted a hand and wiggled her fingers again. Elam did the same. Then, they joined their hands together and intertwined their fingers. "Now the boy has become a man, a general, a warrior chief, and he has a war to wage, a battle to win, so I will curtail my speech and say only one more thing."

As she took a deep breath, she met his gaze. A single tear coursed down her cheek and dangled from her chin. "Elam . . ." Her lips quivered as she steadied her voice. "Elam, I love you."

Elam caught the tear on his finger and touched a tear on his own face, blending them into one. He suspended the droplet from his finger and spoke in a near whisper. "Sapphira, I love you more than my words could ever say, yet I will attempt to put my thoughts into a simple pledge. As our tears are bound together as one, so our lives will become one, impossible to differentiate and impossible to separate." He pulled their clasped hands close to his lips. "What I'm saying is . . . will you marry me?"

Sapphira's tears flowed. As tiny firelets ran across her snowy hair, she nodded. "Yes, Elam. Yes, I will marry you."

He reached into his pocket and pulled out a ring. "This belonged to Makaidos. It's the only one I have, so I hope it will serve this purpose."

She extended her finger and let him slide it on. As he straightened, she lifted her hand and gazed at the rubellite, now as white as a pearl. "I will wear the ring of my great friend, the king of dragons, with gladness."

He pulled her close, and the two wept together again.

Billy felt Bonnie's hand slide into his. As he gripped it, he shifted his gaze absently toward the rampart. What did her touch mean? Did she want him to propose, too? Yes, they were old enough now, and the prophecy was still intact, but was it the right time?

He turned toward her. She was already looking at him, her eyes probing. He studied her expression, searching for a clue. After clearing his throat, he whispered, "We have some things to talk about, too."

"I know." She gave him a tender smile. "We have a war to win. Let's talk when everything settles down."

"That sounds good to me."

Elam touched Billy's shoulder. "Shall we go?"

Billy checked Excalibur's position at his hip. "I'm ready."

"I'm ready, too," Bonnie said, drawing her sword again.

"As am I." Sapphira picked up her sword from the ground, slid it into a hip scabbard, and tossed back her fiery hair with a shake of her head. "I'm going with my warrior chief."

The foursome marched toward the northeast field. Billy walked between Bonnie and Sapphira, turning his head from side to side to speak to both. "We'll have to maintain silence in a few seconds, so I'd better tell you a few things. Walter, Sir Barlow, and Valiant will be out in a field waiting for the shadow people to crawl out over some netting we spread on the ground. Our trio will be stationed at intervals. Valiant will be the farthest out, Walter next, and Barlow the closest to the village. When the shadow people attack each of our warriors, we'll know how far along the net they've come. You see, these creatures are flat like shadows, and they creep along the ground, but they can reach up and drag you down. When they swarm, they can smother you in a hurry."

"So, basically," Bonnie said, "our warriors are acting as bait."

"Exactly. But they'll be bait that fights back."

"Now that's courage," Sapphira said. "Just waiting for the enemy to jump on you."

Billy nodded. "It's courage, but it's also strategy. We want to make sure we trap as many in the net as we can. If we can get some to mass at each point, we'll probably get most of them when we heat up the net."

"Will it hurt our warriors?" Bonnie asked.

"A few burns, maybe, but not enough to leave scars. We tested it on some volunteers, and Ashley declared it safe."

"Ashley?" Bonnie's eyes lit up. "Where is she?"

"At the hospital with your father, getting ready for casualties."

Bonnie grabbed his arm. "So my father *is* here!"

"I should've told you earlier, but, yeah, he's here. I'll tell you more later. It's time to be quiet."

Smiling broadly, Bonnie gave Billy's arm a hearty shake. Billy smiled back at her. As they left the village lights, her face grew dim, but the glow in her eyes remained. Billy bathed in that glow. Seeing her happy was like being in heaven.

When they reached a grassy field on the northeast side of the village, Billy crouched in the darkness and pulled Bonnie down with him. He glanced at Sapphira. She and Elam had stooped as well.

As Billy's eyes adjusted to the moonlit area, more bodies took shape. Dozens of crouching villagers lined up to his left and right, swords and shields ready. Dikaios and Ember stood behind a bushy evergreen. Ember was saddled, but Dikaios had chosen against taking one. His long mane made it easy for a rider to hang on. Although Ember's sorrel coat helped her blend in with the shadows, Dikaios's white body made him stand out, forcing him to stay in his hiding place, at least for now.

Sir Barlow stood at his position on the net about twenty paces in front of the rest of the villagers. Barely visible another twenty paces beyond him, Walter walked slowly from side to side. If not for his movement, he would have been invisible in the darkness.

Billy tried to see past Walter. Pegasus provided enough light to reveal dim outlines, but any one of several phantom shadows could have been Valiant. Standing completely still was his way—a tower of strength, immovable.

Valiant's companion stayed dark. Either the villagers knew to keep their crystals hidden in their hair, or the companions knew not to flash in these dangerous situations. Either way, no blinking lights would betray their presence.

As Billy waited, only his own heartbeat and Bonnie's gentle breathing interrupted the deathly silence. Somewhere out there, a crawling horde of vicious life stealers drew close. Unable to resist the scent of a village victim, they would reach out and attack Valiant, maybe before he could detect their approach.

Still, the miserable wretches would likely squeal, first for joy when they found a victim, and again in agony when Valiant sliced their skinny black arms and legs from their bodies. That would signal the beginning of the battle.

Walter stopped pacing. Now he, too, blended into the darkness. Bonnie held her breath. Even Billy's heart seemed to stop beating. In the growing warmth, the silence felt heavy, oppressive.

A squeal sounded, high-pitched and feverish. Another echoed, and then a third. In the distance, a tall shadow swung an object. More squeals erupted, some fearful and truncated. Valiant, the greatest swordsman among the villagers, was now at work. In just a few seconds, Walter would try to bait them with—

"Hey, you low-life vermin!" Walter shouted. "Come over here and pick on someone closer to your own stunted size!"

Billy whispered to Bonnie. "They should be distracted enough now. It's time to inch closer, but I'm the only one who's supposed to draw his sword. It would be too noisy for everyone to do it."

He rose to his feet and slowly withdrew Excalibur, careful to soften the sound. As he and every villager in their line crept toward the net, Walter shouted again, swinging his sword. "Eat steel!"

Now within a few feet of the net, Billy could see the battle clearly. Valiant fought the dark beasts as he staggered toward the village. With so many shadow people hanging on, it looked like he wore a cape of living blackness.

Sir Barlow called out, "Walter, are you injured?"

Walter trudged toward him. He dragged a host of shadows hanging on to his legs. They bit and clawed as he chopped at them with his sword. "I'm fine. I think I picked up a few hitchhikers. I wish—"

He dropped to his knees. Shadow people swarmed over his body. Their squeals sounded like mice possessed by ecstatic demons. Barlow rushed toward him, but the energized monsters overwhelmed them both in a tsunami of darkness.

CHAPTER 9

THE SMALLEST ENEMY

Valiant struggled toward Walter and Barlow, but with the weight of hundreds of shadow people dragging him back, he would never make it in time to help.

"Get ready," Billy said. He summoned Excalibur's beam and let it soar into the sky. When Cliffside saw the signal, he was supposed to turn on the magneto and fry those fiends. It was time to spring the trap.

The beam's glow lit up the faces around him, including those of Candle and Windor. Wearing anxious expressions, they waited while the battle ahead of them raged on without the expected sounds and smells of cooking shadows. All three warriors faltered under wave after wave of shadow people.

Elam jumped on Dikaios and drew his sword. "I'm going in!"

As Dikaios galloped toward the melee, Sapphira charged after him, her body ablaze. Several other villagers ran to join them, one riding Ember.

Bonnie looked at Billy. "Are we going?"

"Come with me!" Dimming Excalibur to a glow, Billy sprinted toward a corner of the net where the primary node was anchored. Kneeling, he searched through the grass with one hand while reaching Excalibur toward Bonnie. "Hold the sword."

The sword brightened in her grip. Billy glanced at it while continuing his search. "Here it is." He fished the net from the slush-covered grass and held it up. "Now touch the blade to this."

She obeyed. When the metal edge made contact with the net, sparks flew up. Billy dropped it and shook his hand. "Ouch!"

"What's supposed to happen?" Bonnie asked.

"I'm trying to heat up the grid." Now sweating, he nodded at the sword. "Do you know how to summon the beam?"

"I think so. I've done it before." Bonnie closed her eyes. As she concentrated, the blade brightened further. Suddenly, the laser shot out from the tip and burrowed into the ground, raising more sparks and a foul odor. The filament turned orange, then crimson, and the color spread out along the netting, disappearing under the snow and reappearing again as it moved across clear ground.

Holding his breath, Billy watched the battle scene. Thousands of shadow creatures mobbed the villagers. It seemed that someone had dumped a legion of tar-covered demons over their army. The humans fought back—hacking, wrestling, and prying strangling fingers away from throats. They staggered about, desperately trying to keep their balance. Falling into the sea of demons would be a fatal mistake. Companions flashed like strobes, then winked out one by one.

Atop his warrior horse, Elam bent over and sliced at the attackers, while Dikaios stomped with his powerful legs, but Ember and her rider were nowhere in sight. A bright column floated from place to place, Sapphira, her body a flaming fountain. Wherever she went, the blackness fizzled, but she was so small, and their army was so massive. She was like a matchstick in a dark canyon.

When the heat reached the battleground, the batlike squeals changed from joy to terror. Sizzles and pops flew about everywhere, and steam shot up from bubbling black pools.

Billy shouted, "Everyone drop down and roll."

Most heeded Billy's call and pressed the dark attackers against the pulsing red matrix. More squeals erupted. Plumes of steam shot into the air. Two villagers continued staggering, and with their heads covered with black hoods of clawing vermin, they probably never heard Billy's shout.

"Keep the beam going." Billy leaped up and ran toward the battle. When he reached a standing villager, Billy pushed him to the ground. Then, after tiptoeing around several rolling masses of black, he grabbed the second warrior and did the same.

Walking from body to body, he tore away shadow people and stomped them against the heated net. With each uncovering, a village soldier heaved a breath of air and then jumped up to help in the rescue effort. Three of the villagers had to search the blackness and pry their companions from rigid black fingers, but every flashing little egg finally broke free.

As the pungent air grew thick with the stench of boiling shadow people, Billy worked even faster. The lack of oxygen would soon take its toll on their strength. They had to finish up and get out.

Near one corner, Ember walked backwards, dragging a villager by the collar. Now dismounted, Elam ripped a shadow person from Ember's legs while Dikaios stomped another one hanging on to the villager.

Billy tore away another squirming black shroud, revealing Walter. Grasping his friend's wrist, Billy heaved him to his feet.

"Thanks, buddy." Grimacing, Walter peeled a severed hand that had been plastered on his cheek. "I have a good name for these critters. Skunk tape. Sticky and smelly."

"Can't argue with that." Billy nodded toward the village. "Let's get everyone back. I want to sweep the whole net clean with Excalibur."

"I see Elam. I'll ask him to give the order." Walter ran into a rising column of steam and out of sight.

Billy hustled back to Bonnie and reached for Excalibur. "Great job. Time to clean up the mess."

Bonnie turned off the beam and set the hilt in his hand. Her face downturned, she spoke in a sad tone. "I guess if I'm going to fight alongside you, I'd better get used to killing the enemy."

He gazed at her sorrow-filled stance. She was right. A warrior had to be ready to use deadly force against an evil army, and when their numbers overwhelmed those of the innocent, everyone had to take up arms.

After giving her an encouraging clasp on her shoulder, he turned away and summoned the beam again, training it on the net at a forty-five degree angle. When he drew near the bubbling mess, he crouched and swept the beam across the matrix. Wherever the radiance touched, the black pools disappeared in a dazzling explosion of purple sparks.

Some of the closer eruptions sent arcing embers over his body that stung if they happened to land on exposed skin. As he breathed in the fumes, his lungs tried to repel the noxious gas. He coughed and spat, but the residue left a film on his tongue and the back of his throat.

Underneath the vanishing blackness, the net appeared, now fading from red to orange. As the beam moved from one part of the ground to another, it seemed to paint the dark canvas with orange paint until no smudge of black remained. Fortunately, the network of tubing beneath the net would likely be unaffected. Ashley had constructed the second-stage trap out of various plastic and rubber pieces she had found on the airplane, including a box of drinking straws and dozens of feet of wire insulation.

When the final spot disappeared, Billy straightened and let Excalibur fade. A breeze cooled his damp face and brushed away the remaining fog of shadow remnants. His legs shaky, he jogged back to where he and the other villagers had waited for the attack. With Pegasus now high in the sky, the villagers were easy to see, at least twenty standing at the edge of the field, touching each other as they examined their wounds.

Walter greeted him with a hearty pat on the back. "That's what I call cleaning up!"

"I guess so," Billy said as he slid Excalibur back into its scabbard, "but I feel like I need to scrub with lye soap."

"Tell me about it." Walter touched a raw spot on his forehead. "But not lye. Most of us already look like we had a losing battle with a flame thrower."

Elam and Sapphira stepped out of a shadow. "What happened to the plan?" Elam asked.

"No idea." Billy looked toward the southeast where the magneto station lay. "Maybe there's a break in the circuit between here and the magneto."

"Or something's up with Cliffside." Walter drew his sword and began jogging southward. "I'll check on him."

Billy looked out over the field toward Adam's Marsh. In the distance, a single torch drifted away, small and fading, like a lit match dwindling as it burned down to the nub.

"A scout running back to tell the news," Elam said. "Soon Flint will know that his first wave failed."

"Does that mean he won't attack with the rest of his troops tonight?" Billy asked.

Elam tilted his head upward as if trying to get a better view. A criss-cross pattern of thin lines marred his cheek. "That's my guess. We'll station fresh guards, but if our theories are right, the Nephilim will do much better in the daytime, and the warmer season will help them a lot."

"It'll help our dragons, too," Billy said.

"And theirs as well."

Sapphira touched Elam's arm. "I'm concerned about Walter going to the magneto by himself. We should give him support."

"You're right. There might be trouble." Drawing his sword with a sagging arm, Elam waved for everyone to head back to the village. "Sapphira and I will ride the horses to the magneto. The rest of you report to the hospital for some healing salve."

Billy weaved through the crowd. He found Bonnie kneeling next to Valiant and Candle. Both sat leaning against a fallen log, their legs straight out with their trousers rolled up past their knees. Sir Barlow sat on the end of the log. As he pulled black goo from his mustache, he frowned. "Back on Earth, the Caitiffs' sticky blood dissolved after we skewered them. I doubt that we will have the same benefit with these creatures."

As two horses clopped by, Bonnie touched Candle's leg near a long burn. "Will you be able to walk?" she asked.

Sweat glistened on his handsome dark face. "I think so. I just need to rest. I'm not used to the warmth."

Billy reached for Valiant's hand. "Need a lift?"

"I gladly accept." Valiant wrapped his hand around Billy's wrist and pulled himself up. When he gained his balance, he rubbed a finger across a mark on his chin that looked more like a bite than a burn. "I am grateful for your quick thinking, Billy. Those creatures were more ferocious than I realized."

Looking into Valiant's noble face, Billy kept their wrists locked. Watching his courage had sent a charge of bravery through his own muscles. "Good job, my friend," Billy said. "You're a true hero."

After Valiant and Barlow began a stiff-legged march toward the village, Billy and Bonnie supported Candle from each side and helped him limp. They took their time, chatting with him as they shuffled through the damp grass. There was no hurry. He wasn't badly hurt, and listening to him recount his battles with the shadow people gave Billy another boost. This teenaged warrior had a heart the size of a mountain.

As soon as they set foot on the street leading to the center, Pearl and Mantika ran toward them with a stretcher. They set it down and helped Candle lower himself to it.

"Such a warrior," Pearl said as she mopped his brow with a soft cloth. "You were brave and strong for us. Now we will serve you with our healing skills."

Mantika brushed her hand through his mud-caked dreadlocks but said nothing. Even after four years in the village, she still maintained her habit of speaking only when necessary. Yet, her eyes spoke volumes. She loved her adopted son, and her pride in his courage poured forth.

As they rushed Candle toward the hospital, Billy looked around. Several pairs of women hauled other wounded warriors in the same direction. Obviously, Ashley had stationed a battery of stretchers and orderlies at the edge of the village, ready to tend to the wounded.

Billy shuffled to the village's central circle and plopped down on a bench. He leaned forward and rested his arms on his knees. It was dimmer here than on the streets that fed the circle, and it felt good to rest in the shadows, out of the limelight, far from the bustle.

Sitting down next to him, Bonnie touched his arm. "How did you know Excalibur would do that?"

Billy looked at her through the shadows. When his eyes adjusted, he tried to read her expression. She seemed tired, yet charged up by the excitement. "Something that happened a few years back. I'm not sure if I told you about it or not. When I was staying at that old mansion in England, one of the New Table goons attacked me. He was wearing a black cloak that was covered with metallic mesh. When I hit him with Excalibur's beam, it didn't hurt him at all. The mesh just heated up, and it protected him from being disintegrated. Prof looked at the cloak later and said it was jcoated with iron oxide, a fancy term for rust. I thought if Excalibur did that then, it might do it again."

"Good thinking."

They paused, looking at each other in silence. Billy pondered her new expression, meditative, uncertain. For many other people, this would be an awkward moment, but a break in conversation never bothered Bonnie. She often searched for the best words, always willing to risk discomfort in her quest for eloquence, and those who had a chance to listen to her were rewarded for their patience.

As he waited, a woman ran toward them from the direction of the hospital and passed by without glancing their way. Stripped to jeans and a T-shirt, she hurried down the road toward the birthing garden, her slender and muscular form now recognizable.

"Was that Ashley?" Bonnie asked.

"Yep. She was in a big hurry. I guess we'll find out why soon enough."

"I'm sure we will." Bonnie touched the string of beads around Billy's neck. "Did you make that? It looks exactly like mine."

"I found it in the mines. Acacia and I went there looking for you, but the magma chasm had filled with water, so we had to give up." He lifted the necklace and then let it fall back to his skin. "We were worried that you and Sapphira had drowned, but I've been wearing it ever since, because . . ." He looked down for a moment before regaining eye contact. "Well, because I believe in the prophecy."

Bonnie took his hand into hers. "Before we go to the hospital to see my father, I have something to tell you."

Billy studied her expression again. She looked so serious, so grave. Swallowing, he nodded. "Okay. I think I'm ready."

She averted her gaze, apparently focusing on a woman helping one of the wounded soldiers walk past. "I spent over four years in the Valley of Souls training to help Second Eden on the battlefield. And I did a lot of thinking." She looked back at him. "About us."

The lump in Billy's throat grew, this time more painful. "Go on."

"Someone pointed out to me that the prophecy wasn't exactly clear. It might not mean that you and I are supposed to get married."

The lump's pain increased. A tear welled. He fought against the emotions, but they were winning, breaking through to the surface. And although a million words raced through his mind, he swallowed them down. It was better to let her finish speaking her mind.

As she continued, she kneaded his hand with her thumb, and her voice rose to a plaintive pitch. "There are other children of doubt, Billy. There are other virgin brides. Maybe it wasn't talking about you and me. You know, Elam and Sapphira fit the poem perfectly. And Makaidos might be the dragon shorn that lives again."

She paused. Now her eyes searched for a response. It was time for him to say something. But what? His emotions were twisting into a knot. After years of believing he was destined to marry the most wonderful girl in the world, she seemed to be pulling back. She was drifting away. He was losing her.

He breathed a silent prayer. How could he put his feelings into words? Just be quiet? Just ask a question and hope for a clue?

Clearing his throat and hoping to keep his voice steady, he said, "So does that mean you don't want to marry me?" He cringed. Was that too bold?

Her face displayed half amusement and half anguish. "No, no. That's not it at all. I just want to know that I don't *have* to marry you. I want us both to be sure that we *want* to. If you love me, I want you to pursue my heart with your courage, your kindness, and your godly manner. And I want to freely give my heart to you in love, not by compulsion because of a prophecy that seems to chain us together without a choice."

As she continued, tears streamed down both cheeks. "Ever since someone labeled me as the prophetic virgin bride, I was okay with it, because you're such a great guy, but it felt like an arranged marriage. We didn't have any choice. Then, when I heard that the prophecy might not be for us, I felt free. I didn't have to marry you if I didn't want to."

She caressed his cheek, her voice shaking. "But that's a good thing, Billy. If we really do get married, neither one of us will ever wonder about being bound by someone else's words, a predestined edict that denies our free will and forces us to obey its irresistible decree. Instead we can come together by a choice to love that is free and resistible, because if we aren't able to choose to walk away from each other, then our coming together wouldn't be because of love at all, would it?"

As she drew back her hand, a torrent of conflicting emotions flooded his mind. She was so right. Being bound like that wouldn't be love. Freedom to choose a life partner was the basis of love in the first place. Being dragged by fiat into a relationship would be nothing more than bondage. Still, not knowing for sure that he would forever be with this amazing girl nearly tore him apart. Finally, he squeezed out a reply. "I . . . I think you're right. But it's scary. It was kind of . . ." He paused.

The words had to be just right. "It was comfortable, I guess, knowing that you would be in my future. I didn't have to guess what was going to happen."

Her fists clenched in her lap. "But I don't *want* you to be comfortable. I want you to win my heart. I want you to fight for me, sweat for me, bleed for me. I want you to know that you had to pay a valuable price for me, and that I am a treasure in your mind, not a trophy that was handed to you because of a divine proclamation."

Billy looked into her fiery eyes. She had been bold, confident, and true. Again she was right, and he couldn't say a word.

She laid her palms on her chest, covering the sunburst on her uniform. Then, slowly, ever so slowly, she extended her arms, her palms up. "Here is my heart, Billy. It's yours if you want it. But you have to buy it. And since it's the most valuable possession I have, it will be very expensive."

He glanced between her palms and her pleading eyes. "How much will it cost me?"

With a quivering smile, she wept through her words. "Everything. It will cost you your life, your devotion, your commitment to love me for the rest of your life till death do us part." Sniffing back a sob, she added, "But don't answer now. I don't want words. Show me. Show me that you'll pay the price for my heart, and I'll show you that it's worth every drop of sweat and blood you spend."

Billy cupped his hand over her palms, making a covering for her "heart." Firming his jaw, he pushed every ounce of energy he had into his voice, giving it strength, yet a sense of calmness, like a lighthouse in the midst of a storm. "Watch me, Bonnie. We have battles ahead. We have enemies to conquer. And we have women and children to protect from some of the greatest evils imaginable. But I will not neglect this mission. I will show you how much you mean to me, how precious your heart is to mine. And when you see how much I'm willing to pay, then you can decide if it's enough to buy what is priceless."

A new voice broke in. "Billy!"

Her face now striped by tears, Bonnie turned. "That sounded like Ashley."

Billy stood up and looked around. "Ashley! Over here!"

Ashley ran toward them on the southeast road, breathless. "Oh, thank God I found you."

When she arrived, Billy grasped her forearms. Her face was red and glistening with sweat. "What is it?"

"It's Walter." She held a hand against her chest and swallowed. "He was captured by Flint's army. Elam and Sapphira tried to help, but they had a Naphil and a dragon. They barely escaped and came back here for reinforcements."

"An ambush?"

Still trying to catch her breath, Ashley nodded. "They killed Cliffside. That's why our net trap didn't work. Then they waited for someone to check on him."

"That's terrible!" Bonnie said. "The cowards!"

Ashley gasped. "Bonnie!"

Bonnie pulled her into an embrace. "I'm so glad to see you again."

Ashley began sobbing. "Me too, Bonnie . . . but it's so terrible. . . . Did Billy tell you?"

Bonnie pulled away. "Tell me what?"

"Walter." Her weeping nearly overwhelmed her words. "Walter is my fiancé now."

"Your fiancé!" Bonnie pulled her close again. "Oh, Ashley, we'll find him. We'll get him back."

While they held their embrace, Billy pelted Ashley with questions. "Which dragon was it? Did Elam and Sapphira see which way they went? Did either of them get hurt?"

"They're fine." Ashley pushed back from Bonnie, sniffing. "While Elam battled the Naphil, Sapphira rode Ember, trying to follow the dragon when he flew away with Walter, but she couldn't keep up. I don't know which dragon it was. Maybe you should ask Elam. He's with your father and my mother. They're planning a rescue."

Billy grabbed Excalibur's hilt. Redness blinded his vision. He imagined Walter and Elam battling those creeps while he, Billy, relaxed in the village. The thought made his blood boil. "Are they at the garden field or the launching field?"

"The birthing garden. I guess Sapphira and Elam cut straight through from the hospital, so you didn't see them."

"Let's go!" Billy jumped into a quick jog, drawing his sword as he hurried. Of course, holding it now wouldn't do any good. It just felt better to have something to strangle.

Bonnie caught up, half walking, half flying at his side. "Would they take Walter back to their . . . camp, I guess? I don't know where they came from."

"It's a marsh area, and yes, they would probably go there. They know the territory better than we do, and after four years, they might have all sorts of traps set up."

When they arrived at the field, they slowed to a walk. Most of the snow had melted, leaving wet grass, thin and sparse, in the midst of a quagmire. Although Billy's shoes slid at times, slowing him further, Bonnie hovered over the mud and kept him from falling.

Ahead, Elam, Valiant, and Sir Barlow huddled with Dikaios, Ember, and a group of dragons. Billy recognized Clefspeare, Thigocia, and Legossi. Two others blended into the darkness behind them. Sapphira stood a few paces to the side, her arms spread and her body ablaze to add more light to the moon's glow.

As Billy drew nearer, the conversation reached his ears.

"They have us in a bind," Elam said. "If we attempt a rescue, they will have the advantage. The marsh is dangerous enough in the daytime; more so at night. So we can't just march in, and any sign of a dragon or airplane will alert them to our presence."

Valiant gave him a solemn nod. "It seems as if they knew our plans. How else would they know to attack the magneto station?"

"An informer," Billy said as he drew into their huddle. "I think we can assume Semiramis has been lurking."

Elam looked at him. Billy offered a nod of surrender. The warrior chief had the right to say, "I told you so," but he didn't. He was too noble for pettiness.

"I am torn," Valiant said. "My heart burns to rescue Walter, but my brain is shouting that this is exactly what Flint wants. He knows that battles fought in his territory will give him an advantage, and he wishes to deplete our forces. We would bring back a single warrior at the cost of twenty. Flint will gladly make that trade."

Sir Barlow drew his sword and traced a line along the ground. "True, my good fellow, but there is a line we cannot cross. At what cost do we forsake a rescue and allow Walter to suffer alone? Our morals? Our dignity? Our character? We are willing to die to do what is right, and retreating from our purpose now is the very line we should not step past."

"Remember what happened to Shiloh," Billy said. "They won't hesitate to torture Walter."

Ashley joined them. With her arms wrapped around herself in spite of the warmth, she listened quietly, her unkempt hair draped over one eye.

A deep growl rumbled in Clefspeare's throat. "You are correct, son, but he is not a kidnapped hostage. He is a prisoner of war. At the risk of sounding callous, he knew this possibility existed. He is not a boy playing at war with a sharpened stick, and he is prepared to face whatever befalls him."

Billy tightened his grip on his sword, and a growl spiced his own voice. "I agree with Sir Barlow. We pledged to spill our blood for each other. What kind of soldiers are we?"

"Wise soldiers," Ashley said. "Reasonable soldiers."

Everyone looked at her. In spite of the tear tracks, her face seemed peaceful, serene. "Walter and I already talked about this. He's ready to die if he has to, and he wouldn't want anyone else dying to save him. If you try to rescue him, and you lose soldiers in the process, you'll put more people at risk, including women and children. Walter would rather die than let that happen."

Bonnie pushed Ashley's hair out of her eyes. "Would you object to a precision rescue attempt?"

A new tear followed a well-marked track. "A precision attempt?"

"One person, or maybe two. They couldn't walk in safely, but they could fly in."

"Goliath would sense one of us from far away," Clefspeare said. "He would meet us in the air before we had any chance to locate Walter, much less rescue him. I could match him in a head-to-head battle, but the element of surprise would be lost."

Bonnie gave her wings a quick snap. "I could fly in. He might not recognize me as a danger to him."

"Alone?" Billy shook his head hard. "No way."

"Why not?" She touched her sword. "I can fight, and I can fly away if I get outmatched."

Billy looked at her narrowed eyes. How could he protect her without offending her? "But you don't know the marsh, where Flint might keep a prisoner, or—"

"Or where the muskrats roam," Dikaios said.

Billy pointed at him. "Exactly. Elam says they have these huge rodents that are more like bears than our muskrats, and they nearly had him for dinner."

"It's true," Elam said. "I faced several. If I hadn't been lifted out by a dragon, they would have killed me."

"So," Billy continued, "at least you would need an escort."

Elam pointed at him. "But you don't know the marsh either. It's been closed off ever since you've been here."

"He doesn't," Dikaios said, "but I know it quite well. I have already participated in two escapes from there."

Elam stroked the horse's neck. "Are you saying you would be her escort?"

"I would be honored. And her flying ability would allow her to escape if capture or injury seems imminent. And remember, we have two allies somewhere in the marsh, Yereq and Roxil. Perhaps we will be aided in our rescue from within."

Billy chafed. He couldn't let Bonnie ride into the marsh without an armed escort, and he couldn't risk insulting her by suggesting that she wasn't capable of handling the rescue. And if he just let her go, she might think he didn't care about her safety. There was no easy answer. He had to buy time. "Give me a minute to think."

Everyone looked at him. They couldn't wait long. Walter was in trouble, so every second of delay might make rescue even more difficult. But how could he sort out the pros and cons under such pressure? Haste was always a poor general, but delay, based upon fear of doing the wrong thing, was even worse.

He looked at his father's fiery eyes. He seemed to think that rescue was foolhardy; better to risk losing one life than many. Mom would likely agree with Barlow; better to show how much we value a single life and trust that a rescue attempt would work. Seeing her in his mind's eye, now packing a pistol more often than not, he almost grinned. Even with her tender heart, she had become a warrior.

As he concentrated on the image, he focused on his mother's holster. Of course! She still had it, and she had mentioned keeping it with her to protect the hospital in case of attack.

Billy pushed a hand into his pocket and looked at Elam. "We have a weapon Flint won't expect—my mother's gun. She brought one clip, and it has only eight rounds. It's not much good for a war, but it would be perfect for a precision rescue effort, and after fending off the Caitiff back on Earth, I probably know how to use it better than anyone else here."

"You're probably right." Elam shifted his gaze upward, as if trying to remember something. "I had a revolver back when I worked in the shipyard, but I rarely used it."

Billy turned and gave Bonnie a courtly bow. "Fair lady, I do not mean in any way to minimize your capabilities, but, taking notice of your fair gender, I consider it my duty as a knight to offer my services as a pistol-packing flaming torch and as a bodyguard of your person."

Smiling, she bowed her head. "I accept your noble offer."

"I will let Marilyn know of our need for her weapon," Dikaios said. With a quick turn, he bolted toward the village.

Billy looked at Clefspeare. At the sound of "Marilyn," his brow rose for a moment but quickly settled. Their reunion had been delayed by preparations, a battle, and tending to the wounded. Would she now come to the garden field to see her husband? Or was the thought of him as a dragon again too much for her to bear? Maybe the delay had been intentional.

Sapphira let her energy dim to a white aura. With the moon casting its light over her body, she seemed to be a small moon herself. "If our rescue party is captured or killed, our only clue will be that they didn't return."

"If Flint expects a second rescue after a failed attempt," Barlow said, "he might assume that we have depleted our guard at the village. It would be a prime opportunity for an attack."

"Then we'll double our security here." Elam looked at the village. "If we have enough guards remaining."

Ashley raised her hand. "I can implant my tooth transmitter in one of them and stay in touch the entire time. We have plenty of helpers in the hospital and only minor burn cases, so I can go to the radio station and stay in contact with our rescue party."

"As long as you have a dragon guard," Elam said. "You'll need a danger detector. We don't want to lose you, too."

Ashley raised her eyebrows at Thigocia. "Mother?"

"Of course I will go with you," Thigocia said. "Anything to help my future son-in-law."

After a few minutes of discussion, including how they could bolster the guard, Dikaios returned with Marilyn's holster clenched in his teeth. He laid it in Billy's hand. "Marilyn sends her love, and she wishes to convey her appeals for a safe journey. She cannot come right now. Apparently several people have become ill, and she is helping Dr. Conner with . . ." He shook his mane and blew through his flapping lips. "I suppose the best words would be, 'cleaning up messy expulsions.'"

"This is very strange," Valiant said. "We have had no such sickness here before. I have heard of it among the marsh people, but these expulsions are new to us."

Billy turned to Ashley. "Biological warfare?"

As she nodded slowly, her voice turned somber. "Delivered by the shadow people. Maybe Flint implanted something in them."

"Could that be what was growing in the garden?" Elam asked. "Did that weed carry an infection?"

Bonnie shook her head. "A man was inside, not a virulent bug."

"A carrier," Ashley offered. "Maybe they raised up a man to bring the bug into the world."

"So . . ." Billy raised a hand to his chin. "Maybe the shadow people weren't sent to slaughter us. They were sent to *be* slaughtered so they could deliver the infection and be disposed of."

"Semiramis again?" Elam asked.

"Who else?" Billy smacked his palm. "With her spying on us, they're always a step ahead. They knew about the magneto and the net trap, and now they'll probably be content to wait for the infection to take hold. They'll strike when we're at our weakest."

Ashley took on her rapid-fire voice of command. "Valiant, ask Dr. Conner if he saved any of the shadow people remains. We need to culture it. I already showed him how to use my microscope, so if the infecting agent is big enough, he might be able to spot it. We need to isolate the bug and see what we can do to counteract it. If it's fast-spreading, we can't delay for a second. We have to isolate everyone who came into direct contact with the shadow people, including those who took care of the wounded. Put them all in the hospital, and don't let anyone enter or leave without permission, including yourself. I'll be there soon to organize the quarantine and the effort to find a cure."

Without a word, Valiant ran toward the village. As he faded into the darkness, Thigocia touched Ashley with a wing. "What will you do about monitoring the rescue effort at the radio station?"

Ashley stared at her. She seemed lost, perplexed. "I . . . I have to do both. I can't let them try the rescue without someone monitoring their progress."

"You have to help Dr. Conner," Elam said. "I'll man the station. Besides, you took care of the wounded. You're subject to quarantine."

"But so are you," Ashley countered. "We all are."

Billy pointed at himself. "Bonnie and I are leaving the village, so we won't infect anyone."

"And I'll be outside the village at the station," Elam said. "You need to be with Dr. Conner."

Looking at the ground, Ashley furrowed her brow. "It could be that the Second Edeners are the only susceptible ones, anyway. Since they haven't been exposed to diseases, they don't have as many immunities."

"Perfect," Billy said. "Then you can probably take care of them safely."

"And I have a portable receiver," she added. "I'll see if I can pick up your broadcasts while I work in the hospital. It'll help me keep my sanity . . . what little I have left."

CHAPTER 10

BEHIND ENEMY LINES

Billy rode low on Dikaios. With Pegasus almost directly above them and Phoenix rising, ducking into the shade of the overarching trees felt like a good idea. Although the silence gave no hint of any enemy observers, his danger sense told him otherwise. Something lurked close by, something unusual. It didn't feel like an evil presence; more like a natural danger, the foreboding of a storm. Could it be an animal? Maybe Vacants? Their bestial ways seemed more like instinct than premeditated acts of evil.

Bonnie leaned forward on Ember, her arms loosely wrapped around the mare's neck. With her wings folded in tightly, they appeared to be a backpack, though an occasional flutter at the tips ruined the impression.

The two horses stepped quietly through the last strip of forest between the village and the marsh. The trees here were healthier than in most forests in Second Eden. With evergreens dominating the population, only a few rotting logs lay across the ground.

The two moons made the landscape look like a jungle on a stormy evening. It was more like dusk than the middle of the night, barely dark enough to veil the horses' hoofprints in the mud. Fortunately, Billy's cloak covered most of Dikaios's shimmering white coat, and, as before, Ember's coloring blended in with the shadows and the mud below.

Dikaios stopped at the forest's edge and whispered. "The marsh begins in about two hundred human paces. There is only grass between here and there, so we will risk exposure until we reach the bulrushes. Now is the time to send our scout."

"Got it." Billy tapped his jaw. The transmitter vibrated with a barely perceptible hum, accentuating the pain from having the device jammed between his teeth. Ashley had told him he would get used to it, but that hadn't happened yet. Bonnie had offered to wear it, which made more sense. After all, she would be flying reconnaissance alone. But her molars were too close together, forcing them to go with Billy.

"Elam," Billy whispered. "Two hundred paces to the marsh. I'll leave this on for a while."

Elam's voice buzzed. "I'll be listening."

Billy checked the holster fastened to his belt on his right. With Excalibur on his left, he felt balanced, ready to draw a weapon from either side. A bulge in one pocket reminded him of the ring Ashley had given him, the same ring she had found with the bone where Abraham's wall had been. Valiant said the ring once belonged to Flint, a gift from Abraham as a symbol of love.

Even after his rebellion, Flint had kept it for a while, though no one in the village knew why. Valiant noticed it on Abraham's finger after he had turned into a marching column of fire, so it seemed that Flint must have returned the symbol. Everyone agreed that Billy could take it with him, just in case he had an opportunity to use it as a gift of love again. Although Bonnie heard the story about Flint and the ring, she didn't know that Ashley had given it to Billy. That would be his secret, at least for now.

Bonnie slid off her sword belt and draped it over Ember's neck. Then, without a word, she spread out her wings and took to the air.

Ahead, her shadow slid across the grass, black and undulating with the strokes of her wings. Billy tried to find her in the sky but gave up. Watching her shadow was easier.

The dark form glided to the right, circled back, and passed across a cluster of short trees among the bulrushes to the left. After about a minute of back and forth surveying, the shadow began a slow return to the forest. When it disappeared in the trees, Billy looked up. With her wings beating rapidly, Bonnie floated down and landed gently on Ember.

Breathing hard, she swallowed before giving her report. "I saw the central village, but I didn't see anyone there except for two giants." She forked her fingers and pointed at the marsh. "There's an encampment on each side, like lookout stations, with a dragon at each. One is about forty toises to the left of a straight-ahead entry point, and the other is about half that far to the right. I spotted a few tents at each one, but no people."

"Toises?"

"Sorry. My sword trainer always used it. After four years it kind of sticks in your mind. One station is about eighty meters to the left, and the other is forty to the right."

Billy paused and listened. Although the danger signals stayed constant, no sound reached his ears. "Did anyone see you out there?"

"I think one of the giants saw my shadow, but when he looked up, I don't think he could find me. He didn't sound any alarm, so maybe he thought I was a big bird."

"I guess the dragons didn't sense any danger."

"Because I'm not a danger," Bonnie said. "That's why I left my sword belt on Ember."

"I thought it might have been too heavy."

She wrapped the belt around her waist. "Part of my training was to fly with it. I'm a lot stronger than I was that day I dropped Excalibur while flying."

"I'm sure you are. I could tell."

As she rebuckled her belt, a curious grin crossed her face. "You could? Have I changed that much?"

"Well . . . yeah." Warmth oozed into his cheeks. Bonnie's form had definitely changed, and her womanly blossom was impossible not to notice, but he had to keep his mind on the question at hand. "I could see the muscles in your forearms. Those are the first to get toned when you do sword training."

Her smile now radiant in the moonlight, she patted her belt. "I'm ready."

"Wait." Billy set a hand on his sword's hilt. The foreboding sensation suddenly spiked.

"Danger?" Bonnie asked.

"I don't get it. It's strong, like it's real close, but I don't see—"

Something fell on his head. Pressed under a heavy weight, he fell to the muddy ground. He grabbed at anything within reach but could find only air.

"Billy!"

Bonnie's voice! He clutched his attacker's slippery arm, threw the weight off, and leaped to his feet. A Vacant rolled through the mud. Dikaios reared up and stomped it with his hooves.

"Over here!" Bonnie shouted, her voice muffled.

Just beyond Ember, another Vacant held Bonnie around her waist. With one long-fingered hand over her mouth, he dragged her deeper into the forest.

Billy charged toward them. The Vacant stopped, pressed a dagger against her throat, and shouted in a weaselly voice. "Come no closer!"

Billy halted within five feet of them. Setting his feet, he scowled. "What do you want with her?"

His little ovular mouth opened and closed from the sides as he continued in his squeaking, raspy voice. "She is the one our master wants. He has put a ransom on her head that will provide us food and clothing for life."

"Us?" Billy looked back at the dead Vacant near Dikaios's legs. "I think you're outnumbered."

"You are mistaken." He let out an odd croaking sound. From the low-lying shrubs, several more Vacants appeared, each one looking like clones of the first. All carried long spears and shields.

"We know how powerful you are," the Vacant continued, "so we make you this offer. If you leave with your horses now, we will let you live."

Billy wrapped his hand around Excalibur's hilt. If they wanted Bonnie alive, this beast wouldn't be quick to do her any harm. He could afford to be bold. "You can't be serious."

The Vacant's low-set eyes blinked. "You wish not to live?"

"I will die before you take her anywhere." Setting his jaw, Billy withdrew Excalibur. "How many of you wish to stay alive?"

Bonnie bit the Vacant's finger and stomped on his foot. With a lightning-fast spin, she whipped out her sword and cut off her kidnapper's head. In a mad rush, the other Vacants swarmed over her. For a moment, her sword glinted in the moonlight as limbs and spear points flew right and left, but she quickly fell under the mass of bodies.

Billy leaped into the fray, blowing fire. He blasted a Vacant's chest, but the cloak deflected the stream. Using his sword, he whacked off an arm, then plunged the blade through a torso. The Vacant twisted, jerking Excalibur from his hand. Another pulled him into the sea of struggling bodies and threw him down next to Bonnie. The tip of a spear pushed against his chest and pierced his skin. Within seconds, blood soaked into his tunic.

A second Vacant set his foot on Bonnie's chest. Grimacing, she bucked under his crushing weight, but when he pressed down harder, she settled down, her chest heaving shallow breaths.

"Surrender," the first Vacant ordered. He pushed the spear another fraction of an inch into Billy's chest. "Or die."

Billy steeled his muscles. He couldn't let them see an expression of pain. The sting of the cold metal pulsed across his body like an electric shock, but as he remembered Naamah's staurolite blade plunging through his heart, the pain seemed to ease. Nothing would ever be worse than that.

He looked around at his captors. Their numbers had swelled to thirty or more, and they all stared down at him with their big black eyes. These Vacants were dressed strangely. They wore dark cloaks that exposed only their hideous faces. The others Billy had faced wore thick, fur-lined tunics and long woolen trousers. Apparently someone had supplied them with cloaks that would repel his fire.

One of them held Excalibur and stared at it curiously. He wouldn't know how to use its power, but he could still do a lot of damage with its indestructible blade.

Billy glanced at Bonnie. With her brow knit into three tight lines, she looked ready to kill. It was time to show confidence, maybe make them wonder if he had a trick up his sleeve. "Surrender?" He laughed. "If you let Bonnie go unharmed, then I'll let you surrender. We'll treat you like prisoners of war. Otherwise, I will have to kill you all."

Dikaios trotted close. "I advise you to listen to this young warrior. You have said that he is powerful, but now you have angered him by threatening the girl he loves."

"He cannot fight without arms." A third Vacant stomped on Billy's right wrist and thrust a spear into the meaty part of his left forearm.

"Arrgh!" Billy bit his lip. He couldn't cry out again. He had to stay focused. But the spear's blade pressed against his bone, piercing and grinding. It felt like a superheated drill.

When the Vacant pulled out his spear, Billy grunted but managed not to cringe. The release in pressure helped, but the wound continued to shoot bullets of pain up and down his arm.

At his waist, he felt Bonnie's fingers fishing for the gun. Lifting his bleeding arm to point at the Vacant, he kept his glare riveted. He had to keep him distracted. "I repeat. Release us, and I will let you live."

A squeaky laugh spilled from the Vacant's puckered mouth. "I am tempted to let you up to see how well you fight in this condition, but we must return with our prize to the one who hired us."

Billy felt his holster grow lighter. A shot rang out. The Vacant pinning Billy's chest flew backwards. Another shot. The one over Bonnie toppled.

Before Bonnie could shoot again, the Vacant standing on Billy's wrist jerked the gun away. Swinging his legs up and back, Billy caught the Vacant's neck between his ankles and slung him into the air. He leaped to his feet, hoisted Bonnie to hers, and snatched Excalibur while Bonnie scooped up her own sword. Then, standing back to back, Billy and Bonnie stared at the surrounding enemy.

Trying to ignore the pain in his arm and chest, Billy spoke in a commanding tone. "This is my final offer. Leave now or die."

"You are still greatly outnumbered," a Vacant holding two spears said. "You cannot defeat us all."

Excalibur's beam shot into the inky sky. "If you knew what this sword could do, you would think otherwise."

The Vacant tied a sash at his cloak's waist. "Our master is acquainted with your weapon's light, and he assures us that it will do us no harm."

Billy tried to focus on the Vacant's cloak, but it was too dark to discern any details. Did a rusty mesh cover the material? Probably. The uselessness of his fire was his first clue, but there was only one way to find out for sure.

He swept the beam across the Vacant's body. Light splashed, and sparks drizzled on the cloak, but the Vacant stood erect, undisturbed. A matrix of orange and red lines radiated on his cloak, the same effect Excalibur had on the cloaks of the New Table knights.

The Vacant's fishlike mouth spread into a vertical smile. "Will you now surrender the girl? We want her alive, but we will gladly kill you."

Billy let the beam die away and whispered to Bonnie. "Are you ready?"

"Just say the word, warrior." Bonnie's wings flexed against his back. "I'm ready."

Billy looked at Dikaios. The horse nodded and said, "At your command."

Letting his wounded arm hang limply, he tightened his grip on the hilt and shouted, "Now!" He lunged. Swinging Excalibur, he lopped off the Vacant's spear arm. Then, with a quick spin, he cut through another's head at the ear and a third at the base of his skull.

Bonnie thrust her sword into a Vacant's belly, jerked it out, and leaped into the air, her wings lifting her over a hurled spear. Slashing while flying, she toppled four Vacants before settling on Dikaios's back.

Billy ducked under two spears, sliced through the ankles of three Vacants, and plunged through their ranks until he popped out on the other side.

As he raised his sword to attack again, Bonnie extended hers and shouted, "Charge!"

Dikaios bolted into the confused throng and stomped on Vacants, rearing up and crashing down on their bodies. Leaning over from her perch, Bonnie hacked with a two-fisted grip, her wings keeping her balanced as her mount rose and fell. Ember trotted all around the battle circle and gave any exposed Vacant a vicious kick with her back hooves.

Billy dove into the fray again. With powerful, one-armed sweeps, he killed one Vacant after another. A spear point grazed his head. A shaft banged against his ribs. A fist thumped his chest. But he kept swinging with Excalibur's razor-sharp edge again and again.

Vacants pulled and clawed at Bonnie's legs, but she continued flailing away at their groping arms. Finally, a Vacant grabbed her wing, slung her to the ground, and set one foot on her sword arm and the other on her throat.

Billy pulled Excalibur from a dead Vacant's chest and glared at Bonnie's captor. "Let her go!"

Two surviving Vacants scrambled away into the woods. Ember chased them to a line of shrubs before turning and walking slowly back.

The remaining Vacant pressed harder on Bonnie's throat. Gagging, she kicked and thrashed for a moment, but with her wings splayed on the ground, she couldn't get any leverage.

The Vacant growled like a cat. "Drop your weapon."

Billy let Excalibur fall to the ground. "Just let her breathe."

"Very well." The Vacant lifted his foot from her throat, picked up a broken spear, and set the splintered end over her eye. "Now get on your horse and leave."

Bonnie, her eyes closed under the broken spear, cried out. "I'll be all right, Billy. He wants to take me alive."

"I do want her alive," the Vacant said, "but losing an eye will not kill her."

Billy raised his arm. Blood soaked his sleeve from elbow to wrist, and streams ran down to his fingers. He smeared blood across his chest, but his tunic was already soaked from the first spear wound. "Look at me," he growled. "Do I look like I'm ready to just walk away? She is the most precious treasure in the world, and the only way you'll take her is by draining the last drop of blood from my body." Gritting his teeth, Billy set his feet firmly. "Now what do you think my answer will be?"

Another hideous vertical smile broke through. "Yet you dropped your weapon at my command."

Billy kept his stare on the Vacant. Ember had positioned herself behind the monster, her rear hooves set, but he couldn't let his eyes focus on her. "I dropped my weapon," Billy said, "so I could kill you with my bare hands."

Ember hammered the Vacant's back with both hooves. It flew into Billy's arms, knocking him flat. Hooking his arm around the Vacant's neck, Billy made ready to break it, but the body felt limp, like that of a rag doll.

He rolled the body to the side and, rising as fast as his aching bones would allow, he hurried to Bonnie and helped her up. "Are you okay?"

She caressed her throat. "I think so. A few scratches, but I'm okay."

"That one looks nasty." He touched her cheek just above a deep scratch. "Deep and bleeding."

She dabbed her finger in the oozing blood. "It doesn't hurt. I doubt it'll even leave a scar."

"If it does, it will remind me of the bravest girl I've ever known."

"Brave?" She cradled his bleeding arm. "I'm nothing compared to you."

He shook his head. "We both did everything we could. It's—"

Dikaios snorted. "How long will this mutual admiration meeting last?"

Laughing, Billy picked up the gun and slid it into its holster. "At least long enough to thank Ember." He patted the sorrel's neck. "Great job!"

Dikaios bowed his head. "Indeed. A most exquisite strike. I am very impressed."

Ember nuzzled Dikaios's cheek and swished her tail.

"Speaking of mutual admiration," Bonnie said with a wink.

Dikaios shook his mane. "Oh. Yes. Well, shall we continue with our rescue efforts?"

"Definitely. And we'd better hurry. If Flint sent those Vacants, the two that got away will report what happened." Billy put Excalibur away and helped Bonnie find her sword among the dead bodies. Then, using his good arm and getting a boost from her, he climbed aboard Dikaios.

Bonnie flew up to Ember's back, and the foursome returned to the edge of the forest. "There is a channel between the two encampments," Dikaios said. "The depth of the water has probably increased because of snowmelt, so they might not be paying much attention to that path. It would be difficult for intruders to negotiate it without making a lot of noise."

"After all the noise we just made," Bonnie said, "their guards might be on the alert."

Billy nodded. "They had to hear the gunshots."

"I suspect," Dikaios said, "that Flint and company were well aware of the ambush. They likely believe that you and Bonnie are in the hands of their allies. Perhaps now is the safest time to proceed."

"Let's go for it." Billy scrunched down. "But we'll keep a low profile. No use taking chances."

As Dikaios loped along, Ember kept pace close to his side. Since the ground had moistened to soft mud, no telltale clops would travel to the outposts' ears, though a slight squishing sound occasionally reached Billy's.

His wounds aching, he laid his head on Dikaios's neck and looked at

Bonnie. She looked back at him, smiling. Apparently the battle didn't faze her. Compared to running from an insane slayer, being trapped in a candlestone, dying in Hades, and battling demons, this was just another death-defying night.

After a few minutes, the horses reached a line of reeds and walked into the marsh single file. Finding water almost immediately, Dikaios slowed his pace. To keep from splashing, he pushed his legs forward instead of raising them. Ember did the same. Soon, the channel water rose to Billy's knees and stayed at that level.

As they crept along, Billy whispered as quietly as he could. "Elam, we're in the marsh. So far, so good."

Elam's whispered voice tickled Billy's jaw. "After all I heard, I was wondering. But I'll stay quiet. Just give me an update when you can."

Dikaios eased to a stop. As he sniffed the air, he looked around, his ears bending back. "Muskrats," he whispered. "We will have to leave the channel and go directly to Flint's village to the left."

Bonnie leaned so close her leg pressed against Billy's. "It should be safe. I think we passed the encampment."

Dikaios turned and climbed up the incline with his powerful legs. Ember copied his movements, but she slid back, forcing her to spring ahead. With a series of loud splashes, she reached level, shallow-water terrain.

When Dikaios joined her, Ember lowered her head, obviously ashamed. He rubbed his nose against her neck and said, "Do not fret. No one is angry. But we must leave this area immediately."

As they moved on, a whistle sounded from somewhere to the left. Another answered.

The horses stopped. Billy held his breath. Bonnie reached over and grabbed his hand. With the usual breezes deathly still, the marsh fell into complete silence.

About thirty feet away, the tops of the reeds shook, and a deep voice called out. "Muskrats?"

"I see none," another replied, "but I smell them."

"Very strange. I thought we killed the last one." He let out a hearty laugh. "Muskrat hams have a strong flavor, but they taste better than boots."

Billy cringed. They were Nephilim. That distinctive throaty laugh gave them away. He set a hand on his gun but kept it in its holster. Shooting in the dark wasn't a great idea, especially without knowing exactly who or what was out there.

Soon, a face appeared above the reeds. Billy, Bonnie, and the two horses lowered their heads.

"Maybe one traveled here after the wall disappeared," the first Naphil said.

Another head protruded from the marsh's foliage. "Maybe. If you can spear it, I will keep it a secret between us."

"Flint would have our scalps if he found out."

"You have been at your outpost too long. The rules have changed. With the wall of fire gone, we have no energy source, and Flint's people have freedom to hunt beyond the boundary now. Flint will not begrudge us a muskrat that we kill ourselves."

"The survivors are too weak to hunt. The sickness has left none with arms strong enough to throw a spear or legs swift enough to run down a prey."

"The dragons will hunt in their place."

"Roxil, perhaps, but Goliath will guard the prisoner. Flint will not risk losing that little dog."

Another Naphil laugh boomed. "He has quite a bark, does he not?"

"More than a bark. Chazaq is not pleased with the wound the mongrel delivered. From what I hear, this was not their first skirmish. Chazaq is looking forward to when Flint decides it is time to dispose of . . . What was the dog's name?"

"Walter. It will not be long. It seems that the warrior chief has chosen to forsake our prisoner. If Goliath detects no approaching dragon by dawn, we will not have to worry about sharing our muskrat with him. Walter will make a fine meal."

Billy eased his grip on the gun. These guards didn't know any intruders were present. Yet, their conversation seemed odd—forced, contrived, as if they were trying to communicate in code.

Laughing, the two Nephilim parted, each one sloshing through the shallow water. Dikaios took the opportunity to mask the sound of his own movements and plodded ahead. After a few minutes, they reached a clearing. Ahead lay the village, a collection of rundown huts built on a raised area of mud. Some of the homes had partial roofs with perforated thatching and others had no roof at all. A few tilted to the side, the supporting logs either crumbled or missing, the apparent victims of rot or theft. Nearly every home had damage of some kind, though one brick-and-mortar house closer to the water seemed strong and sturdy.

Dikaios nodded at the brick house. "Flint's," he whispered as he continued. When they climbed up the rise, Billy looked from house to house. No movement. No sound. During the past four years, he had imagined Flint's people training for war behind the fiery wall, making ready to attack and kill innocent people, but apparently disease and lack of food had devastated them. No wonder they hadn't attacked. They couldn't. With only a few Nephilim and two enemy dragons, they wouldn't stand a chance. Now the strategy of sending the shadow people alone made sense. They hoped to bring the same devastation to the villagers and win the war through attrition.

Then why capture Walter? They were better off staying in hiding and waiting for the disease to take hold. They must have known that Elam wouldn't attack first, especially after winning the initial battle. Why would they risk bringing the wrath of a host of dragons down on them? They would lose in a rout.

When they came within a stone's throw of Flint's house, the horses stopped. "Ember and I will wait here," Dikaios whispered. "Any closer and our scent will be detected by dragons or humans."

Billy and Bonnie slid to the ground and tiptoed through the mud until they reached the front door. Billy pressed his back against the wall on one side of the door, while Bonnie stooped at the other.

All was quiet. Of course Elam would want a progress report at this point, but the danger was too great. Risking even a whisper now was out of the question.

He edged in front of the door and laid his ear against the panel. Again, not a sound. He looked at Bonnie, pointed at his ear, and shook his head, trying to signal his findings.

As he moved his hand to the door's lift latch, he let his eyes dart around. Both horses stood still, mostly veiled by shadows. A muffled laugh sounded from the marsh, a Naphil likely returning to his post. Sweat streamed down Billy's cheek, and dried blood made his tunic stick to his skin, raising the agonizing sting once again. There really wasn't much choice. He had to go in, ready to fight.

Just as he touched the latch, a hiss came from the side of the house. He jerked his head around. A hooded figure skulked toward him. "Billy," a woman whispered. "Do not go in."

He slid out the gun, pointed it, and spoke with a low, commanding tone. "Stop in your tracks."

The woman halted and let her hood fall back. "It is I, Semiramis."

CHAPTER 11

LOVE NEVER FAILS

"I am your ally," Semiramis said, "not your enemy."

"I doubt that." Billy kept the gun trained on her. "Why did you escape?"

She scowled. "That was four years ago. Are you still holding that against me?"

"If you had waited, we would have let you go. All we wanted was to confirm your story about where Shiloh was being held, and you were right, so—"

"Of course I was right," she said, her voice sharpening. "Why should I acquiesce to imprisonment when I had committed no crime? I helped you once again, did I not?"

"Okay, okay." He lowered the gun but kept it drawn. "What do you want?"

"To deliver your friend, Walter. He is unconscious, so I had to drag him to the corner, but when I saw you, I left him there." She backed slowly away. "Come. You will see."

Billy motioned for Bonnie to follow. When they arrived at the corner of the house, Semiramis stooped next to a body lying face-up in the mud. With the moon shining directly on him, his identity was clear.

"Walter," Billy whispered.

Bonnie gripped Billy's shoulder. "Is he all right?"

"He's been drugged," Semiramis said. "His hands and feet are still bound, but he is fine otherwise. I was in a hurry to get away, so I have not yet cut him free." She withdrew a knife from under her cloak.

Billy extended the gun, watching her every move. With a quiet snick, she cut through the ropes binding Walter's ankles and wrists. "You are familiar with my apothecary skills, Billy. I slipped a powerful sleeping potion into the drinking water, powerful enough to subdue two Nephilim guards, so there is no need for whispers. Unfortunately, it seems that Walter also drank the water, but I think he will recover. He is breathing well."

"We'll see about that." Billy nodded at Bonnie. "Cover me."

As Bonnie drew her sword, Billy put the gun away. Then, lifting Walter over his shoulder, he carried him to Dikaios and Ember. His wounded arm throbbed, and the cut on his chest stung, but he had to push through the pain.

"Lay him over me in riding position," Dikaios said. "Ember will keep him from falling over until you return."

With help from Ember, Billy pushed Walter onto Dikaios and balanced his body. Now semi-conscious, Walter instinctively gripped Dikaios's mane and stayed in place, while Ember stood at his side, watchful.

When he ran back to the house, he pulled out his gun again and nodded at Bonnie. "I'll keep an eye on her now."

Semiramis's brow bent angrily. "I have helped you time after time, Billy. I saved Listener's life, I guided you to Shiloh, I have been spying on Flint, and now I have rescued Walter. What else must I do to prove myself?"

Billy looked at Bonnie again. The confused expression on her face probably mirrored his own. There had to be a way to prove if she was a friend or an enemy. Maybe a prodding for information? "If you've been spying on Flint, maybe you know how he learned about our plans to defend against tonight's attack."

"I do know. Arramos has entered Second Eden." She laid a hand on his arm. "Billy, Arramos is the devil himself. He is crafty and powerful, and if someone is giving away your secrets, you can be certain that Arramos was involved."

"Why would Flint kidnap Walter? I figured out his army is sick, so why would he invite an attack?"

"You are correct. Disease has ravaged this village, and even Flint is deathly ill. He was desperate, so he was willing to listen to Goliath's counsel. I was close at hand only an hour ago, and I overheard the conversation. Goliath and Flint do not believe the warrior chief would attack and risk dropping his village guard. As long as he was unaware of the epidemic here, Elam would always choose to keep his forces in a defensive posture."

She raised a narrow finger. "Remember, the devil is cunning, and he surmised that the two of you would come, because you need someone to fly without alerting Goliath, and you would never let her go alone. With Excalibur and your fire-breathing, you make a formidable army on your own, so the two of you together would be a sufficient rescue party. Once they captured you, it would prove to Elam that rescue attempts were futile and costly, and he would send no more warriors."

"Why would they want us?"

"Not both of you. They want Bonnie. Arramos has longed to have her as a prisoner for years, and he will do anything to capture her."

Billy watched her eyes, sincere and piercing. Did she know about the Vacants' kidnapping attempt? Had she noticed their wounds? Should he probe her to find out if the ambush was planned by Arramos through Goliath and Flint? No. It was probably better to keep the attack to themselves. "So why do they want Bonnie?"

"May I show you something?" Semiramis asked, flashing her knife.

Billy pulled out the gun again. "Just move slowly and let me see your hands at all times."

"You are making me angry." Semiramis pushed the knife into his free hand and spread out her arms. "If you do not trust me, then slay me now. I cannot help you if you are constantly fearful of betrayal at my hands. While it is true that I am already dead, that blade will send me to my eternal punishment."

Billy glared at the knife, a stony blade at the end of a rough wooden hilt. Of course he couldn't take her offer, and she knew it. This act could be a dramatic bluff. Still, if she was bluffing, she was the best actress he had ever seen. What else could he do? He had to play along for now.

He gave her the knife. "Go ahead."

Shifting her gaze, Semiramis touched Bonnie's waist. "Have you ever felt anything odd here, as if something was attached to your body?"

She nodded. "All the time. It started back when my mother and I were running from a slayer. We never figured out what it was, so I just got used to it."

Semiramis glanced at Billy. "It is an invisible line that connects your body to Earth. Flint wants to make sure you stay here, so you can act as an anchor in this world. With the attachment, he will be able to call upon the unredeemed dead in Hades and raise up a new army that you and your dragons will never be able to withstand."

"If the rope's invisible," Bonnie said, "how do you know about it?"

Semiramis lowered her head, her tone weaker. "I was the one who sent Mardon to put it on you."

"Mardon?" Billy repeated. "Elam mentioned him. He's Nimrod's son."

"The same." She looked up at him again. "I used Mardon to do the bidding of Arramos before I rebelled and escaped."

Bonnie brushed her hand across her waist. "I can sense a pull, so why can't I feel it out in front of me?"

"It is so thin now, it passes by your hand like the thinnest of spiders' webs." She showed her the knife. "Only this can cut it. It is a staurolite blade. There are only a few in existence."

As if grabbing a string, she wrapped her hand around the air in front of Bonnie and made a vertical slice. "There," she said, holding up her fist. "I have the rope, and you are now free."

"What will you do with it?" Bonnie asked.

"I must go on a long journey to destroy it. If it stays here, the anchor will be set, and the armies of Hell will gather at the command of Arramos. Yet, I have foiled their plans, and you are free to go and tell Elam that Flint's army is broken and must be routed by a swift and forceful attack."

Billy looked at her face, trying to cut through any feigned sincerity. If this was all a bluff, it was the most cunning bluff he could imagine. If Elam attacked in full force, his own village would be undefended. Then, if Flint's army was actually still intact, they could devastate the villagers left behind. Maybe that was why this place was so deserted. They were lying in wait somewhere, ready to spring their trap. If only there was some way to find out for sure.

Billy reached for the door's latch. "Bonnie, keep an eye on her."

Letting out a huff, Semiramis crossed her arms over her chest, one hand still gripping her knife and the other holding fast to the invisible rope. "You seek truth in strange and deadly places, but if you must see for yourself in order to trust someone who has done only good to you, then step cautiously, for if you arouse those behind this dwelling, your lives, the very lives that I just saved, will be forfeit."

Billy nodded at the horses. "Bonnie, maybe it would be better if you get ready to escape with Walter, just in case."

She walked slowly backwards. "What about Semiramis? Who'll watch her while you're in there?"

Semiramis huffed again but said nothing.

"As long as you're safe," Billy said, "I'm not worried about her."

After waiting for Bonnie to get to the horses, he lifted the latch and peeked inside. It was dark and quiet.

"You will find Flint near the back door," Semiramis said. "After his conversation with Goliath, he returned to the house, and the drug made him collapse on the floor."

"How do you know all of this?"

"Your suspicions never end, do they?"

"Just tell me."

"When Goliath flew away, the drug began taking hold of Flint and his two Nephilim guards, so I was free to walk boldly in their presence. They had no power to subdue me, and since I am leaving to destroy this rope, they will never see me again."

"What about Hunter? Where is he?"

"He is waiting for me in the northlands. We will start our journey by returning him to his home."

Billy wanted to hurry, but another question dogged him. With Semiramis spilling so much information, now was a good time to ask. "Goliath took the weed from the garden. What was in it? Someone who carried the disease?"

"No. The disease began weeks before the wall collapsed. The weed held a warrior, a man of strength and stature. As far as I know, he did not succumb to the illness, but I do not know where he is now."

"Then he might be back soon."

"Indeed. In fact, he was riding Goliath when he flew away. Perhaps they went in search of food. If so, their return could be at hand."

"I'll be ready." Billy withdrew his sword and let its glow shine brightly as he entered the house. Tiptoeing, he waved the blade from one side to the other. The front room was spacious but empty, with holes in the walls that exposed decaying lattice work. Dikaios had mentioned seeing the inside of Flint's house and described it as relatively rich in décor, but it was certainly far from rich now. Without furniture or wall decorations, and with piles of nondescript debris lying here and there, it seemed no more than an abandoned shack.

As he pushed deeper into the house, the sounds of creaking footsteps followed. He looked back. With her hood again covering her head, Semiramis walked a few steps behind.

"Curious?" Billy asked.

"A better word would be, 'Cautious.' If Goliath returns, perhaps I can be of service, in spite of your never-ending suspicions."

"Have it your way." Leading with Excalibur, Billy picked up his pace until he reached the back wall where he found a blond-haired man lying faceup on the floor next to a wooden table and a single chair. A cup sat atop the table along with a pile of dried fruit, apparently partially eaten.

He leaned through an open back door and looked around. As expected, two Nephilim lay stretched out in the mud, one with an empty cup still in his hand. He walked closer and examined their sleeves. Neither wore Ashley's band around his arm.

Billy curled his fingers tightly around the hilt. It would be so easy to kill them and take out two powerful enemies without risking anyone else's blood. But, of course, he couldn't. The professor's wisdom had been emblazoned on his heart. *A knight opposes his enemy face to face. A stab in the back is the way of the coward. If you must fight, attack your enemy head-on. That is the way of valor.*

Killing a sleeping giant would be the coward's way, the way he killed Palin. And he would never return to the life he had left behind.

He pulled back into the house and knelt next to the man's body. At the end of a necklace, a glass egg, much like a villager's companion, lay on his chest, dark and lifeless.

Billy looked up at Semiramis. "Is this Flint?"

When she nodded, her hood fell back again, revealing her long tresses, shimmering in Excalibur's light. "He is drugged to be sure, but he was quite ill before my potion took effect. He will likely remain unconscious for a long time."

Billy used his tongue to feel for the tooth transmitter. It still buzzed. "Elam, I'm inside Flint's house. We rescued Walter. He's out of it, but I think he'll be fine."

Elam's tiny voice tingled in his jaw. "That's great, but how did you get into Flint's house? What's going on?"

"It looks like they have no army. The disease killed most of Flint's people."

"What about Flint himself, and the dragons?"

He turned away from Semiramis and whispered. "Flint's here, and he's out cold, but the dragons aren't around. Semiramis is here, and she explained—"

"Not her again. Did you wonder why she showed up?"

"Yeah. Kind of convenient, wasn't it?"

"Exactly. She was probably assigned to wait for you and tell you the story they want you to hear."

"Yeah, I thought of that, but we have an ace in the hole."

"What's that?"

Billy turned back toward Semiramis. She was looking out the open back door. Was she listening? Probably. She had already admitted to being an expert eavesdropper. "We have Flint."

"You mean you'll take him prisoner?" Elam asked.

"As a prisoner of mercy. Can you send three dragons? We'll need extra cloaks that can be made into litters a dragon can carry underneath. Be sure to send my father. If Goliath shows up, he might be the only one who can handle him."

"How many sick people are you talking about?"

"I don't know. I haven't searched their village."

"Perhaps six or seven," Semiramis said. "But I also have not searched everywhere."

Billy glared at her. "So you *were* listening."

"You did not say it was forbidden. I cannot hear Elam, but I can deduce what he is saying."

"I'm not surprised." After putting Excalibur away, Billy pulled Flint up and carried him over his shoulder. He marched quickly toward the front, hoping to keep Semiramis and her radar ears far enough behind. Although it was now dark, his memory of the empty room guided him toward the moonlight peeking through the open front door. "Elam, I'll send the horses back with Walter, and we'll wait for the dragons to arrive. And make sure Sorentine is in the group. This is a perfect job for her."

As Billy hurried out the front door and closed in on the horses, Elam replied. "What will the horses do if trouble shows up?"

"That shouldn't be a problem." Billy laid Flint next to Bonnie and, rising again, smiled at her. "I'll send a winged transport with them, someone in whom I have complete confidence."

"Okay," Elam said. "I think we have enough dragons. We can spare three. I have to leave the radio station to call them, so you might see the dragons before you hear from me again."

"Great. Thanks."

Semiramis called from the doorway. "I will be leaving you now, Billy. It grieves me that you never learned to trust me, but perhaps in later years when you remember these days, you will find it in your heart of love to look upon me with greater mercy." She raised her hood once more and walked slowly toward the marsh. With every step, her slender form faded into the darkness.

"She mentioned a staurolite blade," Bonnie said. "I have one of those." She touched a sheath at her hip. "According to Sapphira, it once belonged to Morgan, but my trainer in the Valley of Shadows thought I should keep it."

Billy eyed the narrow wooden hilt. "Maybe it will come in handy, but if Semiramis uses one, I wouldn't be too sure it's a good idea."

"You still don't trust her?" Bonnie asked. "I don't feel that pull anymore. She must have been telling the truth about that."

Billy moved to her side and watched Semiramis's shadow meld with the darkness. "I'm not sure what she's planning to do with that rope, but I thought it would be better for her to have it than to keep it tied to you. And I just wanted to get her out of here. It's better if she doesn't know what we're doing. If Arramos is so good at predicting our actions, we have to do the unexpected."

"Is that why you're taking Flint?"

"Right. Drugged or sick, their general is in our hands. If Semiramis is in a conspiracy with Goliath and Arramos, then she's too evil to expect us to show mercy."

She hooked her arm around his and laid her head against his shoulder. After sighing deeply, she whispered, "Love never fails."

Billy took in a long breath. Her touch felt good, a touch of approval, a blessing, maybe even a hint of an opening door. When she had said that he needed to win her heart, he imagined a dramatic rescue by which he suffered horrible wounds and shed a gallon of blood to prove himself worthy of her most precious gift. Yes, he had delivered that sacrifice, and gladly, but now this moment felt even more important.

Standing in the glow of a brilliant moon, it seemed that Pegasus illuminated more than a devastated village and a muddy marsh. It revealed the truth about an enemy. Flint needed healing.

Billy looked down at Flint's pallid face. Yes, if necessary, he would have gone to war against this pitiful man, but the opportunity to offer him medicine instead of the tip of a sword seemed like medicine to Billy's own soul. More than four years of preparing for battle, toning his muscles and sharpening his skills, had made him a formidable soldier in the eyes of his enemies, ready to go to war to protect the innocent. Four years spent away from the opulence of life on Earth and, instead, worshiping with the villagers in their simplicity of life and faith, had honed his heart into one that longed for peace.

"Bonnie?" he whispered.

"Mmm?" She kept her gaze locked on the marsh.

"We're alone now."

"How can you say that? Dikaios and Ember are here."

"I meant we're the only awake humans."

She laughed gently. "Okay. I guess that's close enough."

He slid his hand into hers and faced the two horses. "Before you take Walter back, will you be our witnesses?"

Both horses nodded. "What will we be witnessing?" Dikaios asked.

"A question from my heart to hers." Still holding Bonnie's hand, Billy lowered himself to one knee and looked into her eyes. Pegasus sparkled in her irises. A warm breeze tossed her blonde-streaked hair, making it flow behind her like a banner of tawny linen embroidered with gold. Oh, if only he could borrow some of this beautiful woman's eloquence, something that would pour out his heart in a sonnet of love, words that would bare his soul and allow her to see the man of God he had become. Silently he begged for those words, if only for these next few moments.

After clearing his throat, he spoke loudly and clearly, unafraid. "Bonnie Silver, together we have plunged into the heart of territories unknown, and, with love as our sword, we have captured the captain of those who threatened to harm the innocent. He was a rebel who shook his fist at the one who showed him love and mercy in spite of the rebel's clenched fist. Two thousand years ago, the Lord of the universe entered a world of rebels and washed the feet of those who denied him in both word and deed. Because of your witness, the life you have lived in your words and in your deeds, I was able to clearly see this God who became a man. Because of the purity you displayed, I witnessed a reflection of the sinless life he lived. Because of the light you shone every moment you were in my presence, his light was able to break through my stubborn shell."

He swallowed, trying to loosen his tightening throat as he kept his gaze on her lovely face. Tears streamed down her cheeks. She squeezed his hand but said nothing as he continued.

"The day I opened your journal and read your prayer was the day I saw that light in all its glory, and I never wanted to depart from its blaze. I thought being with you would be the only way to walk in the sunshine. Yet, strangely enough, while I spent more than four years without you, I learned something very important. The light of Jesus shone wherever I went, and spending that time away from you strengthened me in ways I never imagined. I learned how to find the light that God planted within me. I learned how to seek his power without looking to you for instructions." Swallowing again, he raised his eyebrows. "Do you understand?"

Her chin quivering, she nodded.

"So, Bonnie Silver, now that I have spent those years without you, and I have learned what those days were designed to teach me, I never want to live another day without you. I want to spend the rest of my life with you." He withdrew Excalibur and summoned a strong glow. "So here, in the heart of darkness, I shine my light without fear. Instead of looking to you as my source of illumination, I look to God alone, and I will lead you through the darkest of places, arm-in-arm and heart-to-heart, as together we storm the gates of the enemy and rescue those he has taken captive."

Now trembling, he rubbed her knuckles with his thumb. "What I'm trying to say, Bonnie, is this." With his own tears flowing, he returned Excalibur to its scabbard, pulled out the ring, and lifted it between his thumb and finger. "Will you marry me?"

Her eyes sparkled. The moon bathed her milky cheeks in a soft glow, highlighting the trickling tears. She took in a deep breath, and spoke, her voice as smooth and lovely as her spirit. "Yes, Billy Bannister. I will marry you."

Taking in a deep breath, he pushed the ring onto her finger. Since it was far too big, it slid easily over her knuckles. She rolled her fingers to keep it in place, smiling as she gazed at the red stone.

He rose to his feet, his legs shaking. Just as he opened his mouth to speak, a clapping sound made him turn.

Walter leaned against Dikaios, clapping his hands. "Bravo! That was simply fabulous!"

Bonnie laughed. "How long have you been listening?"

"Let me think . . ." Walter shrugged. "Ever since you said you were all alone, I think. But it's kind of fuzzy. The water here really packs a wallop. Good thing I only took a sip."

Billy pulled Bonnie close, leaned his head against hers, and extended his hand to Walter. "Come here."

Staggering slightly, Walter joined them in a tight huddle. Billy kissed Bonnie's head, then Walter's, and wept. "I'm with my best friends in all the world. I couldn't be happier."

After a minute or so, Billy pulled back and looked at his friends in turn. “We have a lot to do, so . . .” He sniffed and wiped his eyes with his sleeve. “So let’s start with checking on Flint.”

Walter’s brow shot up. “Maybe we’d better draw our swords.”

Billy lowered his voice and slowly withdrew Excalibur. “Did you hear something?”

“Yep. After listening to those Nephilim, I’d recognize them anywhere, even the sloshing of their big, ugly feet.” As if working in tandem, Walter and Bonnie pulled their weapons. A shimmer of light ran along the metallic blades, and the two warriors set their feet.

A huge figure crashed through the wall of reeds and rushed toward them.

Billy lit up Excalibur’s beam. “Stop!”

The Naphil halted and raised his hand to block the brilliant light, revealing Ashley’s band on his arm. “Billy? Is that you?”

“Yereq!” He let the beam fade. “Where have you been?”

The giant crossed his massive arms. “For the last half hour I have been keeping the other Naphil guard away from you. You have been making a great deal of noise.”

“Where is he now?”

“I subdued him. He will not be a threat any longer.”

Walter slapped Yereq’s back. “Thanks. We owe you one.”

“Perhaps more than one. The two Nephilim who were asleep behind the house woke up, so I had to put them to sleep again. And when you rode here with the horses, I kept the other guard from finding you. Did you not hear me?”

“We heard,” Billy said, “but I didn’t know who you were.”

“I spoke as a witless monkey, loud and obvious. I hoped you would recognize that I was trying to send you information. We heard gunshots, and I convinced the other Naphil that it was likely just a series of thunderclaps. Fortunately, that giant did not possess more than a squirrel’s brain.”

“We were wondering about that. Thanks for covering for us.”

“Well, I see that you learned what has been afoot here. Goliath never intended to use Flint or his people as part of his army, but he speaks about another army that he hopes to gain by capturing Bonnie, something about anchoring her in Second Eden."

"Let's save that thought for a minute. Did you figure out who was in the plant?"

"I never saw him, but I heard his name. Sir Devin. Your mother told me many stories about him, so if he is here, we have another great concern."

Billy breathed the name quietly. "Sir Devin . . ." Years ago that name would have given him a shiver. Now it seemed little more than a bad memory, and the miracle of his resurrection seemed commonplace, just another villain back from the dead. "How did he get into the plant?"

"A traitor in the village had a companion that was actually a seed of sorts. It contained Devin's life energy, and the traitor planted it in the garden."

"A fake companion?" A thousand thoughts raced through Billy's mind—Hunter falling in the garden, his lost companion, Semiramis protecting the plant, finding Shiloh only to lose Acacia, and now . . .

Billy kicked at the mud. "Semiramis has the rope!"

"Yes," Bonnie said. "What do you mean?"

"This is exactly what she wanted. We followed her plan from start to finish. They didn't want Bonnie; they just wanted the rope. And only Semiramis knew how to cut it and what to do with it. She'll anchor Second Eden to Earth and Hades herself."

"So their army's on its way?" Walter asked.

"Probably." Billy searched the dark edges of the marsh. Every shifting shadow seemed to hide a crouching warrior. Although the potential danger was real, nothing prodded his alarm, just a bit of background uneasiness. "We need to get out of here."

Bonnie marched toward the nearest hut. "Then we'd better search the homes and find the survivors. Our dragons might be here at any minute."

Looking at Walter and Yereq, Billy let his shoulders slump. "You're right. Let's do it."

"I'm still kind of woozy," Walter said, "so I'll stay with Flint and the horses and watch for our dragons." He pulled Billy's gun from its holster. "But I might need this."

Billy and Yereq caught up with Bonnie, and after searching through at least twenty houses, they found three women and two men between thirty and fifty years old. All five were either unconscious or too sick to walk, so Yereq carried them to Walter. By the time they brought the fifth patient, three dragons had arrived: Clefspeare, Thigocia, and Sorentine.

After Billy and Bonnie wrapped the five in cloaks, Thigocia and Sorentine snatched up two bundles each and took to the sky.

As Billy laid Flint on a cloak, his body jerked. His eyes blinked open, and he stared at Billy. "Who are you?"

"Relax. I'm a friend. I heard you're sick, so I'm taking you to a hospital."

"What hospital? The only hospital I know of is . . ." A frown bent his face. "Abraham's village?"

He tried to get up, but Billy pushed him back to the cloak. "Don't worry. We're taking you there to help you."

Venom laced his voice. "I cannot accept help from Abraham. He kept us trapped in a circular prison of flames. We had so little food, we were always weak. We had no way to fight disease."

"You're not accepting help from Abraham," Billy said. "He's gone forever, so you won't have to swallow your pride. Just take it easy and let us get you and your people to the hospital."

Closing his eyes, Flint gave a nod of resignation. "I am too sick to fight. Do with me what you will."

CHAPTER 12

FINDING SHILOH

Floating several inches above the lake, Gabriel pushed forward. Of course, using his mental power to travel in his light energy state was never physically tiring, but it put a drain on his brain. Yet, that didn't matter. Finding Shiloh and Acacia couldn't wait for him to sit and rest. And now that he had found the lake, this was no time to slow down. The portal was probably only moments away.

After crossing a snow-covered valley, he found a large boulder that matched the description Billy had provided. He let his hand float above a letter *X* on one side. No doubt about it. This had to be the place.

He drifted around the area. The sixth circle village was pretty large, so its location shouldn't be hard to find. The problem wouldn't be sniffing out a portal if it was still here; it would be breaking through. It might take all his energy, but he had to find Shiloh and Acacia. Nothing was more important.

Something moved near the boulder, a human crouching at the base. Gabriel eased closer. The man, shorter than average, seemed to be manipulating something with his hands, as if tying a knot with an invisible line.

When the man straightened, his oval face came into view. Badly scarred from burns, he wore glasses over his narrow eyes, and his scant white hair blew back in the cool breeze, uncovering a nearly bald head. He pulled against his invisible rope, as if testing the knot he had fastened at the base of the boulder.

Gabriel studied his countenance. He seemed to be too serious, too focused to be a madman. Yet, what sane man would be playing an imaginary game of tug-of-war with a boulder?

The man withdrew a bottle from his pocket, pulled out a stopper, and poured a shining yellow liquid onto his "rope." A splash of sparks sizzled in the air and shot out from the boulder like a lit fuse, following a line until it disappeared far away.

Suddenly, Gabriel's body dropped. He looked down. His shoes made indentations in the snow, and his energy field gave way to physical legs and torso. Quietly, he patted his chest and stretched out his wings. It was true! He had regained his body!

The man gasped and jumped back. "What are you doing here?"

Gabriel raised his hands. "Hey. Don't be scared. I know I have wings, but—"

"I am not frightened of you. We have met before."

"We have?" Gabriel narrowed his eyes. "Now that you mention it, you do look familiar. Did we meet before your burn accident?"

The man snorted. "Accident. That's a laugher. The only accident is that you're here, so now I have to decide what to do about this unfortunate meeting." He withdrew a dagger. "I doubt that I could catch you, so it would be better for both of us if you would leave as quickly as possible."

Gabriel gave his wings a quick flap and scooted away. As the man's voice and manner registered in his mind, everything grew clear. This was Mardon, the mad scientist who tried to lasso Heaven and join it with Earth, and the dagger looked like the staurolite blade from

Dragons' Rest, though the hilt was slightly different. "Where'd you get the knife?"

"Don't play me for a fool with your small talk. I wasn't born yesterday." Mardon looked upward, apparently in thought. "Upon reconsideration, it might be advantageous for us to work together. As you can imagine, I am not happy with what happened to my face, and I want to exact revenge upon the beast who did this to me."

"Beast? What beast?"

"The devil himself. He masquerades as Arramos, one of the dragons of old. If I could get back to the Bridgelands, perhaps I could find him and use this dagger to end his charade. My sources tell me that only a staurolite blade is able to cut through his scales, and such a cut will force that devil from his body so that he won't be able to deceive or maim anyone else."

"Well," Gabriel said, "I'm all for taking a shot at him, but I have to find some friends who were trapped in the sixth circle of Hades. Do you know anything about that?"

"I know more about your friends than you do."

Gabriel resisted the temptation to roll his eyes. Mardon's dramatic pause was annoying, but he had to play along. "Well, then, please tell me where they are now and how to find them."

"I will tell you, if you will agree to help me foil Arramos's plans."

"Yeah. Sure. As long as it doesn't conflict with what I need to do."

"We will not be at cross-purposes." Mardon nodded toward the boulder. "I have anchored a line that attaches Earth and Hades to this realm. I did it here because, when I transported from the Bridgelands, this is the point where I appeared in Second Eden. I thought it best to try to return by this route. Shiloh, too, was here, so it stands to reason that she might have gone there as well. Therefore, your journey is tied to mine. My sources tell me that you are also seeking Acacia. Although I have not seen her, the story of her disappearance would indicate that she is likely with Shiloh. Finding her would serve my purposes well."

"Why is that?"

For a moment, he paused, nervous, uncertain. "I gave her life in my laboratory thousands of years ago. So, of course, I want to see her again."

Gabriel studied Mardon's uneasy manner. He had balked. Was he lying? Either way, it didn't really matter. He had to complete his mission. "Right," Gabriel said. "I heard about how you did that with Acacia, and Sapphira, too."

Closing his eyes, Mardon took in a deep breath and let it out slowly. "Yes, Sapphira. I wish to see her more than any other. She was a wonderful assistant to me, intelligent, thoughtful, kind, even when my father brutally misused her." He shook his head as if tossing off a wayward thought. "In any case, if we work together, perhaps we can signal the Bridgelands that we are here and request safe conduct to that realm."

"Signal the Bridgelands?"

"Yes, my mother knows the gatekeeper there, and he monitors attempts to enter. If we can make an attempt to open the portal, whether successful or not, perhaps he will come and see who is, shall we say, knocking at his door."

"Fair enough." Gabriel looked around for a loose piece of wood. "What do we do? Spin a flame like Sapphira does?"

"Exactly. I was able to do it when transporting from Shinar to Hades, but that was a wide-open portal. I'll wager that this one won't be so easy. Otherwise, the people of this land would have gone there long ago. So, I am hoping you will fly around with a flame. Perhaps that will attract the gatekeeper's attention."

Gabriel shrugged. "Sure. I don't have any other way of getting there."

"Very well. I brought flint stones and parchment, so I will start a fire, while you search for a suitable firebrand. There are fallen trees within a mile, so with your wings, I assume you can locate a branch and return quickly."

"I'll see what I can do." Gabriel lifted into the air and scanned the valley. As Mardon had said, several trees had succumbed to the long winter, leaving rotting logs with spindly branches reaching upward like a man drowning in frigid water. He zoomed down to one, snapped off a branch, and again rose into the air.

As he flew, memories of battling Mardon's giants flowed back into his mind. This madman had been the cause of so much trouble over the centuries, including very nearly destroying the entire world. Would it be right to help him? Was there really any choice?

Gabriel eased into a descent. The air carried a nasty chill, but the prospect of working with this snake in the grass made him shiver even harder. He had to keep a close eye on Mardon's every move, a very close eye.

* * *

Acacia searched for an appropriate branch, something easy enough to break from a limb, yet thick enough to hold an enduring flame. Although nothing seemed suitable so far, the search had been relaxing. The woods here were always a delight— shade from the never-setting sun, a breeze tossing the treetops into a melodic swish, and blossoming vines to flavor the air with hints of honeysuckle and jasmine.

Ever since their transport to this realm and the subsequent vanishing of the sixth circle's village, life had been sweet and easy. With Shiloh for company, as well as a variety of animals, both familiar and exotic, including unicorns, every day brought new sources of pleasure and mental stimulation. But with her strength still ebbing daily, any strenuous exercise taxed her body. Even breathing seemed to erode her from within.

Although she didn't need food to survive, she occasionally took small meals to see if something would revive her energy. They brought some strength at first but later burned like fire in her bones. Shiloh was always worried and daily cajoled her into a few more mouthfuls of this fruit or that herb, warning her that she had grown so thin, her Second Eden garments now hung like rags on a skeleton.

Not only that, thoughts about worried loved ones haunted them both. Shiloh spoke about them more often, especially Gabriel.

Acacia crouched next to a bush that bore a yellow flower the size of her hand. She took in the lovely fragrance—sweet, mellow, and buttery. This was one of the edible flowers, but the thought of eating it made her feel queasy.

She looked back at Shiloh as she worked on her latest effort to contact Gabriel. She had abandoned any pretense about her love for him, choosing to believe that he would be the one to find her and sweep her off her feet. Years ago he had watched over her and proven his devotion. Even after all this time, he wouldn't have forgotten his commitment to keep her safe.

And now new hope had arisen. They finally learned where they were. Although Acacia had long suspected this to be the case, a strange old man had confirmed today that they were in the Bridgelands. She had been here before when she, Joseph, and Ruth came through, but they had been in such a hurry, and Ruth's condition had so dominated her thoughts, she didn't pay much attention to the details of this world.

During their journey, Joseph, while carrying Ruth, led Acacia across a bridge over an apparently bottomless chasm. Yet, the bridge Acacia more recently found here was very different, so she wondered if it was the same one. Most of the planks connecting the supporting ropes were either gone or broken, and the ropes themselves were so frayed, in some sections only a few strands held them together. With every gust, the span swung wildly, making the broken steps clack and creak. If this was the same bridge, there seemed to be no way to get to the other side where Heaven's Gate awaited.

The old man said just moments ago that they need not make an attempt to cross the bridge. Why? In his strange and mysterious way, he hinted at bringing someone from another realm, but he just cackled merrily when she or Shiloh tried to press him for details.

As a heftier breeze swept past, Acacia looked up. A limb hung low with a protruding branch that seemed perfect. She reached up and snapped it off. It was time to give their new plan a try.

After exiting the woods, she held up the arm-length tree branch and called out, "Ignite!" A flame erupted at the end and burned steadily. Lowering it to eye level, she showed it to the withered old man seated on a stone. "Will that be sufficient, Glewlwyd?"

Glewlwyd eyed the flame and spoke in a squeaky voice that sounded more like a rusty hinge than a man. "Perhaps. Perhaps. We shall see. When the circle of stones is complete, we can test it."

Shiloh pointed at the stone Glewlwyd sat upon. "May I use that one? I can't find any others close by, and I need one more."

Smiling, the old man pushed on a cane and rose to his feet. "I will be most satisfied when this is finished. The body I received has aged slowly while in the Bridgelands, but not slowly enough to keep these old bones from complaining."

Shiloh picked up the stone in both arms and, with knees bent, carried it to a flat, grassy area nearby. She had already set out eleven similarly sized stones in even intervals, one short of creating a circle with a diameter roughly matching hers and Acacia's combined heights. After letting the stone roll out of her arms and onto the grass, she shoved it into place. "There. That should do it."

Acacia walked to the center of the circle. "So how will we know when someone passes through this spot in Second Eden?"

"That is where you need my help." Glewlwyd shuffled across the perimeter boundary. The moment he passed the stones, his body morphed into a transparent, liquidlike substance. Only his slow movements allowed them to detect his presence at all.

When he stopped at the center, he seemed to disappear, but his voice was clearer than before. "I am the gatekeeper of the Bridgelands, and I am able to discern if anyone is trying to pass through an entry portal. Since this is the spot that you appeared, a portal remains, and that is why I asked you to build this new gateway. Someone, indeed, is at the gate, and the stones will create a dome of safety for the traveler." For a moment, he paused. His liquid head shifted slowly from side to side, as if he smelled something odd. "This is a strange portal. I cannot discern what is different about it, but it feels . . . dead."

"'Dead' might be a good word," Shiloh said as she joined them in the circle. "When I was in that old ghost town in Hades, Semiramis told me only dead people could travel through the barrier."

"Hades is an unusual place, but when it merged with Earth, all the rules of travel changed. The dead were able to pass into the lands of the living, but the living ones were still shackled by their corporeal existence."

Acacia raised a finger. "But I'm not dead. Clefspeare, Billy, and I were able to open it, and I fell through the barrier."

Glewlwyd's barely visible head nodded. "A most perplexing mystery. Perhaps there is something about your existence that even you do not yet know. In any case, I am the gatekeeper here, so I have the power to open any portal in the land, and now I will peer into Second Eden to see who is about." He took the branch from Acacia and waved it over his head. It seemed that a flaming, crooked stick floated in midair. "Take heart. I will return as soon as I am able."

The old man, or what was left of him, disappeared, along with the branch.

Shiloh let out a breath and sat on the grass. "Well, since he's gone, at least we know the portal still works."

"True enough." Acacia sat next to Shiloh and took her wounded hand in both of hers. "Have you been keeping track of time?"

Shiloh gave her a shrug. "Not really. Since my watch quit working and since we have constant daylight, it seems impossible. I kept track for a while by watching my body changes, you know, counting my cycles, but even those got out of whack. Maybe it's the food here. I don't know."

"I've been watching." Acacia looked up at the sky. "Even though this world's sun never goes down, it still makes a circuit in the sky. If that equals a day, then we've been here between four and five years."

"Sounds right. It didn't make much difference in Hades, but now I'm finally aging, so the passing of time feels more important than before."

Acacia caressed Shiloh's cheek. "You still look very young, no more than twenty years old, and you're as lovely as ever."

Shiloh looked down and plucked a blade of grass. "When Gabriel shows up, I hope he thinks so. In reality, I'm practically a senior citizen."

"And he's even older." Acacia gave her a gentle push and laughed. "Come now, Shiloh, don't fret. He loved you before; he will love you now."

Still looking down, Shiloh let a smile break through. "I hope you're right."

"I am. Trust me. He will sweep you off your feet and fly you to the wedding altar. After all you've been through, I'm certain God will reward you with the desires of your heart."

"After all *I've* been through," Shiloh said, pointing at herself. "What about *you*? You've been around for thousands of years, suffering loneliness and pain for a lot of that time, and you've never had anyone, no husband to lift you up when you're down, to offer you a shoulder to cry on, or to . . ." She looked away. "Or to give you babies."

"Oh, Shiloh, is that what's troubling you?" Acacia turned Shiloh's face toward her. "Don't worry about your womb. I'm sure it's as youthful as your face, and Gabriel will prove to be a marvelous father. You have nothing to fear."

"There you go again," Shiloh said. "You're always concerned about me, never about yourself."

"That's because I'm not sad about these things. Although I have often longed for strong, embracing arms, I have them in my Lord Jesus. Day after day I needed a shoulder to cry on, and he gave me one that never tires of hearing my lamentations. And now that I have seen him, I know that his presence was real every moment."

"You've seen him?"

Acacia looked up at the sky. "Only once, but it was so strange. One day while I was praying at Heaven's Altar, a group of martyrs rose up and cried out, 'How long, O Lord, holy and true, will you refrain from judgment and avenging our blood on them that dwell on the earth?'

During that moment, I could look up into Heaven itself and see the Lord, and he instructed an angel to give each martyr a white robe." She shifted her gaze back to Shiloh. "You see, I'm not a martyr, so I wore a blue cloak while I was there, but when new martyrs come to the prayer room, they are given white robes. Anyway, that's when I heard his voice. He said, 'Rest, my beloved, for a little while longer until your brethren who will be killed as you were fulfill their purpose.'"

"Wow! That must have been amazing!"

"Oh, Shiloh, I can't even begin to describe it. But here's my point. Ever since the day Sapphira restored me after my fall into the chasm, I learned to turn my focus outward, never inward, and I find complete fulfillment in serving others. I have no need of a husband or children. All I want to do is make my savior, my only husband, happy with me, so that when I finally get to meet him, to touch him, he will smile and welcome me into a physical embrace and ensure that I never need a shoulder to cry on again."

Looking up into the sky, Shiloh breathed in the fragrant air. "Just think. It's going to be even better than this place." Then, half closing one eye at Acacia, she added, "Do you think they'll have unicorns in Heaven?"

Acacia shrugged. "I don't see why not. Maybe they'll even let you take Cornelius with you."

"Speaking of Cornelius," Shiloh said as she rose to her feet, "have you seen him lately?"

Acacia pointed. "He was grazing in a meadow just beyond the stream we crossed. He seemed to like the clover there."

"Let's bring him over here. Maybe Glewlwyd will be back by then."

Shiloh ran through the calf-high grass. Acacia followed, though more slowly. Her legs hurt too much, and today they felt worse than ever. Her body seemed empty, like a sail without wind. Her flames had been adequate for starting campfires, and she could still fashion a small fireball, but the days of creating blazing infernos seemed to be over.

Was age finally creeping up on her after all these centuries? Did her years in Heaven's Altar leave her pining away for the sweet fellowship of the martyred saints and another glimpse of the Holy One, the blessed Messiah Jesus?

Urging her legs into a quicker walk, she searched for Shiloh. There she was, petting Cornelius, the leader of the unicorns, at least the leader of the herd that grazed on this side of the chasm. After Cornelius and Shiloh met, he left his herd to stay with her, apparently realizing that she needed a strong, tactile companion, someone who could physically return the love she poured out.

Acacia stopped and waited while Shiloh led the unicorn back. Acacia crossed her arms over her chest and smiled. The way Shiloh treated Cornelius proved that Gabriel would someday have a sweet, gentle wife, a real treasure. All would be well.

A tear dripped from Acacia's eye, and she quickly swiped it away. Yes. All would be well.

CHAPTER 13

A DOUBLE PLUNGE

Holding the flaming branch, Gabriel landed next to Mardon, out of breath. "I don't think . . . it's working. I did . . . about thirty orbits."

"Yes, I know." Mardon glared at the dwindling flame. "Thirty-two, to be precise."

A squeaky voice broke in. "I counted exactly thirty."

Gabriel turned toward the voice but saw nothing, only the snow-covered ground he had flown over so many times. "Who's there?"

A vague outline took shape and slowly filled in. After several seconds, a stooped old man stood barefoot on the snow carrying a flaming branch similar to Gabriel's. His brow suddenly scrunched tightly, and he looked down at his feet as he lifted them in turn. "If you don't mind, please state your business quickly. Since you are not trying to enter from Hades, I will bypass the usual required examination protocol."

Mardon stepped forward. "Glewlwyd, I request—"

"So you know my name, do you?" He pointed his branch. "Let me know yours before you make your requests."

"Very well." Mardon cleared his throat. "I am Mardon, son of Semiramis."

Glewlwyd's eyebrow shot up, but he said nothing.

"I seek passage to the Bridgelands," Mardon continued, "in order to provide a great service for all the realms. I intend to find the devil who assumes the body and the great name of Arramos so that I may slay him. He must no longer bring shame to dragons."

"A noble task. Impossible, but noble." Glewlwyd turned to Gabriel. "And who might you be, winged boy?"

"I am Gabriel, son of Makaidos and Thigocia. I am searching for two friends, and they were last seen here before they disappeared through a portal. We suspect that they might be in the Bridgelands."

"I assume you mean Shiloh and Acacia."

Gabriel nearly leaped out of his shoes. "Yes. Are they there?"

"Indeed, they are." Glewlwyd waved his branch. "Come nearer, and we will go immediately. I have not stood in the snow since the days of Arthur. I did not like it then, and I do not like it now."

Gabriel and Mardon stepped close, one on each side of the strange old man. Then, with a quick, snappy motion, Glewlwyd waved his firebrand. Instantly the snow scene disappeared, replaced by a field of green grass and lush forests as well as a surrounding circle of stones.

Inhaling deeply, Gabriel took in the warm, fragrant air, allowing it to chase away every shiver. "So," he said as he turned to survey the new scene, "where should we start looking for—"

"Gabriel!"

He spun toward the sound. Shiloh and Acacia were riding toward him on a unicorn, but it suddenly stalled, as if frightened. A slight tremble ran across the ground, gentle but noticeable.

Shiloh slid down and ran, her arms outstretched. Gabriel gathered her into an embrace and pressed his cheek against hers. "Shiloh! Praise the Maker! I finally found you!"

While they hugged, Acacia dismounted and stood nearby, smiling as she looked on.

Gabriel studied her petite frame—thin, fragile, almost cadaverous. Although pale and gaunt, her face was still lovely, yet it carried a morbid sort of beauty, like a comely child dying of cancer.

As another tremor, stronger this time, rolled through the meadow, Gabriel extended his arm. "Acacia, it's good to see you as well."

Acacia glanced at Glewlwyd. He had dropped to his knees and set his palm against the ground, his head tilted upward as if listening. She joined in an embrace with Gabriel and Shiloh for a moment before pushing away, her eyes narrowing. "Your traveling companion looks familiar."

Gabriel looked over his shoulder at Mardon. The mad scientist was staring at Acacia, seemingly mesmerized, or perhaps appalled at her appearance.

Acacia stepped closer to him, her face drooping into a piteous frown. "Hunter, I see you never found your companion. I hope—" She paused and stared. "You look different here . . . more distinct, more focused."

Mardon held out his hand. "I was worried that you would recognize me in Second Eden, but apparently there are no secrets here in the Bridgelands, so I will no longer disguise my voice. My usual voice is hampered by burn damage, but you will likely recognize it."

Gasping, she raised her fingers to her lips. "Mardon!"

"Yes, my child." Mardon stepped closer and gazed into her eyes. "You are wasting away."

Acacia inched back and pulled her tunic higher on her bony shoulders. Her voice lowered to a whisper. "I have been ill."

A tear slipped down Mardon's ravaged cheek. "I created your genetic blend. Perhaps I can do something to help you if you will let me examine you thoroughly."

"Uh . . . thank you, but that won't be necessary." She shot Gabriel a look that seemed to communicate, "Why are the two of you together?" but she said no more.

Gabriel stepped between them. "Mardon and I sort of ran into each other while I was looking for you." He gave his wings a quick shake.

"For some reason, I got my body back in Second Eden. Mardon says that Second Eden has now combined with Earth and Hades, so that would explain the change."

"And your explanation," Glewlwyd said, rising to his feet, "tells me all I need to know."

Gabriel slid his foot across the grass. "Is that what all the shaking is about?"

"Indeed, and it will increase to catastrophic proportions. In fact, the portal by which you entered here has already dissolved." Glewlwyd waved his arm. "Come. The Bridgelands will crumble. We must go to the bridge. It is our only hope of escape."

"The bridge?" Acacia said. "It's in ruins."

Glewlwyd's voice grew animated. "Do not judge by appearances, for salvation often comes in broken vessels."

"How far is it?" Gabriel asked.

"If we hurry on foot, perhaps fifteen minutes by your measurements. If, however, the ladies ride the unicorn and you fly, the three of you will get there more quickly. Mardon and I will get there when we can. We are both already dead souls, so the worst that can happen to us is a quicker entry into our ultimate destination."

"The worst is right," Mardon said. "I hope to convince Elohim that I be allowed into Heaven. My current destiny is one that I would like to avoid."

Gabriel flapped his wings and drifted behind Acacia. "I'll carry her, and Mardon can ride with Shiloh. But what do we do when we get there?"

Glewlwyd raised a pair of fingers. "You have two choices. You may cross the bridge and go from there to Heaven's Gate where you may petition for entry into the altar, or you may go into the chasm, which would lead you to Second Eden. The problem is that if you are unable to slow your descent, you will be crushed when you arrive."

"I might be able to carry two," Gabriel said, "but not all three."

"Then the ladies should go, and Mardon will cross the bridge with me. That way—"

"No!" Mardon shouted. "I must return to Second Eden! I must complete my mission!"

"What mission?" Gabriel asked. "To convince Elohim that—"

"Never mind." Mardon thrust a finger toward Acacia. "I know what's wrong with her, and I can heal her. But if you refuse to let me come, I cannot help, and she will surely die."

"But you're probably as heavy as both girls combined. I can't carry everyone."

"Gabriel," Acacia said. "Have no fear for my health. I have lived for thousands of years, and I am glad to go to my Lord. Our embrace has been delayed far too long. Take him and leave me to Glewlwyd's care."

Firming his jaw, Gabriel wagged his head. "I will not trade you for this mad scientist! I'd rather leave him here and have you die in my arms!"

"Then leave me," Shiloh said. "I'm not afraid to die."

A strong tremor raced across the ground, nearly knocking them from their feet. Gabriel grasped Acacia's arm and helped her stay balanced. "We can't keep arguing. I'm carrying Acacia and Shiloh, and that's the end of it."

"Then more will perish," Mardon said, shaking his fist. "Sapphira has identical genetics, so she will suffer the same fate Acacia does unless you take me to her."

His words hit Gabriel like a hammer. How could he let both Oracles waste away like this? These twin beacons couldn't be allowed to fade. No! It just couldn't happen!

"Gabriel," Shiloh said softly as she eased up to him. "Take Mardon and Acacia. After you jump into the chasm, I will wait two minutes and follow. When you land safely, fly back up and catch me."

"But what if I can't—"

"You will catch me." She laid her head against his chest. "I trust you with all my heart."

Gabriel drew in his lower lip. How could he let her take such a risk? Impossible! Yet, there seemed to be no choice. He had to trade one impossible situation for another.

Laying a hand on the back of her head, he whispered, "I'll do it. Your faith in me is beyond anything I have ever seen."

After getting directions from Glewlwyd, Gabriel flew Acacia to the chasm and waited near the edge for Mardon and Shiloh to arrive. In the distance, the muscular unicorn galloped across the expanse of green, a magnificent sight.

Another tremor shook the ground. Again Gabriel held Acacia in place. As he grasped her shoulders, the reality of her emaciated state crushed his heart. She was so thin, so frail. How much life could be left in this broken jar of clay?

As if sensing his dismay, Acacia turned and, staring at him with her still brilliant blue eyes, spoke with firm resolve. "Fear not, Gabriel. Although I am now but dust in the wind, I still have one gift remaining that I might yet use to great purpose in Second Eden."

"What gift? And how will you use it?"

"The gift will remain my secret. How I will use it, I do not yet know, but I assume when the opportunity presents itself, I will recognize it."

An even stronger quake rocked the earth. Acacia's legs gave way, but Gabriel caught her and lifted her into his arms. He beat his wings and hovered in place, now immune to the unstable ground.

A loud groan sounded from across the chasm, a low, creaking grumble of rocks grinding against rocks.

Acacia whispered in his ear. "There is a portal here. It's making me sicker than ever. But my eyesight is sharp, and it appears that the other side of this chasm is coming this way."

"The chasm is closing?"

"Not quickly, but steadily." She seemed ready to say something else, but she just leaned her head against him and sighed.

When Shiloh and Mardon arrived, they dismounted and stood with their feet spread apart. Shiloh petted the unicorn and pointed in the direction they had come. "Cornelius, wait here for Glewlwyd. He'll figure out how to get you to safety. And thank you for allowing Mardon to ride."

As the unicorn's head bobbed, Gabriel studied the splendid creature. The legends revealed that they couldn't be ridden by anyone but a virtuous maiden. Apparently Cornelius was willing to make an exception for Mardon.

Gabriel elevated to about three feet off the ground. "Mardon, you'll have to hang on to my legs, but you'd better hang on tight, because we'll be dropping like a rock. I won't put on the brakes until I see the ground."

Mardon wrapped his arms around Gabriel's legs. "I am ready."

As he rose higher and lifted Mardon, he looked at Shiloh. She blew him a kiss, but, straining against Mardon's weight, he could return only a grimacing smile.

Flapping his wings mightily, he drifted over the chasm. Mardon trembled and squeezed so tightly, Gabriel's legs ached. The chasm groaned again, and now the narrowing of the gap was easy to see. The bridge drooped farther, and rocks tumbled in from either side. Shiloh crouched to keep her balance. The quake was really rocking this world now.

Gabriel took a deep breath. It was time to go for it. He lunged horizontally, then folded in his wings. Instantly, they plunged. Mardon's weight eased, though his death grip continued. Acacia buried her face in Gabriel's shirt, but she showed no other signs of fear.

As the wall on each side raced by, rushing air whistled in Gabriel's ears. He tried to breathe, but the wind snatched away most of any mouthful he could grab.

Soon, their surroundings grew dark, too dark to see the walls, much less any sign of ground below. Would he be able to see it in time? Even if he could, would he be able to grab the hurricane-like wind and put the brakes on three hurtling bullets?

After a minute or so, the darkness faded, and they floated for a moment in a clear blue sky before descending once again. Although they dropped quickly, that brief pause seemed to start the process over again, so the plunge wasn't as fast as it had been earlier.

Acacia whispered, "I see the ground, but it's still far away."

"Yep. I'd better start slowing down now." He let his wings out a few inches at a time and tried to catch a slowly increasing amount of air. The wind beat against the webbing, and everything heated up, from his toes to his face to the tips of his wings.

The ground drew closer. He stretched his wings farther. The blast of air lessened, and Mardon's weight seemed to increase until he felt three times as heavy as before. Acacia sagged in Gabriel's arms. Fingernails dug into his legs. Pain flooded every limb.

Gabriel gritted his teeth. He had to make it. There just wasn't any choice. Letting out a loud groan, he spread his wings fully. The raging wind ripped against his canopy. Agony shot from his wings to his spine. Below, Mardon screamed and dug his nails farther in.

Finally, just a few hundred feet above the ground, they slowed. His wings aching, Gabriel swung the trio into a controlled, spiral fall until they landed in a muddy field. Mardon dragged on the ground for a few seconds until he let go and slid in the mud. Then, settling his own feet, Gabriel lowered Acacia gently to the ground.

"I'll be right back," he said, stretching out his wings again. "Wait for me here."

He shot up into the sky. As he rose higher and higher, he searched the blue ceiling, desperately trying to spot the tiniest speck, the slightest hint of a plunging human body. Of course, the greater the elevation, the better chance he had of slowing her down enough to prevent injury, but since she would be plummeting at an enormous rate, and he would be ascending, timing their meeting would take incredible precision. Fortunately, the physics of Earth didn't match the rules here, and the brief pause would likely work in their favor. Otherwise, he would have no chance of catching Shiloh. She would be dropping much too quickly.

Once he reached about five thousand feet in the air, he caught a glimpse of a speck much farther above. It had to be Shiloh.

He hovered for a moment, trying to gauge her rate of descent. Stretching out his wings, he used them as a parachute and descended slowly. As Shiloh approached, he drew them in a little at a time until he dropped in a feet-first plunge. She had spread her arms and legs, slowing her descent just enough to match his.

When she came within a hundred feet, her face clarified, wide-eyed and flushed. He reached up for her. She reached back, her fingers groping.

Slowly, the gap decreased. Gabriel glanced down. The muddy field rushed toward them. Acacia was already easy to see, her white hair a beacon of danger.

Gabriel let out his wings another inch. Shiloh dropped into his arms. Stretching out fully, he slammed on the brakes. Again, agony shot up and down his spine. The base of his wings strained against his back, feeling as though they might rip away.

Finally, his feet slammed into the mud. The soft turf absorbed some of the momentum, but as he rolled, he couldn't keep Shiloh from getting a face full of sloppy soil.

When they came to a stop, he helped her up. Her face, chest, and arms were covered with mud.

"I'm so sorry." He tried to wipe her cheeks with his sleeve but managed only to smear more dirt.

Shiloh laughed. In fact, she laughed so hard she couldn't speak. She wrapped her arms around Gabriel's waist and buried her face in his muddy shirt.

He laughed with her, feeling light and carefree, but only for a moment. As wonderful as it felt to land safely, they had to figure out what they should do next.

He set his hand on the back of her head and looked at Acacia and Mardon. "So, where are we?"

Acacia stooped next to a strange plant. With two big leaves pressed against each other and a lump in between, it seemed to be praying. "This is the birthing garden where once-dead people are given new bodies for life in Second Eden."

"I guess that means we made it. Is anyone hurt?"

"I'm fine." Acacia straightened. "How about you?"

After breaking his embrace with Shiloh, Gabriel pulled up a pant leg, revealing a long, deep gash. "It looks worse than it feels."

"If anyone cares," Mardon said as he tucked something away under his tunic, "I am unharmed."

Gabriel eyed Mardon. It was better not to trust even his slightest movements. "What are you hiding?"

"I am hiding nothing." Mardon withdrew the object, a long strand of white hair. "I persuaded Acacia to give it to me so that I may confirm my theory about her illness."

"You can tell what's wrong from her hair?"

"And from the skin cells still attached. I believe her genetic structure has been altered. This will be sufficient."

Gabriel offered an approving nod. What could it hurt? Maybe he could help Acacia and Sapphira. He looked around at the surrounding field and bordering walls and forest. "So if we can find a place to clean up, maybe—"

"Oh, my!" Acacia jumped up and away from the plant.

Behind the two praying leaves, a bright rectangular light flashed, like sunlight shining through a window. As the rectangle grew, its edges drawing away from the center, its brilliance dimmed, and a transparent circle took shape at the focal point, growing at the same rate the entire box expanded.

After a few seconds, it looked like an enormous sheet of glass, easy to see through, like a window into another world. On the other side, a stooped old man and a unicorn appeared, standing in a room that looked like an old library.

Shiloh clapped her hands. "Glewlwyd and Cornelius! They're safe!"

Glewlwyd bowed. He moved his lips to speak, but no sound came through. As he straightened, his stoop disappeared, his face smoothed out, and his hair filled in, turning from white to brown.

Gabriel bowed in return. He reached a hand toward the window, but a sharp tingle made him draw it back. "I guess we can't go that way."

"Is that Heaven's Gate?" Mardon asked.

Touching her chin, Acacia studied it. "When I last saw it, it was blue, but I recognize that room. It's the antechamber that leads to the altar. Since the Bridgelands are likely gone now, maybe it's the same gate."

Gabriel stared at the barrier. The chamber faded away, as did the man and unicorn, leaving a transparent glass-like sheet. Glare from the sunshine provided the only hint that it was there at all. Now the back of the garden came into view, as if the gateway to another world had become a window.

"We should go to the village," Acacia said as she pointed toward a forest on the other side of a field. "It's just beyond those trees. We can get cleaned up and find someone to look at the scratches on your legs."

Gabriel looked at his filthy body. Acacia was right about cleaning up, but it was more important to get Mardon's research going than to get a doctor to look at a few scratches. With only a strand of hair and some skin cells providing clues, Mardon might need help in figuring out what was wrong with Acacia. Could Ashley provide what he needed? Maybe. Certainly by now she would have advanced the technology in this world.

"Okay. Let's go." Walking between Shiloh and Acacia, he took their hands and headed toward the trees. Mardon followed quietly. As Gabriel glanced back at the dirty, scarred mad scientist, a tingle ran up his spine. Maybe trusting him was a mistake, but there seemed to be no choice. Acacia was dying, and saving her was all that mattered.

CHAPTER 14

THE CALM BEFORE THE STORM

Billy lay on a hospital bed, a proper bed with sheets and a blanket, far better than the cots in the old triage hut. A leather bandage wrapped around his ribcage several times, covering his otherwise bare chest. After pushing the blanket down to his toes and stripping to thin, pajama-like trousers, he had done all he could to stay cool. For some reason, the room had grown much too warm.

Underneath his arm bandage, sweat stung his wound. That was by far the deeper of the two cuts, but the spear didn't rip any tendons, so it would heal fine.

Ashley bustled in, carrying a thin stack of parchments and a feather pen. After scratching a few marks on the top page, she smiled. "Are you ready to check out?"

"You bet." Billy sat up. "Only five hours in a hospital. That has to be a new record."

"The record is the temperature outside. My homemade thermometer says thirty-two degrees Celsius."

He half closed an eye. "So that's about ninety Fahrenheit?"

"Very good. It's eighty-nine point six, but my meter isn't exactly precise, so give or take a couple of degrees."

He let out a whistle. "The locals must be roasting."

"They are, especially the sick ones." She poked his shoulder with her finger. "That's why I want you out. You got a few hours' sleep. That should be enough for a warrior like you."

He gave her a thankful smile. "What's the rush?"

"We're taking the hospital back into the air. It should be cooler up there, and if the new army shows up, everyone will be safer."

A knock sounded at the door, and a sweet voice sang out, "I have something for you." Bonnie walked in with a bundle of clothes, his village battle uniform. As her wings waved at him, she patted the top of her pile. "All clean and ready for my warrior."

Billy reached for her hand. Her own uniform looked sharp, obviously freshly laundered, though a rip in her right sleeve revealed that she hadn't had time to mend it. The scratch on her cheek was already healing nicely. Although it probably wouldn't leave a scar, it made her look like the sword maiden she was.

He caressed her knuckles, causing her to grimace. "Oh. Sorry." He looked at her hand. A deep gash ran across her knuckles from her index finger to her pinky.

She pulled her hand back and examined her wound. "It's not bad. Just superficial. But I didn't want a bandage. I need to keep my fingers free."

"I don't blame you. A sword maiden needs her hands to be unbound."

Smiling, she showed him her other hand. "And I hope you don't mind. I moved the engagement ring for now. It irritates the wound."

"I don't mind at all."

She touched the bandage on his arm. "How's your wound?"

Billy nodded at Ashley. "Better ask the doctor."

"It's pretty deep, but he'll be fine." Ashley took the clothes from Bonnie and tossed them on Billy's legs. "Get up, tiger. Bonnie and I'll meet you outside."

Giving him a wave and a smile, Bonnie spun on her toes and hurried to the door with a bounce in her step. When the door closed, Billy got up and put on his long-sleeved undershirt. Wearing all three layers would be warm, but necessary. The second layer, the metallic shirt, would chafe his skin without protection, and the tighter over-tunic held everything in place.

When he pulled up the uniform's green pants and tucked in the shirt, a loud knock sounded. He buckled his belt and called, "Come in."

The door swung open, and Bonnie ran through. Alarm filled her eyes. "They're coming!"

"Goliath's army?" Billy threw the mail shirt over his head and pulled it down.

She nodded briskly. "Your father was on patrol and saw them leaving the marsh."

"Did he describe them?"

"They look like something out of a history book; Romans from Caesar's time, Egyptians from the days of Moses, Chinese from an ancient dynasty, and they have full armor, horses, and chariots."

Billy stuffed his head through his tunic and thrust the hem down his torso. As he looked into her wide eyes, he spoke in a calm tone. "How many?"

"Two hundred, maybe. But that might be just the first wave. They're not marching very fast, but they could be here in about forty-five minutes."

"Let's move!" Billy grabbed his sword belt, Excalibur still attached, and swung it around his waist. As he buckled it on, they hurried through the hospital's long hallway. "Were they wearing cloaks like the Vacants had?"

"No," she said as she jogged at his side, "but your father said they seemed to be coated with something reddish, like powder."

"Rust." He burst through the double exit doors, held one for a moment while Bonnie hurried through, then ran across the dragon landing platform. Taking Bonnie's hand, he leaped to the ground three feet below, bypassing a makeshift stairway.

"Hey! Wait up!" Walter jumped down and joined them. "Ashley sprung me from the hospital. I'm ready to roll."

"Did you hear about the army?" Billy asked.

Walter shrugged. "What's a few hundred historically misplaced soldiers? They won't even speak the same language. They have to be as confused as a herd of cows landing on Mars."

"Charging bulls, maybe, but good point. We'll see." Together, all three dashed into the village. When they reached the central circle, Valiant, Elam, and Sapphira stood next to the bell, each wearing full battle gear as well as somber faces. With the bell still and silent, they obviously hadn't sounded an alarm.

"Where's everyone else?" Billy asked.

Flexing his forearm, Elam strangled the hilt of the sword protruding from its hip scabbard. "Sick or helping with the sick. It looks like Ashley was right. Only the Second Edeners are getting it. They don't seem to be immune like we are."

"We're guessing it's a bug from Earth," Sapphira said.

Elam took Sapphira's hand. "We speculated that it came with the rubellite Billy's mother sent. The timing would be about right."

"A bug actually on the gem?" Billy shook his head. "That doesn't make sense. It would have to survive exposure and then a trip through a fiery wall."

"Or maybe," Elam said, "a certain witch introduced the virus through one of her witch's brews."

Billy shifted his weight from one foot to the other. Elam was probably right again. Semiramis had been following a plan from day one, and this disease was likely just part of the scheme. The huge army they were building proved that she didn't need Flint or his people. They were pawns, and their sickness provided a way to spread the virus, both through the shadow people and through the survivors in Flint's village. Ruth's illness had been short-lived and her symptoms were quite different, so that seemed unrelated. This was definitely biological warfare.

"No matter who brought it," Elam continued, "it's here, and we have to deal with it. Since most of our villagers have it, the remaining healthy women and children are taking care of the sick. Valiant is one of the few Second Eden warriors left standing."

"Candle will join us soon," Sapphira said. "He's flying the plane to get an update on troop count and movements, and Yereq and Sir Barlow are at the field by the birthing garden waiting for him to return."

Billy imagined a thundering horde stampeding toward the little village—iron chariots, charging horses, and savages with blood-thirsty hearts. "That's just not enough," he said. "How can we possibly defeat so many?"

Lifting a hand, Valiant looked up at the clear sunny sky. "Only by faith. Without help from above we are doomed. Listener is organizing a prayer vigil in the hospital. When Candle returns, we will gather and send our prayers into the sky as an appeal to the Father of Lights."

"So we have . . ." Walter lifted his fingers in rapid succession. "Me, Elam, Billy, Bonnie, Valiant, Candle, Yereq, Sir Barlow, and Sapphira. That's nine of us and the dragons." He let out a whistle. "I don't know about you, but if we're facing hundreds of crazed warriors trained to kill, I'd like at least ten."

"You got it!" Ashley strode toward them wearing an oversized battle uniform and clutching the hilt of a sword at her belt. Stopping at Walter's side, she squared her shoulders. "I'm not as skilled as any of you, but I've sparred enough with Walter."

Walter grinned. "I won't argue with that!"

She nudged him playfully with an elbow. "Don't get me started."

"What about the patients?" Bonnie asked.

"They have Doc, Patrick, Ruth, Steadfast, Marilyn, and Listener taking care of them," Ashley said, "and one very interesting addition. It turns out that Hunter is really Mardon, the crazy scientist who tried to bring Heaven and Earth together. It's a long story, but Gabriel met him while trying to find Shiloh and Acacia. Gabriel's body has been restored, and he brought all three back here."

Sapphira nearly leaped off her feet. "Acacia's here?"

Ashley nodded toward the hospital. "She's here, but she's not well. She has some sort of degenerative disease." She touched Sapphira's arm tenderly. "I don't think she'll last much longer. Doc's working with Mardon to figure out what's going on. If anyone can solve the puzzle, I think they will."

"We can't trust Mardon," Elam said. "He's been posing as Hunter and working with Semiramis for years. You can bet that he'll use his research against us. He just wants to get into Heaven by force."

Ashley laughed under her breath. "Believe me, Patrick and Marilyn already accused him of every crime in the book. He claims that he has always loved the two Oracles, and he won't betray them. There are plenty of people in the hospital to watch his every move."

Sapphira looked up at Elam, tears brimming. "Isn't there any way we can let him try? If he can save Acacia, then maybe we can stop him from doing anything else."

Tightening his jaw, Elam gazed at Sapphira for several seconds. It seemed that a battle was raging in his mind, a struggle between judgment and mercy. Finally, he nodded. "Only if Acacia stays away from him."

"Don't worry about that," Ashley said. "Gabriel won't let him touch her. Mardon has a strand of Acacia's hair to work with, and that's all he'll get. But it should be enough. He and Doc will use my lab equipment in the hospital, and they'll be floating high above the village while Gabriel, Shiloh, and Acacia stay here."

"So, where is Acacia now?" Sapphira asked.

"Getting cleaned up. Shiloh's helping her in the ladies' washroom, while Marilyn's patching up Gabriel. He got some nasty-looking scratches on his legs."

"Did my mother ever get to talk to my father?" Billy asked.

Bonnie touched his arm. "While we were rescuing Walter."

"I was there," Elam said. "It was pretty good. I think you could call their interaction 'subdued joy,' but they talked more about you than each other."

Biting his lip, Billy nodded. He could picture the scene. Mom hadn't seen Dad in almost five years, and now he was a dragon again. They probably just looked at each other while they talked, both aching to embrace. But the scales-on-skin contact would have been like acid, a reminder that they were still worlds apart. Mom's love was still as strong as ever, but the blend of joy and pain had to be tearing her heart in two.

"Anyway," Ashley continued, "back to the original topic. We weren't able to isolate the bug, but I mixed up an elixir that might help. There's really not much more I can do. Doc knows more about cell structures and medicines than I do." She curled her arm around Walter's. "And I want to be with my fiancé. Someone has to watch his back."

"I'm glad to have you with me," Walter said, "but I'm afraid I might be watching out for you more than fighting the bad guys."

She raised a finger near his eyes. "If you do, I'll kick you in the backside. And if you're going to die, I'm coming with you. You're not going to Heaven without me."

Walter raised his hands. "I wouldn't dream of it."

"Besides," Ashley said, "I have to make sure our fuel trap works."

"Are we sticking with Candle flying the plane?" Billy asked. "If their troops are protected with rust, Excalibur won't do much good, so maybe I should fly it."

Elam touched the hilt of his sword. "We still need Excalibur in the battle. Maybe some of the enemy won't be as protected as others. Windor's sick, but he still wants to be the bombardier for Candle, so we'll go with the original plan."

"Good thing they didn't bring Nazis with machine guns and tanks," Walter said. "I'm not sure who's in Hades, but you've got to figure some of them were."

"So, where are the dragons?" Billy asked.

Elam nodded toward the northeast. "They're lining up along the village border. Since most of our dragon riders are sick, we'll have to fill in. Dikaios is with the dragons, and he's supposed to meet us with a new report soon."

"Sounds good," Billy said. "We'll just have to do the best we can."

"Let's get moving." Elam gripped Billy's elbow and led him down the street. "There's something I have to show you, something strange in the garden."

As the others followed, Billy tried to read Elam's face. "Have you taken care of the plants?"

"All but the one I planted. Before he got sick, Windor dug them up and hauled a lot of the soil to the new garden in the hospital." Elam broke into a jog. "You'll have to see what I mean."

Billy kept pace. Behind him, the sounds of running footsteps echoed in the empty village. When they reached the field, now completely free of snow and basking in warm sunshine, they slowed to negotiate the mixture of mud and grass. Yereq and Sir Barlow stood at the far end of the field, looking up at the sky. The low buzz of a propeller sounded from somewhere, signaling Candle's approach. With the snow gone and the mud drying, his landing wouldn't be as difficult as usual.

Ahead, something shimmered in the garden, a rectangular shape so large, it seemed to have no borders on either side or at the top.

Elam quick-marched along a furrow while Billy followed in the one next to it. With the plants gone, no one had to worry about tripping and hurting one of the babies.

Coming to a sudden stop a few paces away from the shining rectangle, Elam stretched out his hand and waved it over the light. "It's like a force field. It tingles when I get close, so I wasn't sure if I should touch it. It reminds me of the wall I saw at the Bridgelands, but it was blue there, and you couldn't see through it. This one's transparent."

Billy shielded his eyes. "It's like sunlight on water, almost blinding."

"And look at this." Elam pointed with the toe of his shoe. The only remaining birthing plant stood just inches in front of the base of the wall. The leaves, although green on the surface, emanated a reddish glow from within.

"Too close for comfort?" Billy asked.

"Right. Windor moved the others before this wall showed up. I told him to leave this one here, because I thought there might still be a chance of resurrecting Makaidos. I hope it's okay where it is."

When the others caught up, Sapphira stepped close to the force field. "It's a portal. I can sense it."

"Your eyesight?" Elam asked.

"My sight and the feeling of sorrow." She knelt next to the plant. "I can see inside this fragile shell. Our dear friend Makaidos is within, but unlike other unborns at this stage, he cannot survive without two essential catalysts that will give him life. We can provide one of those now." She looked up at Ashley. "Do you have the crystal egg I formed out of your father's tears?"

"Always." Ashley pulled a thin necklace and lifted a glassy egg from behind her tunic.

Sapphira extended her hand. "May I have it? This is the first catalyst."

"Of course." Ashley reached behind her neck, unfastened a clasp, and laid the necklace in Sapphira's palm. "Anything for my father."

"I hope I'm doing this correctly. Our teacher in the Valley of Souls had no egg to demonstrate with." Sapphira closed her fist around the crystal. For a few seconds, a flaming halo encircled her hand. When she spread out her fingers, the egg glowed with a blinding white light. Using a finger, she dug a shallow hole directly under the roots and pushed the egg in. As soon as she covered it over with soil, a stream of light crawled up the stem, as if an iridescent dye flowed vertically through its channels. When the stream flowed into the pair of leaves, they vibrated with a rhythmic beat.

Soon, the light faded, and the plant returned to normal. Sapphira petted the leaves softly. "I see a heart beating. Perhaps it was there before, but it's clear and strong now."

"What's the second catalyst?" Elam asked.

She rose to her feet, her expression sad and forlorn. "A sacrifice. Someone will have to give his or her life for Makaidos to be reborn. My teacher said that I must apply the blood of our willing victim to the plant's leaves."

"Who will it be? Has it already been planned?"

"Our teacher wouldn't tell us," Sapphira said. "It's hard to explain, but, in the Valley of Souls, the concept of planning is very strange."

A ripple of light ran across the wall, and a voice sounded as if echoing the tremors of energy. "The lamb has been preparing for this sacrifice for many years, though he or she does not yet know it."

Directly behind the plant, a vertical line of dazzling light split the wall. A leg protruded, then an arm. Finally, a man appeared. He stepped around the plant and stood with his arms crossed over his Second Eden-style leather tunic and breeches. His white hair and thin white beard dressed him with many years, but his sparkling eyes told of youthful vigor.

"Father Enoch!" Sapphira hugged him around the waist. "It's wonderful to see you again!"

He laid a palm on the back of her head. "And you, dear child."

"It's good to see you again," Elam said, shaking Enoch's hand. "I assume you're aware of the coming army."

"Indeed. And you are ill prepared. They outnumber you at least a hundred to one."

"A hundred to one!" Elam looked at each member of his company. Billy read Elam's dismay. It felt like a stab in the gut. All of their planning now seemed like spitting into a hurricane.

"They are still gathering their forces," Enoch continued. "Many have been summoned from a great distance, and Arramos, whom I will now call by his real name, Satan, has timed their arrival for this date and hour."

"Why do they need so many to conquer two little villages like ours?" Elam asked.

"Oh, they haven't assembled this army to conquer you." Enoch spread out his arms and called out. "Gather around, everyone, and I will explain. We can take the time, for I must give you a solemn charge."

Yereq, Sir Barlow, and Candle, who had been standing at the edge of the garden, walked toward them. Billy, Bonnie, Walter, Ashley, Elam,

Sapphira, and Valiant formed a semicircle in front of Enoch, leaving room for the three others to join in.

Enoch touched the wall, raising a bright light around the outline of his hand. "The army has come to attack Heaven itself. The alliance with Flint was merely a vehicle, a stepping-stone of sorts. Satan often uses willing fools in his quest to bring down Heaven's throne. He makes them feel important for a time, then casts them down when they are no longer needed. Now the evil one finally has the means to attack Heaven's Gate with the legions of warrior slaves he has collected throughout history."

"So is this the same Heaven's Gate I saw in the Bridgelands?" Elam asked.

"It is. The Bridgelands were nothing more than a buffer that separated the realms of Earth, Hades, and Second Eden. When the realms joined, the buffer collapsed and brought all three to Heaven's doorstep. The single world now is a blend of three realities. Because of the temperature, my guess is that where we are standing is a temperate or subtropical zone on Earth, and the residents there have been forced from their usual abode and must find a suitable habitat. Fortunately for us, we blended into Earth's environment in a zone that was inhabited by very few humans."

"Do we have other Earth dwellers here now?" Elam asked.

"And Hades dwellers. Except for this barrier to Heaven, all portals have been destroyed. There is no limit to travel between the realms."

Billy looked at the wall at the east side of the birthing garden, the only barricade separating them from the advancing army. "Are you going to send warriors from Heaven that'll mow down the forces of Hades?"

Enoch pulled Billy's sword from its scabbard and lifted it high. Even in the bright sunshine, its glow created a brilliant aura. "We have thousands of angels, and they could wipe out this horde in short order, but that will not be God's way. Since Satan is bringing an army of his followers and not his demonic host, Jehovah wishes to counter with his own servants and not with his angelic advantage." He slid the sword back into the scabbard, extinguishing its glow. "Those who live by faith are always more powerful than those who live by sword and sinew."

Billy again imagined the attacking army, hundreds and hundreds of warriors armed to the teeth. "I guess it makes sense, but I don't see what's wrong with having a few angels on our side."

"Angels on your side?" Enoch chuckled. "I suppose you could say that. Although they are neither Cherubim nor Seraphim, the two faithful witnesses who felled the giants' tower to Heaven are working behind the scenes to help you in whatever way they can." He added a wink. "In fact, I think you know them, an especially spunky redhead and a petite songstress. Although they cannot come out here for the battle, they are at this very moment behind that wall planning their strategy."

Billy looked at Ashley standing near the end of their semicircle. Her broad smile said it all. She knew who the redhead was, her sister Karen. And Elam's melancholy expression revealed his recognition of the songstress Naamah.

"So what do we do?" Elam asked.

"Defend this gate. Repel the attackers. Take courage, knowing that you have been prepared for such a time as this, and even if some of you die in battle, you will not be forsaken. You will simply pass through this barrier and take your place with the saints who cheer you on from that side of eternity." Enoch raised a finger. "And there is one more issue. It is crucial that you bring Flint to the battlefield. Jehovah wants him to see what his decisions have wrought."

Elam nodded at Sir Barlow. "Will you see to that?"

"With pleasure." Barlow lumbered toward the village.

"Now," Enoch said as he stepped back toward the wall, "I must leave you in order to advise our two angels." He paused and looked at the plant, a sad expression sagging his features. "Until the lamb comes to complete the sacrifice, you will likely suffer great losses. Pray that she comes soon."

With that, he turned and disappeared through the split in the wall. Then, as if closed by a zipper, the line sealed from bottom to top.

Billy glanced at Bonnie, then at everyone else. Had they picked up the clue? Enoch said, "She." Who could be the female who would act as a sacrifice that would bring Makaidos back to life?

Bonnie whispered into his ear. "It's better not to guess. Let the one who is called do what she must do."

A low hum sounded from the village. Above the trees, the hospital rose slowly into the sky. With the sun shining on its metallic shell, the glint blinded them for a moment, but when it turned and continued to ascend, the luster faded. Soon, it shrank to the size of a mechanical pencil.

Elam locked wrists with Valiant. "Are you ready, my friend?"

"I will be, after we pray." Valiant's muscular forearm rippled as he firmed his grip with Elam. "With the enemy closing in, a moment in prayer will feel like another layer of armor."

From the forest near the village, two figures appeared, Barlow with his arm around Flint. As the two drew closer, Elam faced Heaven's Gate and lowered himself to his knees. The others joined him in another semicircle. Forming a chain of hands, Elam on one end and Valiant on the other, they waited for Barlow to arrive.

Billy looked at Bonnie. Kneeling with her at Heaven's Gate felt like the fulfillment of the greatest dream of all time. Someday, when their engagement time reached its climax, they would kneel at an altar of marriage, but could it ever match this heavenly altar?

When Barlow and Flint arrived, Candle released Walter's hand at the middle of the line. Barlow knelt, took Candle's hand, and looked up at Flint, who stood shakily. "There is always room for one more," Barlow said.

Crossing his arms, Flint offered a timid shake of his head and stepped back a few paces. "I am ill, and I don't want to infect Candle or Valiant."

"Very well." Barlow grasped Walter's hand and closed the line.

At the end of the row on Billy's left, Valiant lifted a hand and called out in a loud, vibrant voice. "Father of Lights, creator of all, hear our plea. We kneel at the doorstep of Paradise and ask you to grant us more strength than we have in our muscles, more courage than we feel in our hearts, and more endurance than our feeble arms and legs now possess. We are humbled by your confidence in us, that you would deem us worthy to suffer, bleed, and die for the sake of defending your glory. Although you could sweep this rabble away with a breath, you have blessed us with this great honor. Let us be your breath. Let us be your might. Let us be your hand of wrath upon your enemy."

Valiant took a deep breath and continued in a softer, gentler tone. "And let us be your hand of mercy as we extend your grace to Flint, an offer of forgiveness if he would only turn from his rebellious ways and allow himself to be embraced by your love."

Billy sneaked a look at Flint. He kept his stare locked on the eastern wall, shaking in spite of the warmth.

Lowering his hand, Valiant ended with a quiet, "Let this prayer be answered according to your wisdom, by which we all strive to live."

Bonnie whispered, "Amen." Several others echoed with quiet amens of their own.

Pulling on each other's hands, they rose as one. Valiant walked over to Elam and grasped his upper arm. "Warrior Chief, the command is yours."

Elam looked around at his little army, his muscles flexing and his eyes flashing. "Candle, are the bombs ready?"

The teenager's dark face lit up with a brilliant smile. "They are on the airplane. Windor is aboard. He was too sick to come out."

"Get in the air. One or more of the dragon riders will guide your bombing runs." Now animated in his delivery, Elam thrust a finger toward Ashley. "Is the fuel apparatus ready?"

She nodded. "We'll burn the whole village before we'll let them into the garden."

"Excellent." Elam grabbed Barlow's hand with both of his. "My good friend and noble knight, are you ready to go to battle on a dragon?"

Barlow's smile lifted his mustache. "By all means! May I ride on my old friend Legossi?"

Deepening his voice to mimic the knight, Elam said, "By all means!" Adding a laugh, he pointed toward the village. "You go ahead of us and tell the dragons that we'll be there soon. They're probably getting anxious by now."

While Barlow hurried away, Elam paced back and forth in front of the others. "When the enemy comes within reach, Billy will try Excalibur's beam. When he has done all he can with it, he will ride Clefspeare into battle. Walter will ride on Firedda, Ashley on Thigocia, Bonnie on Hartanna, Valiant on Yellinia, and I will take Sorentine. Remember to watch for weakness in the dragons. That would indicate that the enemy has candlestones, and we will have to call off our dragon cavalry. And remember this. If your dragon falls to that evil gem, and you survive the fall, but the dragon is incapacitated, you must leave the dragon and hurry back here to help with guarding Heaven's Gate. There is nothing more important. Our dragon friends will understand."

Billy gauged everyone's expression. Bonnie, in particular, grimaced at the thought of leaving her mother behind, but they all seemed to understand that this strategy was necessary.

"Sapphira will stay on the ground," Elam continued, "and ride Dikaios to light the fires when the enemy gets close enough to our trap. Yereq will stand here at the wall as the final guard. Any enemy who gets past our defenses will have to face him."

He stopped pacing and, with a serious bend in his brow, faced his troops. "Any questions?"

"I have one." Bonnie pointed at the forest near the village. "What are we going to do with her?"

Like a timid deer, Listener peeked out from behind a tree. Dressed in the village's battle uniform, she walked slowly toward them, her head low and the spyglass in her grip. With sleeves and pant legs overlapping her hands and boots, she looked like a soldier who had shrunk while wearing her clothes.

Bonnie whispered, but her voice was loud enough for everyone to hear. "I know what she's doing."

"The lamb?" Elam asked.

Bonnie nodded. "At least she thinks she is. She overheard me talking to Sapphira about the need of a sacrifice to resurrect Makaidos. Since she feels like she should have died in his place, she wants to be the one."

As Listener approached, the image of her nearly lifeless body on the surgery cot came back to Billy's mind. During those torturous hours, everyone had worked so hard to keep this precious girl alive. Makaidos had given his own life in her place, choosing flames and forfeiture of his soul to let her live.

Billy shook his head. No way. There was no way he would let her die now.

"Bonnie," he said, keeping his own voice low, "can you fly her up to the hospital?"

"I can try, but—"

"No time," Elam said. "We have to go to war. And, besides, the choice of the lamb isn't our business."

Billy gritted his teeth. Like Valiant had said earlier, they were going to battle for little girls like this. How could they let her die now?

Dikaios galloped out of the forest. When he caught up with Listener, he stopped, helped her climb to his back, and carried her to the garden.

"Their army is now complete," Dikaios said when he arrived. "Clefspeare estimates at least nine hundred armed men, perhaps a thousand, along with two hundred horses and fifty chariots. He expects them to arrive within fifteen minutes."

Elam looked into the horse's eyes. "My good friend, when we met in the Bridgelands, did you know that we would be facing such an army together?"

"No, Elam. I was called to serve my master, and that is all I need to know. If I must sacrifice limb or life, I do so gladly, for there is no greater joy than to die in my master's hands."

"Well stated." Elam looked down and dragged his shoe across the drying mud. He seemed ready to speak again, but he just sighed and whispered, "Well stated."

"I have come to help Timothy resurrect," Listener said from atop Dikaios. She sucked in a breath and squared her shoulders. "I can fight almost as well as Candle. I promise not to die on purpose."

Billy turned away. Watching that girl's determined, yet piteous expression would make him laugh or cry, or maybe both at the same time.

"Let her come with me," Sapphira said to Elam. "She can help me set the fires. We certainly can't leave her alone in the village."

"I guess that will have to do." His face melancholy, Elam looked at Billy. "I'm going now. You have a couple of minutes if you need more time with your friends."

Billy nodded. "Yeah. Thanks."

Elam stood face to face with Sapphira. She looked up at him, her eyes moist. He looked back at her. They neither moved nor spoke.

Billy slid his hand into Bonnie's. He could feel the heartache. Elam and Sapphira had waited thousands of years to come together, often in the abyss of loneliness. Now they had to separate once more, and who could tell if one or both of them might die in battle?

Elam lifted his hand and wiggled his fingers. A tear emerged from Sapphira's eye. A spasm shook her body, and as she wiggled her own fingers, she broke into sobs, but she didn't say a word.

Turning abruptly, Elam signaled for Valiant. They each took one of Flint's arms and marched him out of the garden.

Bonnie embraced Sapphira and kissed the top of her head, then, with Ashley's help, boosted her onto Dikaios's back with Listener. Without a word, Dikaios turned and trotted away.

Walter clapped Billy on the shoulder. "You ready?"

"I think so." Billy gripped Excalibur's hilt and looked around. Yereq stood in front of the plant, his feet set firmly and his arms locked over his chest. The great giant was now the only one in the garden besides Billy, Walter, Bonnie, and Ashley.

"We'd better go." Billy reached for Bonnie's hand. "How about you? Are you ready?"

Her eyes a blend of sadness and determination, she nodded. "I am."

Walter pulled Billy and Ashley closer, and Bonnie joined them in a tight circle. "Listen, guys," Walter said with a shot of confidence in his voice. "This is just like old times, the four of us fighting the bad guys. We've battled the forces of Hades before; we can do it again." He put his hand in the middle of their huddle, palm down. "If you don't believe we're going to win this thing, then don't join your hand with mine. But if you think that the God who took us to Hades and back is going to help us kick these guys' butts, then let's see it."

Ashley laid her hand on top of his. "I believe it with all my heart!"

Bonnie's hand came next. "Whether I live or die, I am the Lord's, and he will win the battle."

Billy looked at each set of joyous eyes. What faith! What sincerity! They exuded the overflowing confidence they had been learning through all their incredible adventures. And now, when called to face almost certain death, they showed no hint of hesitation. How could any army, no matter how great, conquer a God who could instill such supernatural courage in his soldiers, no matter how few?

Billy laid his hand on top. He then set his other hand underneath and pressed the layers closer. Reaching for the same confident tone, he let his gaze pass across each face. "Nothing will ever separate us, neither life, nor death, nor the armies of Hell. If I don't see you again on this side of the heavenly wall, I will see you on the other."

CHAPTER 15

THE INVASION

Billy stood next to Clefspeare. Both stared into the northeastern field, the same field where they had battled the shadow people.

In the daylight, everything seemed so different—bright, cheery, almost peaceful. Yes, *almost.* Billy's danger alarm was already burning in his stomach. A rise in the landscape prevented them from seeing beyond a half mile or so, but a low rumble from somewhere in the distance agreed with the alarm. Something big was on its way.

Hartanna's recent surveillance report had said that a marauding army was now marching faster and would crest the rise in less than three minutes. Chariots rolled in the front line along with dozens of bowmen and spearmen. The war they had awaited these four years was now upon them.

Billy lifted Excalibur and let it glow. Hartanna had confirmed the rust coating on most of the troops, but not all had been protected. Maybe he could take out enough soldiers to slow them down, or at least spread a little panic.

Hiding in the forest at the left side of the field, Dikaios waited with Sapphira on his back. Nearby, Listener rode Ember, her pigtails swinging in the warm breeze as she carried an unlit torch in each hand. Dikaios pawed the ground with a hoof. The warrior horse was ready for action.

On the right side of the field, Ashley and Thigocia also hid among the trees. Ashley held a hose that led up into a tall evergreen where it split into several feeder tubes attached to bags of airplane fuel. In the other direction, the hose split again into a web of tubes that spread out over the field. Ashley had drilled tiny holes throughout the tubing network and laid it in the grass several weeks before she and Walter covered the field with the filament net. Now, with the net removed, the tubes would be ready for the attack.

With her hand on a valve, she waited for the right time to open it. Gravity would force the fuel into the tubes and spray both the ground and the invaders. Then she and Thigocia would take to the sky while Sapphira set everything ablaze. Her timing would have to be perfect.

Above, Merlin flew back and forth over the expanse between the fire trap and the rise. Candle and Windor were ready. The bombs would soon be falling.

To each side of Clefspeare, dragons had lined up in a row, leaving a gap of about ten paces between them. Bonnie sat atop Hartanna to their left, and Elam rode Sorentine to his right. To Elam's right, Walter sat high on Firedda's neck, his muscles flexed. He was ready to go to war. Beyond him, Sir Barlow rode Legossi. She had brought her head back toward him, and he was whispering something in her ear. Dragon and warrior grinned, both apparently in good humor.

To Billy's left, beyond Hartanna, Valiant rode Yellinia. Both were stoic, perhaps even sad. As many times as Valiant had gone to war, it seemed strange that he appeared to despise it so much. Such was the character of nobility—a hatred for violence, yet a willingness to perform it to protect the innocent from its jaws.

Billy tried to settle his heart. As soon as Excalibur disintegrated as many enemy troops as possible, the ground on which they all stood would erupt with dragons flying into battle.

Behind the line of dragons, Flint sat against a tree. Still very sick, his arms hung loosely at his sides. Obviously, he couldn't do anyone harm, and Elam and Valiant wanted him to witness the trouble his alliance with Goliath had caused. If the attacking army managed to break through, Flint would be at their mercy, though no one thought they would show him any.

In a cloud of dust, a chariot appeared at the top of the rise and halted. Two horses reared up and stomped the newly dried mud. Four other chariots joined the first, and the lead driver steered his horses to the side, allowing him to view the land ahead.

Billy clenched Excalibur. Just a few were in sight. It would be best to wait as long as possible. Besides, he had never tested the beam's power from this far away. Still, with the restored rubellite in the hilt, it would probably work.

The lead driver shouted. His horses wheeled the chariot around and charged. The other four pursued in a wild gallop. Like a rush of ants, men clad in dark armor swarmed over the rise and flooded the landscape, some on foot and some on horseback. Brown dust flew all around, masking their churning legs. At least three invaders stood taller than the others, the surviving Nephilim, and the oddly shaped heads of a few Vacants were obvious in the midst of the throng.

Elam drew his sword. "Billy, you may attack when ready."

As battle cries pounded his ears like a sonic hammer, Billy lit up Excalibur's beam and pointed it straight up. The horde's front line would be in the fuel trap in less than two minutes. It was time to thin them out.

A flutter of wings made him look back. Gabriel flew horizontally along the ground and settled between Billy and Elam. Dressed in the village's battle uniform, he withdrew a sword from a scabbard at his hip. "I'm reporting for duty."

"Excellent," Elam said. "We can always use another warrior."

"Warrior?" Gabriel waved his sword. "I have zero training, but I might be able to take someone out from the air."

"Where are Shiloh and Acacia?" Billy asked.

Gabriel pointed toward the village with his thumb. "Behind me. I told them to stay put, but I'm not sure they will. Acacia thinks she can muster up a little more fire, but—"

"No more time to talk." Billy angled the beam toward the rushing mass and swept it from right to left across the field. As soon as the beam made contact with a soldier, sparks flew. One man disappeared, but four surrounding him continued running, though the one following had to leap over the tumbling armor.

As if jumping from place to place, the sparks erupted in a ragged pattern. A horse vanished, sending its rider flying. Three men running side by side disintegrated, but the next five merely glowed red.

Finally, the last line charged over the rise. A lone man rode a horse at the top of the crest. Tall and dressed in black from head to toe, he stopped and watched the scene, apparently content to let the advance troops do the dirty work before he came to add to the carnage. His entire body seemed to sparkle in the sunlight, as if he had been painted with reflective powder instead of rust.

Two red dragons flew over his head, one half the size of the other. As they zoomed toward the village, a third dragon with tawny scales trailed them.

Billy swept the beam back across the invaders. More disappeared, but far fewer. Gaps dotted the black sea. The disintegrating laser made it seem as if a rain of arrows had fallen among them, taking out about a fourth of the troops—not nearly enough.

"I think that's all I can do." Billy ran up Clefspeare's tail and sat at the base of his neck. "Let's go!"

In a massive flurry of wings, six dragons lifted into the air. As Clefspeare rose in a tight circle, Billy tapped his jaw and shouted into the transmitter. "Candle! Make a bombing run!"

Elam called from Sorentine's back. "Tell him to take out the lead chariots!"

"Got it!" Billy kept his grip on his sword and clutched his father's spine. "Bomb the front row, Candle. Send the charioteers on a ride they'll never forget!"

Clefspeare leveled out at an elevation high enough to avoid the expected onslaught of arrows. As soon as they sailed over the attackers, arrows zinged into the air, but most fell back to earth before reaching their altitude. A few made it that high and finished their ascension in lazy arcs. One pinged harmlessly off Clefspeare's scales and another drifted past Billy's ear, too slowly to do any harm.

He looked back at their takeoff point. Acacia and Shiloh now stood there, Gabriel in front of them with his wings spread and his sword in front of him. In the rush, Elam hadn't told Gabriel what to do, so he would have to fend for himself and hope Ashley's firetrap warded off the invaders.

Clefspeare drew his head close to Billy. "Candle is making his run. Are you ready?"

Bending low, Billy nodded. "Let's smoke 'em!"

Clefspeare angled downward. To his right, five other dragons did the same. The plan was to follow Candle, fan out, and blast fire at anything the bombs didn't stop. So far, the dragons seemed strong, and no one on the ground flashed any glittering gems. Maybe they didn't have candlestones after all. Still, the lone man on the ridge held up a fist as he patiently watched. Was he Sir Devin? He was too far away to tell for sure. Could he be holding their ultimate weapon? If so, what was he waiting for?

As they dove, the airplane came into view. A bomb dropped, a leather bag loaded with fuel and explosive powder that would ignite on impact. Before the first one landed, five other bags flew out the airplane's door.

With the warm wind stinging his eyes as he and Clefspeare zoomed downward, Billy squinted. The bombs exploded one by one, the first one blasting a chariot to bits and sending a cloud of fire and smoke skyward. The cloud obstructed their view, but the loud bangs and thick plumes told the story.

Danger alarmed from every direction. Death lurked in too many places to count. Dodging the smoke, Clefspeare took aim at the invaders to the rear of the bombing run. Just as he drew in a breath, a red dragon blasted out of the cloud and slammed into Clefspeare's flank.

Clefspeare rocked to the side. Billy jerked with him but held on. As the attacking dragon bounced away and righted himself in the sky, Clefspeare beat his wings to keep his balance. "Goliath!" he roared. "Only a coward like you would attack from a cloud!"

Goliath wheeled around and zoomed toward him again, shouting, "It is not cowardly to attack when I am so outnumbered in the sky."

Fire gushed from Goliath's mouth. Clefspeare folded in his wings and dropped. Billy hung on. The stream of flames flew just above his head, and Goliath's claws snatched at his hair, barely missing. As they fell, Billy's stomach pressed up toward his throat. When Clefspeare spread his wings again and caught the air, Billy's organs surged into reverse and dove straight down into his pelvis.

Now that they flew close to ground level, the details of the battle came into view. The bombs had blown craters in the ground, and iron wheels and broken pieces of several chariots lay strewn about. The surviving invaders in the front lines were now scrambling around the holes, while five dragons swooped, one after the other, flooding the field with fire.

Clefspeare added his own barrage. Men became torches—flags of flames as their horses galloped away with them, terrified. Still, at least a third of the attackers broke through the wall of craters, fire, and smoke and charged toward the village, now within seconds of reaching the final barrier, Ashley's trap.

Above, Goliath gave chase, his laser eyes aimed at Billy. Obviously he knew Clefspeare's greatest vulnerability was his son.

"Dad!" Billy shouted. "Take me to where we launched! I have to protect Shiloh and Acacia! You'll fight Goliath better on your own!"

Without a word of objection, Clefspeare veered away and beat his wings madly. Like a shot out of a rifle, they zoomed toward the village.

Billy looked back. Goliath followed but at a slower rate. Behind him, Karrick blew a stream of flames at Legossi, but she shook them off and slapped him across the face with her tail, sending him tumbling downward with a shriek.

From atop her back, Sir Barlow shouted, "Well struck!"

Goliath banked and flew toward the point where Karrick fell. Smoke engulfed both dragons, blocking the view.

As they rocketed past the lead runner and horses in the invading horde, Clefspeare swooped low and flew so close to the trapping field, the tips of his wings touched the ground at the bottom of their down sweeps, even brushing the tubes that lay in the dead grass.

He tore past Ashley to the left and Sapphira to the right as they continued waiting in the bordering woods. At the launching site, Gabriel sprang out of the way. Rearing up, Clefspeare beat his wings furiously and landed on the run, fanning Shiloh and Acacia as he passed by.

Before he came to a stop, Billy leaped to the dried mud. "I'm down! Take off!"

Clefspeare banked, his feet clawing the ground and his wings swerving his massive body. Then, in another flurry, he vaulted again into the sky.

The stampeding army swarmed over the booby-trapped field, chariots rumbling, horse hooves thundering, men shouting. Billy dashed in front of Shiloh, Acacia, and Gabriel and raised his sword. "Get down! Now!" Billy gave Flint a quick glance. He sat motionless against the tree, his eyes wide, but he showed no other signs of alarm.

In the woods, Ashley twisted the valve, then mounted Thigocia. As they scrambled from the forest, thin fountains spurted across the field. A few soldiers slipped and fell under the tromping feet and hooves, but the rest charged on.

Dikaios leaped into action, carrying Sapphira in a mad gallop. Ember and Listener followed close behind. At the near end of the field,

Sapphira tossed a ball of fire to the ground. Listener slung a flaming torch.

Like a blast from a dragon, the flames shot across the muddy grass, creating a fiery wall. As Dikaios ran along the field's left boundary, Sapphira threw ball after ball, igniting the fuel that coated the ground and the sea of soldiers. Listener tossed her second torch, then ducked low and rode Ember at a gallop.

Chariots, men, and horses burst into flames. Cries of anguish filled the air. The inferno spread throughout the forest-bounded field and roasted every creature caught in the trap.

Standing close enough to feel the searing heat, Billy kept Excalibur raised. The three Nephilim broke through the fiery wall. Two were completely ablaze while the third batted at his flaming legs, apparently in too much pain to fight. Another two men, normal in size and wearing Roman-style armor, jumped out from the forest, their clothes merely smoking. They charged, but there was only one clear path to the village, straight through Billy and Excalibur.

As they sprinted toward him, one threw a spear. With a quick swing, Billy slapped it out of the air and ran to meet them. Just as he heaved in a breath, ready to send a volley of fire, a ball of flames surged past him and splashed in one attacker's face, knocking him back. As he writhed on the ground in a blaze, the other swung a sword. Billy parried and dropped to a crouch. When the man's momentum carried him over Billy's body, Billy shoved upward with his shoulder and sent the man tumbling.

The attacker climbed back to his feet, dazed. Gabriel strode in front of him and spread his wings. Wide-eyed, the man drew back his sword, but Gabriel drove his own sword through the man's belly. He collapsed in a heap.

Exhaling heavily, Billy scanned the area. The other four attackers, including the three Nephilim, lay on the ground, burning, and no one else had broken through the fire trap. He hurried to Shiloh, Acacia, and Gabriel. "Thanks for the help."

Her face pale and gaunt, Acacia gave him a nod. "It was the least I could do."

Gabriel nodded. "Same here. That guy was so scared of my wings, I think he was having a heart attack."

"We have to get you guys out of here," Billy said. "That was our last trap. There are so many of them, more are bound to break through."

"And the fire's spreading into the forest," Shiloh said. "What are you going to do about Flint?"

Billy looked at the pitiful man, still leaning against the tree. "Nothing. Elam's orders. I wish I could take him, but I can't disobey."

Gabriel wrapped his arms around Shiloh from behind. "I can carry one. Just tell me where to go."

A gust blew back Acacia's snowy hair. Thigocia landed with a thump, breathing heavily. Atop her back, Ashley shouted, "Our dragons are faltering! Someone must have a candlestone!"

Billy pointed toward the fire. "I saw someone dressed in black behind the lines, probably Sir Devin. It looked like he was waiting for something."

"Likely to see if I was anywhere in sight," Thigocia said. "I am immune to the candlestone, and if I had seen him, I would have cooked him on the spot."

"Then let me ride with you." Billy stepped toward Thigocia. "I'll show you which one he is."

Ashley shook her head. "You're not immune, but I am. I know what the creep looks like."

"We have to hurry," Thigocia said. "I stopped here to let you know that Goliath is trying to lead a wave of invaders to the birthing garden by a different route. Clefspeare is opposing him, and they are doing battle, but they are getting closer to the garden by the second. If Elam and Valiant are still alive, I will warn them. Otherwise, as queen of the dragons, I will order our survivors to break off this attack and hurry to the garden. We must protect Heaven's Gate."

Billy nodded. "Have you seen Bonnie?"

A streak of pain crossed Ashley's face. "We saw Hartanna from a distance. She was still flying, but she had no rider. That's all we know."

As Thigocia beat her wings to take off, Ashley kept her gaze on Billy. She mouthed the words, "I'm sorry," and then rose into the air.

His legs now trembling, Billy turned to the others. "We have to get to the garden and warn Yereq."

"You bet." Gabriel flapped his wings, but Billy pulled him back.

"I think you'd better take Acacia," Billy said. "She probably can't run as fast as Shiloh."

Gabriel shifted his arms from Shiloh to Acacia. Looking at Shiloh, he whispered, "I'll see you soon." Then, taking a deep breath, he flapped his wings again and took off.

Billy slid Excalibur away and grasped Shiloh's hand. "Come on!"

As they ran toward the village, Billy glanced at her every few seconds. Her lovely profile and blonde-streaked hair shot pain through his heart. If only Bonnie could be running at his side. Would it be all right just to imagine her presence for a moment? Would it ease the pain of not knowing where she was and cast away the images of her lying dead on the battlefield while those demons from Hell did whatever they wished to her body?

As she began to pant under the strain of their sprint, Shiloh pulled her hand away, a hand with a missing finger. The stump shattered his daydream. Her lack of wings ripped his heart. This wasn't Bonnie. She was still in danger . . . somewhere.

After running into the village at the northeast side, they skirted the tree-lined border to the north and rushed into the garden's field. Gabriel had already arrived and stood with Acacia in front of Yereq.

Billy and Shiloh joined them. While Billy caught his breath, he scanned the sky. As expected, two red dragons battled overhead, maybe a quarter mile away. If Goliath was leading part of the army this way, the invaders would be here in moments.

Breathless, Gabriel nodded at the plant between Yereq's massive legs and Heaven's Gate. "Ashley filled me in on a lot of your story, but what's the deal with the wall and the plant?"

"We think Makaidos is in the plant," Billy said, "and we figured out that a girl is supposed to give her life to resurrect him. Listener thinks she's the one, but I know Makaidos would not want to live if Listener has to die."

"Is Listener supposed to come here?" Acacia asked.

"If they follow the plan, they should be here any minute. We're all supposed to fall back and protect Heaven's Gate."

Acacia set her hand close to the shimmering wall. "Perhaps we will be entering it very soon."

"Now that's strange," Shiloh said, pointing at the sky. "Storm clouds in one spot and nowhere else."

"They're over the battlefield." Billy took several steps toward the village. The cloud spread out from the northeast and stopped maybe two hundred yards away. A purplish tint between the cloud and ground indicated heavy rain.

Suddenly, the ground shook. A massive explosion sounded from the north. In the distance, a dense cloud of black soot and ash poured into the sky.

"Mount Elijah!" Billy shouted. "It blew its top!"

A fast stream of air in the upper atmosphere jetted the debris into the storm and mixed the ash with the boiling cloud. The purple tint turned darker, almost black. A bolt of lightning forked into three jagged green lines as it crashed to the ground. Rolling thunder followed, deep and menacing.

Billy stared at the ominous cloud. The weather in Second Eden had been strange for years, but this was the strangest yet. With all the supernatural events going on, it had to mean something, but what?

CHAPTER 16

THE SLAYER RETURNS

With a sudden jerk, Hartanna tilted to the side. Bonnie fell from her back and plunged. Just before smashing into the ground, she unfurled her wings, grabbed the rising air, and landed with a heavy, feet-first thump.

A man wearing a head scarf charged. Ducking under his swinging sword, she stepped to the side and gashed his thigh with her own blade. As the man toppled, another swordsman ran toward her. With help from her wings, she leaped over his thrust and kicked him square in the nose. When he crumbled, she dropped on his shoulders and pierced him through his chest.

Swinging her head from side to side, she looked around. The invaders had all passed her except a single man atop a black horse. Apparently she had fallen at the back of the ranks and only this straggler remained. She looked up. Hartanna flew erratically, jerking back and forth as if disoriented or blind.

"Mama!" she called. "What's wrong?"

Flying in a ragged circle, Hartanna descended, finally landing in a rough slide. Bonnie ran toward her mother, but the horse bolted and cut her off.

Bonnie looked up at the man, a muscular specimen draped in black chain mail. He seemed to sparkle from head to toe, as if coated by glittering dust.

He removed his cowl, revealing his face and hair. "So we meet again, demon witch." He extended a hand. Dangling from a thin chain at the ends of his fingers, a gem swung back and forth. "Does this look familiar?"

Pain stabbed her stomach, a hot poker jabbing again and again. She steeled her body. She couldn't double over. Not now. Giving Devin any sign of weakness could be fatal.

She quickly scanned the battlefield. Four dragons had fallen to the ground and were now staggering and beating their wings in their attempts to escape the candlestone's energy drain. She had to come up with a plan to save them, something he didn't expect.

"It does look a bit familiar," she said. Battling the tremors in her arm, she raised her sword and pointed at him. "Would you like to come down off your high horse and let me have a closer look?"

Devin laughed. "You always had a lot of spunk. I admire that."

"Don't patronize me. If you really admire me, then put that stone away and prove it. Fight me sword to sword, unless you're too scared to fight a woman."

"And revive the dragons?" Devin shook his head in a scolding manner. "Bonnie, come now, you know I am not a fool. Your bravado is comely, to be sure, but I do not wish to become dragon fodder."

"You won't. I can arrange it." Bonnie turned toward her mother. She was now fully stretched out on the ground, but her eyes were open, two sad orbs glowing dimly. "Mama, if Devin puts the candlestone away, do you promise to take the other dragons and leave us?"

"Bonnie," she called with a hoarse voice, "we cannot sacrifice you to save ourselves."

"If you don't, all is lost, Second Eden, the garden, Heaven's Gate. If I don't defeat Devin and the candlestone, all the dragons will die, and we will be overwhelmed by their army."

"But Bonnie, he is an expert swordsman, and you are—"

"Do not underestimate me!" Summoning all her energy, she shouted, "You must let me do this! Promise it now!"

Blowing out a weak stream of smoke, Hartanna eased her head to the ground. "Very well. I give my word. If we revive, I will take all the dragons to the birthing garden and leave you here with the slayer."

"There you have it," Bonnie said, looking back at Devin. "If you want your demon witch, then let the dragons go, and come and get me."

"On one condition." Devin slid off the horse and drew his sword. "I had hoped to kill all four of these dragons. What is the head of one demon witch in exchange for four others? I admit that your lovely head would be an excellent trophy, but it cannot replace four dragon heads."

Bonnie squinted at him. "What are you trying to say?"

He raised a gloved finger. "Before I battle you, I will allow three dragons to escape, but I must kill one of the others first. Let us say that this is a demonstration of my intent and resolve."

She gulped. As the candlestone glittered in her eye, pain roared through her body, numbing her senses. With tears welling, she lowered her arm and forced out a weak, "Which dragon?"

"Well, obviously not your pitiful mother. She is the one who has to enforce her promise. One fact I have learned about the dragons who pretend to be good, they keep their word, hoping to veil the evil intentions of their hearts."

Leaving his horse behind, Devin marched about thirty paces to one of the other dragons. Her tawny scales revealed her gender, but since she lay motionless on her side, Bonnie couldn't figure out who she was, especially with her vision blurred by the candlestone's influence. And this dragon's rider, by Elam's orders, had fled to the garden to shore up the defense there.

"Wait!" Bonnie cried. With the candlestone farther away, the pain eased a fraction, allowing her to think more clearly, but the awful idea that one of these brave dragonesses might soon feel the demon's blade made her body tremble. Could she do this? The cost was so terrible! "If . . . if I agree, will you keep the candlestone put away until we finish our battle?"

Devin flashed an evil smile. "I will." Setting the point of his sword against the dragon's underside, he thrust the blade deep into her belly.

"No!" Bonnie screamed. "I didn't say *I* agreed, I was just asking—"

"Too late." His eyes now wide in a maniacal stare, he twisted the blade and jumped back as he pulled it out, dodging the gushing fluids.

"You fiend!" Bonnie shouted, shaking her fist. "You could've waited a few more seconds for me to decide!"

"The candlestone obviously has had a greater effect on your mind than you are letting on. If you had agreed, I would have killed her. If you had not agreed, I would have killed all four. Waiting a few more seconds would not have altered this dragon's fate." He shifted to the dragon's head and set the blade against her neck. Again smiling, he lifted his sword.

Bonnie turned her head. She couldn't bear to watch. But what could she do? In her condition, she couldn't fight. She had to stay strong to save the other three.

A dull thwack sounded in her ears. Pain knifed through her stomach and soul. One of the valiant dragons had just given her life, and all Bonnie could do was stand there.

Suddenly the pain in her belly eased further. The slayer's shuffling footsteps grew close. Turning toward him, she raised her sword again and backed away.

Devin showed her his empty palm. "As you can see, the candlestone is now hidden. It is on a neck chain behind my mail."

She set her feet in ready position. "When my mother leaves with the other dragons, we can begin. Not before."

Whispering a "tsk, tsk, tsk," he shook his head. "You are such a fool. I didn't have to make this deal at all, and I could alter it at any time."

Bonnie glanced at her mother. Quietly, the weak dragon rose and used her wings to help the others get up. Their heads swayed, and their legs trembled, but the absence of the candlestone seemed to be helping.

"You and your kind are of the devil," Devin continued, "and I will exterminate every scaly beast by any means necessary, including deception."

Bonnie kept her sword out in front. "Even if it means proving yourself such a coward that you couldn't even fight a girl?"

"Ah, yes!" Devin said, laughing as he drew closer. "The clichéd challenge, the appeal to my pride as a gentleman and a knight." He spat in her face. "That's what I think of your theatrics."

Keeping her eyes on him, Bonnie wiped her sleeve across her cheek, again refusing to grimace. "If you're not enamored with my acting ability, then what *do* you want?"

Devin looked at the three surviving dragons. One by one they lifted up into the sky. Hartanna called as she flew away. "I will see you again, my love."

A new tear welled in Bonnie's eye. She blinked, letting it fall to her cheek. But where would they meet? Here, or in Heaven?

"What I want," Devin said, turning back to her, "is something that I have tried to get for many years."

"Now you're the one who's being theatric. Just tell me."

In the sunlight, his eyes glinted—evil, hungry, bloodthirsty. "I want the mongrel. I want Billy Bannister. And I want his father, the great Clefspeare. Now that I have you, it will be much easier to lure them into my clutches."

A surge of anger swept through Bonnie's body. Her muscles

flexed—the arms, legs, and abdomen she had trained four years to harden into steel. Now feeling much stronger, Bonnie stepped back. "You don't have me yet, and I'll never let you take Billy."

"We'll see about that." Devin raised his sword. Like a raging bull, he charged. Bonnie jumped to the side, but Devin tripped her, sending her into a backward somersault. At the end of her spill, she leaped to her feet and shot into the air, barely avoiding his sword as it swiped just underneath.

She landed behind him and lunged, aiming her sword at his back. He spun and blocked her blade with his. As the two locked, his eyes narrowed. "You are much too strong for a girl of your stature. The blood of demons flows through your veins, but I will puncture the witch with enough holes to drain every drop."

Bonnie narrowed her eyes to match his. "If your theatrics continue, you will soon have to take a bow. Don't think for a minute that your diatribe can scare me. I have been in every realm—Earth, Heaven, Hades, the Valley of Souls, and now Second Eden—and God has been with me every step of the way. It would take more than the venomous spewing of a viper to make me tremble."

"It is not God who slinks like a serpent at your side, it is—" Devin glanced upward. A slight bend in his brow piqued Bonnie's curiosity. She gave the locked blades a shove, jumped back, and looked up. A cloud formed low in the sky, boiling, swelling, darkening. Within a few seconds, it grew to a raging black cumulonimbus that began spreading toward the village.

A tremendous explosion rocked the ground. In the northern sky, a geyser of black shot into the air and flowed southward into the brewing storm. The two clouds mixed into a purple and ebony swirl.

Bonnie stared at the roaring eruption. Ashley had mentioned a volcano called Mount Elijah, but she had said nothing about how active it might be.

As penny-sized raindrops began to pelt her head, Bonnie set her feet again. Should she attack? Wait for his next move? She tried to gauge his level of aggression, but he just stared toward the village, his scowl deepening. Was it a ploy to get her to strike? She mentally shook her head. Even though he was the foulest creature ever to walk the face of Earth or Second Eden, she couldn't attack while he wasn't looking. Billy had taught her that lesson a long time ago.

Something stung her hand, a minor sting, like a mosquito pricking her exposed skin. Was it the rain? She pulled her sleeves down over her wrists. It was really nothing. Maybe the volcanic ash had created an acidic rain.

Devin looked at her again. "You could have run me through just now. Why didn't you?"

"Because I'm not a cowardly snake. I won't stab a man while he's looking away." She pointed her sword at him and shouted, "En garde!"

Devin lowered his sword. "I am looking at you now. Feel free to strike. This is your only chance. If you fail, I will take out the candlestone and imprison you with it."

Bonnie studied his expression. Was this a trick? Did he think she wouldn't do it because she was a girl and too squeamish to run him through? Well, if he did, he thought wrong. Setting her feet, she lunged and thrust the point directly at his chest. When the blade struck his mail, it made a loud pinging sound and deflected away.

She swung it back with all her might and hacked at his bare neck, but the blade bounced again and quivered in her grip. His sparkling aura flashed momentarily before settling back to normal.

"This is getting tiresome." Devin reached behind his mail shirt, withdrew the candlestone, and let it sway at the end of the chain around his neck. "I'm in a hurry, and you're too skilled to defeat quickly."

The stabbing pain returned, worse than ever. She staggered, dizzy. Turning, she tried to run, but a sharp pain tore across her scalp. Her neck bent, and her head snapped back. She lost her balance, but as she toppled backwards, something stopped her fall. She twisted to find out why. Devin was dragging her by the hair.

As the rain increased, her heels made ruts in the moistening mud.

Reaching back, she hacked weakly with her sword, but he just swiped it away with his own, and her blade thudded to the ground at her side.

His nauseating snicker rose above the intermittent splashes. "I might risk losing your pretty head as a trophy, but having you as bait for the grand prize is worth it. First, I capture the mongrel, then I will use him to lure the most powerful dragon of all." He laughed loud and long. "I can already picture the heads on my mantle, side by side by side. I will let you keep your scalp so your lovely hair will flow all around."

She jerked her body downward, freeing her hair from his grasp, but when her head hit the ground, new pain ripped across her skull. She gasped for breath. Her heart raced, feeling like it did the moments before she died in the Circles of Seven.

"Get up, witch!" Devin grabbed her belt and hoisted her up to his horse's saddle. The feeling of his hands on her waist and backside as he pushed her into place made her want to vomit, but she couldn't. Inside, she felt a void, an aching emptiness. She could barely move at all.

Mounting behind her, he spread out her wings and pushed close as he settled into the saddle. With the candlestone now resting on her back, the agony spiked, and with his body pressing close to hers, the nausea churned to a sickening swill.

Rain poured. The wind howled. Green lightning flashed from cloud to ground with a crackling pop. As water streamed from her hair to her folded hands, all seemed lost. She was a maid being dragged to the stake. Soon the fire would be set, and all her hopes would go up in smoke.

As they trotted past the slain dragon, its head lying a few feet from its body, Devin let out a snort. "I will collect that little trophy later."

Lightning flashed again. Rain fell in sheets. The wind whistled in her ears, and it seemed to form a tune, a familiar tune. What was it? Could it be? Yes, it was the same tune she had always used for her favorite psalm.

Words filled in, but not the usual psalm. A gentle feminine voice sang new words in a vibrant contralto that poured in like the driving rain.

Within the gem your light had ebbed,
Entrapped in crystal prison lair.
You cried for help from God on high;
You sang in faith that he was there.

The candlestone, a pseudo-gem,
The bogus beauty now exposed;
By lies, deceit, the hidden heart,
A wolf in wool, the killer's clothes.

For prophets false are like the gem;
They dress in collar, frock, and silk,
Pretending beauty, while within,
They soil their garments, prove their ilk.

The prophets false are but a breeze;
The chains they carry, but a string.
They shackle those who don their garb,
But never children of the King.

The crystal fools the sightless ones;
They give their light away for free,
And even prince and princess have
Become ensnared unknowingly.

But when you sing the faithful song,
The gem will lose its blinding grip.
Defeated foes cannot endure
When faith invokes the master's whip.

After the tune faded, the voice continued, now merely speaking. "Brick upon brick, your song will build your faith until you become an impenetrable fortress. You have already conquered this crystalline enemy. Sing the words again, for the master of that deceiving gem cannot have so soon forgotten the child of God who has already repelled him within those walls. He is a defeated enemy, but you must claim this truth by faith, for only then will the invisible chains be broken forever. Let no shackles bind this valiant daughter of the lamb. Let no darkness overcome the light within an Oracle of Fire."

Nodding with the horse's gait, Bonnie hummed the tune. Then, ignoring the bullets of pain shooting through her heart, she began to sing.

Whither shall I go from thy spirit? Or whither shall I flee
from thy presence?
If I ascend up into heaven, thou art there: If I make my bed in hell,
behold, thou art there.

"Stop the singing!" Devin slapped the side of her head. "Or I'll start carving you now."

Bonnie's ear rang, but she barely felt the slap. "I'm going to sing. You'll have to kill me to stop me."

He grabbed her hair and twisted her head halfway around. For a moment, he stared at her with hate-filled eyes, but soon, his expression slackened, and he shoved her cheek. "Go ahead and sing! What do I care?"

Taking a spasm-filled breath, Bonnie began again, picking up where she left off.

If I take the wings of the morning, and dwell in the uttermost parts
of the sea;
Even there shall thy hand lead me, and thy right hand shall hold me.
If I say, Surely the darkness shall cover me; even the night
shall be light about me.
Yea, the darkness hideth not from thee; but the night shineth as the day:
The darkness and the light are both alike to thee.

When she finished, she let out a sigh. The pains eased. Her heart slowed to a steady rhythm. Energy roared back into her muscles. Though the candlestone still lay on her back, it no longer had any effect.

So what now? Devin had a sword, and she didn't. Her only hope was to take him by surprise.

As the horse cantered, Bonnie looked up. About a hundred yards away, the sky was clear, though rain continued pouring from overhead. Above, two red dragons battled at the boundary between storm and calm, while the remaining army, perhaps four hundred, gathered nearby, all soaking wet and standing in mud.

Bonnie watched the up and down movements of the horse's head. Her timing had to be perfect.

She reached out, set her palms high on the horse's neck, and pushed with all her might, thrusting herself upward. She slapped Devin's cheeks with her wings, kicked him in the chest with both feet, and propelled her body up and away.

As Devin hurled obscenities, Bonnie flew with all her might toward the garden. The downpour beat against her wings, but at least the weather would keep the invaders from looking up and spotting her. She didn't want to have to dodge their arrows now. That would be nearly impossible.

CHAPTER 17

THE SACRIFICE

Billy stared at the strange contrast in the sky, clear over the garden field but stormy just beyond the eastern wall. The battling dragons drew ever closer. With the invaders following Goliath's lead, they couldn't be more than two minutes away. Soon they would be scaling the walls or pouring in through the narrow path from the village.

The sound of hooves made him turn toward the path. Dikaios and Ember galloped into the field, Sapphira and Listener riding. Walter ran behind them. Holding his scabbard to keep it from bouncing, he favored a leg, but it didn't seem to slow his pace.

When they stopped, Sapphira leaped off and ran to Acacia, shouting, "Oh, my dear sister!" But when they drew close, Sapphira halted and stared at her. She took Acacia's fingertips and lifted her arms. Acacia's tunic rode up, exposing her emaciated frame. "Oh, Acacia!" Sapphira wrapped her up in a tight embrace. "I'm so glad you're here! I'll nurse you back to health. I promise."

"I'm sure you'll try," Acacia said, "but there seems to be no explanation for my decay. Perhaps the fruit I ate from the Tree of Life has finally lost its power."

"How could that be? I am still hale and hearty." Sapphira looked at Billy. "She can't die unless someone kills her with violence, and that can't happen unless she's betrayed by someone who loves her. Even if someone spills a drop of her blood, her attacker will die."

"Elam told me those stories," Billy said. "Let's hope they're true here in Second Eden."

Breathing heavily, Walter clasped Billy's arm. "My dragon fell near the back of the invading line. I killed seven of their goons while trying to defend her, but then the other dragons faltered, and Valiant and Elam were grounded. After we cleared out the enemy stragglers, Elam ordered me to come back here."

Another man ran onto the field, shorter and slower than Walter. Sapphira recognized him immediately. "It's Mardon! I thought he was supposed to be in the hospital."

As Mardon drew close, Billy stepped out in front of the others. "What are you doing here?"

Wringing his hands, Mardon bowed his head to Billy and then to the two Oracles. "I have come to confess everything. I sneaked out of the hospital before it departed, because I never had any intention of working with your doctor. There is no cure for Acacia's disease. I altered her genetics in order to study her indestructibility. Even in this state, she will not die, but she will waste away and live on as a walking cadaver." He withdrew a white hair from a pocket. "You see, it's important to study the genes before and after the alteration in order to decode the secret to her power. I plucked a hair from her long ago when I exposed her to the decaying light, so I have the older set of genes and—"

"We don't want a science lesson," Billy growled. "Just get to the bottom line."

"Very well." Mardon put the hair away and again wrung his hands. "My mother, Semiramis, conspired with Arramos to bring this army to Heaven's Gate. I was supposed to use the genetic encoding to make ourselves and our troops indestructible, but I have already learned that without a blood sample, that will be impossible. Her blood likely contains the final clue that will solve the puzzle, but when I considered the possibility of coercing some fool into taking blood from her, I finally woke up to my folly. I was actually willing to kill an innocent lamb to further my own desires!"

He clenched his fingers into a tight knot. "I have been such a fool! I have been following the commands of a dragon who ruined my face and a mother who cares only for her own advance. Now I wish to appeal for mercy and join forces with you. Perhaps with time, I can learn how to reverse Acacia's degeneration."

Billy looked at the two Oracles. Sapphira gave Mardon a skeptical stare, while Acacia gazed at him with forgiving eyes.

Gabriel crossed his arms and shook his head, while Shiloh just glared at Mardon, her stub of a finger obvious as she let her hand dangle at her side.

"What should I do?" Billy whispered to Walter.

"No time to decide." Walter pointed toward the sky. From over the tree line, Thigocia flew in with Ashley, followed immediately by Legossi, Firedda, Hartanna, and Sorentine, each of those four without a rider. All but Thigocia flew haphazardly and flopped to the ground when they landed.

Billy scanned the weakened dragons. Yellinia was missing. Since Valiant was no longer riding her, she must have fallen out in the battlefield and was unable to return.

"They have been weakened by a candlestone," Thigocia said as she settled gracefully. "There is no fight remaining in them, and the storm left them disoriented. The rain carries an unusual odor that has made them dizzy."

Legossi lifted her head. "As long as I have strength to breathe, I will fight."

"And that won't be long," Ashley shouted from atop Thigocia, "unless you rest at least a few minutes."

Billy and Walter ran to Thigocia and helped Ashley down. "We've been routed," Ashley said. "Elam, Valiant, and Barlow are on their way, and Roxil is creating walls of fire between them and the invaders."

"Roxil?" Walter pumped his fist. "Yes! She's fighting for our side now!"

"Not exactly. She's creating an escape for our people, but she won't destroy any invaders. I guess she thinks that's part of her vow." Ashley pointed at Mardon. "What's he doing here?"

Billy took in a breath. "It's like this. Mardon was—"

A ball of fire erupted in the village. A beige dragon flew almost straight up from the blaze as if launched by the explosion. She bent into a sharp turn and flew toward Clefspeare and Goliath.

"Roxil's heading for the big fight," Walter said. "I don't know if that's good or bad."

Elam and Valiant hustled into the field with Flint in between them. Flint's feet barely touched the ground as his two supporters ran. Sir Barlow followed, backing toward the garden and fighting sword to sword with an armor-clad invader.

New flames shot from the treetops. With much of the forest dead and tinderbox dry, the fire roared from one tree to the next.

Elam and Valiant joined Billy and the others at the edge of the garden. They set Flint in a sitting position in a grassy area. Looking sicker than ever, Flint let his head droop close to his crossed legs.

"We couldn't hold them off," Elam said to Billy, panting. "I think the invaders will be here any minute." He glared at Mardon for a brief moment but said nothing.

"I'll help Barlow." Walter drew his sword, but Elam grabbed his arm.

"He's fine. Stay here. We have only a minute to execute our final plan."

"Final plan?" Acacia asked. "What might that be?"

"We have to resurrect Makaidos before it's too late. We learned that a female has to sacrifice herself and offer her blood to energize his rebirth from the plant."

"And I'm the one," Listener said as she slid down from Ember. "He died in my place, so now it's my turn to die for him."

Ashley pointed toward the sky. "Look! Roxil's trying to break up the fight!"

Above, Roxil flew between the two combatants like a battering ram. Both sets of claws from the male dragons scraped against her sides. As she faltered in the air, Clefspeare made a quick turn as if to check on her, but when he exposed his underbelly, Goliath attacked, his teeth and every claw extended. When they collided, blood sprayed from Clefspeare's belly, red and sparkling.

Thigocia launched into the air. "I will help Clefspeare."

As she zoomed upward, Billy wanted to scream at Goliath, but his throat clamped shut. Enraged, he clenched a fist and shifted his stare to another part of the sky. Something appeared from the storm cloud, a human with wings.

Swallowing hard, he managed to whisper, "Bonnie?"

"We don't have time to watch the battle," Elam said. "We have to decide now. Who will be the sacrifice?"

Acacia raised her hand. "I am already weak, and my body is deteriorating."

"No!" Mardon stalked into their huddle and grabbed Acacia's forearm. "You cannot be the sacrifice or someone else will die. Why destroy two lives?"

"Why do you care?" Acacia asked. "I was just a science experiment to you."

Mardon glanced between her and Sapphira. Beads of sweat popped up on his balding head. "You two were the only ones I really cared about. You were wonderfully created by a miracle that went beyond mere genetic logic. It was clear that I had to protect you. By defending you in the face of Morgan's threats, I saved your lives countless times."

Acacia gazed into his eyes and breathed a low, "I see."

A man at the burning tree line screamed. Barlow yanked his sword from the invader's stomach and hurried to the garden. "The fire is keeping them from entering through the forest," Barlow said, "so they are building a ramp to scale the walls. We have a little more time, but not much."

In a spray of wind and water, Bonnie flew down and settled next to Billy. Breathless and dripping wet, she rattled off her story. "I fought Devin . . . He has a candlestone . . . and he's invincible. One of my blows should have cut his head off, but the blade just bounced away."

"Bonnie!" Hartanna called as she shuffled on her wobbly legs. "Stand still while I dry you off. At least I have the energy to do that."

While she blew a jet of hot air across Bonnie's body, a black horse and a black-garbed rider burst through the wall of flames at the forest entry. A sparkling aura surrounded his body, making him appear ghostly.

"Speak of the devil," Walter whispered. "Just replace the *l* with an *n*."

Devin eased the horse into a high-stepping trot and approached the gathering. "I see my trophy has flown to a safer haven. It's not wise to send little girls out to battle alone."

Billy jerked out Excalibur and summoned the beam. "Stay back, or I'll fry you and your horse together."

"Oh, don't take out your anger on my horse. He never did you any harm." Devin dismounted and drew his sword. "I, on the other hand, have done you much harm, and I intend to do a great deal more."

"He's so cocky," Bonnie said, "he was spewing dramatic lines non-stop while we fought. I think he knows that Excalibur won't hurt him."

"There's only one way to find out."

Billy swiped the beam across Devin's body. Sparks erupted, but the slayer stayed upright. A grin spread across his face as he set his feet and raised his sword. "I have come for you, Billy Bannister. You have been a thorn in my side for far too long."

"He will taste my steel," Sir Barlow growled. The muscular knight charged and hacked at Devin's midsection with his sword, but it rebounded. Barlow lost his balance and dropped to his knees. With a swift turn and thrust, Devin drove his sword into Barlow's midsection and jerked it back out.

"Sir Barlow!" Bonnie cried. "Oh, dear God! Help him!"

His eyes wide, Barlow clutched his belly and toppled over. Blood spilled between his fingers. Walter and Ashley ran to him and, gripping him under his arms, dragged him back toward the garden.

Ashley peeled away Barlow's fingers, pulled his shirt up, and laid her hand on the wound.

Barlow opened his eyes and winced. "How bad is it, my lady?"

Pressing her lips together, Ashley shook her head. "It's bleeding quite a bit. I can't tell."

His smile revealed a set of crooked teeth. "I am sure your touch will seal it fast. I have confidence in you."

"Sapphira!" Ashley called. "We need to try a healing."

Elam stepped forward. "Billy. Walter. Valiant. Gabriel. Yereq. Let's see if the six of us—"

"No!" Billy waved everyone back. "He's mine!"

"Billy," Bonnie said, staying at his side. "You can't beat him. He's invincible."

He pushed her gently away. "I'll keep him occupied long enough to stop him from killing anyone else, at least for a while. The others can stay alive for the more important battle."

Billy charged and swung his sword. Devin's blade met his with a loud clank. Grunting, Billy pushed away and set his feet to run again, but a deep female voice erupted from the direction of the burning forest.

"Desist!"

A woman emerged from the flames. Dressed in a long red cloak, she marched toward them, lowering her hood as she drew near.

"Semiramis," Ashley said. "No wonder I didn't sense her approach." She covered Barlow's abdomen with her body and looked up at Sapphira. "It shouldn't take too much. Let's try to make it quick."

Semiramis grabbed Devin's arm, scowling. "Didn't I tell you not to seek revenge until the battle was over?"

Billy glanced at Elam. Their gazes met. Again, the son of Shem had every reason to say, "I told you so," but he just averted his eyes. After all her pretense, Semiramis was finally coming out in the open, proving that every good deed she had done had been an illusion.

Devin jerked away. "I have plenty of protection. I can dispatch this mongrel and everyone else in this pitiful company."

Semiramis pointed a finger at his nose. "You will do as I tell you and nothing more."

"You sound just like Morgan." Devin spat on the ground. "And you know where she is now."

"And you refused to listen to her precise instructions. Shall I recount your losses?" Semiramis raised two fingers. "You were imprisoned in a candlestone, not once, but twice."

Growling, Devin aimed his sword at the garden boundary. "Then where are my allies? Let us proceed with the battle and collect our trophies."

"The ramps are in place, and the troops are awaiting my command to storm this refuge." She looked up. "As you can see, the remaining dragons are returning."

Above, Clefspeare and Thigocia descended, Clefspeare dripping blood. When they landed, Clefspeare's head flopped to the ground, and Thigocia immediately covered him with her wings. "Hartanna," she called. "Between you and Legossi, you should have enough firepower to coat me with healing flames."

"I'll put a stop to this," Devin said as he reached for a thin chain around his neck. "I want that devil's head."

Ashley leaped up from Barlow, rushed toward Devin, and grabbed the chain. Devin spun on his heels and swung his sword, but Ashley threw herself backwards, avoiding the blade and breaking the chain. Now holding the candlestone, she slid away on her backside, her cheeks as red as embers.

"Why, you little . . ."

Devin took a step toward her, but Semiramis pulled him back. "Stand down until I am finished with my business here!"

Flashing a fake smile, Devin bowed. "Then be my guest, your royal highness."

Ashley covered the candlestone with both hands and hurried back to Sir Barlow and Sapphira. "This will help us heal him." She let a drop of her own blood fall from her scraped hands to the gem.

As the flames from the forest crawled out to the field and began devouring the scant brown grass, Semiramis turned toward Billy and company. "With whom shall I speak? I need someone who will make wise and just decisions."

Elam stepped forward. "Say what you've come to say, and then leave."

Her eyebrows lifted. "Ah! My old friend, Elam. You made it safely across the chasm, proving your arrogance; you came to Second Eden, proving your desire for fame; and you forced a grieving widow to lie and face humiliation, proving your misogyny, which you also willingly heaped upon me when I came as a mother in search of help for her son." She let out a contemptuous laugh. "And now what are you? You are the warrior chief of a ragtag gang of weak dragons and sick humans. Will you rally this pitiful menagerie to battle a trained army? While it's true that you have thinned our ranks, we still number over four hundred strong. How long do you think you will last? Five minutes? Three?"

"Like I said . . ." Elam's brow dipped low. "Say what you've come to say, and leave out the venom."

"Very well." She pointed at Mardon. "Bring the Oracle of Fire forward. I want to speak to her."

Elam looked back at Acacia. "Just to talk. Nothing more."

"Just to talk?" Semiramis repeated. "We shall see."

Holding Acacia's hand tenderly, Mardon guided her to the front of their company. Acacia glanced at Sapphira, who was still on her knees next to Barlow.

The line of fire drew closer, but since the flames were only inches tall, they seemed to pose no danger. Anyone could easily step over them.

Thigocia lay on top of Clefspeare, her scales reddened by the flames of other dragons. Motionless and quiet, she waited for the healing to take effect.

Semiramis's eyes narrowed. "Which one are you, Sapphira or Acacia?"

Elam gave everyone a firm shake of his head. Obviously he didn't want anyone to answer.

Billy glared at Mardon. If this creep really wanted to help Acacia, now was the time to prove it. Obviously Semiramis asked this question for a reason, so giving away Acacia's identity wouldn't be a good idea.

Acacia pulled free from Mardon and dipped into a curtsy. "If you please, my lady, kindly tell me why you wish to know my name."

Her eyes narrowing further, Semiramis glanced between Acacia and Sapphira. "It is my understanding that one of you is ill. I selected you because you appear malnourished, and I wish to make an exchange. Once we learn the secrets behind your DNA structure, we will gladly restore your health. Yet, if I choose the wrong Oracle, everything we worked for will be lost."

"Begging your pardon," Acacia said, "but I do not wish to aid whatever ends you have worked so hard to achieve, so I will maintain my silence regarding my identity."

Sapphira shuffled over to Mardon's other side, adding a pronounced limp to her gait. "We will never help you. We are Oracles of Fire, and we were created to serve God alone."

"Fools! I need no help from you." Semiramis glared at Mardon. "Which one is Acacia?"

Mardon took Acacia's hand and caressed it, then did the same to Sapphira. Keeping his head low, he said, "Even if I told you which one is Acacia, you would not be able to use her genetic changes for your purposes without my expertise."

"Mardon! We are moments from our final triumph. Your father dreamed about this day, the day we would rise up to Heaven, assault its very gates, and demand an audience with the Almighty. You know as well as I do that we cannot complete the assault unless we equip our army with angelic invincibility. Are you now going to forsake that dream, that passion born in his heart millennia ago? Are you going to throw away your place at the throne of the universe because of a foolish infatuation with a pair of pretty pets? Have you gone mad?"

Mardon looked up at her. "They are not pets. Each one sprouted from embryonic cells I put together with my own two hands. If I turned Acacia over to you now, it would be as if God himself turned his back on his own daughter."

Semiramis reached out her hand. "You are my son, and my loyalty is to you. If we can extract this knowledge from Acacia, not only can we become like gods ourselves, your own face will be healed, and we can exact revenge upon the monster who maimed you." Her voice transformed to a tone of entreaty. "Don't you see, my son? If we get Arramos to kill Acacia, he will die because of the Oracle's curse, and then we will be free to harvest her ova for our purposes. You will be whole, and revenge will be yours, delivered in a package of bloody red and snowy white prepared by your own hands."

Mardon touched the scars on his face. His ears flushed red. As new beads of perspiration gathered on his forehead, he grasped Acacia's arm and strode toward Semiramis. "This one is Acacia." Acacia stumbled along with him, apparently too weak to resist.

"No!" Billy lunged toward Mardon and swung Excalibur, aiming for his neck. Devin thrust his own sword in between and blocked the stroke.

As they pushed against each other's blades, glaring eye to eye, Walter charged and stabbed at Devin's side, but his sword merely bent and sprang back. Walter lost his balance, stumbled several steps backwards, and fell to his seat. Billy leaped away from Devin and ran with Bonnie to Walter's side.

Still holding Acacia's hand, Mardon passed Devin and joined Semiramis.

Yereq bellowed from Heaven's Gate, his sword drawn. "Say the word, Warrior Chief, and I will kill all three of these villains."

"And I will join him," Valiant said. "They cannot stand against us."

Gabriel flew over and landed next to Valiant. "Count me in."

Elam held up his hand. "You might hurt Acacia."

Billy and Bonnie helped Walter up. "Let's go after Mardon and

Semiramis together," Bonnie whispered. "They won't hurt Acacia on purpose, and if we're quick enough, one of us can snatch her away."

"I'll push Devin to the side," Billy whispered back. "You and Walter can take care of the rest."

When all three rose, Devin rushed toward them. He kicked Billy in the groin, knocked Excalibur away, and set the tip of his own sword against Billy's throat. "I see no one has trained you for a dirty, underhanded attack."

In spite of the pain, Billy refused to double over. He wanted to swallow, but the blade was already cutting into his skin. He growled without moving his throat. "We fight like knights here."

"As if I care." Pulling back the blade slightly, Devin turned toward Elam. "Now you will leave Mardon and Acacia with Semiramis, or I will skewer this mongrel where he stands. If you acquiesce, Semiramis will signal our troops, and at least he will have a fighting chance to survive."

Billy glared at Devin. "My friends will likely want to save my life, but it's not their choice. Whether your troops come or not, you will take Acacia over my dead body."

Devin laughed. "Your demon witch girlfriend complains about my theatrics, yet you drool that pathetic cliché."

"Take it or leave it, you cowardly sycophant. You were under the thumb of a sorceress for centuries, and you still cower behind the skirts of one now. If you weren't covered by her dark magic, you would be tucking your tail and running like a terrified puppy."

"Her dark magic?" Devin laughed again. "How little you know!"

Semiramis took a step closer to Billy and crooned. "Do you want to know how Devin was able to gain his invincible shell?"

Billy finally swallowed, brushing his throat against the sharp blade. "Why should I care?"

"Because it was by your hand. Fool that you were, you added Shiloh's blood to the plant, exactly as I requested, and her blood, which carried an extraordinary immunity, added the precise element we needed to provide our seedling a cloak of invulnerability. And all this time, you thought we wanted Bonnie, when we really needed Shiloh. You were such a fool."

"Am I?" Billy knitted his brow. He had to figure out a way to rile Devin, somehow get him to rebel against Semiramis, or at least get him angry enough to make a mistake. "Devin is the real fool. He's still just your toady, nothing more than a fat lapdog that you pet with your bloody fingers. What bone did you toss to get him to lick your filthy boots?"

"You have your Oracle," Devin growled at Semiramis. "Signal our people, and let me kill this rodent."

Semiramis let out a shrill whistle and waved her hand. "Very well. Feel free to take his head. You have earned that reward."

"With pleasure. First a stab through his heart." As Devin pulled back the hilt, Acacia jerked away from Mardon and leaped in front of Billy. Devin thrust his sword. The blade punctured her chest, ran through her body, and slid out her back, pricking Billy's skin.

Devin yanked it out. "Stupid girl."

Acacia slumped. Blood poured from her wound. Billy slid his arms around her chest and lowered her gently to the ground and himself to his knees. Heat blazing in his cheeks, he shouted, "You . . . you . . ." He couldn't think of a word vile enough to describe the slayer. As he stared at the foul beast, the aura surrounding his skin and black chain mail fizzled and disappeared.

"Sister!" Sapphira screamed as she ran to Acacia.

"No!" Bonnie raised her sword and charged.

As Devin stared at her, a cocky smile bent his lips. "The demon witch comes again—"

"Shut up!" With a mighty swing, Bonnie swept her sword at his neck. The blade struck bare flesh and sliced cleanly through. Devin's head toppled over and dropped to the ground, his eyes wide as it rolled. The mail-clad body crumbled in a heap of black.

Pointing her sword at his eyes, Bonnie added, "Forever."

"We can still use Acacia!" Semiramis shouted. "Get her body!"

Bonnie aimed her sword at Mardon, her arms and voice shaking. "Make one move, and you're dead!"

Mardon backed away a step, then turned and ran toward the village, leaping over the low fire. Semiramis raised her hood and followed. She seemed in no hurry, likely realizing that no one would attack an unarmed, retreating woman.

Flint rose to his feet and hobbled toward Devin's body. He picked up the slayer's fallen sword and propped it against his shoulder as he faced Elam. "Allow me to fight for you."

"You're too sick," Elam said. "You can't possibly survive."

His eyes glistening, he managed to straighten his body admirably. "After all I have seen here, I must demonstrate my repentance. Whether I live or die is of no consequence."

Elam nodded. "Let it be so." He stooped close to Sapphira and touched the white rubellite ring on her finger. "During the four years of waiting here, I think I figured out a prophecy. You'll probably have to use that gem to resurrect Makaidos, but I'll get you another." As he rose, he pointed at Ember. "Take Listener to the far side of the field."

Walter boosted Listener onto Ember's back. As she settled in place, she said, "Sapphira, please tell Acacia that I'm sorry. I'm sorry that I was too slow to take her place as the sacrifice."

Her face twisting in grief, Sapphira nodded. "I . . . I will tell her."

Gabriel wrapped his arms around Shiloh. "I'll take her to safety with Listener, but I'll be back to join the battle."

As he lifted into the air, Ember followed his path toward the field's western boundary.

Walter shouted, "Get ready! Here they come!"

At the eastern wall, invaders climbed over the top and, one by one, then two by two, dropped to the ground, their weapons drawn for battle.

Thigocia lifted her body off Clefspeare and tugged on his wing with a clawed hand. "Are you able to rise?"

With a lurch, Clefspeare rose to his haunches. For a moment, his neck wavered, but he quickly steadied it and roared. "Follow me!" He vaulted into the air, beating his wings with all his might.

Thigocia followed. Hartanna and Legossi struggled to their feet and flew after them, but much more slowly. Firedda and Sorentine stayed on the ground. They seemed to be trying to get up, but their wings flailed helplessly.

Elam waved his arm toward the eastern boundary. "Defend the garden!"

"Let's do it!" Walter said as he leaped after him. Valiant broke into a full sprint and kept pace at Walter's side.

Yereq shouted from Heaven's Gate. "Take courage, my friends. If any of the snakes slip through your fingers, I will be here to relieve them of their heads."

Dikaios ran to Barlow and lowered his body. "Come, valiant warrior. If you are strong enough to ride, let us go to battle like the knights of old."

"By all means!" Barlow climbed to his feet and crawled over the horse's back.

Dikaios shot up to his full height and jumped into a gallop, Barlow shouting a battle cry as he waved his sword.

Clefspeare stormed toward the garden's boundary. Fire shot from his mouth and nostrils and blasted the invaders as they trickled over the top. Like a dragonfly, Thigocia flew from place to place, seemingly pausing in midair to cook the invaders who had already dropped onto the field.

Merlin the airplane buzzed overhead. A fuel bomb dropped on the opposite side of the wall and raised a fiery explosion. The stream of invaders slowed, but only for a moment.

As Merlin flew away, Billy watched the action, dazed as he held Acacia's body. Was that the last of Windor's bombs? Would Candle land somewhere and try to make more? He ached to join his fellow warriors, but holding the sacrificial Oracle seemed far more important. He had to guard her body until Sapphira did what she had to do.

Sapphira pulled Acacia into her arms, weeping. "Oh, my dear sister! Oh, my sweet, wonderful sister!"

Ashley laid her hand over the wound, but it did no good. Blood continued to pour from Acacia's twitching body.

His heart pounding, Billy looked at his blood-covered hands. Acacia's blood. The sacrificial lamb's blood. She had completed her purpose, her millennia-long journey. For this death she had been born, and for this saving sacrifice she had been waiting all her life.

His hands trembling, Billy rolled his fingers into fists. He couldn't fight. He couldn't even speak. His arms felt like rubber, and his legs were numb.

Groping fingers ran along his arm and found his fist. He loosened his fingers and let the weak hand slip into his.

"Billy?" Acacia whispered.

He leaned close to her as she lay cradled in Sapphira's arms. He had to swallow before he could answer. "Yes. . . . Yes, I'm here."

Her lips, now light blue, trembled as she spoke. "I gave my life to save yours."

"Yes." He folded her hand into both of his and forced his body to stop shaking. "Thank you."

Her voice weakened. "It was the greatest thing I have ever done."

He pressed his lips together. As tears dripped, the lump in his throat swelled. He couldn't answer.

"I never had a man in my life," she continued as she raised a hand to his cheek. "But after our talk in the mines, I knew that if I were ever to choose, I would want someone like you at my side."

Her eyelids closed. After a final heave, her chest became still. Acacia, the great Oracle of Fire, had died.

Billy raised her hand to his lips and kissed her knuckles. His tears flowing freely, he whispered, "Goodbye, Acacia. Thank you for saving my life. I will be forever grateful." Then, his voice strengthening as new energy flowed through his body, he added, "I will fight in your name."

"Can we try a healing?" Ashley asked.

Her face stained with tears, Sapphira shook her head. "This is what she wanted. I have to use her blood now to resurrect Makaidos."

"I'll go with you," Bonnie said. "You apply the blood, and I'll guard your back."

As Sapphira lowered Acacia to the ground and rose to her feet, Bonnie touched Billy's arm. "The rain washed the rust off. You need to get to work."

"Right." He scanned the ground and spotted Excalibur a few feet away. Rising on his wobbly legs, he stumbled toward it and snatched it off the ground. He summoned the beam and looked at the battle near the eastern wall.

Goliath had flown in, and as he and Clefspeare fought once again, more invaders and their horses spilled over the top, like rats crawling out of a flooded sewer. Five armor-clad horsemen kept Thigocia at bay with thick spears while fending off her flames with shields. The weaker dragons continued spewing fire at the arriving troops, but they were unable to keep up with the flow.

The battleground resembled a sea—waves of slashing swords, roars of battling men and dragons, and a tidal surge that pushed the entire group toward the middle of the burning field.

He let the beam die away. With everyone fighting in close quarters, using Excalibur would be dangerous. He would have to save it until he met the invaders face to face.

Ashley strode to his side, her sword drawn. "Mind if I join you? I have to keep my fiancé in one piece."

"By all means."

She set a hand on his shoulder and lifted her sword. "For Acacia?"

Tightening his jaw, he nodded. "For Acacia."

CHAPTER 18

WHEN DEATH BRINGS LIFE

Cradling Acacia's body in her arms, Bonnie pulled the dead Oracle's blood-soaked tunic up just past her ribcage and held it there. Blood oozed from under the material, and when it reached the end of her ribs, it dripped down to her scant waist.

Sapphira cupped her hands and collected it drop by drop. Her arms trembled, but she kept them in place. She had to angle her head away to keep her tears from spilling in.

As the blood filled Sapphira's hands, Bonnie wept. This portrait of one sister gathering the blood of another was too much to bear. They had loved each other for thousands of years. They longed to be together, but calamity after calamity had kept them apart. And now, when they finally met again, they were torn asunder only moments later.

"Do you think I have enough?" Sapphira asked.

Bonnie took a deep breath and tried to compose herself. "I don't know, but since her heart's not beating, I don't think you'll get much more." She lowered the tunic and mopped Acacia's waist with the hem. The red liquid against her pale skin painted a stark contrast. Although both colors signified death, maybe one would soon bring life.

With the sounds of a raging battle behind her, Bonnie slid both arms fully under Acacia's body and rose to her feet. The little Oracle was so thin, she seemed no heavier than a bag of bones. Heaving a sigh, she nodded at Sapphira. "We'd better hurry."

Sapphira padded toward Heaven's Gate, glancing back and forth between the plant and her cupped hands. When they arrived, she knelt in front of the plant, while Bonnie set Acacia next to the transparent energy field. Although the wall cast a sharp tingle across her skin, it seemed appropriate to lay Acacia as close to Heaven as possible.

Bonnie sat next to Sapphira, one leg curled under, one knee raised, and the point of her sword planted in the dirt so she could thrust herself to her feet if danger arrived. Yereq took three sideways steps to give them room and watched, his sword clutched in both hands. He, too, would be standing guard. They would be safe, at least for a while.

The bones of Makaidos lay strewn about, so dry and stripped white, even a dog wouldn't bother with them. Lifting her head, Bonnie looked at Heaven's Gate. It shimmered in the vibrant sunlight. Somewhere just beyond that barrier, the God of all creation awaited their fellowship in the glory of eternal light, a place she had visited briefly, but with war raging in the sky and on the ground behind her, the splendor of Paradise seemed so foreign . . . distant. How could perfect peace abide so close to demonic discord?

Sapphira laid her palms on the leaves and began massaging them in an up and down motion. As blood dripped to the ground, the leaves changed from green to red. The white gem in her ring, stained now with blood, began to glow with a swirling radiance of red and white. She pulled the ring off and forced it under the roots. The radiance pushed up through the stalk's channels, as if red and white phosphorescent paint flowed upward through its veins.

After a few seconds, she straightened her torso, though she stayed on her knees. Then, lifting her hands, she shouted, "Ignite!"

A ball of radiant white appeared in each palm. She swirled her arms, making the balls grow. They burst open, and the radiance spilled to the ground. As the light crawled along the soil, bubbling and sizzling, the bones absorbed the energy and began to glow, turning whiter than ever. The brilliance followed the red and white channels up the plant's stalk and burrowed into the middle of the praying leaves, lighting up the entire womb.

The blood on Sapphira's hands burned away. Like a sponge soaking in water, the plant drew in the blood from the praying leaves. Thin lines of scarlet pierced the membrane, as if creating capillaries from the outside to the life inside. Soon, the redness disappeared, leaving only vibrant green. As wave after wave of energy flowed from the soil, the bones dwindled to thin sticks and finally vanished.

When the last sparkle of radiance winked out, Sapphira shouted, "Makaidos, we call you to resurrection. The sacrifice has been made, and the blood of the innocent has purchased your new life." Weeping once again, she cried, "Come to Second Eden and help us rid this land of the corruption that has spoiled the new beginning that Abraham tried to maintain for so long."

As if erupting from the deepest recesses of her soul, words spilled from Bonnie's lips, unbidden words, passionate words that seemed set on fire from the Paradise that lay beyond the gate.

Makaidos, dragon, strong of heart,
Bereft of daughter, son, and mate,
Arise and take thy crown and throne,
Become again the potentate.

Deceivers fly to wrest thy place,
To steal thy seed, thy brood, thy fold;
Forbid the theft, this love betrayed,
And seize the souls from demons' hold.

Bonnie snatched in a breath. For a moment, she had lost her sense of reality. She had to concentrate. As the shouts, roars, and clanking of metal on metal grew louder, she glanced between the raging battle and the plant.

Reaching for the leaves, Sapphira looked at Bonnie. "I suppose I should just peel them back."

Bonnie nodded. "I think it's now or never."

Sapphira pinched the tops and pulled the leaves away from the center. An egg-shaped, transparent ball sat on top of the stem. No bigger than a small pumpkin, it glowed orange. Inside, a miniature dragon tried to spread its wings, but the glass boundary squeezed in the tips. The dragon reared up on its haunches and clawed to get out.

Sliding her hands under the ball, Sapphira lifted it to eye level. She gazed at it, her brilliant blue eyes shining and reflecting its glow.

Hoofbeats sounded. Bonnie glanced toward the battle, barely able to take her eyes off the plant's offspring. Dikaios thundered toward them, riderless and shouting, "Watch out for Goliath!"

Bonnie looked up. A red dragon swooped, his claws extended and fire blazing. Yereq leaped ahead and blocked Goliath's dive, slashing the air with his sword. Bonnie dove on top of Sapphira and spread out her wings. Heat coated them, and something sharp dug in, but it didn't rip her wing.

A loud whinny clashed with a dragon's roar. Bonnie jumped to her feet. Dikaios had reared up and was battling the dragon, hooves against claws and teeth, and Yereq jumped into the fray with powerful sword thrusts, but the nimble dragon dodged every jab.

As Goliath drew in a breath to scorch his opponents, Sapphira rolled over and threw a ball of flames into his eyes. Goliath beat his wings and flew backwards, then headed high into the air, apparently making ready for another diving attack.

Dikaios trotted up to Bonnie. "Ride with me to the battle. Yereq and the Oracle will protect the dragon king. Your beloved needs you."

"Billy? Is he all right?"

"He is alive, but there is no time to explain. Just come."

With a flap of her wings, Bonnie jumped onto Dikaios's back and looked at the egg. Now on the ground, it had swollen to four times its original size and was growing at an astounding rate. The outer shell cracked and flaked away. The dragon's snout poked through, then his wings. Surpassing Dikaios in size, he shook away the shell fragments, then, extending his neck, let out a trumpeting call.

Dikaios turned toward the battlefield and took off in a gallop. Bonnie looked back. Above, Goliath dove toward Sapphira. She raised her hands and created a dome of light around herself and the growing dragon while Yereq stood in front of her, his sword raised.

Goliath blasted a stream of fire that splashed against Yereq's chest. With a swipe of his tail, he smacked Yereq to the ground, snuffing the flames. Then, reaching out with his claws, he broke through the light, snatched Sapphira's arm, and jerked her off the ground. As he rose into the air, Sapphira screamed, but her voice thinned out in the distance.

The newly birthed dragon, now almost normal size, shot after them. Bonnie jumped to her feet on Dikaios's back and zoomed upward. "Makaidos!" she called. "Attack Goliath! I'll catch Sapphira!"

Now at least a hundred feet in the air and closing in, Makaidos roared. "Release the girl, Goliath, and prepare to feel my wrath."

Goliath flew in a slow orbit another fifty feet higher. "Long ago, you vowed not to fight alongside the human race. What has become of your cherished integrity?"

"I am not fighting alongside them. I am here to reestablish my kingdom, and you are the usurper. Now release the girl, and let us see who is the rightful king of the dragons."

"As you wish." Goliath opened his claws. Sapphira plummeted, but she didn't scream. Her arms and legs flopped helplessly. She seemed unconscious, or worse.

Bonnie flew underneath, caught Sapphira, and pressed her ear close to her mouth. "Thank God," Bonnie whispered. "She's breathing." As she eased her to the ground near the open plant, she looked at the

Oracle's face. A dark bruise marked her forehead, but that was there before. Apparently all the jerking around had knocked her out. Someone had to stay to protect her.

Bonnie looked at the battlefield. In the sky, Makaidos fought with Goliath, colliding, snapping, biting, then circling around for another violent collision. A smaller red dragon joined in and helped Goliath. Thigocia dove down from above and snatched him out of the sky with her claws and threw him downward.

On the ground, the invaders had made a ring around the village defenders, but Bonnie couldn't see through to the center. Flames shot here and there, indicating that some dragons were within, apparently holding the attackers at bay. With only Billy and a few other warriors remaining, how long could they hold out against such an onslaught?

Still, the invaders seemed far fewer than before. Had Billy thinned them out with Excalibur? Where was its beam now? If he was hurt, as Dikaios had implied, he wouldn't be able to fight. Yet, she could take his place. If she could locate the sword, she would be able to fly into the circle, summon its beam, and disintegrate men and evil dragons.

Merlin flew over the field again. Another fuel bomb dropped and exploded among the invaders, but it was smaller, obviously something Candle and Windor had pieced together in a hurry. Still, it punched a significant hole in the attacking troops. As the plane flew away, perhaps to try to reload again, Windor stuck his head out the open cargo door and shook his fists, a blend of triumph and worry in his expression.

Something touched Bonnie's shoulder. Twisting her neck, she looked at it—a man's hand, large and gentle.

"Go to him, Bonnie," a soft voice said. "I will watch Sapphira."

Tilting her head upward, she gazed into Enoch's eyes. "You'll protect her? How?"

He set a duffle bag down next to the plant. "Yereq is recovering, so you need not worry."

Bonnie looked at the giant as he struggled to his feet. His uniform was soiled and scorched, but as he straightened and lifted his sword, he seemed strong and alert.

Behind Enoch, the gate had split slightly, allowing a brilliant light to radiate from within. "Go now. The glory of Heaven is an effective deterrent. No one will dare approach while Yereq and I guard the Oracle."

She grabbed his hand, kissed it, then leaped into the air. Flying as fast as she could, she lifted over the invaders' siege circle and landed at the center, dodging a ball of flames launched by Clefspeare. The great red dragon stood next to two fallen men lying under a lean-to of battle shields, ferociously guarding them with a barrage of fire against any invader who dared to draw near.

Hartanna and the other females spewed their own flames, weaker but effective. The invaders held up shields to protect themselves, but they had to stay back.

Elam, Valiant, Barlow, Gabriel, and Flint jumped and jabbed at the closest enemies, each with shields up to ward off arrows and spears. Flint seemed invigorated by the battle, though his movements lacked the crispness and vigor the others displayed.

Ashley knelt near Billy and Walter, making sure the shields over their bodies stayed in place while holding another shield over her own head.

"Where is Excalibur?" Bonnie shouted.

"Over here!" Ashley waved her arm. "Get under cover!"

As Bonnie ran, an arrow whizzed by her head. An invader charged toward her. Valiant slung a dagger and pierced the attacker's neck, instantly felling him. Five more attackers charged. Valiant raised a shield and, like a battering ram, drove into them, pushing all five far into the crowd. In a mad flurry of swords and spears, Valiant disappeared.

"Valiant!" Bonnie cried.

Flint ran after Valiant, swinging his sword to cut an opening. As if swallowed by the attackers, he, too, vanished.

Ashley yanked Bonnie down to a crouch. "Stay low! We can't help them now!"

"Are Billy and Walter all right?" Bonnie asked.

Ashley shifted the shield, partially covering both herself and Bonnie. "Billy got knocked unconscious, but I don't think it's serious. He's been mumbling your name. Walter's alive, but not for long. I need Sapphira to help me do a healing."

Bonnie shook her head. "She's out cold, but she's safe."

Ashley pulled Excalibur from Billy's grip and passed it to Bonnie. "Go get 'em, tigress."

Billy raised his head and called out with a groggy, "Bonnie?"

"Hush." Ashley pushed his head back down. "You're in no shape to help."

"I'll do you proud, Billy." As Bonnie rose to her feet, Dikaios burst into the circle and joined them. "Karrick has fallen, but when Roxil flew to protect him, Goliath knocked her down. The coward is up to his old tricks and now stands with a claw on Roxil's underbelly threatening to kill her if Makaidos and Thigocia approach. They are at a stalemate."

"We can't do anything about that now." Picking up a shield from the ground, Bonnie used her wings to mount Dikaios. "Let's make like a clock, if you know what I mean."

Dikaios bobbed his head. "I do. Proceed when ready."

"You're a sitting duck up there," Ashley said.

"But I'll get a better angle on the enemy." Holding the shield in one hand and Excalibur in the other, she summoned the beam. The brilliant light shot into the air. For a moment, the surrounding invaders became stone silent. Their wide eyes told Bonnie that they had seen what the beam could do, and now that they were within range and no longer mixed in with the village troops, she could wipe them out in a hurry.

While Dikaios turned in a circle, she swept the beam over the heads of her allies and into the crowd of invaders. The dragons ducked as the beam passed by. Clefspeare blew fire at any invader who lowered his shield to load an arrow or throw a spear.

In explosions of sparks, the enemy troops vanished—fifty, seventy, one hundred. Some retreated while some managed to shoot arrows.

A few pinged against her shield, but one hit Dikaios's front leg. He grunted but continued his rotation.

Bonnie kept the sword in place. Fifty more vanished. Another twenty. As invaders ran for their lives, the remaining ones shot their arrows wildly. Clefspeare and Hartanna flew into the air and chased the retreating men, blasting their unguarded backs, while Elam, Gabriel, and Barlow pursued the stragglers. Now it seemed that only thirty or so remained.

An arrow whizzed in and knifed into Bonnie's sword arm. She drew her arm back and dropped Excalibur. As the sword fell, the beam died away. Flapping her wings, she jumped off Dikaios and lunged for the hilt, the arrow protruding from her forearm, but a hand scooped Excalibur up before she could reach it.

One of the attackers, a tall muscular man in ancient Egyptian garb, swung Excalibur at Bonnie's neck, but just before the blade could strike, a shield blocked it with a loud clank. The shield bearer lowered his shoulder and bulldozed the attacker, knocking him flat on his back and sending Excalibur thudding to the ground. As Bonnie's defender snatched it up, a dragon flew by and smothered the attacker in flames.

The defender turned and smiled. "That was a close one."

"Billy!" Bonnie gave him a one-armed embrace. "Thank you!"

He whispered into her ear. "You did me proud. Now let's finish the job."

She flew up to Dikaios's back and, using her good arm, helped Billy mount in front of her. With Excalibur's beam once again surging, Billy shouted, "Let's round them up!"

Dikaios leaped ahead. As he passed one fleeing invader after another, Billy raked the beam across them. When a man vanished, his armor kept running for a moment before crashing to the ground. Soon, he had cleared the field of enemy troops.

After dousing the beam, he jumped off Dikaios and ran to Ashley while Bonnie followed, flying a foot or so off the ground. Ashley had tipped the shields over, exposing Walter's pallid face to the sun.

Billy knelt next to him and touched a deep gash across his forehead, placed there by an enemy sword. "How is he?"

She shook her head. "Not good, and Bonnie says Sapphira's not available." She looked at him, her eyes wet with tears. "Can we try a healing with Excalibur?"

"In a heartbeat." He stepped a few paces back. "Everyone stand clear!"

Clefspeare rose into the air. "I must see what I can do about my father's new threats," he said. "I suggest you join us after you restore your friend."

Ashley covered Walter's body and slid her arms underneath. "I'm ready."

Billy reignited the beam, but just as he angled it toward the ground to send its energy through the soil, someone shouted, "No!"

With a quick jerk, Billy raised the sword again. He turned toward the voice. In front of Heaven's Gate an elderly man waved an arm. "With the gem intact," the man called, "Excalibur is too powerful in this realm. It will likely heal him, but it will bring great harm to the healer, perhaps even death."

"I'll risk it," Ashley shouted. "Walter's dying."

Billy squinted at the old man. "Is that Enoch?"

Bonnie nodded. "We'd better listen to him."

"Bring him to me!" Enoch said, gesturing for them to come. "I will tell you what to do."

Billy let the beam die away and ran to Walter. "Come on. Let's get him on Dikaios."

Bonnie, Ashley, and Billy hoisted Walter in place, and Ashley mounted with him, holding his limp body in a sitting position. She gave Dikaios a gentle kick. "Let's move!"

As Dikaios galloped toward Heaven's Gate, Billy reached for Bonnie's hand and nodded at a gathering of dragons. "Elam and the others are already there. Come on."

"You go. I have to check something."

He pointed at the arrow protruding from her upper arm. "How bad is it?"

"Just break it off for me, but leave a few inches."

Taking a deep breath, he grasped the shaft. "Here goes."

She closed her eyes and clenched her teeth. The arrow snapped. Pain stormed from her arm, through her spine, and down to her toes, but it quickly eased to a dull throb. As tears welled, she nodded. "I'm okay. Thanks."

While Billy ran toward the garden's western wall, Bonnie scanned the ground and eyed each nearby body. She spotted one of the village's distinctive orange and red uniforms dressing a body that lay underneath a tall thin man sprawled facedown with his limbs splayed.

With a beat of her wings, she half ran and half flew toward the pair. She fell to her knees, rolled the top man over, and slid his blood-spattered body to the ground. His blond hair, dirty and matted, brushed back from his face. He blinked, revealing blue eyes, glassy and dilated. A companion attached to a thin chain floated out from under his shirt and hovered next to his ear. It flashed a dim blue light. As if in response to its light, Flint smiled weakly.

"Flint," Bonnie whispered. "Can you hear me?"

Grimacing, he choked out gurgling words. "Valiant. You must help Valiant."

Bonnie shifted to the other man and, with a heave, turned him over. Valiant's dark curls waved in the warm breeze, but the rest of his body stayed motionless. He was breathing, but with multiple wounds in his chest and his belly oozing blood, he wouldn't be breathing for long.

"I have to get you both to Ashley." Bonnie slid her hands under Flint's back.

"No." Flint clutched her sleeve, pulling the arrow and sending a new shock wave of pain through her body. She tried not to let it show, but a grunt pushed through.

"Take Valiant," Flint said, his voice slightly stronger. "You cannot take us both, so allow me this one sacrifice to make amends for my many sins against Abraham . . . my beloved father."

Bonnie looked at her engagement ring. Sunlight made the red gem light up with brilliant sparkles. She pulled the ring off and slid it onto Flint's finger. "Abraham gave this to you long ago, and he kept it with him, even as he burned. For some reason, he left it behind. I think he wanted someone to give it back to you."

Flint drew his hand close to his face. He smiled again, then closed his eyes and let his head droop to the side. As his chest drew in a final breath, the companion settled there, and its light faded away.

Tears once again flowing, Bonnie shifted back to Valiant and slid her hands under his armpits. Using her legs and wings, she dragged him to Heaven's Gate where Ashley sat next to Walter's body. Yereq stood guard in front of the two Oracles, while Enoch knelt over Walter.

Panting, she nodded at Valiant. "No time to talk. Please take care of him." Without another word, she flew to the western end of the field and joined Billy.

Goliath stood over Roxil, a clawed foot resting on her underbelly. Clefspeare and Makaidos stalked around him, apparently searching for a way to catch him off guard, but Goliath's head rotated with them, and when his neck twisted beyond its limits, he snapped it back around and began following them again.

"You must stand down, son," Makaidos said. "Even if you kill Roxil, you can never escape. Between Clefspeare and me, you stand no chance."

"Give me my son back," Goliath growled. "Allow me to fly away with him, and I will release my mate. I will never return to haunt your pathetic tribe again."

Billy whispered to Bonnie, "This has been going on ever since I got here. The words have changed, but the standoff remains the same."

Bonnie searched for Karrick. She spotted a splash of red scales surrounded by Thigocia, Hartanna, Legossi, and Firedda. She then scanned the field again. Two dragons were missing, Yellinia and Sorentine. Bonnie had guessed that Yellinia was Devin's victim out on the battlefield, but what had happened to Sorentine?

Listener had dismounted Ember and was now standing near the ring of dragons, though she appeared to be back far enough to avoid danger.

Gabriel and Shiloh stood behind her, while Elam and Barlow, both with swords drawn, watched from the opposite side of the circle.

"Karrick is under our protection," Makaidos said. "He has seen your traitorous ways, your brutal betrayal of his mother, and has requested asylum among us. We will not give him over to you."

"This is new," Billy whispered to Bonnie. "Just keep your eyes and ears open and be ready for anything."

A low growl erupted from Goliath's throat. "You know our law. He is not of age, so he cannot consent to join with you. As his father, I decide his fate."

"I know the law, and the king can overrule a father's rights if a son applies for asylum." Makaidos extended his neck, bringing his head close to Goliath's. "And I am the king."

Goliath spat a wad of fire on the ground. "The king of pride. The king of arrogance. You lord your authority over all your subjects, just as you did over Roxil and me. Your insane loyalty to corrupt humans incited us and other dragons to seek to protect our own kind."

Makaidos snorted. "And you say this with the claws of death ready to rip open your own mate."

"I am willing to sacrifice one for the good of many others. You did that yourself."

"You speak as a fool! I sacrificed *myself*, not someone else." Makaidos stretched out his wing and gently pulled Listener into his webbing. "This is the precious girl who asked to die for the sake of my daughters, but I could not allow her to pay the price of blood for dragon children she did not even know." He touched the other wing tip to his chest. "Roxil and Ashley were bone of my bone and flesh of my flesh. If they were to find deliverance in the ultimate Messiah, I had to be the one to give up my own blood to show them the way."

"It is true," Roxil said as she lifted her head from the ground. "I agreed with you during our days of foolishness, but when I saw our father burn in flames, his joy increasing with every painful moment as he gave his life for my sake, I knew that our rebellion was folly. Our father's every act, whether we agreed with it or not, was fueled by love, and when I saw that love, I knew that his love for humankind was pure and righteous. He loved humans, corrupt and stupid as they were, just as he loved you and me, though we never ceased in our rebellion. It took his suffering and death for me to finally see past my hatred, but now I understand what love really is."

Goliath blew out a stream of sparks. "He was grandstanding. He knew he would come back to life and lord his self-righteousness over us once again. But he cannot fool me. I am wise to his trickery. I can see—"

"My son!" Thigocia pleaded. "The Nephilim spirits are speaking these lies to you. Can you not see their schemes? No matter how great your father's deeds of sacrifice, the spirits burn them into scornful ashes. He can do nothing good in your sight. Your controlling spirits will not allow it."

Goliath's eyes flashed. "There are no spirits! No one has control of me. I am autonomous."

Listener broke away from Makaidos, ran to Goliath, and petted his scales as she looked into his eyes. "Daddy?" she cried out. "Is that you?"

Everyone stared, mesmerized. The little girl was now out of reach, beyond rescue.

"Daddy?" Goliath drew his head back. "This child is proving her madness once again. She who sought to die for her betters now wonders if one is her own father."

"But Daddy . . ." Listener laid a palm on each side of his head as she continued staring. "I see you in there. I have not forgotten when you told Candle and me stories in front of the fire. We used to snuggle, and you would look at me with those same red and flashing eyes as you told of the dragons of old who would breathe fire instead of ice and help the humans battle against enormous angels called Watchers who had enslaved the world."

Goliath's words stumbled out like those of a stuttering drunkard. "Many know these . . . these stories. It . . . it wasn't I who told them to you."

"But you did. I will never forget the one about a great red dragon who spoke these vows to his new mate, the same vows you spoke to my mother, Angel."

Listener folded her hands, and, looking up, she spoke in a singsong chant. "Sweet are the days of those in love, yet too short for the breadth of love's endurance. When death comes to end our story, the words of love I write will find another page, for—"

"For our book of affection can have no end," Goliath finished. His eyes now seemed glazed over, a duller shade of red.

She set her hands on his face again. As dragon and girl stared at each other, Listener added, "Those were the words of my father's vow to my mother. He said he would love her even after death."

A thin line of smoke rose from Goliath's nostrils. Almost incoherently, he mumbled, "Even after death."

She pulled his head closer, so close he could have killed her with a single puff. "Do you still love her?"

Goliath's eyes rotated toward Roxil, then back to Listener. He seemed lucid now, though his tone was much gentler than Goliath's normal tenor. "Your mother was your father's mate, not mine. He died. She died. Why raise the issue?"

"Are you the great red dragon my father told me about, the one who spoke the vows?"

Goliath drew back again. "How did you learn these words of mine? I composed them, but I never spoke them to my mate. I chose a different vow."

Roxil spoke up, still underneath Goliath's foot. "Your vow was similar, but not exactly the same. You said, 'When death comes to end our story, the words I write will find another page.' You said nothing about love or affection."

A scowl bent Goliath's brow. He snatched Listener's clothes with his wing's claw and set her down next to Makaidos. "This is trickery," Goliath said. "You are filling my mind with confusion."

Thigocia pleaded again. "My son, Listener is reminding you of your true nature. When you were here as a human, you were kind and noble and good. When you are in your dragon form, the spirits of the Nephilim control you and tell you lies. Listen to Listener, for she has listened to you and learned of your integrity. Fight against the demons who have controlled you for all these centuries. If you truly want to think for yourself, then you must win this battle."

Goliath looked at Thigocia. Again his eyes turned dull as he whispered, "Mother, I . . . I cannot fight them. . . . Help me."

"Father!" Ashley ran into the gathering, her eyes wide and streaming tears as she reached her arms around Makaidos's neck. "Walter is dying. Enoch says that only another sacrifice will allow the birthing garden to restore him."

CHAPTER 19

ANOTHER SACRIFICE

Makaidos nuzzled Ashley's cheek. "But there are no remaining bones. How will the garden be energized?"

Ashley dug a bone from her pocket, the finger bone she had found at Abraham's wall of fire. "There is this one. Maybe it will be enough."

Makaidos lifted his foreleg and looked at a gap in his clawed hand. One appendage was missing.

He let out a long sigh. "It will be enough."

"Makaidos?" Thigocia spread a wing toward him. "What do you intend to do?"

"I intend to save another life." He turned toward Heaven's Gate. "If my son-in-law dies, a valiant warrior will perish, and my daughter will be heartbroken. I cannot allow it."

"You have already given so much," Thigocia said. "You have died thrice. Will you be able to cheat death again?"

As he shuffled toward the garden, he shook his head. "No, my love.

There will be no more bones, for the ones that fill my frame now have no resurrection power."

She dipped her head. "Very well, my darling. I shall not try to persuade you to turn against the love in your heart."

"It seems that our reunion is short-lived." He stopped and looked at her. "But when we meet on the other side of that gate, we will never be apart again."

"Let it be so." As Makaidos continued his march, Ashley at his side, Thigocia turned back to Goliath. "Is it grandstanding you perceive now, my son? Do you see a charlatan, or a loving father?"

Goliath wagged his head back and forth as if trying to cast off a spider's web. "I . . . I cannot see. I cannot hear."

"Concentrate!" Thigocia set her wings on each side of his head. "Look at me and focus on my eyes."

Goliath's eyes flashed back to their more vibrant color, but his manner stayed calm. "I am focusing."

Now speaking softly and slowly, Thigocia continued. "Release your mate."

Goliath lifted his foot. Roxil rolled out from underneath and rose to her haunches.

"Good, my son. Now listen to my words. Your father loves you. He has always loved you. Just as you love your own son and do not want to lose him, so your father never wanted to lose you. You know the pain you suffered in your heart when Karrick chose to leave you. Oh, my son, it was ten times worse for your father, for instead of his wise teachings, you chose to listen to the foul song of demons. His firstborn, the crown prince of the dragons, decided to follow the Prince of Darkness, and how great the darkness has become. Because of your rebellion, his life has been but one death after another, each one a result of a series of events you set in motion. Yet, he has borne these sorrows and suffered these deaths willingly, for ever since you left his loving embrace, he died in his spirit every time he awoke from slumber to find that you were still a rebel."

Sparks drizzled from Goliath's nostrils. "How will he die now? Who will kill him?"

Sudden pain shook Bonnie from a trance. Billy had brushed against her arm and the still-protruding arrow. Since he was also mesmerized by the dragons' conversation, he hadn't even noticed the pain he had inflicted.

Bonnie studied Makaidos's shuffling gait as he closed in on the garden. Goliath's question was valid. Who would kill him? Every enemy had been vanquished.

She looked at Excalibur, the hilt still clenched in Billy's grip. Would he have to do it? Could he bring himself to take the life of a king in order to save Walter?

"Come," Thigocia said. "We shall see what the king of the dragons has in mind."

Still encircling Karrick as he walked, the female dragons half shuffled and half flew to the garden. Goliath and Roxil trailed them, while Bonnie and the other humans followed, Elam in the lead and Gabriel bringing up the rear.

Bonnie sidled up to Billy and whispered. "Are you thinking what I'm thinking?"

"I think so, but I can't see how anyone here could kill him."

From his other side, Sir Barlow spoke up. "Nor I, William. It is a terrible task indeed. Perhaps it will fall to the duty of the warrior chief."

Elam shook his head. "After all we've been through, I would rather die myself."

"Billy, you'll probably be called upon to energize the bone," Bonnie said. "I think Sapphira's still unconscious."

Billy nodded. "I can do that, but let's see what Enoch says."

When they had all crossed the garden and drew near to Heaven's Gate, Billy weaved through the crowd, stepped ahead of Makaidos and Ashley, and dropped to one knee in front of Enoch. "I have brought Excalibur." He laid it on his palms and lifted it up. "A few years ago, Professor Hamilton traveled from Oxford to a little town in West

Virginia. His faith in me led to the salvation of all dragonkind, and without his guiding hand, I would never have had the spirit or the courage to give my life for a race that spawned a few traitors who tried to kill me. So now I cannot dishonor the professor by lifting my hand to destroy the great king of the race for which we both sacrificed so much."

"Well spoken." Enoch grasped the hilt and lifted Excalibur. Then, touching Billy on each shoulder, he said, "By the power vested in me by the Majesty on High, I dub you a Knight of Heaven, for although a few precious souls might be willing to die for a friend, anyone who gives his life for those who hate him surely possesses the spirit of the ultimate Messiah."

Billy looked up at Enoch. "I will do my best to wear that title with honor and integrity."

Enoch gestured for him to rise. Lifting Excalibur high, Enoch spoke with a commanding voice that seemed to echo throughout Second Eden. "When Billy energizes this final remnant from the bones of Makaidos, the birthing garden will have the power to regenerate all who stand on its soil, including Gabriel, who lost his physical body in the earthly realm. As before, when the dragons passed in front of the Great Key, all who have dragon traits will be able to choose their form, a state they will keep for the rest of their natural lives, but this time, they must bear witness to that choice before we begin. Each of you will speak the words that God's spirit will reveal to your hearts."

He pointed the sword at Billy. "Take the hand of your fiancée, for the two of you will speak first. Have no fear that the wounded are in travail, for God will watch over them until we are finished." He looked at Bonnie's arm. "We will tend to that arrow very soon."

Bonnie joined hands with Billy. As he looked into her eyes, Billy said, "I choose to stay as I am, the way God made me. I will breathe fire and sense danger for all my days."

She pulled their clenched hands close to her chest. "And I choose the same. I will be content to be hounded by the media and to be called a freak." Breaking into a big smile, she added, "I will be a freak for God."

Gabriel raised a hand. "I'm with you. Being a winged wonder is very cool. I never really wanted to be anything else."

"And now you, Ashley," Enoch said as he shifted the sword toward her.

Ashley knelt beside Walter's body. As blood drained from the gash on his head, he heaved shallow breaths.

Enoch leaned down and touched her shoulder. "Fear not, my child. God will sustain him."

A hint of a smile broke through. "I agree with my brother and with Billy and Bonnie. I would like to stay as I am."

"Very well." Enoch moved the sword's point from dragon to dragon.

"I will no longer be Irene Silver," Hartanna said. "I will be Irene Conner, for my husband has returned, and he has restored his good name. I am proud to wear it again."

Clefspeare bowed low. "I will again be a husband to my dear Marilyn and a father to my noble and courageous son. I hope soon to take a daughter-in-law under my proverbial, if not literal, wing. I choose to be human."

Legossi lifted her head high. "I was born a dragon, and I will stay a dragon. If humans continue to despise my form, then so be it. I will show them the spirit of true integrity as I guard their backsides whether they like it or not."

"I am sorry, my old friend," Firedda said. "I was never very skilled at being a human, but I wish to return to Earth as a human to continue searching for my youngling."

Enoch shifted the sword and pointed it toward the sky. Everyone turned and looked. Another female dragon flew toward them, carrying two wriggling bodies. When she landed in the garden, she kept a foot planted on each one.

Bonnie grinned. It was Sorentine! And she carried Semiramis and Mardon in her claws!

"I apologize for my absence," Sorentine said. "When I saw these two escaping, I thought it better to make sure they caused no further trouble."

"And what of Yellinia?" Thigocia asked. "Have you seen her?"

Sorentine's head dipped low. "The slayer beheaded her. I assume the others did not tell you because of their grief."

A tear dripped from Thigocia's eye. "She was a valiant warrior." She turned toward Enoch. "Can Yellinia be brought back from the dead when the garden is energized?"

"Sadly, no," Enoch said. "This energy will not restore life or severed body parts."

Everyone stayed silent for a moment. Listener hugged Elam and wept. As he patted her gently on the back, he nodded at Sorentine. "Well done, good dragon. You are among the wisest and noblest of your race."

"You honor me too well," she replied, lowering her head further.

Semiramis, her red cloak now smeared with dirt, grunted from underneath Sorentine's foot. "If you will stop all this chatter for just a moment, I would like to plead my case."

Elam drew his sword and pointed it at Semiramis. "You have borne witness against yourself. We will hear no more from your lying lips."

Mardon stayed still as he stared at Elam. "Perhaps they will hear me. The three realms are still joined, and I know how to sever the rope that binds them. If you will grant me mercy, I will show you how."

"I will address that issue later," Enoch said. "For now, we must continue. Sorentine, what is the desire of your heart? Do you wish to remain a dragon or will you return to your human form?"

"I have learned that my precious little one is alive here in Second Eden, so I would like to become human and be her mother for as long as I can." She bowed her head again. "If that pleases you, honorable prophet."

"It pleases me," Enoch said, smiling. "Now, I need a volunteer who is not going to transform. Kindly take these two miscreants to the village, find a place that isn't in flames, and guard them there until you receive further instructions."

Legossi shuffled over to Sorentine. "With pleasure." She grasped Semiramis and Mardon and lifted them into the sky. Mardon shouted, but only the words, "Sever the rope," survived the buffeting wind.

Enoch moved the sword to Roxil. "And you, dear dragoness?"

Roxil looked at Makaidos and Thigocia in turn. "I have long disparaged the human race, so it is important that I make up for my errors. If I become human again, I would show that I love mankind by becoming one of them, but it was as a dragon that I spat on their shadows, so I will stay a dragon and become what I should have been all along, a servant in scales to the human race."

When the sword pointed at Thigocia, she looked up at Enoch. "What of my other offspring, Carboni, Alithia, and Martinesse?"

"They are humans on Earth, and in that place and state they will remain. Many adventures await them there. They have already located other dragon offspring, but that is not for us to consider at this time."

"And Valcor?"

Enoch smiled. "Patrick's desire to remain human and stay with Ruth prevented him from becoming a dragon here in Second Eden. That decision will not change."

"Very well." Thigocia looped her tail with Makaidos's and spoke with a trembling voice. "When my mate completes his sacrifice, he is going to be with you in glory, so I will stay a dragon and honor his memory within a suit of scales. Since my remaining days will be spent in sadness, let them be days that give tribute to the great Makaidos, king of the dragons."

Makaidos laid a wing over her back. He nuzzled her cheek but said nothing.

"And you, Makaidos," Enoch said, shifting the sword again, "what form do you wish to take? For even in death your body would be left behind."

Makaidos fixed his gaze on Thigocia. "Although my love for humans is well known, my love for my mate and my offspring exceeds all loves, save for the love I have for the Maker. Let me die as a dragon, and let the legacy of my service to both species be preserved forever."

Finally, Enoch pointed the blade at Goliath. "What do you wish to be? The dragon named Goliath, or the human who was called Dragon?"

Goliath looked at Makaidos, then at Listener. Although his eyes seemed filled with confusion, he spoke with clarity. "I will not tell you."

Riveting his gaze on Goliath, Enoch raised his voice. "You must!"

Goliath growled through his words. "I . . . will . . . not!"

Enoch bent his brow. "Then we will have to proceed without you."

"But how do we proceed?" Billy asked. "Who here would kill Makaidos?"

Enoch nodded at Ashley. "Do you still have the dragons' bane?"

She lifted a chain from around her neck and pulled the candlestone from under her uniform. The moment the crystalline facets appeared, Billy flinched. Every dragon showed signs of pain, some grimacing and others drawing back a step.

The chain dangling under her hand, Ashley wrapped the gem in her fingers, concealing it.

"You will give it to the sacrificial dragon," Enoch said, "for he is called to suffer great torment. Every ounce of energy he has gained in this life will be delivered bit by bit to the ones for whom he is dying. This will demonstrate once and for all the great love that he has for humans, and since love covers a multitude of sins, every evil act by dragonkind that has ever been incited against the human race will hereby be nullified in the memories of mankind. Tales of this sacrificial act will be told to generation after generation, and the story will remind them that the evils of the past have been washed away."

Keeping her grip on the chain, Ashley released the gem and let it dangle underneath. Now sobbing, she rose to her feet and held it out for Makaidos.

Bonnie looked at Billy. He was biting his lip. The pain had to be terrible, but he could bear it. If the pain in his heart was the same as the horrible ache in hers, it was much worse than anything the candlestone had ever delivered.

As Makaidos reached out with a foreleg, Goliath beat his wings and shot forward. He snatched the candlestone in both clawed hands and held it close to his chest. "I could not choose a form," he said, his eyes flashing wildly. "For I have chosen death." He settled to his belly, holding the candlestone underneath. "Let the Maker decide what he will."

Thigocia lunged toward him, but Enoch waved her back. "Stand aside!" he shouted. "The Maker's purposes will be fulfilled through this dragon, and every word I spoke will come to pass, for the evils perpetrated through dragonkind had their source in him."

Goliath lay still. His eyes pulsed. Smoke poured from his nostrils. Although his tail and wings twitched, he gave no other signs of suffering.

Makaidos dropped to his belly next to Goliath and draped a wing over him. "My son, I love you." Spasms shook his body. "I love you more than I could ever say."

Thigocia did the same from the other side. Sobs punctuated her words. "Oh, my dear son! My dear, dear son. My love for you has never diminished, and my memory of you will never die."

Clefspeare and Roxil guided Karrick in front of Goliath's eyes. "Father," Clefspeare said. "For many years my thoughts of you have been dark, but now they will be filled with light, for I have never witnessed a nobler act."

Tears falling to the ground, Roxil stretched out her neck and nuzzled Goliath's cheek. "Now I will look forward to eternity. Our love will truly survive death, and when I see you in Heaven, we will forever celebrate what you have done."

Karrick nuzzled Goliath from the other side. "Good-bye, Father. I have known you for only a few years, and now I will live the rest of my years as you have lived your final minutes, in sacrificial love for those around me."

Enoch gave Excalibur back to Billy. "It is time to energize the garden's soil, so please move Walter, Valiant, and Sapphira close to Goliath."

Gabriel and Sir Barlow lifted Valiant, while Bonnie and Elam carried Sapphira. As they laid the two limp bodies side-by-side, Sapphira's feet almost touching the dragon's snout, Yereq carried Walter and placed him next to Sapphira.

Enoch pointed at Makaidos's plant. "Set the bone on the ground near the roots."

Ashley laid the tiny white fragment next to the thick stem. "Like this?"

As he nodded, Enoch reached for Bonnie. Cradling her arm, he looked into her eyes. "Prepare yourself, sword maiden. This will hurt terribly, but you will soon be healed."

Gritting her teeth, Bonnie watched Enoch as he pushed the arrow the rest of the way through her arm and pulled it out the other end. Pain jolted her body once again. For a moment, she felt dizzy, and nausea churned in her stomach, but both sensations quickly eased.

Enoch threw the bloody arrow to the ground. "Now we must hurry. We don't want Bonnie or anyone else to lose too much blood before the healing takes place." He turned to Billy. "Summon the beam and cover the bone with Excalibur's energy."

Billy aimed the beam at the spot. The laser coated the bone with light and dug into the soil.

The finger of Makaidos glowed so brightly, Bonnie pulled a wing in front to shield her eyes. The energy spread across the ground and flowed into every human and dragon.

"Now," Enoch said, "the healer must cover the wounded."

Ashley lay on top of Sapphira and spread her arms over the other two. The light crawled up over all four, coating them with a pulsing glow. Beams of light shot out from Ashley's eyes, and, as she guided the beams from body to body, she wept. Her tears sizzled as they fell to Sapphira's chest.

Bonnie held Billy's hand. Her arm had already stopped bleeding, and the entry point seemed to be closing. "The light stings, doesn't it?" she asked.

"Yeah, but it's a good sting."

Goliath groaned but quickly stifled it. Makaidos and Thigocia patted him on the back and whispered into his ears, but their voices were too quiet to be heard.

A violent spasm jerked Goliath's body. A stream of black fog flew out of his nostrils and, like a frantic phantom, darted back and forth, stopping at each human and dragon as if seeking refuge.

Enoch pointed at the stream. "Billy! Strike the foul spirits of the Nephilim! They have tormented both dragons and men for far too long."

With a flick of his wrist, Billy zapped the fog with Excalibur's beam. The beam's energy enveloped the blackness with a halo of sparkling radiance. It evaporated the entire stream in an instant.

Enoch gave Billy an approving nod. "You may now let Excalibur darken."

He obeyed and lowered the sword.

"While the power of light does its work," Enoch said, "one of you must summon the hospital and bring it down to rest. Then, bring everyone to Heaven's Gate. Let them bathe in the radiance, and all will be healed."

Elam raised his hand. "I can run the magneto. I'll set them down in the field." He jumped onto Dikaios, and they rushed toward the forest path to the village. The fire had dwindled, allowing them to pass.

"The transformations will now begin," Enoch said with a bow. "When all is completed, I will come back. I have something very special prepared, and I ask that everyone return here ready for a celebration." Smiling, he added. "Including a good washing."

With that, Enoch turned, passed through a brief rift in the gate, and disappeared.

Hartanna lifted her wings. "I feel something."

"As do I," Clefspeare said.

Firedda and Sorentine stretched out their necks. "I feel smaller," Firedda said. "My neck is shrinking."

Clefspeare's scales smoothed out, and his tail and snout began to shrivel. Hartanna's spines flattened. Blonde hair began to sprout at the top of her head.

Bonnie picked up the bag Enoch had left near the plant. "I'll bet I know what this is." She pulled out a beautiful sky blue dress. As she held it up off the ground, Billy reached in and withdrew a man's suit, black with pinstripes.

"Uh . . ." Billy said as he looked in the bag, "there are two more dresses in here, underwear, too. Men's and women's."

Giving Billy a wink, Bonnie placed the bag in front of the dragons and turned toward Heaven's Gate. "Let us know when you're done," she called.

Bonnie gazed at the transparent gate. Although she could see through to the rear of the garden, it seemed that faint shadows passed across the plane, like human phantoms of light scurrying from one place to another. It seemed that much more was going on behind the scenes than met the eye. The precise timing of so many events proved that loving helpers lay behind that shimmering barrier.

"We're ready!"

Billy and Bonnie turned. Jared Bannister, dressed in a perfectly fitting suit, bowed. Holding her ankle-length dress up to keep it from touching the dirt, Irene Conner curtsied. Dallas and Tamara copied her motions but with a bit less grace.

Bonnie ran to her mother and wrapped her up in her arms. "Oh, Mama, I'm so glad you chose to be human!"

Billy walked up to his father and extended his hand. "Dad, I—"

Jared pulled Billy into a tight hug. "Son, I watched you in battle. You and Walter both sacrificed yourselves for Ashley and Listener. I'm so proud of you, I might just explode."

As he returned the embrace, Billy laughed. "Don't explode. You'll mess up your new suit."

He pushed Billy back and brushed off the dirt Billy's uniform left behind. "Kind of overdressed for this place, aren't we?"

"You heard what Enoch said. He's planning something special."

Bonnie looked down at her uniform, caked with dirt and blood from her collar to her pant cuffs. "We'd better get cleaned up."

As the radiance continued sparkling on the ground, Goliath also shrank. Within seconds, he had turned into a man, now motionless. Makaidos and Thigocia kept their wings over his naked body from his shoulders to his ankles. Roxil lay down and stretched her neck over her mother.

Listener knelt near the man's head. "Oh, Daddy! It really *was* you!" She ran her fingers through his thick locks and tried to look into his eyes. "Daddy, it's Listener, your daughter."

Tears welling again, Bonnie pulled in her lip. This was too sad for words. The poor little girl had lost her father once again.

Tamara joined Listener and rubbed her back. "My precious little one. I will take care of you now. I cannot replace Angel or your father, but I promise to love you with all my heart."

While they embraced and wept together, Tamara's dark tresses fell over Listener's pigtails. The two colors were perfectly matched. Mother and daughter had finally reunited after over a thousand years.

Ashley lifted herself off Sapphira and helped all three patients rise to their feet. With her hair tossed about, her cheeks scarlet, and her shoulders slumped, she seemed ready to collapse, but when Walter smiled at her, her own smile lit up her tired face.

Rubbing his head, Walter looked around. "Wow! What did I miss?"

"When we hit the washroom," Billy said. "I'll tell you all about it."

Valiant bowed toward Ashley. "Thank you, healer. I am forever in your debt."

Sapphira ran to Acacia's body and fell to her knees. "Oh, my dear sister! I was hoping it was just a nightmare!" She laid her head on Acacia's chest and wept.

As her cries rose into the air, another sound drifted down from the sky, a low hum. Like a slender blimp, the long, tubular hospital descended toward the field. Merlin eased in for a landing as well. Candle threw down the back airstair and helped Windor hobble toward the garden.

Bonnie touched Billy's arm. "I'll stay with Sapphira. Why don't you and the others help the hospital patients come for their healing in the garden. Then we'll all get cleaned up."

"Good idea. I can hardly wait to see Dad and Mom get together."

While Billy, Walter, Ashley, Shiloh, Barlow, and Gabriel headed to the field, Bonnie stooped and touched Sapphira's shoulder. "I will never, ever forget your sister's sacrifice," Bonnie said. "She saved my fiancé, she stripped Devin's invincibility, and she rescued Earth and Second Eden. I have seen many wonderful sacrifices, but never one as beautiful, noble, and loving as hers."

Sapphira looked up at her. Tears poured from her shining blue eyes. "Thank you," she said, barely above a whisper. "That means a lot to me."

Bonnie rose and turned toward the field. Pearl and Marilyn had just carried a patient on a stretcher through the hospital doors and onto the landing platform. Ashley took Marilyn's place at the stretcher and pointed at Jared.

Marilyn pressed a hand against her chest, let out a squeal, and very nearly flew into Jared's arms. Billy and Walter laughed, but Ashley got them back to work in a hurry as she barked out her usual rapid-fire orders.

Carrying a stretcher, Patrick and Ruth emerged, with Steadfast walking alongside and holding an IV bag. Whoever that patient was, he or she must have been very sick.

When Bonnie's father came out, carrying a dark-skinned little girl in his arms, Ashley caught his gaze and nodded toward Heaven's Gate. As Sir Barlow took the girl, his resonant voice carried across the garden. "Your wife is waiting for you."

His mouth agape, Bonnie's father ran to Irene, then stopped and stared at her for a moment. After an exchange of inaudible whispers, they embraced warmly. Soon, they pulled apart and, holding hands, walked back to the hospital.

As stretcher after stretcher headed toward the garden, Bonnie leaned over and caressed Sapphira's hair. "I'd better check on our water supply and see if we have any clean clothes. The fire might have burned everything."

"Wait!"

Bonnie followed the sound of the voice. Enoch stepped out of a new rift in Heaven's Gate, carrying a pile of clothing draped over both arms. "I apologize for this last-minute detail, but some good friends of yours have been rushing this project to completion. Karen and Naamah were particularly fussy about your dress." He nodded at the pile. "They guessed correctly that you would keep your wings, but they had to pull out some fastening devices they had put in the back, just in case."

Bonnie touched the dress on top, a gorgeous white satin gown with a silk train. "It's . . ." She lowered her voice to a whisper. "It's a wedding gown."

Keeping his voice low, Enoch winked. "I had to wait for Billy to leave. Tradition says that a groom should not view the bride's gown until the appropriate time."

Bonnie kissed Enoch's cheek. "Thank you so much!"

"And there is a fine suit here for Billy and proper attire for everyone. I'm sure you will find that they all fit perfectly. We have access to very accurate information inside Heaven's Gate."

Smiling, Bonnie ran her hand along the hefty load of clothing. "I see two more wedding gowns here. Who else—"

"They are all labeled, my dear." Enoch began walking toward the edge of the garden. "You are all much too dirty, so I will carry these to the village. I will meet you at Abraham's old hut when you're ready."

A surge of joy blended with a fountain of sadness, and both rushed through Bonnie's mind and heart. As she surveyed the garden and adjoining field, scenes of life and death flooded her senses. Her mother and Billy's father were again human—happy, healthy, and content. Billy and Walter hauled sick villagers to the garden to be cured in a bath of life-giving energy. Dikaios and Elam galloped back into the field, and Elam joined in with the helping hands. Listener's father and Acacia lay dead, both a true blend of joy and sadness, and both precious portraits of the tragedy and victory of heroic sacrifice.

Tears flowing yet again, Bonnie heaved a sigh and marched toward the edge of the garden. With every step through the radiant soil, the sadness melted away, giving rise to fuller and fuller joy. Every tragedy, every moment of suffering, had led to life and peace, just as the suffering and death of her Lord Jesus had brought the same to every man, woman, and child on Earth who called upon his name.

She gave herself a firm nod. In this truth she could rest, knowing that the God of the universe had guided her and Billy every step of the way. And now, a final journey lay before her, a new adventure with her beloved, the young man who had proven his worth time and time again.

As Billy and Walter passed by with a patient on a stretcher, Bonnie smiled. Billy smiled back. Turning to the village again, she wrapped her arms around herself, holding the memory of that smile close. Yes, that wonderful man had proven his undying love, and their union would now come about by an act of the will, not a prophetic destiny. He was hers, and she was his, by choice. Could she scream that truth from the rooftops? Her heart felt like it was about to burst.

She unbuckled her sword belt, let it fall to the ground, and walked onto the field. The first step on the final path couldn't come soon enough.

Dikaios and Ember trotted up to her, Listener riding on Ember's back. "Would you like a ride?" Dikaios asked.

Bonnie grinned. "I think I could float back to the village, even without my wings."

"I can see the joy in your eyes." Dikaios bowed his head. "After the celebration, I will enter into Heaven to forever be with my master, so please do me this honor."

Bonnie flapped her wings, rose into the air, and settled on Dikaios's back. "The honor is all mine, great horse." She looked at Enoch as he walked across the field. Even from the garden, she could see the wedding gown on top of his pile of clothes.

Smiling, she stroked Dikaios's neck and cried out, "Let's fly!"

CHAPTER 20

TILL DEATH DO US PART

Lush grass, ankle-high and as green as emeralds, now covered the birthing garden and its adjoining field. Only one flaw interrupted the verdant carpet, a rectangular mound of dirt, a grave for Dragon, formerly Goliath. Since he had expelled the Nephilim in the garden, everyone agreed that his body should be laid to rest here, though all knew that his spirit was now rejoicing somewhere beyond Heaven's Gate.

Bonnie stood at the edge of the field and contemplated the recent events.

Just an hour ago, Enoch guided Bonnie back to Heaven's Gate. A golden rope had appeared, parallel to the shimmering gate and extending out of sight to the right and left. He instructed her to cut it with her staurolite dagger, which he had found buried in her dirty uniform. When she did, the rope snapped and disappeared. The ground shook. Although the sky stayed clear, the air cooled, though not enough to bring a chill.

Enoch explained that cutting the rope separated the three realms, but he wouldn't say what happened to Semiramis and Mardon, only that they would receive exactly what they deserved.

At that moment, thick green grass began to shoot up in the garden's soil around Bonnie's feet, replacing the burnt grass. Enoch went on to tell of several new birthing gardens that would be created so that Second Eden could be populated more rapidly as the inhabitants explored beyond the old boundaries and established new settlements.

Earlier, Thigocia and Legossi burned Yellinia outside the village, along with the bodies of the invaders. Billy and Walter buried Devin in an unmarked grave far from any footpath or water source. When they returned, they seemed stoic, lacking any joy at finally disposing of one of the darkest beings in all of human history.

"Let's just forget about him," Billy had said. "He's not worth the energy to speak his name." And he and Walter refused to tell anyone where they had buried him.

Following the village's custom for fallen warriors, Elam and Valiant burned Flint's body and buried his bones. Instead of the burial grounds outside the village, they created a small plot behind Abraham's former hut. Valiant sang a beautiful song of lament that carried a theme of hope. No one knew the condition of Flint's soul when he died, but the revival of his companion, his apparent change of heart, and his heroic sacrifice spoke volumes.

The two village chiefs also burned Cliffside's body. Taking Emerald along, they interred Cliffside's bones in the traditional burial grounds. Valiant's song prophesied the coming of another Second Edener, a child who would learn the same rock-solid dedication to service and unshakable love of the smallest ones, the unborn lives in the garden. Emerald wept for quite some time, and Valiant stayed with her, both on their knees as they prayed for comfort.

Enoch himself had taken Acacia's body through Heaven's Gate, saying something about preparing a "Welcome Home" celebration for an Oracle of Fire. As the prophecy indicated, since Elam never returned to

Earth with Acacia to search for Sapphira, Acacia's life became chaff, a sacrifice of love on behalf of others.

Just before Enoch took her body, Elam asked about the prophecy.

* * *

"I don't understand. When was I supposed to take Acacia to Earth?"

"When Billy took Acacia and Listener, you could have gone instead of Billy. If you had kept the prophetic words in mind, you might have realized that."

Elam pointed at himself. "So is Acacia's death my fault?"

"Of course not. Devin killed Acacia. You merely made a mistake. You had set your mind on training the troops. You did not intentionally disobey."

"But what if I had paid attention? Would Acacia still be alive?"

"Yes, my son." Enoch set a hand on Elam's shoulder. "But Sapphira would have perished instead."

"Sapphira? But how could—"

"Shhh . . ." Enoch stooped and picked up Acacia's body. "I can tell you no more of things that might have happened. Rest assured that God is not angry about your choices. You came to a fork in your journey, and you chose the path that you thought would be most likely to please him. It is a heart of obedience that God cherishes, and yours burns with passion like few others."

He turned toward the gate, and as he passed through a shining rift, Acacia's body burst into flames. Then, they both disappeared.

* * *

Bonnie sighed. One tragedy in exchange for another.

She shook her head and tried to cast off the sorrow. Only tears of joy would be allowed for the rest of the day. After all, a great celebration was about to commence.

Before she had cut the rope, in anticipation of the celebration, the youngest villagers had washed naked in the fountain. Enjoying the newfound warmth of their land, they scrubbed themselves and each other in perfect innocence. Their parents joined in, not caring that their wet, filthy clothes weighed them down. They made sure their toddlers exited the fountain clean from head to toe. Wearing broad smiles, it seemed that everyone was washing away the past—the conflicts, the deaths, and the sadness of days gone by.

Bonnie and the other Earth inhabitants had chosen to bathe in the private washrooms. Those buildings and half of the others survived the fire, but to the villagers, the losses seemed no more than broken jars. The huts were merely things, temporal and replaceable. They would share their dwellings and the labor of rebuilding what they had lost. Such was the loving character of these precious people.

Now, less than half a day after the climactic battle, Bonnie stood on the field that led to the birthing garden. A line of six bridesmaids and matrons assembled in front of her, temporarily shielding her from the groom who waited for her in front of Heaven's Gate.

They walked ahead in time with the slow music of a trio of pipers playing near the edge of the garden. It seemed appropriate to stretch out the occasion. Her wedding gown felt so heavenly, why not let these moments last for hours? The satin, dazzling white and as soft as silk, brushed against her body from her bare feet to her neck. With Ashley at her left and Sapphira at her right, each also wearing a beautiful white gown, the sensation was like walking among angels in the clouds.

Karen and Naamah knew the hearts of the brides and designed the gowns accordingly. Although they bore many similarities—modest necklines, fully covered shoulders, long sleeves, and ankle-length skirts—the gowns displayed the individuality of each bride.

The lace that covered the bottom third of Ashley's skirt lacked symmetry, but a closer inspection revealed a complex design within the delicate fabric, a tiny mural of scenes from her adventures—a miniature

Apollo, a representation of Larry the supercomputer, and a portrait of her departed grandfather.

Sapphira's lace bore images of flames sprouting from plants, scrolls from the museum, couples dancing with fountains of water spraying over their heads, and a blossom from the tree of life. As she pushed each foot forward, the sun seemed to make the flames come alive, the tongues sparkling with her every movement.

Bonnie looked down at her own dress. Of course, Karen and Naamah had cut holes in the back for her wings, but they had added something far more important. Although the satin was already brilliantly white, when the sun struck the bodice and skirt at the right angle, something still brighter gleamed—text stitched in silver thread, her song from Psalm 139. As she read the opening words, though it was upside down in her perspective, tears filled her eyes.

Whither shall I go from thy spirit? Or whither shall I flee from thy presence?
If I ascend up into heaven, thou art there: If I make my bed in hell, behold, thou art there.

Yes, whether living on Earth, visiting Heaven, trapped in Hell, or in the midst of battle in Second Eden, God had always been with her no matter what.

As they neared the garden, Bonnie peeked through the line of escorts. Billy stood in front of Heaven's Gate, facing her and wearing a stunning white tuxedo, a jet-black sword belt, and a freshly polished scabbard with Excalibur sheathed within.

She smiled. With his hair brushed back, his handsome face clean and shaven, and his broad shoulders squared, he looked fine indeed. Oh, yes, very fine indeed.

To Billy's right and Bonnie's left, Walter stood ramrod straight, alternately folding and unfolding his arms. Also wearing a white tux, he kept his eyes focused on the ground, shifting his weight constantly, apparently too nervous to behold the lovely treasure he would soon receive.

Elam stood at Billy's left, his hands folded at his waist. Also dressed in white, he moved from side to side, obviously trying to catch a glimpse of Sapphira behind the bridal party wall.

The villagers sat in the grass, as did the dragons and humans from Earth, all facing Heaven's Gate, yet looking back at the approaching procession, every eye wide with anticipation.

Billy's parents sat in the front row next to Bonnie's, all four so close to Billy, he could have reached them with two steps and an outstretched arm. Makaidos and Thigocia sat on their haunches close to Walter, with Roxil behind them, all three wearing draconic smiles.

Bonnie also spotted Patrick and Ruth seated near Elam. Patrick still felt very close to Elam, though he was much younger. Watching over Elam, or Markus as he was called at the time, had made him feel like a father long before Shiloh was born.

When the bridal party arrived at the front edge of the garden, the escorts stopped. The pipers' song faded, and, except for the cool breeze creating a gentle rustling of nearby trees, silence ensued.

Bonnie let her gaze drift from left to right along her line of escorts—Mantika, Tamara, Dallas, Shiloh, Listener, and a village girl about Listener's age. The two Second Eden maidens began to sing, trilling words in an unfamiliar language. They had explained earlier that Abraham had written the song centuries ago at a time when they did not yet speak English, and it became their traditional wedding song. Of course, he later translated it, but to this day they still sang the first verse in the original language, and that was the cue for Bonnie, Ashley, and Sapphira to lower their bridal veils over their faces.

After the beautiful yet mysterious words ended, the three matrons on the left shifted into single file, and the girls on the right did the same, as if opening a gate to the brides they had veiled with their bodies.

Bonnie and her companions stepped through the gap. The villagers and Earth visitors rose to their feet, gazing in silence. Even the breeze fell to a hush.

All three grooms stared. Walter's mouth dropped open. Tears streamed down Elam's cheeks. Billy's jaw quivered, and his fingers worked Excalibur's hilt. With his gaze locked on Bonnie's, he smiled.

Goose bumps covered Bonnie's arms. That smile . . . that wonderful smile—content, satisfied, filled with joy that a great journey was over and a new one, perhaps even more exciting, was about to begin. And now, they would travel the new road together as husband and wife.

She returned his smile, hoping to reflect the same excitement, the same joy, a joy so overflowing she could barely keep from bouncing on her toes.

Listener stepped out from her line of maidens and stood directly in front of Bonnie. Now the processional would begin, Listener leading the way, singing the English version of this realm's wedding song, altered slightly for the triple union of brides and grooms.

As she and the maidens proceeded, followed by the three matrons, Bonnie paused for a moment, took in a deep breath, and led the brides, stepping in time with the song's gentle rhythm.

The brides are ready, sound the call,
With spotless virtue, virgins all;
Let pipers pipe and angels sing,
Let shouts resound and anthems ring.

Extend your hands, O grooms of light,
And be their noble, worthy knights;
With arms of holy strength embrace
Your brides with honor, love, and grace.

When the song ended, Bonnie took her place in front of Billy, facing him and Heaven's Gate, though they didn't yet touch, as was the Second Eden custom. Ashley stood in front of Walter, and Sapphira faced Elam.

Immediately to Bonnie's right, Listener knelt and gazed at Billy with a broad smile. As Shiloh, the gap in her fingers still obvious, took a seat with Gabriel, and the village maiden sat with her parents, the crowd buzzed, some displaying questioning glances.

Tilting her head, Bonnie gave Billy a quizzical look. Why did Shiloh and the other girl do that? They were supposed to copy Listener's pose, one kneeling in front of Walter and the other in front of Elam, virgin females to attend each of the couples, a Second Eden tradition.

Billy seemed to understand her silent question, but his expression said he didn't have an answer. Obviously Shiloh and the other girl knew something the marrying couples didn't. A surprise, maybe?

A bright vertical line appeared in Heaven's Gate. As expected, Enoch stepped out. Instead of his usual tunic and breeches, he wore a multicolored cloak tied at the waist by a purple sash. With his white hair brushed neatly back, he appeared regal and holy, certainly looking like a man qualified by Heaven itself to perform the wedding ceremonies.

As Enoch lifted his hands, the crowd quieted. Speaking with a deep, resonant voice, he said, "I assume you are wondering why the young ladies have broken tradition and not taken their places as attendants." He flashed a coy smile. "I made this agreement with them earlier, so they are following my instructions. Through special arrangement by the Majesty on High, we have two replacements, one whose purity is unquestioned and another whose virtue has been restored."

He stepped away from the rift in the gate and looked at it expectantly. A young woman's head came through the opening, her hair red and shining. As if frightened by what she might find, she set her foot down timidly on the garden's soft turf and looked around, her eyes wide. When her body fully appeared, a shining aura surrounded her sky blue gown, making her look like a radiant angel.

Bonnie bit her lip. She wanted to squeal, "Karen!" but it wouldn't be right. This was a moment reserved for Karen and Ashley.

Lifting a hand to her mouth, Ashley let out a gasp. As Karen's gaze locked on her, Ashley's knees buckled. Walter grasped her arm and held her up, his smile trembling. "It's okay," he said. "It's just Karen. She's—"

Walter swallowed his words. Karen, every step touching the ground as if set there by a princess, glided toward him. She knelt at her position and looked up at him with sparkling eyes. With a voice like a strummed harp, she said, "She's what, Walter?"

"She's . . ." As he looked at Ashley, his jaw firmed. "She's amazing!"

Another woman, raven-haired and petite, stepped through the rift in Heaven's Gate, wearing a gown every bit as blue and shining as Karen's. Even more timid, she glanced around as if wondering if she would be unwelcome. When her gaze fixed on Elam, she bowed her head.

"Who is that?" Bonnie whispered to Billy.

"I remember Elam's description. She has to be Naamah."

Bonnie mouthed her name. Naamah. Sapphira had told stories about her evil mistress, Morgan's seductive minion. After all she had done, how had she gone to Heaven? What would Sapphira think about this wicked woman kneeling in the place of a virtuous attendant? What did Elam think?

Keeping her head low, Naamah took short, quick steps to her spot in front of Elam and knelt. Sapphira looked at him, her expression asking the questions Bonnie had already raised in her mind.

Suddenly, Heaven's Gate flashed. The transparent wall grew opaque, and a grassy meadow took shape. A woman with dark hair knelt in the field, her body so low she seemed curled in a trembling ball. As she shook, a song emerged, a lament that drifted across the wedding party like a gentle wind.

O who will wash the stains I bear
The harlot's mark of sin I wear?
Exposed and shorn of all I prized,
And now I beg for mercy's eyes.

O Jesus, look upon my strife
And spare this foolish harlot's life.
I bow, surrender, pour my tears;
Forgive my sins and draw me near.

The scene shifted abruptly. Elam stood at the crest of a rise looking out over the expanse. Naamah, wearing an oversized cloak, stared at her hand, standing, waiting, hoping. Elam extended his own hand, grass-stained and bloodied.

She ran to him and dropped to her knees. Grabbing his hand, she kissed his palm, her tears flowing. "You won't regret this, Elam," she said. "I promise, you won't regret your mercy."

He pulled her to her feet and spoke softly. "To be wanted and not lusted for. To be loved and not pitied. To be asked and not commanded." He pushed his hand through her tangled hair, then slipped it into hers, touching their palms together. "Is that right?"

As Naamah's cheeks flushed, she smiled. "And to be believed, even after all my lies."

The scene faded away, and the gate reverted to transparency. Sapphira leaned over and took Naamah's hands. Letting out a little gasp, Naamah looked up at Sapphira and allowed her to raise her to her feet.

Bonnie bit her lip again, trying not to cry. The sight was such a contrast! Although both women stood no taller than five feet, they seemed like giants, one with snowy white hair, pure and undefiled, the other with the shadow of Morgan hanging over her, a raven dressing her locks with memories of darkness, torture, and abuse. Did Naamah's mocking songs still ring in Sapphira's ears? Did the whip and briar nettles still sting like angry hornets up and down her back? Could Sapphira forget all the years of humiliation she suffered at the hands of this servant to a sorceress?

Sapphira lowered herself to her knees and looked up at Naamah. "Will you forgive me?" Sapphira asked.

Naamah's chest heaved. Tears streamed. She swallowed and choked out her words. "Me? Forgive you? I . . . I don't understand. I need you to forgive me."

Sapphira kissed Naamah's fingers. "I hated you for centuries. I cursed your name both in whispers and shouts. I wanted you to die." Her voice pitched higher. "But then I watched Bonnie Silver. Even though her father treated her with contempt over and over again, she never cursed his name. She never stopped loving him, even after he betrayed her mother and caused her death as well as Bonnie's suffering in foster homes. And when he asked for forgiveness, she gave it, showing the kind of love I needed to learn."

Bonnie looked at her father and gave him an "I love you" sign with her fingers. He returned the sign, his eyes glistening. Her mother took his hand and clenched it tightly, nodding at Bonnie with trembling lips.

"So," Sapphira continued, "that's why I ask you to forgive me. Because of Bonnie, I learned about the same Jesus you sang about, and that's when my hatred for you just melted away. But I have ached for your forgiveness ever since, and now that you're here . . ." She kissed Naamah's hand again and looked up at her. "Will you please forgive me?"

"Oh, yes! Yes!" Naamah pulled Sapphira to her feet and wrapped her arms around the white-haired bride. "And please do not withhold *your* forgiveness. My wickedness toward you was not in response to anything evil you did. It sprouted from the depths of my black soul."

"And now your soul is clean," Sapphira said. "As white as snow."

They kissed each other's cheeks, smearing the tear tracks. Naamah withdrew a handkerchief from her dress and dabbed Sapphira's face. "Enoch said I would probably need this," Naamah said. "He was right."

Enoch clapped his hands. "Now if everyone will take your places . . ."

Her smile as broad as an ocean, Naamah knelt at Sapphira's right, glancing back and forth between her and Elam.

Bonnie's father stood at her left. Makaidos shuffled forward and sat next to Ashley. The fathers of two brides were now ready to give away their daughters.

Bonnie looked at Sapphira. She had no father, no one to give her away. They had already wept together, knowing she would need a surrogate, but the one she chose certainly stood head and shoulders above any father. Yereq, dressed in a tailored Earth-style suit, walked up and took his place at her side. Being a brother, of sorts, spawned from the same genetic code and the same soil as her own origin, surely he had the right to offer her to the groom.

Smiling, she reached up and held his hand, barely able to wrap her fingers around three of his.

Heaven's Gate shimmered. Now, instead of a window to the other side of the garden, it became a window to another world. Dozens of people lined up on the other side, watching the ceremony.

Bonnie let her gaze linger on each face. She spotted Acacia, Dorian, Brogan, Joseph of Arimathea, and many other souls who had passed away during her many adventures, a band of heavenly witnesses who would be watching over all of them for years to come. She tried to find Professor Hamilton, but with people lined up at least five deep, he was probably hidden from sight.

"Now," Enoch said, "in order to make sure each union receives its proper recognition, we will perform the ceremonies one at a time."

Bonnie grinned. Enoch didn't mention the fact that the best-man situation made it impossible to perform all three at once, but that would become obvious very soon.

Enoch walked to Walter's side. "You seemed surprised to see Karen," Enoch said.

"Shocked would be a better word. I didn't know you could just pop out of Heaven and into Second Eden like that."

"Well, be prepared for another shock. Now that some of the portals have been restored, I sent a certain pair of couriers to collect other special guests from the cave in the Valley of Shadows." Enoch lifted a hand to his ear. "And if those are hoofbeats, they are right on time."

Everyone turned toward the village. Dikaios and Ember trotted across the field, Dikaios carrying Walter's parents, Carl and Catherine Foley, and Ember carrying Shelly, Walter's sister. All three were dressed in sharp riding outfits. When they arrived, the three Foleys took places in the front row, Carl using a cane to walk. Catherine blew Walter a kiss as she sat down.

Walter grinned and gave them a thumbs-up. "About time you got here!"

When the laughter subsided and Billy took his place at Walter's side as his best man, Enoch looked over Ashley's shoulder at the sea of onlookers. "Who gives this maiden to be wed to this warrior?"

Makaidos nodded at Thigocia, then at Enoch as he laid a wing over Ashley. "Her mother and I do."

Enoch bowed. "So be it."

Ashley pressed her veiled cheek against Makaidos's. "Thank you . . ." She paused, her voice spiking. "Daddy."

She threw her arms around his scaly neck and pulled him close, but only for a moment. When he took his place with Thigocia, Enoch folded his hands at his waist. "Since only one of you has dragon blood, we will proceed with the traditional vows of humans in your culture."

After reciting the vows, saying "I do," and exchanging rings Enoch provided, exquisite gold rings from Heaven's forge, Walter and Ashley knelt in front of Enoch.

He laid a hand on each head. "Seeing that you have made this commitment to one another in the sight of God and these witnesses, by the authority vested in me as a prophet of the Most High God, I now pronounce you husband and wife, or as the Second Eden residents say, 'Adam and Eve.'"

He gestured for them to rise and nodded at Walter. "You may now kiss your bride."

Walter lifted Ashley's veil with both hands. Karen smoothed the veil out behind Ashley's hair, another Second Eden custom. He paused, staring at her lovely face as if hypnotized. Finally, Ashley laid a hand behind his head, pulled him close, and kissed him, a tender lip caress that lingered for several seconds.

Laughing, Enoch turned the couple around and announced to the crowd. "Ladies and gentlemen, dragons and dragonesses, I present to you, Mr. and Mrs. Walter Foley."

"All right, Walter!" Billy shouted, clapping his hands. "You're a married man!"

Walter pointed at him. "You're coming up, buddy!"

"Indeed." Enoch waved for Ashley and Walter to sit with their parents. As he walked toward Elam and Sapphira, he passed Bonnie, whispering as he breezed by. "You are radiant, my dear."

Warmth rushing into her cheeks, Bonnie smiled. Having that wise old prophet performing their ceremony would be wonderful. He was so gentle and kind.

With Patrick as best man, Enoch performed a similar ceremony for Elam and Sapphira. When he asked them to repeat the vows, they spoke in Hebrew. Looking into each other's eyes, Elam pressed his left hand against Sapphira's right. Their fingers didn't wiggle. That expression of longing for togetherness had ended. Now they had come together, their union as husband and wife only seconds away.

After Enoch repeated his pronouncement, declaring them a wedded couple, he turned them toward the audience and said, "These two have waited thousands of years for this blessed day. When the final ceremony is complete, we will have a celebratory feast to end all others."

Everyone rose to their feet and cheered, most clapping while a few children leaped into the air.

"Now," Enoch continued, turning to Elam, "you may kiss your bride."

Elam pushed Sapphira's veil up and paused for a moment while Naamah smoothed it out. Then, without another second's hesitation, he kissed Sapphira, keeping his hand pressed against hers.

Standing on tiptoes, she wrapped her arms around him. A faint glow coated her body, and a ripple of flames ran from her head to her toes.

Elam pulled back and gazed at her. Sapphira's eyes sparkled with a more radiant blue than ever. They both smiled, the two most beautiful smiles Bonnie had ever seen—pure joy, simply pure joy.

From under his robe, Enoch withdrew a journal and gave it to Elam.

"A friend of Sapphira's and Bonnie's asked that I restore this to its owner. She said to tell you that 'The Maid' will pray for you both for as long as you live."

Elam and Sapphira caressed the journal's worn cover, their faces beaming. After they sat with Patrick and Ruth, Enoch turned toward Billy and Bonnie. Bonnie stiffened. Now it was their turn. Would Enoch have any surprises for them? Visitors from Earth? Other special guests?

As soon as Walter took his place as Billy's best man, Enoch stood in front of them, his arms crossed and his expression somber. "I am afraid, my two wonderful anthrozils, that I will be unable to perform your ceremony."

Billy drew his head back. "What? Why?"

"The Majesty on High has forbidden it, and someone has been chosen to take my place."

Enoch stepped aside and joined Elam and Sapphira in the audience. The wall to Heaven split vertically again, and a tall, lanky man strode out. Dressed in a multicolored robe similar to Enoch's, an aura shimmered around his body. He bowed, mussing his silvery white hair. "Greetings, my friends."

Bonnie could barely breathe. Now it was her turn to shout out the name of their surprise visitor, but she couldn't get her tongue to move.

Billy spoke his name for her. "Professor Hamilton?"

The professor smiled and dipped again. "William, Miss Silver, I am delighted to see you."

Bonnie ached to embrace him, but would it be proper? He was a heavenly being, not the familiar teacher of years gone by.

As a tear slipped down the professor's cheek, he stretched out his arms. "Come, my three friends. I cannot hold back my affection any longer."

Billy, Bonnie, and Walter eased into his embrace. Bonnie laid her head against the professor's shoulder, but in the warmth and joy of his presence, no tears emerged, only the bliss of feeling those wonderful arms again and hearing his lovely voice.

After releasing them, Walter backed away, and the professor gestured for Billy and Bonnie to turn. When they looked out upon the audience, still standing in response to the previous wedding, he spoke with power. "These are the witnesses to your coming union, and since you both have dragon blood, we will create a covenant veil."

The professor nodded at Walter. "If you would be so kind, Mr. Foley, please split them into two groups with an equal number of dragons and humans on each side."

"You got it!"

While Walter waved for everyone to get together, and Ashley helped him count and separate them into two groups, the professor reached for Listener's hand. "Are you ready to lead them through, my dear?"

Listener nodded. "Should I just do what you said in my dream?"

"Exactly."

Smiling, she reached up and lifted Bonnie's veil. "To pass through the covenant," Listener said, "all other veils must be removed, for your soul is laid bare through your unfiltered eyes."

When everyone assembled, Bonnie's parents on the left, Billy's on the right, and a host of others evenly divided on either side, Professor Hamilton again lifted his voice. "When I say the vows, I want everyone to repeat them by speaking through the gap in between the groups."

The people and dragons on each side faced each other. When the rustling stopped, the professor spoke again, now with a more powerful voice than ever. "I, Billy Bannister, do take thee, Bonnie Silver, to be my wedded wife."

With a joyous outburst of voices—men, women, children, and dragons—the words rocked across the garden in both directions. The gap in between the groups sparkled and began to glow, creating an arching aura. It looked like a shimmering membrane, thin and brilliant, nearly as tall as Yereq and wide enough for two people to pass through.

The professor finished Billy's vows as well as Bonnie's, waiting between each phrase for the witnesses to repeat them. With every utterance, the aura grew brighter, stronger. When the final words sounded forth, the arch pulsed with white energy.

He nodded at Listener. "Now, dear child, you may lead them through."

She stepped in front of Billy and Bonnie. "Each of you lay a hand on my shoulder," she said quietly.

As soon as they complied, Listener marched slowly forward, in step with the cadence of the professor's voice.

"The covenant veil is established, and the bride and groom will be able to pass through only if the words of the vows are true in their hearts. They, too, will speak them as they walk, fulfilling the human tradition."

Bonnie let the words pour from her lips. "I, Bonnie Silver, take thee, Billy Bannister, to be my wedded husband."

Billy echoed with his vows. "I, Billy Bannister, take thee, Bonnie Silver, to be my wedded wife."

As they spoke the final phrases, they reached the energy field. Not even slowing down, Listener led them into its light. Taking Billy's hand, Bonnie looked at him as they finished their vows together with "Till death do us part." They passed through—easily, as if gliding through a silk curtain. The radiance tickled Bonnie's skin, forcing her to smile.

When they emerged on the other side, Bonnie blinked. Billy stood at her side, gazing at her as they held hands.

The veil dissipated. A fountain sprang up in its place. Shooting seven streams high into the air, it sprayed a fine mist over everyone within a few paces. While most of the crowd moved away from the water, Sapphira and Elam held hands and stayed under the mist, allowing the tiny droplets to dress their hair and clothes in sparkling raiment.

The professor waved for everyone to gather around in a circle. "William. Bonnie. I have desired to do this for a long time." Setting his hands on their shoulders, he turned them toward each other. "By the authority vested in me as an emissary of Heaven, I now pronounce you husband and wife."

He paused. Bonnie looked at him, noting the gleam in his eye as he winked. When would he say those final, wonderful words?

Smiling, the professor took a deep breath and spoke with clarity and passion. "William, I will now dispense with formalities and call you by the name your bride cherishes." He paused again, his smile broadening. "Billy Bannister, you may now kiss your bride."

Billy set his hands on Bonnie's cheeks. Tears welling, making his hazel eyes sparkle, he drew close. Then, Billy and Bonnie kissed, a slow, satisfying kiss—soft, tender lips touching for the first time.

A shiver ran down Bonnie's spine. All the dangers, pain, deaths, and sorrows melted away. All the waiting, prayers, and lonely vigils had been worth it. She was now the virgin bride, spotless, unspoiled, and pure for her warrior husband, a noble knight, equally unblemished and holy.

When their lips parted, Professor Hamilton turned the newly married couple toward their parents. As Walter, Ashley, Elam, and Sapphira looked on, the professor called out, "I now present to you, Mr. and Mrs. Billy Bannister!"

Epilogue

Carrying Bonnie's lunch in a paper sack, as well as a stack of about fifteen envelopes, Billy hurried along the hospital corridor. He had left Bonnie in her room too long, having told her he would return in less than an hour. But Walter had stopped by his house with an important message, and Larry kept interrupting their conversation with updated communications from Second Eden. Establishing an open, cross-dimensional channel had worked out great most of the time, but Listener had a habit of reporting every event in Second Eden, no matter how trivial.

Ever since Earth, Hades, and Second Eden separated more than a year ago, everything should have returned to the peaceful paradise that realm had longed for. But Elam and Sapphira, established as king and queen of Second Eden by Enoch's orders, made sure life there stayed hopping with technology updates and deeper explorations of their cleansed world through expeditions led by Yereq, Legossi, Mantika, and Windor.

When Legossi learned that Angel was her resurrected daughter, she felt more at home in Second Eden. She spent many evenings hearing Listener's stories about Angel's love and wisdom.

Valiant relished being relieved of his duties and often took Candle on long journeys, both for physical training and spiritual instruction. Having recently become Emerald's Adam, Valiant felt like he was in training himself. Fatherhood awaited. He and Emerald had won the lottery for an upcoming birth, and both were as happy as they could be.

The companions of those who had died in Second Eden became communication portals between Heaven and Second Eden. The widow or widower, along with any children, could speak to their loved one in Heaven, fulfilling Abraham's word that keeping the companions would someday bring his people joy.

Sharing authority in Second Eden, Makaidos and Thigocia ruled as king and queen of the dragons, with Roxil and Karrick as their ambassadors to Earth. Since every slayer had been vanquished, they hoped to acclimate both worlds to the idea of dragons in their midst, but that would take a while.

On the Earth side, the castle museum run by Sir Barlow and his knights flourished. They no longer hid their identities as knights from the time of King Arthur, thereby attracting more visitors than they could handle. Barlow, in particular, enjoyed the exposure. Every day he would tell a long tale to a gathering of hundreds of children, a tale of knights, dragons, and slayers.

Walter's new message was hilarious, as usual. After he and Ashley resumed her computer business, she built another super-computer in their home—Lois, a new generation, faster and with a greater learning capacity than Larry. According to Walter, Larry found out about Lois by reading Ashley's e-mail to Billy, and now Larry was "requesting" an upgrade by sending Lois thousands of messages per minute with the same words, "Give me parity, or give me death."

As he reached for Bonnie's hospital room door, Billy laughed to himself. Walter was as funny as ever, and he and Ashley were as happy as any two love birds around. Although as different as night and day, their conflicting ways somehow seemed to mesh, and they never spoke a cross word to one another, though they still playfully fought with snow, water, and anything else that would cause no damage.

Billy pushed open the door and strode in. "Sorry I'm late."

As soon as Bonnie saw him, her face lit up. "Don't worry. I was fine. I just finished feeding the babies." Reclining in a partially raised bed, Bonnie used her wings to push higher, trying not to disturb the infants, one nestled in each arm. Her multicolored necklace draped a blue hospital gown that matched her pretty eyes. "Charles went right back to sleep, but Karen's a little fussy. I couldn't get her to burp."

"I'll give it a try." Billy held out the sack. "I brought your favorite sandwich."

She waved with a wing. "Thank you! You're my knight in shining armor!"

He set the bag on her stomach along with the stack of envelopes. "Christmas cards," he said. "Lots of great news."

While Bonnie opened the first card, Billy set Karen against his shoulder and patted her on the back. The image of tiny wings appeared in his mind. Of course, she was much too young for any wings to sprout, but it was possible, someday. Maybe she would take after her mother.

Now that society had accepted Bonnie Bannister, the strange dragon girl, as well as Gabriel and Shiloh Drake, two more recently married oddities from the dragon line, and now that Earth was negotiating with Roxil for the reentry of friendly dragons into the world, Karen would never have to worry about hiding wings in a backpack.

"This *is* good news," Bonnie said. "The orphanage is well-supplied, and Patrick and Ruth are both healthy and happy."

As Billy continued patting Karen's back, Bonnie showed him a photo from the next card. "Shiloh looks just like me when I was pregnant."

"Stands to reason," Billy said. "Did you read the sales' leads?"

She nodded. "Gabriel thinks he has a buyer for two of them. Do you know which ones?"

"He called me a few minutes ago. He sold 'The Faceless Protectors' and 'The Wedding Ball.' He's really proving to be a great agent."

"And you're a great artist."

Billy smiled at her loving expression. No matter how many times she built him up with her encouraging words, her compliments always felt good. Yet, the wedding painting, in particular, really was a work he could be proud of. Drawing Elam and Sapphira dancing under the spray of a fountain, with a wedding party of dragons and humans surrounding them, had been a labor of love, and it turned out beautifully. The price Gabriel was able to get would pay the bills for quite a while.

Karen burped, and heat from her spittle scalded Billy's shoulder. Holding her at arms' length, he gazed into her eyes. "Did you and your brother pull a switcheroo on us?"

She just stared at him, her purplish eyes wide. Billy set her back at Bonnie's side and reached for his son.

"What are you doing?" she asked. "He's asleep."

Billy pulled away. "I just wanted to check for—"

"Wings?" Smiling, she winked. "I already checked. Nothing yet."

He set a hand on the bedrail and gazed at their two newborns. "So now that Alithia and Dallas found their offspring, how many does that make, humans born to dragons or former dragons, I mean?"

"Eleven?" Bonnie guessed.

Billy raised a finger for each name he rattled off. "Ashley, Gabriel, Shiloh, Listener, Thomas, Mariel, Karen, and Charles. That's eight. If Angel were still alive, that would have made nine, but I'm counting only living anthrozils."

Bonnie pointed at him. "And you and I make ten."

"Right," he said, laughing under his breath. "I almost forgot."

"And Ruth's and Patrick's son makes eleven."

"But he doesn't count, does he? They're both fully human."

Bonnie wrinkled her nose. "True. I didn't think about that."

Resting his hand on the rail again, he blew a sad sigh. "I wish Prof could have lived to see our little ones."

Bonnie caressed Karen's feather-soft blonde hair. "I'm sure he's seen them. Enoch would make sure of that."

"I guess so. With his portal viewer, he can—"

A knock sounded at the door. "Maintenance."

"Sure," Billy said. "Come on in."

An elderly man dressed in clean blue coveralls walked in, pushing a cart that carried lightbulbs, paper towels, and bathroom tissue. Brushing back his white hair, he nodded at a flickering light in the ceiling. "I heard that you might want a bit more illumination in here."

Bonnie's face lit up. "Enoch!"

He pressed a finger to his lips. "I suppose my disguise lacks authenticity."

"No," Billy said, laughing. "It's great. We just have, I guess you might call it, a heavenly advantage."

"Did you come to see our little ones?" Bonnie asked.

Enoch waved a hand. "Oh, I've seen them, and so have many in Heaven. When you announced their names, more than one tear coursed down your professor's cheek, and Karen's aura shone like the sun." He patted Billy on the back. "Your kindness to their memory is very much appreciated."

Billy grasped Enoch's arm warmly. "So, to what do we owe the blessing of your visit?"

Enoch gazed at the infants. "Just to deliver a prophecy. Be sure that your offspring forge friendships with the others, especially Listener, Thomas, and Mariel. It is clear that their paths, should they choose the way of faith and righteousness, will lead them toward many adventures."

"Dangerous adventures?" Bonnie asked.

"Oh, yes. Of course." A wry smile spread across his face. "I assume you wouldn't want it any other way."

Billy slid his hand into Bonnie's. "After all we've been through together, and after all God taught us . . ." He shook his head. "No. We wouldn't have it any other way."

ACKNOWLEDGMENTS

It would be impossible to thank every person who offered a helpful hand in the creation and polishing of these works, so please forgive any omissions.

Thank you to my wife and children. You helped me in more ways than I can count, from conception, to gestation, to birth. This story would have remained a crazy dream without you.

This book, part two of the longest in all three series, required the editing prowess of many willing helpers, including some of my faithful readers, so I send my thanks to Peter Blaskiewicz, Connie Wolters, and Holli Herdeg for poring over the two hundred thousand words and offering their suggestions.

And most of all, thank you to my Lord and Savior, Jesus Christ. You implanted the flame within me that helped me understand what an Oracle of Fire is. Without You, I would be nothing.

For every Oracle of Fire who reads this, I pray that your heart's flame blazes once again as these words reignite a passion that can never be extinguished.

About the Author

Bryan Davis is the author of fantasy/science-fiction novels for youth and adults, including the bestselling Dragons in Our Midst series. Other series include The Oculus Gate, Reapers, Dragons of Starlight, Tales of Starlight, Astral Alliance, Time Echoes, and Wanted: Superheroes, several of which have been bestsellers.

Bryan was born in 1958 and grew up in the eastern US. From the time he taught himself how to read before school age, through his seminary years and beyond, he has demonstrated a passion for the written word, reading and writing in many disciplines and genres, including theology, fiction, devotionals, poetry, and humor.

Bryan is a graduate of the University of Florida (BS in industrial engineering). In high school, he was valedictorian of his class and won various academic awards. He was also a member of the National Honor Society and voted Most Likely to Succeed.

He continues to expand his writing education by teaching at relevant writing conferences and conventions. Although he is now a full-time writer, Bryan was a computer professional for over twenty years.

Bryan and his wife, Susie, homeschooled their four girls and three boys, and they work together as an author/editor team.

THE
CRESCENT
STONE
MATT MIKALATOS

THE
HEARTWOOD
CROWN
MATT MIKALATOS

THE
STORY
KING
MATT MIKALATOS

wander